The Devil's Lieutenant

The Devil's

M. FAGYAS

Lieutenant

G. P. Putnam's Sons, New York

To the memory of my father, First Lieutenant Géza Fagyas of the Austro-Hungarian Army, killed in action on October 9, 1914

ADVANCEMENT LIST

November 1, 1909

IMPERIAL AND ROYAL AUSTRO-HUNGARIAN ARMED FORCES

The following first lieutenants, graduated from the War College, class of 1905, have been promoted out of turn to captains and permanently assigned to the

GENERAL STAFF CORPS

RANK IN CLASS	STATIONED
1. AHRENS, Robert Stefan	Second Infantry Regiment, Eger
2. EINTHOFEN, Ludwig Alexander	Thirtieth Infantry Regiment, Budapest
3. SCHÖNHALS, Karl-Heinz	Thirteenth Mountaineer Brigade, Mostar
4. GERSTEN, Johann Paul von	Thirty-first Infantry Brigade, Brassó
5. WIDDER, Franz August	Third Infantry Regiment, Graz
6. HOHENSTEIN, Prince Rudolf Eduard	Fifth Dragoon Regiment, Wiener Neustadt
7. DUGONICH, Titus Milan	Fifth Dragoon Regiment, Wiener Neustadt
8. MADER, Richard Emmerich	Eighth Uhlan Regiment, Cracow
9. LANDSBERG-LÓVY, Baron Otto Ernst	Fourth Dragoon Regiment, Enns
10. HRASKO, Wacław Jas	Fifth Infantry Regiment, Sarajevo
11. TRAUTMANNSDORF, Georg Hermann	Twenty-eighth Infantry Regiment, Nagykanizsa
12. MOLL, Carl Günther	Thirteenth Landwehrdivision, Vienna
13. MESSEMER, Gustav Johann	Sixty-fifth Infantry Brigade, Györ
14. OBLONSKY, Zygmunt Alexander	Third Uhlan Regiment, Bruck
15. HODOSSY, Zoltán Géza	Thirteenth Hussar Regiment, Kecskemét

I

On THE afternoon of November 17, the last day of his life, Captain Richard Mader left his office at the Ministry of War an hour earlier than usual. Anna Gabriel had promised to be at his flat at six, and he needed time to change and relax before she came. There lurked a hint of anxiety under his pleasure at seeing Anna again. Several times during the day he had been tempted to send a porter with a message to Anna, then was afraid the letter might fall into her husband's hands.

As a rule, Richard Mader was even-tempered and in full command of his emotions. Women liked him because he was thoughtful and handsome and men, because they could trust him. As a soldier, he possessed the kind of quiet courage that under certain circumstances might prove a man a hero, but never a swashbuckler. Throughout his life he had known very little pain, mental or physical, and enjoyed a fair amount of success. To be a captain in the Kaiserliche und Königliche—the Imperial and Royal—Austro-Hungarian Army and assigned to the General Staff Corps at the age of thirty was quite a remarkable accomplishment for the son of an obscure Viennese bureaucrat.

Fate had spared him the disappointments and dilemmas that often take the steel out of the best of men. His sex life was satisfactory and uncomplicated. Over the years he had been in and out of love with nice girls, married women, minor actresses, and once —only once—at sixteen, with a prostitute. He gave his feelings the romantic definition of love, although they were nothing more than a young man's lust, curiosity or—at best—infatuation. With the nice girls he held hands, took long walks, exchanged quick kisses in dark doorways or whenever a chaperone left the room; with the rest he entered into passionate, though mostly short-lived, liaisons. He never became emotionally involved and was cool-headed enough to let an affair taper off the minute the woman displayed matrimonial intentions. Army regulations called for a marriage bond of thirty thousand kronen from a first lieutenant and sixty thousand from a General Staff captain. Impecunious officers like Mader had three choices: to resign from the service, to marry wealthy girls, or to remain single. Captain Mader chose the third solution, at least for the time being. He liked his independence, the uncomplicated, orderly routine of his life. There was nothing more soothing than a quiet evening spent in his flat after the departure of a woman he had made very enjoyable love to earlier in the afternoon. But now, for the first time since his adolescence, the prospect of sleeping with a woman did not hold its usual promise of pleasure. On the contrary, it made him tense and unsure of himself.

It was a good thirty-minute walk from the ministry to Hainburgerstrasse, where he lived. He could have taken a fiacre—there was a stand on Michaelerplatz—but decided against it, hoping the exercise would soothe his nerves.

At a florist's shop on Schubertring he bought chrysanthemums. He had asked for pink roses, Anna's favorites, but the florist was out of them. November was a bad month for everything except chrysanthemums. They seemed to be the only flowers in existence, and Vienna was full of them. All Souls' being the day when the dead are remembered and their graves decorated, there was a veritable flow of chrysanthemums in the direction of the cemeteries, and the sight of floral offerings, no matter how lovely, reminded one of death.

The weather had been murky all week, and the gas lamps were lighted by the time he reached Hainburgerstrasse. He liked the street, mainly because of its suburban atmosphere. The houses, no higher than three stories, were built around rectangular yards with old-fashioned fountains, reminders of the not-too-distant past when life in Vienna had not included indoor plumbing or running water.

His was a two-room flat on the second floor of Number 56, rather sparsely furnished because he had been transferred from Cracow only a few months earlier and had been too busy to buy more than the essential pieces. His mother had offered to help, but—gently and firmly—he had turned her down. He wanted a place reflecting his own taste, airy, uncluttered and modern. He had already had the walls papered, the study in pale green and the bedroom in gray, both in delicate Art Nouveau patterns, much too expensive, but wonderfully decorative. He very much enjoyed shopping for the flat, and this was one of the reasons he had tried to do it in easy stages. With a wisdom rare in the young, he preferred to stretch out his pleasures.

"They stink like funeral candles," József Boka, his orderly, had commented when the captain told him to put the flowers in a vase.

Boka was a stocky young man from the Hungarian plains, practically illiterate, but shrewd and resourceful as only a peasant could be who during the first eighteen years of his life had learned to outwit nature and during the following eight the Austro-Hungarian military. Without doubt, he was the ideal orderly for an officer: quick, clean, untiring and dependable. Before his stint with Mader he had attended to the needs of three officers, among them a Czech count who had molded him into the perfect specimen he now was. The scar above his left eye was a reminder of the shoe tree hurled at him when he had failed to polish a pair of riding boots to the count's satisfaction.

Without mentioning or admitting it to themselves, a deep manly affection existed between the captain and Private Boka, but the relationship did not keep Boka from making small profits on the captain's purchases. Mader had an inkling of the situation but closed his eyes to it. Only officers were expected to be high-principled and incorruptible; enlisted men were not.

At a quarter past five Mader gave Boka five kronen and sent him to Wolf's, a gourmet foodstore on Stubenring, for a pound of cold ham, rolls, *pâtisserie* and two bottles of Gumpoldskirchner.

So it's Mrs. Gabriel again, Boka thought as he descended the steps to the street. Mrs. Gabriel was cold ham and wine; the dark-haired, nervous wife of the general, champagne and goose liver; the little chorus girl from the Theater an der Wien chocolate cake and sweet liqueur. A tacit agreement existed between Boka and Mader that the orderly was to ignore the captain's love life. Whenever Mader entertained a woman, Boka stayed out of sight, yet he could not fail to see the lady coming and going since the window of his cubicle overlooked the staircase. His male solidarity and innate decency kept him from breathing a word about the visitors to anyone, including the captain.

On this afternoon, Boka noticed a touch of nervousness in Mader. Usually, the captain was full of exuberance before a rendezvous, especially a rendezvous with Mrs. Gabriel. She was the kind of woman, he, Boka, wouldn't have minded sleeping with, which, judging by what he had heard about her sex life, was no impossible dream. Although she was the daughter of a cavalry major, she was not adverse to having an affair with a man in the ranks. Some people insisted that her indiscriminate sexual appetite was the reason for her father's retirement from active service rather early in life.

She was a slim woman with an unfashionably boyish figure—delicately boned and almost flat-chested. Her skin was ivory-colored, her almond-shaped eyes were coal black, and her mouth was much too big for the narrow oval of her face. Her most attractive quality was her childlike gaiety, an infectious friendliness few could resist. During Mader's two years at the War College, her father, Major Baron Johann von Campanini, had been chief riding instructor. Twenty years old then, Anna had looked like a shy and scrawny fifteen-year-old. An impressive number of her father's pupils, among them Mader, had learned by experience how deceptive her looks were. In bed she proved neither shy nor scrawny.

Despite her reputation, it was inevitable that sooner or later one of the young officers would succumb to her magnetism and propose to her. First Lieutenant Friedrich Gabriel, a brilliant and promising graduate of the War College, was the man with enough love and determination. Of course, marriage to Anna meant the sudden end of his army career. Even if he could have produced the thirty-thousand-kronen marriage bond demanded by regulations, the husband of Anna von Campanini could never have been assigned to the General Staff Corps. At best, he would have been delegated to some obscure army post in Galicia or Dalmatia.

For Anna, First Lieutenant Gabriel made the supreme sacrifice: He left the army and—as his training did not qualify him for anything more lucrative and distinguished—took a job as a postal clerk. People considered it a damn shame and pitied him. Thus he became the second officer to have his career wrecked by the riding instructor's daughter.

Despite all predictions to the contrary, the marriage turned out to be very happy. At least, this was the consensus among the friends who still maintained contact with the couple.

After their marriage, Mader lost sight of the Gabriels. Then four years later, on an afternoon in October, he had bumped into Anna in front of the pastry counter at Demel's. From there he took her straight to his flat and into his bed.

During November she had visited him twice. Her lovemaking was as expert as ever, though a lot more exhausting. She possessed a hunger that first flattered, then disturbed Mader. It pained him to realize that he was no longer a match for her. The discovery came as a bitter shock, especially since it was not the first time his performance as a lover had not been up to his old standards.

During September he had had a mild flirtation with the wife of a general. One day, to his utter astonishment, the lady had accepted his facetiously extended invitation to come up to his flat and see his Art Nouveau wallpaper. It had been an unseasonably hot, sultry day, and she had arrived wearing a high-collared white lace dress trimmed with black velvet ribbons and exuding the strong scent of lilies of the valley. Mader abhorred strong perfume, preferring natural odors, sun-dried linen or feminine skin after a good scrubbing with soap and water. The air was heavy in the room, and the woman's presence penetrated every corner.

"How kind of you to come," he murmured because nothing more original occurred to him.

He unbuttoned her right elbow-length kid glove and planted a kiss on the moist rose-colored skin of the exposed wrist. Peeling off the glove, he repeated the procedure with her left hand. This was always an effective curtain raiser, a symbolic introduction to whatever play was to follow. It was at this moment, however, that Mader began to feel uneasy. There should have been a flutter of excitement within his body, a vibration at his throat, in his loins, a signal that his male organ was ready for service. There were times when he became aroused by the mere glimpse of the calf of a girl boarding an omnibus. Now he was alone with a very attractive woman who had come to his flat with the explicit purpose of making love and he felt as cold and lifeless as a marble slab on an old man's grave.

They stood in the middle of the room. He still held her hand. She smiled at him expectantly. She had good, healthy teeth, somewhat unevenly spaced incisors and sharp canines, which gave her otherwise handsome face a wolflike cast. Her hair was coal black, and there was the hint of a mustache above her lips. Because of the Oriental opulence of her looks and her preference for bright colors and showy jewelry, in army circles she was nicknamed the Odalisque. Her father was a banker of Jewish extraction who had been converted to Catholicism when his three daughters reached marriageable age. One was now the wife of a cabinet minister; another was a nun. The third was Mader's visitor, Lily Wencel.

"Won't you sit down?" Mader released her hand and pulled up a chair.

Her expression clearly indicated that she was ready to dispense with the social niceties. He busied himself, however, with uncorking the bottle that waited in the cooler, pouring the champagne and serving the goose liver pâté. Thirstily she downed two glasses of wine, refusing the pâté.

"This heat is brutal!" She fanned herself nervously with the small fan which dangled from her wrist on a gold chain and was made of the same lace as her dress. "Do you think it would help if you opened the window?" Then, as he rose: "No, don't! It would be worse. I shouldn't have worn this dress. You men don't know how lucky you are." She began fumbling with the hooks at the back of the high neck. "I think all couturiers hate women; that's why they bone everything. I'm sure my skin is rubbed raw. Would you be shocked if I asked you to unhook me?" Then she added with a giggle: "Of course, just the neck."

Dutifully he went around her chair, reached under the heavy chignon, and searched for the top hook. Her skin felt hot under his fingers. She rose and moved in front of him. Slowly, methodically, he worked one hook after the other down to her waist. Like an overripe melon, the tight garment split open.

His touch sent a shiver through her and accelerated her breathing. Her excitement alarmed him because he was still unable to respond. And the fault was not hers. The skin of her exposed back, smoothly velvet, exuded a warm, animal fragrance. His hand reached inside the thin silk chemise and groped for her breasts. They were full and firm, and the nipples turned hard beneath his fingers.

Richard Mader had always loved the magic in the discovery that there was a warm, live woman hidden beneath the many layers of clothing prescribed by current fashions: the long skirts, high-necked blouses, boots, stockings, corsets and camisole tops. Now, however, with Lily Wencel, he could not detect the slightest stir of desire within his body.

He was stunned. At thirty, he could still outrun, outswim, outride any of his fellow officers, and his brain worked with the precision and promptness of a well-oiled automatic gun. He could think of no reason why in the very prime of his life he should become impotent.

The term frightened him. With a violence that made Lily Wencel cry out, he pulled her close and pressed his lips against hers. She responded by forcing her tongue through the barrier of his teeth. For a long moment, they stood holding each other, she panting like a bitch in heat and he feeling the cold sweat trickle down his back. Suddenly it became bitterly clear to him that unless he stopped his playacting, the afternoon would end in humiliation and ridicule for him.

He freed his mouth, released her, and backed away. She remained frozen in a pose of surrender, her lips parted and her eyes closed. Then she gave him a startled look.

"What's the matter?" she asked in a hoarse whisper.

Ignoring the question, he picked up the champagne bottle, filled her glass, and handed it to her. Obediently she took it but stared at it as if she had never before seen a glass. Her heavy-lidded eyes remained clouded with a thirst the wine could not quench.

"What's the matter?" she asked again. "Don't you like me? I thought you did."

"Oh, I do—very much. You've always been most kind to me. Both of you."

She frowned. "Both of us?"

"You and the general. And I'm very grateful."

She began to understand.

"Don't be ridiculous," she snapped. "You loathe him. All subalterns do. As if I didn't know!"

She was right. General Wencel was the least liked officer ever to head the Judge Advocate Corps.

"You're mistaken," Mader responded lamely. "I have great respect for the general."

"Is that why you lured me here? To tell me that?" Her voice grew loud and strident.

Oddly, anger became her. She was a fascinating sight. Her cheeks were flushed, her eyes blazing, and where the unhooked dress exposed her neck and shoulders there was the pale translucence of milk glass.

He told himself she was alluring and desirable, but it did not help. Only his mind responded.

"The general is a fine officer. One of the finest," he muttered, feeling ashamed.

She put down her untouched glass. Half the wine spilled on the tabletop.

"That's a very touching attitude. He'd be very pleased if I told him so. You want me to?"

"That's up to you," he shrugged.

"Impertinent, too." She looked around for her gloves. As she began to pull the left one on, she realized that the back of her dress was still open. "Hook me up, damn you!"

He complied. When the task took him too long, she threw him a disdainful look over her shoulder.

"Next time I'll remember to bring my maid along."

The high neck of the dress was still open when she flounced from the flat.

Following her downstairs, he offered to take her home, but when he hailed a fiacre, she told him that she preferred to ride alone. After the clip-clop of the horses' hooves died away in the direction of Stubenring, he returned to his flat feeling defeated and miserable.

*   *   *

The church bells of Landstrasser Hauptstrasse struck five thirty. There was still a half hour before Anna Gabriel's arrival.

The pills, Mader thought, then again discarded the idea. They weren't really pills, but—as far as he could tell through the carefully glued red tissue paper wrapping—they were capsules. He had received them in the morning mail at his office. The envelope they had arrived in also contained a hectographed circular, the text of which was outspoken even for an era when similar products were openly advertised in newspapers. Richard Mader was no prude, but the word "coitus," printed in clear black letters, shocked him.

"Take two capsules with a glass of cold water half an hour before coitus," the text read. And in the next paragraph: "Effects stupefying!" The rest was pseudoscientific jargon advertising a nerve stimulant guaranteed to restore man's waning virile powers. The circular was signed by "Charles Francis, Pharmacist."

Mader's first reaction to the letter had been annoyance tinged with embarrassment. He suspected a practical joke. Then later in the morning he learned that two fellow officers, Prince Rudolf Hohenstein, and Hans von Gersten, both captains, had also received the Charles Francis circular. They had read it aloud, and with obvious glee, in the men's room. They told Mader that a fourth officer on the floor had also been sent the capsules. The information relaxed Mader. It had not been a practical joke after all, only a promotional device to sell a patent medicine. The prince had thrown his envelope and contents into the toilet, which he then flushed. He evidently was not curious about the "stupefying effect" promised by the capsules.

Mader wondered if Anna would be on time. He decided to finish the letter he had started the night before to a young woman named Ingrid Fiala. Ingrid was the kind of girl he would probably have married if it had not been for the army. Blond and blue-eyed and piquantly snub-nosed, with the disposition of an angel, she would have made a wonderful mother to all the little Maders who were destined to remain unborn because their presumptive father was a member of the General Staff Corps of the Imperial and Royal Austro-Hungarian Army.

Mader thoroughly understood that the army was more than an institution, a religion, a race or a fraternity. It was an alien organ implanted in the body of the monarchy, nurtured by its nation's life fluid, but functioning in complete independence. The General Staff Corps was the very center of the organ. Once a man became a member, he ceased to be the master of his own destiny. He could not take Ingrid Fiala to be his lawful wedded wife because Ingrid Fiala was a vaudeville artist, one-third of the Dancing Leonardo Triplets, who were neither triplets nor Leonardos, but three former strangers at present performing in a variety show in Frankfurt, Germany. Of course, the corps had no objection to its officers' sleeping with Ingrid Fiala—provided the affair did not end in a scandal.

"My dearest Angel," read the first paragraph of the letter. "Three weeks ago the painters finally finished papering the flat. The work turned out beautifully. I cannot wait for you to see it. As I remember, you were somewhat unsure about the pattern for the bedroom, but you'll love it now. It is a great deal more impressive on a wide surface than in a small sample. I have bought the desk we admired at Horn's. It was delivered last week and now the room looks almost furnished—"

Mader lighted the candle on the desk and sat down. He wrote: "Last night I went to Lilli Lehmann's concert, but left after the intermission. There is no pleasure in listening to beautiful music alone. I can't stand it much longer without you. You promised to come here after your Frankfurt engagement, which means no later than the first of December. I won't accept any excuses. I need you, Angel, more than—"

The church bells struck five forty-five. He put his pen down and rose. On both past occasions Anna had been on time. If he now allowed a quarter of an hour for the preliminaries—"You look lovely. May I take your coat?" "What's new at the Ministry? Have you heard the latest gossip?" . . . "Do you think there will be a war between England and Germany next year?" . . . "Isn't it too bad about the czarina's illness?"—it would be around six fifteen by the time she unbuttoned her blouse and dropped her skirt to the floor. The circular read: "Thirty minutes before coitus." If he wanted to try the damn capsules, he had to take them without any delay! After all, at the worst, they contained powdered sugar. Perhaps Charles Francis, whoever he was, counted on the psychological effect of his "stimulant." Provided nothing was physically wrong with a man and he merely lacked confidence in himself, the concoction was as good a cure as any.

The envelope was still in the pocket of his greatcoat where he had slipped it in the morning. He took out the small flat box. Carefully—as the instruction cautioned—he tore open the red tissue paper and dropped the capsules onto the palm of his hand.

Boka had lighted the gas lamps in the room, but the entry and kitchen were dark. Mader had to feel his way to the cupboard for a glass and from there to the sink for water. He placed the capsules on his tongue and washed them down quickly. He was about to light the entry lamp when he remembered the circular on the table in the study. He went back and threw it, the envelope, red paper and small box, into the fire of the large tile stove.

Pulling from his trouser pocket the flat gold watch his father had given him after his graduation from the Military Academy, he saw that it was ten before six. He decided he had better slip the unfinished letter under the writing pad. Not that he wanted to keep Anna from seeing it. No, it was, in some strange fashion, the other way around. He felt it would have been wrong to let the letter witness whatever was to happen between them in that room. Anna did not love him, but Ingrid did. This was the crux of the matter.

He moved to the desk, but as he reached for the letter, he was suddenly overcome by dizziness. The next moment he felt a heavy weight pressing against his chest. He gasped for air.

I am drowning! was the thought that flashed through his mind.

"Boka!" He tried to shout, but no sound came from his throat. His heart skipped a beat, then started pumping again. The pressure on his chest grew more unbearable. His heart expanded until it seemed to fill his chest with its bulk. A fierce pain gnawed at his intestines, and his body jerked as if manipulated by the strings of a demented puppeteer.

"Boka!" This time the sound came, but no response.

"Help! Help!" He screamed with terror as the pain climbed to his throat and burned his mouth.

"Water—" He started blindly for the kitchen. If only he could reach water to extinguish the fire. There had to be a fire—nothing less could cause the murderous pain which consumed his entire body.

"God. Oh, God, I'm dying!" In a flash of insight he realized that the capsules had contained poison.

He failed to reach the kitchen, collapsing in the dark hallway, writhing and gasping and emitting loud, piercing screams whenever he was able to fill his lungs with air. He tried to rise and could not. In agony, he dug his fingers into the parquet flooring. Splinters tore the flesh under his nails, but the gnawing inside his bowels was so excruciating that he became insensitive to the lesser pain. Before losing consciousness, he cried out once more, after which his pulsebeat slowed to a faint quiver and his respiration to an erratic wheeze. The spasms continued a few seconds longer. Death arrived swiftly after complete paralysis.

Private Boka was at the bottom of the stairway when he heard the scream. It was a high-pitched sound that could have been emitted by a woman or even by an animal. He did not take time to analyze it since he was already late getting back from the store. Wolf's had been crowded with shoppers, and on the way home he had run into a man from his village, also an officer's orderly, and they had had a pleasant talk. The church bell striking a quarter to six made him take a quick leave from his friend and rush home.

He mounted the steps by threes. He had trouble fitting the key into the front door lock because of the parcels he carried. After crossing the dark hallway to the kitchen, he deposited them on the table. There was silence in the flat, so he assumed the visitor had not yet arrived. Intending to ask the captain how to serve the ham, he recrossed the hallway to the study. There was a strange, bitter smell in the air, something that had not been there before. The captain wasn't in the study, the bedroom, or the bath. Gaslight burned in both rooms, and a candle was lit on the desk. Puzzled, Boka looked around, then suddenly remembered the animal cry he had heard coming upstairs. He picked up the candle. Even before reaching the hallway, he felt that something dreadful had happened to Captain Mader.

He found the body in a corner near the kitchen door. It lay in a fetal position, the legs pulled up to the chest, almost touching the chin. Only the hands were not in line with the rest of the body. They still clung to the floorboards, blood dripping from the mutilated nails.

"Jesus Christ, Captain! What's the matter with you, sir?"

Boka dropped down beside the lump of clothing and inert flesh and attempted to lift the body. Mader's face was a bluish red, but his skin felt hot. Boka tried to detect a pulsebeat. He pressed his ear against Mader's chest but was unable to tell whether the throbbing he heard was that of his own heart or the captain's. Boka was a strong man, and it was no effort to gather the body in his arms. In the bedroom he deposited it on the bed, and covered it with a comforter. Then he raced from the flat, out the front door and across the street to the third house, where a doctor's sign hung at the door.

Two patients were seated in the waiting room when Boka burst in. After some confusion, the receptionist managed to sort out the facts from Boka's garbled German and called the doctor. He was an elderly man with a salt-and-pepper beard and tired, red-rimmed eyes set under the high dome of a wrinkled forehead. Without bothering to slip on the overcoat his receptionist held out for him, he threw a few instruments into his black bag and followed the impatient Boka from the room. For a second he paused on the threshold.

"Call the police precinct," he shouted to his receptionist, then, on second thought: "and the Military Command!"

He crossed the street trying to keep up with Boka. As they reached Number 56, they found a group of people, mostly tenants, clustered around the janitor's wife. She must have seen Boka dash from the house and, with the unfailing instinct of all janitors' wives, had guessed that something unusual had occurred in the captain's flat. Now she barred Boka's way and, with the authority of a landlord's deputy, demanded to know what had happened.

At that very moment Anna Gabriel, in a dark-green wool suit, her skirt the new short length, was approaching Number 56 from the direction of the Ring. Her wide-brimmed hat, a mass of velvet petals, was the same color as her suit. Despite the four pins that held the hat to her chignon, she had trouble keeping it straight in the sudden gust of wind that swept down the street. She was slightly out of breath and in very good spirits. Her cheeks were flushed, and she hummed the latest Leo Fall song. When she spotted Boka and the white-smocked old man surrounded by a group of women, she halted abruptly.

Boka saw her, too. He had been about to enter the house after having unceremoniously pushed the janitor's wife out of his way. Later he could never explain what prompted him to stop on the threshold and shout at Anna Gabriel: "Go home! Get the hell out of here! Go back!"

After that, he entered the house hurriedly, the doctor following him.

Anna remained standing as if petrified. She felt hostile and searching eyes fastened on her. Their crossfire lasted only a moment; then she heard the people shuffle upstairs and stop in front of the captain's door.

She felt a mad urge to follow them. It took all her willpower to turn and walk away. Her walk had much less bounce than before. She knew that something dreadful had happened to Captain Mader and that Private Boka's warning had probably saved her from the same fate. She had been standing on the brink of an abyss, and he had called out to her just before the rock gave way beneath her feet. At the nearest hackstand she hailed a fiacre, gave the coachman her address, and told him to hurry.

Dr. Bruck threw a perfunctory glance at the face framed by the soft pillow on the brass bed and knew that his services were no longer needed. The man was dead. He bent over the corpse, and as he lifted the comforter, the nauseating stench of excrement mixed with the smell of bitter almonds hit him. A trickle of blood appeared at the corner of the man's mouth and spotted the open collar of his coat. Violent death, Dr. Bruck knew, was a messy affair.

"Cyanide," he said to himself.

Boka stood at the foot of the bed, his hands clasped on the brass rail, his face as pale as the knuckles of his clenched fists.

"I was gone only thirty minutes," he reported. "There was nothing wrong with him when I left."

"Of course not." The doctor nodded. "This thing works pretty fast. Sometimes in less than a minute."

Boka suddenly erupted. "Goddamn it! Don't you just stand there! Do something!"

The doctor was a civilian and, as such, inferior to anyone in uniform, even to an officer's orderly. Civilians could be shouted at, unless they were larger and stronger than the soldier, which was not the present case.

The doctor riveted his tired eyes on the orderly's face. He saw desperation and grief on it and forgave the lack of manners.

"There is nothing I can do." His gaze returned to the corpse. "You had better find a priest. I assume the captain was a Catholic." When Boka didn't move, the doctor added: "This is the time, young man, when one has to shift one's concern from the dead to the living. In this case—the family."

"Will you stay with him?" Boka asked. He realized he would have said "with the captain" if Mader had still been alive. Now Mader was just "he." Not because of any lack of respect, but because Boka was unable to identify the crumpled form under the heavy comforter and the bloody, pain-distorted face with the man he had left in the apartment only a half hour before.

"I will," the doctor promised and sat down in the armchair beside the bed. He was sixty-nine years old and felt one hundred at the end of each day.

As Boka was leaving, Police Lieutenant Horn arrived accompanied by two of his men. Having been told by the doctor's receptionist that the accident victim—she had described the case as an accident—was a member of the General Staff Corps, the police lieutenant had already notified the Ministry of War, the Security Bureau and the local Military Command. Not that he liked their meddling, for he was convinced that if left alone, the police could work a lot more efficiently, but because there was no way of excluding them.

At first glance the affair appeared to be a suicide: the fast-acting poison, the unfinished letter on the desk, the orderly dispatched on an errand before the victim swallowed the poison. The candle by which the dead man had written the letter still burned with a vivid flame. A vase contained a bunch of chrysanthemums, and on the kitchen table were several unopened delicatessen packages.

"What a pity," the doctor commented. "Such a handsome

young man. I remember seeing him a few times in the street. Always in the mornings. I usually start out for my house calls at a quarter to eight. That was when he left for wherever he worked."

"At the Ministry of War." The lieutenant nodded.

"That's right. His orderly told me he was on the General Staff. Why did he do it, Lieutenant?"

"Do what?"

"Kill himself. Probably over some woman. How utterly foolish of the young. To throw away an irreplaceable treasure for a commodity so abundant that it constantly gluts the market."

The lieutenant did not answer. He stepped into the study to read the unfinished letter. He read it twice, then slowly put it back on the desk. One of the detectives was going through the contents of the wastebasket; the other searched the garbage pail in the kitchen. The lieutenant pulled out the desk drawers. Stacks of stationery, photographs in boxes and albums, pens, pencils, stamps, a package of tobacco, cigarette paper, a cigarette machine, a small dossier with bills, all marked PAID, receipts, several bunches of letters tied with gold string, the captain's service revolver, everything neat and in order.

"Why didn't he shoot himself?" the doctor asked. "Why such a painful way?"

Extreme unction was administered to the dead man by Father Jellinek, the tall, husky chaplain of the church on Landstrasser Hauptstrasse. His altar boy must have been summoned hastily from an empty lot where he played soccer, for his shoes were caked with fresh mud, and throughout the sacrament mucus threatened to trickle from his wind-bitten nostrils.

Boka kneeled at the foot of the bed, his glassy stare fastened on the hand-painted copy of Michelangelo's "Holy Family" on the wall. Captain Mader had bought it in Florence on his way home from a horse show in Rome. He told Boka he had visited the Uffizi and spotted a young artist copying the original. The captain had offered to buy the finished work and was thrilled that the artist was willing to part with it. Boka remembered Mader's delight when he had unwrapped the canvas after his return. He seemed a great deal more proud of it than the prize he had won at the horse show. At that time Boka had not understood the captain completely, but now the remembrance of that moment brought tears to his eyes.

"What time did you say the captain sent you to the delicatessen?" the lieutenant asked.

Priest and acolyte had left. The police lieutenant was sitting on the settee; Private Boka stood facing him. Dr. Bruck had resumed his seat beside the bed, which he had tactfully left while extreme unction was administered by Father Jellinek.

"Around a quarter past five. Just as I told you," Boka replied.

"And when did you return?"

"Half an hour later. I remember that I was near the house when I heard the church bells strike quarter to six."

"How can you explain staying away that long when the shop is only a ten-minute walk from your house?"

"There were a lot of people in the store. And even though you're next in line, if a lady comes in and wants a pound of caviar or a gentleman a case of champagne, they're always served first and you must wait."

Boka's accent was heavily Hungarian, and his vocabulary limited. As his native tongue knew no genders, he simply disregarded the German way of distinguishing between feminine, masculine or neuter and restricted himself to the pronoun meaning "he," whether he spoke of the ham he had bought, the shopgirl who sold it to him, the street he walked home on or the church bell that reminded him of the time. Neither did he pay attention to the conjugation of the German verbs, using the present infinitive whether he spoke of now, yesterday, tomorrow or a hundred years before. As a Germanic linguist, he was letter-perfect only when it came to blasphemy. He could out-curse any top sergeant in the local infantry regiment or any riding instructor in the dragoons. His speech mystified the doctor, but not the lieutenant. A Viennese policeman's ears were tuned to all the accents and grammatical eccentricities of his racially heterogeneous city, blessed or burdened with more than two million inhabitants.

"Why did the captain send you shopping?" the lieutenant asked.

Boka shrugged. "We ran out of things, sir."

"Was he expecting a visitor?"

"Maybe he was." Whenever Boka felt himself on dangerous ground, he played the dumb peasant, his face taking on the vacuous expression of a dead fish.

"Was he or wasn't he?"

"I don't know, sir." Boka despised all civilians, including the police, but cautiously avoided conflict with the latter.

"Didn't he tell you anything?"

"He did," Boka agreed readily.

"What was it?"

"To get a pound of ham, a dozen rolls and two bottles of wine. That's what he told me, Lieutenant—sir."

"Didn't it occur to you that this was too much food for one man's supper?"

"No. The captain was a big eater. Besides"—through the open door he threw a glance at the lifeless form on the bed, and his throat constricted with a pain that was not entirely physical— "what he ate I ate, too. That was how he wanted it."

The sound of footsteps and loud voices came from the corridor. Arriving at the flat simultaneously were the judge advocate Captain Kunze, and Dr. Ruppert, a regimental physician. While the captain waited in the study, Dr. Ruppert, a slight, nervous man, who wore a pince-nez and the expression of a rodent on the lookout for traps, examined the corpse. Ruppert had granted a hurried handshake to Dr. Bruck but from then on pointedly ignored him.

"I'm afraid we'll have to wait for the results of the autopsy before we can form an opinion about the cause of death," Dr. Ruppert proclaimed. "It might have been an epileptic seizure, apoplexy, embolism, heart infarct, food poisoning—anything."

The thin, tired voice of Dr. Bruck spoke behind him. "Nonsense, Doctor! It was cyanide poisoning."

Whirling about, Dr. Ruppert glared sternly at the civilian doctor. "Let's not jump to conclusions!"

"It was cyanide poisoning." Dr. Bruck repeated the diagnosis, his low voice carrying conviction and authority.

"You mean suicide?" Ruppert asked.

"That's not for me to decide."

Captain Kunze listened to the exchange with a slight frown. He was a slender man with the face of a Hamlet who had survived the poisoned foil and was nearing middle age. The word "suicide" coupled with "cyanide" worried him. He knew the army would prefer a stroke or heart attack. If an officer—especially a member of the General Staff—felt like putting an end to it all, he was expected to send a well-aimed bullet through his head and leave the more vulgar methods, such as lye, rat poison, the razor, jumping from high windows or in front of moving locomotives, to the civilian population.

"Thank you, Doctor, for your prompt assistance." He offered his hand to Dr. Bruck. "As far as your fee is concerned, the Paymaster General's Bureau will take care of it."

"That won't be necessary." The old man shook his head. "I did not have the honor of meeting Captain Mader—that is, while he was alive. Nevertheless, we were neighbors, and I consider it my duty to be at my neighbor's service should he need me. I only wish I could have done more for him."

A policeman reported that the ambulance had arrived. Covered from head to foot with a heavy blanket, Richard Mader's body was taken on a stretcher to the Military Hospital morgue, where the autopsy was to be performed. Captain Kunze instructed Lieutenant Horn to get in touch with Chief of Police Brezovsky and Police Inspector Dr. Weinberger—liaison to the Security Bureau —and make detailed reports to both. Boka was ordered to withdraw to the kitchen and wait for further instructions.

"Now that we're *entre nous*"—after the police had departed, Captain Kunze turned to Dr. Ruppert—"I feel it my duty to inform you that Mader did not commit suicide." He picked up the unfinished letter to Ingrid Fiala. "Mader was writing this letter when he collapsed. It doesn't sound like a farewell note to me. The poor fellow was making plans for the future. Besides, a man who has just taken or is about to take a lethal dose of poison doesn't write to his girl about wallpaper and Lilli Lehmann's concert. No, sir, whether we like it or not, this is no suicide."

Dr. Ruppert adjusted his pince-nez.

"It might have been an accident," he mused. "Why not? A man wants to take an aspirin, reaches for the wrong bottle, and takes a dose of rat poison. Anyway, I'm not ready to accept the poison theory. I don't doubt that a general practitioner of Dr. Bruck's limited experience is capable of diagnosing a sore throat or appendicitis, but to decide that a person has died of poisoning—no,

Captain, that requires more than just a cursory look at a body. So I suggest that we wait for the result of the autopsy and proceed from there."

Captain Kunze did not reply. It was not the first time he had observed Dr. Ruppert in action and judged him to be a poor physician and a pompous fool. Against the background of horror, the stench of violent death and the sight of a young man's body crushed like an oversized insect, Kunze resented his pettiness more than ever before and was irritated by the manner in which Ruppert had treated Dr. Bruck, a benign old owl, very Jewish and very wise. More than that, the whole case appalled him, and he hoped he would not be assigned to it.

Anna and Friedrich Gabriel lived in a walk-up flat on the fourth floor of an old house behind the Burgtheater. Negotiating the narrow, steep stairway with its worn steps was almost as tiring as a climb to an Alpine summit, and by the time Anna reached her front door she was short of breath, as usual. She hoped Fritz, as she called her husband, was not yet home, but when she entered the hallway and saw the light in the sitting room, she knew her hope had been in vain.

"What happened?" he asked her. "I thought you had an appointment with Dr. Lorentz."

That morning she had told him that she would be home late because her dentist could not see her before six.

"Oh, he was called away on some emergency case. His receptionist sent everyone away and closed the office." She lied quickly and without groping for words. There was no need to be cautious with Fritz, for he never questioned her. Not because he was stupid and gullible, but because he trusted her implicitly.

"What have you done all afternoon?" he asked.

They were in the habit of giving an account of their hours spent away from each other. He worked in the post office on Mariahilferstrasse near the Western Railroad Station. It was a busy place, frequented by all types of people, and he usually recounted some incident that he thought would amuse her. She enjoyed listening to him, although she could not shake off the suspicion that he was trying to convince her that work at the post office was great fun and that he felt no regrets over having sacrificed his army career for her.

They always had midday dinner at home. Supper was usually leftovers or cold cuts and tea. She had only a part-time maid and spent her mornings shopping, cleaning, cooking; from two in the afternoon till seven she was free. Of course, her account of these hours was not nearly as complete and truthful as his. Like the censored newspapers of a police state, it contained gaping spaces.

They had little contact with their old army crowd. Their current friends were writers, newspapermen, musicians, all of whom liked him and admired her. She enforced a strict rule of never sleeping with men who had any connection with their present circle.

"You haven't told me what you did all day," he reminded her.

She seemed nervous, which was unusual. Their evenings together were always the happiest, most relaxed hours of the day, but now he sensed a restlessness in her he found disturbing.

"Oh, nothing special." She shrugged. "I saw Mother for a few minutes. She says Father's gout has been acting up lately. Oh, yes, I had a glimpse of the emperor just as his carriage turned from Mariahilferstrasse into the Ring. He must have been coming from Schönbrunn. I thought he looked rather pale. Of course, it was hard to tell since he was riding in a closed carriage."

Her speech, too, was different, erratic and disconnected. Something must have upset her, he thought and wondered why she didn't tell him about it. He decided to pretend not to have noticed her mood.

"We had quite a laugh at the post office today," he said when the silence in the room became oppressive. "A man came in and wanted a thousand ten-heller postage stamps. He looked like a simple fellow in work clothes—a bricklayer or a cabinetmaker—so I asked him what he needed the thousand stamps for. You'll never guess what he answered! He'd heard that the letter rates would be raised to twelve hellers and decided to lay in a supply of ten-heller stamps and sell them for profit after the price rise. Incredible, isn't it?"

Her reaction was a much too eager laugh, as she tried desperately to hide the turmoil raging in her. Something alarming had happened to Mader, but this wasn't the aspect that disturbed her.

It was her narrow escape. Had she arrived a few minutes earlier, she would have been in his flat, perhaps even in his bed, when the accident—surely it was an accident—occurred. For years now she had been able to pursue her own amusements without endangering her marriage. It was not even difficult, especially since Fritz was so touchingly trusting. She had grown bold and careless, forgetting that a slip of the tongue or a chance meeting could destroy her wonderful marriage forever.

"I love you, Fritz," she told him.

He threw her a surprised look. Neither of them was demonstrative by nature. He took her affection for granted, just as she did his. There was no need to proclaim it in words. They kissed when they met or parted and made love often. Aside from being husband and wife, they were also good friends.

"I know you do." He tried to sound casual but felt ill at ease. Her sudden confession of love had the same effect on him as her earlier nervousness. He crossed to the stove, where he fumbled with the fire grate, but she did not drop the subject.

"I love you more than my life," she added. "Don't ever forget that. No matter what."

Prince Hohenstein was tall and thin with the face of an El Greco Spanish grandee. In motion he resembled a thoroughbred horse. When he approached a chair, one rather expected him to vault over it instead of sitting in it. He was courteous and unassuming and possessed a brilliant mind. Although his forte was mathematics, family traditions demanded that as a second son he choose a military career rather than a university. It was to the army's credit that it recognized his qualities and found a niche for him on the General Staff.

"That meeting in the men's room, was it the last time you saw Captain Mader yesterday?" Judge Advocate Emil Kunze asked the prince.

They were seated in Kunze's office in the Military Lawcourt Building on Hernalser Gürtel. Earlier in the morning the captain had received an order assigning him to the Richard Mader case.

Hohenstein reflected for a moment.

"No, it was not. Around four thirty in the afternoon, I passed him in the corridor. Our section, Decoding, adjoins his, the Telegraph Office. I was taking a cable to be sent out when I saw Mader. He was in his greatcoat, shako and gloves. I dropped a remark about his leaving so early—playing hooky or something like that. He grinned and said he had to hurry home because he was expecting a visitor."

"Man or woman?"

"He didn't say. I don't recall his exact words. He probably said 'visit.' No gender."

"Do you know of anyone else, besides Captain von Gersten, who received the Charles Francis circular?"

"No, I don't. But that doesn't mean that no one else did. I share an office with Gersten, and we were both in the room when the mail was delivered. And as for Mader—it was a coincidence that he entered the men's room just as Gersten and I were disposing of the trash."

"I wish you hadn't!" Captain Kunze commented. "Incidentally, why did you throw the envelope and it contents into the toilet instead of the wastebasket? I hope, Rudolf," he added quickly, "you don't misinterpret my question. I'm merely trying to find out what the damned thing looked like."

Although they had never met before, they were on first-name terms. The familiar *Du* was the rule among officers of the same rank and of superiors addressing a subordinate except when the situation called for a formal tone.

"An ordinary envelope containing a circular and small box. In the box, two capsules, filled—so the circular said—with a nerve tonic. We, Gersten and I, assumed that the sender was some kind of quack. That's why we thought the safest place for his tonic was the WC."

"Of course, we still don't know if there is any connection between the tonic and Mader's death," Kunze went on. "From all I've heard about him, he seemed too intelligent a man to fall for a cheap trick like that."

"A very decent chap and a wonderful comrade. We will miss him at the corps," the Prince said.

After seeing Hohenstein out, Kunze returned to his desk. After opening a slim dossier, he carefully studied the six handwritten sheets within. Captain Richard Mader's life was recorded on the six pages, all data that could be hastily assembled: his annual fitness report, a précis of his career, his service background, also some confidential information on his way of life. A character analysis on the last page contained all the elements to make a parent's heart swell with pride and frustrate an investigator. Not a hint of shady activities or involvements, sexual or mental aberrations, feuds or hostilities. *Un chevalier sans peur et sans reproche.* Why would anyone kill a man so perfectly harmless and kind that one wondered how he could ever have become a member of the General Staff?

Later in the morning a policeman brought Frau Czepa, the janitor's wife from 56 Hainburgerstrasse, to Kunze's office for questioning. She was haggard and thin-lipped, resembling, in silhouette and coloring, the implement of her calling: a long-handled twig broom.

For some time she rambled on about trivialities. Kunze listened drowsily until a remark of hers brought him wide awake.

"Dr. Bruck and Private Boka were just coming down the street," she was saying, "when this young lady reached the house. When Boka noticed her, he turned white in the face and shouted at her to go away."

"What do you mean, turned white in the face?" Kunze asked.

"Just that." She shrugged. "White as a sheet." She waited a second, then lowered her voice to a whisper. "It looked like he didn't want her around when the police came. Maybe she knew something he didn't want her to tell them."

Frau Czepa harbored a secret grudge against Boka. Soon after Captain Mader had moved in, she and Boka had an argument regarding the amount of trash a janitor was supposed to collect from a tenant. Boka, the uninhibited son of the Hungarian plains, had dropped a few crusty remarks about the Austrians in general and their negative attitude toward physical exertion in particular, at which time Frau Czepa questioned the legality of his parents' marriage. Captain Mader's timely arrival had kept the incident from turning into an assault and battery case, and there remained a feeling of hostility between the two of them.

"You referred to her as a *young lady,*" the captain said. "Did she look like a respectable woman to you?"

"She didn't look like a whore, if that's what the captain means."

"In your opinion what could have been the connection between her and Private Boka?"

"In my opinion they were thick as thieves. When he yelled at her, she looked kind of surprised, then turned and ran."

"Had you ever seen her before yesterday?"

"Just once. On the staircase. She was coming from Captain Mader's flat."

"Was the captain home at the time?"

"I don't know. He might have been. It was around seven in the evening. He was usually home by then."

If Mader had been home, it was clear the woman visited him, not his orderly, Kunze concluded.

Earlier that day both the police and the military had received the result of the autopsy performed on Captain Mader's body. Death had been caused by cyanide poisoning. Although the postmortem examination had not yet been completed, the pathologists were of the opinion that the dose had been powerful enough to kill a dozen men.

After dismissing Frau Czepa, Captain Kunze asked the sergeant on duty to find out whether Dr. Max Bruck had a telephone. The sergeant returned with the number. Kunze had to wait a few minutes before hearing the old man's voice croak from the receiver. He asked the doctor whether he remembered the mystery woman taking flight after the orderly's warning.

"I'm afraid I don't," Dr. Bruck replied. "From what the orderly had told me I gathered the captain's condition was critical and that we had to hurry. We had trouble getting through the crowd in front of the house. I heard the private shouting, but I assumed he was telling the people to get out of the way. I'm sorry, but that's all I can recall."

"Don't worry, Doctor. If there was a woman, we may find her yet. I want to thank you once more for your assistance. And," he added, "to tell you that your diagnosis was correct. Captain Mader *did* die of cyanide poisoning. Potassium cyanide."

"There was never any doubt in my mind about that." The doctor chuckled.

"I know. But I thought I'd tell you just the same."

Kunze wished he could tell Dr. Ruppert, too, but that wouldn't have served any purpose. People like Ruppert could easily stumble, then continue without missing a step, head high, eyes daring the world to call their bluff.

Captain Kunze gave orders to have Private Boka brought to his office for questioning. While he waited he felt a migraine headache lodge itself—like a voracious rodent—in the cavity behind his right eye and begin gnawing on the bones of his skull. His stomach felt queasy, although he hadn't eaten a bite all day. Lately these attacks had become more frequent, and he wondered why. His was a pleasant and well-regulated existence, containing all the basic ingredients for the condition commonly known as happiness: a healthy constitution, satisfaction with his work and harmony at home.

Emil Kunze had entered the regular army late in life. The opportunity was offered to him—after he had taken part as a second lieutenant in the reserves in the 1902 maneuvers—by General Hartmann, an old acquaintance, practically a friend, although the nature of their relationship did not quite warrant the appellation. Kunze's mother had been the Hartmanns' housekeeper for fifteen years, and he had grown up in the Hartmanns' comfortably unpretentious villa surrounded by a huge and neglected park.

Wilhelmine Kunze, the daughter of a schoolteacher, had been slim, not unattractive, with the undernourished, sexless look of a medieval saint. Well educated, she had the faultless manners of a lady. People often wondered why she had chosen to work in another woman's house, instead of trying to find a husband who could provide her with a home of her own.

Twenty-five when her son, Emil, was born, she had been married briefly to Staff Sergeant Herbert Kunze of the Viennese Deutschmeister Regiment, who—shortly after the wedding—disappeared from her life as quietly as he had entered it.

"Don't you ever start looking for him," she had told her son when, as an adolescent, Emil questioned her about the mysterious sergeant. "He was a decent man and a good soldier. That's all you have to know. The name he gave you was a respectable name. If in the future, someone comes to you and makes demands in the name of Staff Sergeant Herbert Kunze, show him to the door.

You don't owe the sergeant anything. Neither money nor affection. Always remember that."

It had been an odd way of talking to a boy about his alleged father, but Emil Kunze had become used to his mother's odd ways. He had also learned to respect her need for secrecy. She worked hard for every penny she earned, which was less than that which other housekeepers, who didn't have growing sons living with them, were paid. She held a unique position in the household, was neither a servant nor a member of the family. The relationship, too, was of her own design. Ironically, it had been the mistress who had a deep dependence on—even a slight fear of—the housekeeper, not the other way around.

Kunze suspected that his mother had had access to some extra money, which she spent on his education, clothes, medical care and twice a year, photographs taken of him by an expensive photographer. Not a penny on herself. On her Sunday afternoons off, she would take him on long walks in the woods or along the Danube and on his—and again on the emperor's birthday—to the amusement park in the Prater. Twice a year, when the photographs were ready, she would ask Frau Hartmann for an extra afternoon off, dress with special care, and leave for town. She would return in a few hours and, during the following days, would be even more taciturn than usual. The habit of her twice-a-year absences were kept up until her death. By then Emil had his law degree and was employed by the highly reputable firm of Teller and Bauer, Attorneys. Despite his insistence that she retire, his mother still kept house for the Hartmanns. It was a heart attack that put an end to her servitude and to her life. To Kunze's great surprise, he found that she had close to ten thousand florins saved. "For my dear son, Emil," she had written in her will, "to make amends for the unhappiness of a fatherless childhood."

He often wished he could tell her how wrong she had been. He had never felt unhappy, never wanted to be anyone else but Emil Kunze, Frau Wilhelmine's boy. General Hartmann, his wife, daughter and two sons accepted him as a member of the family. Also, somewhere there was a man who had fathered him and kept a watchful eye on him. No doubt, the Teller and Bauer law firm offer had been the result of his patronage, as was the commission in the Judge Advocate Corps. The man seemed to reside on

Olympian heights, declining to descend to the level of mortals. In his younger years Emil Kunze was very often filled with the impatient desire of a Phaëthon to find his Helios. One thing appeared certain, Staff Sergeant Herbert Kunze, whose name he bore and whom he had never met face-to-face, was not Helios.

He remained a bachelor, but his good fortune granted him the benefits of marriage without any of its burdens. The woman he lived with, Rose von Siebert, embodied the best of all wifely virtues. She loved him tenderly, loyally, tactfully, understandingly and eternally. He considered himself rather average-looking, well preserved for his thirty-eight years, but with a face that in its pale softness appeared more priestly than soldierly. His thinning hair was dark blond and turning white at the temples. His eyes were like the waters of the Danube, described as blue in songs, but actually a lackluster gray. He never really cared much about the impression he made on others. He was clean and orderly, though somewhat remote, a boy, once tolerated in the house of strangers, now grown into manhood.

He had known Rose for three years. He had met her first when he rented two rooms in her high-ceilinged, luxuriously cluttered apartment on Zaunergasse. It had taken her a year of cajoling to get him to sleep with her. As lodger turned lover, he insisted on strict business arrangements, paid a high rent for his rooms, also half the household expenses and the servants' salaries. In return he demanded absolute privacy. She was not to enter his domain unless invited or expect him to meet her friends or attend her parties. At first she tried questioning his rules, but when he threatened to move out, she accepted them.

He had made it clear to her at the beginning of their affair that he could marry her only after having reached the rank of full colonel, which meant a wait of at least twenty years. She was the widow of a cabinet minister and lived on the pension she received from the state. Officers of the K. and K. Army basked in glamor and prestige but received very modest salaries. Regulations also called for a generous marriage bond, and neither he nor Rose could produce that. Only from the rank of colonel up were officers paid well enough to marry without having to put up any security, provided the bride had an immaculate reputation. Rose farsightedly had had her brother-in-law take over the tenancy of the apartment so there would be no evidence of her relationship with her lodger. The ruse was commonly practiced all over the monarchy. It amused Kunze that the army code of honor did not object to an officer's living in sin, only to his making it legal later. It was one of the strange contradictions that sometimes made the army seem like a giant retarded child.

"Who was the woman?" For the fifth time during the interrogation Captain Kunze asked Private Boka.

For the fifth time Boka replied, "What woman, sir?"

"Goddamn it, Boka, you know very well whom I mean."

Boka responded with a rambling account. He found Captain Mader on the floor in the hallway, carried him into the bedroom, ran for help, and returned with the doctor. The story contained no new details, and besides, Boka told it in rather bizarre German that was hard to understand. The captain wondered how Mader had ever been able to communicate with his orderly. Finally, losing his patience, he called in the Hungarian Lieutenant Szabó, one of the judge advocate candidates, and told him to interrogate Boka in their mother tongue.

While in disposition and bearing Kunze was jurist rather than army man, Szabó was army from head to toe. Short and squat, with a thick mass of unruly hair and a drooping mustache, he looked like a puli, the fierce little sheep dog of the Hungarian plains. He sounded like one, too, barking his questions in a loud, shrill voice that made Kunze's head spin. There was a moment when he feared Szabó's bark might be followed by a bite.

It was to Boka's credit that he resisted the barrage for more than an hour. At the beginning, he shot back his answers in a strident drill-ground tone; then his voice lost its thunder, became hesitant, and finally thinned to a whisper.

Exactly seventy-two minutes after Lieutenant Szabó's appearance Boka revealed the name: Mrs. Friedrich Gabriel.

Captain Richard Mader's name first appeared in the Viennese press on November 19, 1909. The leading morning paper printed the following story in its city news section:

On November 17, around six o'clock in the evening, Captain Richard Mader, one of the most brilliant young officers of the General Staff, was found dead by his orderly. Since Captain Mader had from all appearances been in perfect health, a police investigation is now in progress to clear up the circumstances of his sudden death.

Next, there was an item about an accident on Kärtnerstrasse. The horses of Paul Horner, fiacre owner, had bolted for no apparent reason, causing the passersby to scatter in panic. In the turmoil, a seventy-three-year-old tobacconist was slightly injured. The horses were brought under control by the valiant efforts of Police Officer Michael Rosner.

Although the two items had been given equal space, the reporters who swarmed around Chief of Police Brezovsky's office weren't there to hear about the tobacconist's condition. For a few kronen, pressed into the palms of plainclothesmen waiting for assignments in the anteroom, the reporters learned about a hastily called conference taking place behind the padded doors of the inner sanctum with the participation of General Kutschera of the Vienna garrison; Captain Emil Kunze, judge advocate; Police Inspector Weinberger, liaison to the Security Bureau; and General Karl Wencel, head of the Judge Advocate Corps. The subject of the meeting was the death of Captain Mader.

The police had discarded the possibility of suicide and were concentrating on the search for the poisoner. They examined all clues pointing to his identity and motives. He might have been the member of an antimonarchist organization, a Serb, a Croat, a Hungarian, a jealous husband, a noncommissioned officer bearing a grudge or a rival. He might not have been a "he" at all, but a "she": a jilted woman perhaps. The rumors and guesses proved too vague and contradictory, and not even reporters of the sensation-hungry boulevard papers dared print them.

At ten thirty in the morning, a dark-haired young woman, wearing a chic green suit, was escorted by a detective up the wide stairway through endless corridors and crowded anterooms to the chief's office. Although her face was hidden by a thick veil attached to a gaily decorated hat, one of the reporters recognized her.

Her name was Anna Gabriel.

The reporter belonged to the Bohemian circle the Gabriels frequented and was shocked to find her present in the Police Presidium for interrogation. Elbowing his way through his colleagues, he caught up with her in front of the chief's door.

"Frau Gabriel! For heaven's sake, what do they want from you?"

She halted and stared at him as if he were a suddenly materialized bill collector. Behind the heavy veil, her eyes seemed even larger and darker than usual. Her fear and embarrassment were obvious.

The detective stepped between them. "The lady is not supposed to speak to anyone, Herr Swoboda." The phrasing was polite, but the tone was not. The reporter stepped back, and the two disappeared behind the padded door.

In the course of their long army careers General Wencel and Baron von Campanini saw each other frequently at both official and social functions. The general had watched Anna grow from a chubby girl into a disturbingly attractive woman. He was also aware of her premarital escapades and, as a member of the military judiciary, had had a hand in her father's forced retirement from active service.

Now the Anna von Campanini who, years before, had bespattered the good name of the Austro-Hungarian officers' dependents with her indecorous conduct, stood before him as a witness and possible suspect in what appeared to be a disgusting murder case.

General Karl Wencel was having a bad day. His peptic ulcer was acting up again, most likely triggered by the latest escapade of his mistress, a minor actress from the Theater an der Wien. While supposedly visiting her sick grandmother in Graz, she had been seen in the company of an Italian count in Monte Carlo.

Now as he faced another naughty young woman, he was tormented by the physical pain at the pit of his stomach and the mental pain which accompanied jealousy and frustration. Jealousy alone was bad enough. What disturbed him even more was the astonishment he felt at the disloyalty of the young. He was fifty-six, far from old, yet anyone under thirty—man or woman— seemed to him disturbingly and incomprehensibly alien. The

young of the new century—his mistress no less than the rest—
appeared greedy, ungrateful and blasé. They did not appreciate
what his generation had created for them: a peaceful and pros-
perous monarchy where every man willing to work had a fair
chance. The lower classes engaged in senseless and noisy street
demonstrations and in strikes organized by the Socialist Party,
and the upper classes spent their time in absurd pranks, dueling,
dissipation and promiscuity. There was a great deal of talk about
the imminent war. He, like most of the military, felt that it was
inevitable. More than that, he longed for it, considering it the
only cleansing agent that would free the monarchy from filth and
pollution and reestablish its onetime order and moral purity.

To his worries over his mistress was added the change in his
wife's attitude toward him. Throughout their twenty years of
marriage Lily Wencel had remained ambitious for his career, undemanding and patient with his extramarital escapades. She had
inherited not only her father's money, but also his sophistication
and the detachment—or was it arrogance?—of the rich. Then,
suddenly, she became moody and neurotic. At first he blamed it
on the weather, the unseasonably hot spell in September, but the
weather turned cool and her restlessness remained. He had no
other solution but to attribute her sudden contrariness to meno-
pause and add that to his problems.

After the usual preliminaries—name, marital status, occupation,
residence—were out of the way, Captain Kunze began the questioning.

"Frau Gabriel, what were you doing in front of Number Fifty-
six Hainburgerstrasse on the seventeenth of November at six
o'clock in the evening?"

Anna's husband had read an item about Mader's death in the
morning paper. She had still been in bed when he had come into
the room, shaken and pale, and told her the news. He and Mader
had been classmates at the War College and served together later
as field officers with the Fifteenth Infantry Regiment in Brassó.
Although they had lost contact after Gabriel's resignation from
the army, his ex-friend's tragic death saddened Fritz deeply. He
also felt a touch of remorse. Mader was one of the few who had
wished him well after his marriage. But Gabriel had never thanked
him, having thrown away the address book of his army days and

with it expurgated his memory of all the people whose names were listed. Suddenly he realized how wrong he had been. Mader had reached out to him, but he had ignored the gesture. Now Mader was dead, and there was no way to make amends.

Anna repeated the question. "What was I doing on Hainburgerstrasse?" Until the moment she was ushered into the room she hadn't been quite sure what the police wanted with her. When she recognized General Wencel and noticed two other uniforms in the group of solemn men staring at her, their eyes cold and mistrusting, she realized that their inquiry was connected with Mader's death. Naturally, she had no idea how much they knew of her affair with him. She only knew she had to be cautious and avoid a trap.

"Just walking," she answered.

"Do you know a Private József Boka?"

She frowned. The name sounded familiar. Then she remembered. Boka was Mader's orderly. He was the man who had shouted at her in front of Mader's house. Her memory dipped even deeper into the waters of the past. Years before, this same Boka had been one of the soldiers she had seen frequently around the riding academy where her father taught. Boka must have been an officer's orderly then, for she had never seen him working in the stables.

"No, I don't know a Private Boka," she answered with a hint of indignation. After all, the daughter of a cavalry major was not supposed to remember a private just because he used to loiter around the riding academy.

"Why then did you turn back when he told you not to go up to Captain Mader's flat?" Kunze asked.

"I don't know what you mean. What makes you think that I had any intention of going up to Mader's flat?"

"Didn't you visit him on the sixth and again on the twelfth of November?"

Petrified, she stared at Kunze. Someone, probably the damned orderly, had told them. Or had it been Mader himself? *God, oh, God,* she thought, *don't let Fritz find out!*

"What if I did?" she asked defiantly. It would have been foolish to deny it as her inquisitor appeared to have all the facts. But why go to pieces? After all, she had nothing to do with Mader's murder. Quite evidently murder it was, or there wouldn't be all this fuss. If she convinced them that she was in no way involved, they would have to let her go. She reflected for a few seconds on how much she should admit.

"Yes," she told them finally. "I went to his place on the two occasions you mentioned. Each time when I left, he was very much alive. The day before yesterday, I wasn't even near him. That's what you've just said, isn't it?" She waited for a reaction, but none was forthcoming. "I don't see any point in bringing me here and questioning me about matters that have no bearing on the case."

"That is for us to decide, Frau Gabriel," General Wencel snapped. "Now what about Captain Karl Moll?"

The previous evening Captain Moll, also newly assigned to the General Staff Corps, had reported the receipt of a Charles Francis circular. He had not destroyed his copy but had handed it in, complete with poison capsules, to his command post.

"What about him?" she asked. For a moment she could not place the name.

"During the months of April and May, 1909, you were frequently seen entering and leaving his flat on Singerstrasse."

Now she remembered. Moll was one of those faceless men she —already married to Gabriel—had slept with. She had never really cared for him and never thought of him again after the affair ended. The unexpected mention of his name terrified her because she failed to understand the connection.

"Is he dead, too?" she asked. She could never explain to herself or anyone else what had prompted the question. Nevertheless, it must have fitted into the chain of assumptions the five dour men used as a guideline in their interrogation, because they suddenly lost their waxworks detachment and exchanged meaningful glances.

"No, he survived," General Wencel told her. "And so did Prince Hohenstein."

Another name out of the blue. *What are they trying to do to me?* Anna asked herself. First Moll and now the prince. Are they going to excavate my past as though it were an ancient city buried under the dust layers of centuries, bring up every broken amphora, cracked mosaic, no-longer-revered idol, and label it?

She sat up straighter and stuck out her chin the way she had as a child when submitted to unwarranted punishment. Her head was spinning, and she clenched her right hand with the left firmly in order to keep them from trembling. The room was silent. General Wencel was obviously waiting for her answer, but she refused to comply.

Judge Advocate Kunze broke the silence. "When did you last see Captain von Gersten, Frau Gabriel?"

A third name. This time she was completely baffled.

"I don't think I know any Captain von Gersten."

"He was one of your father's pupils at the War College, class of 1905."

"So were another hundred. I knew a few of them, not more than three or four. And I'm not even sure they were all class of 1905."

Again there was an exchange of glances among the men.

"But you did know Prince Hohenstein?"

"Yes. He was introduced to me." She nodded curtly.

"You had an affair with him, just as you had with Captains Mader, Moll and von Gersten."

"Not with Gersten! I told you I don't even know him!"

"But you admit the others." General Wencel pounced.

He needn't sound so triumphant, she thought. Admitting three lovers had been no slip of the tongue. She had done it deliberately. She was still in the dark about the purpose of the investigation. However, one thing was certain—they had thoroughly explored her private life and somehow had discovered affairs that she had hoped to keep secret from her husband. They could not bring the law down on her for having slept around—if they could, a good portion of Vienna's female population would have been in jail—but they could certainly inform Fritz Gabriel, and that would be the end. She had to make a deal with them, buy their silence by telling them all they wanted to know.

"Yes, I admit the others." She took a deep breath. "I honestly don't know what you are searching for, gentlemen. I wish you would tell me, because I could be of more help. It is very difficult for me to—"

General Wencel interrupted her. "Is your husband a very jealous man?"

"No, I don't think so." The tempo of her heartbeat accelerated again. "No, he is not. Why do you ask?"

The general ignored the question.

"You mean to tell me he doesn't mind your—your having affairs?" Wencel grunted. "With men who at one time were his classmates or served in the same regiment with him? He must be either an imbecile or entirely without honor."

Anna felt a stir of hot anger. "Kindly leave my husband out of this!" she shouted. "He is a wonderful person—with very high moral principles!"

Chief of Police Brezovsky entered the discussion. "A person of very high moral principles who condones his wife's licentiousness." Up to now Brezovsky had been sitting upright, his hands folded in front of his embonpoint, motionless, except for eyes that darted from face to face and thumbs that at times twirled nervously, reminding Anna of angry cats swinging their tails from side to side.

"No, he doesn't." Anna felt herself on the verge of tears. "I mean—he certainly wouldn't if he knew, but—"

Her voice broke, and she couldn't go on, suddenly speechless with fear of these five stern men and of what they could do to her marriage. Her eyes came to rest on Wencel's face. He was the only one she knew among them; she knew his wife and also his reputation for being a middle-aged Don Juan. She remembered him from her childhood. He and his rich, elegant wife, Lily, had attended some of her mother's gatherings. He used to pick her up and joke with her. Once he had brought her a box of bonbons.

"I know this is hard to understand," she spoke in a low voice to General Wencel, trying to forget that there were others in the room. "I love my husband more than anything in the world. But I—I just can't stay faithful to him. It's odd—I know it is—I often thought of . . . of seeing a doctor about it—only what doctor?"

"Are you aware of the sacrifices your husband has made for you? When he informed his commander that he wanted to marry you, he was given the choice between you and his army career. And he chose you. Are you aware of that?" the general asked.

"I am. I've always been—"

"But that didn't keep you from cheating on him, did it?" Wencel wagged an accusing finger at her.

She could not find the words to make it clear to this tribunal of righteous men that the two—her love for her husband and her extramarital excursions—had no bearing on one another. She realized that according to society's moral laws she ought to feel guilty about her "licentiousness," but it seemed to her as though she were two persons, the model wife of Friedrich Gabriel and the trollop, disciple and practitioner of sexual freedom and that neither could be made responsible for the other's deeds. Now the wife had been dragged before the tribunal and ordered to plead the trollop's case.

"You haven't answered me, Frau Gabriel," General Wencel reminded her.

She shrugged. "I don't know what to answer." It was useless to argue with him. She was the adulterous woman whom he wanted stoned. And Christ was not present to save her. Contrition might prove to be the only way out, and she was willing—not for her own but for her husband's sake—to resort to it.

"I know I made a terrible mistake—"

"Use the plural, Frau Gabriel." The chief of police chuckled. Wencel responded to the quip with a grin; the others remained stony-faced.

"All right, I made terrible mistakes," she went on with a touch of acrimony, "but I can't change that now. All I can do is mend my ways and pray to God that my husband never finds out." She turned once again to Wencel. "General, there is only one thing I beg of you—let me save my marriage. You don't know my husband. He is the kindest, most considerate man on earth, but if he found out that I've deceived him, he would—"

"Kill you?" General Wencel cut in sharply.

The harshness of his tone startled her.

"Maybe not. Oh, no—certainly not—but—"

Wencel rose and stepped closer to her.

"Or kill your lovers! Is that what you wanted to say?"

She shrank back.

"No, no! It wasn't! Don't put words into my mouth! No such preposterous idea ever occurred to me!"

"Isn't it possible that he found out about your infidelities and, in a moment of rage and bitterness, decided to take revenge on the men you had deceived him with?" The general's shout caused her to jump to her feet and seek refuge behind a chair.

At last, she realized what the tribunal was after, and the realization was a shock. Someone had murdered Mader, had also tried to kill Moll and the prince. By a weird coincidence they all were lovers of hers. For this reason, Fritz appeared to be the most likely suspect. Appeared? Mother of God! They couldn't be right. If her husband had found out about Mader and the others, she would have known it; she would have noticed the change in him. Feverishly she tried to recall that morning. Every detail. The way he had come into the bedroom, quite shaken, to read the news to her. If he had merely been testing her or setting a trap, he would have acted differently. He would have watched her to see if she betrayed herself. But no, he had paid no attention to what she said, was simply and understandably shocked by the sudden death of a friend. On the other hand, two days before, when she had returned from Hainburgerstrasse, he was rather insistent that she tell him about her afternoon. He always asked her about her day, but on the seventeenth he had seemed especially insistent.

The general leaned across the back of the chair. She was aware of his hot breath, reeking of tobacco smoke and gastric odors.

"Is it, Frau Gabriel?" His voice was a whisper.

"No! You're wrong! Fritz didn't kill Mader or anyone else! He couldn't have. I've been married to him for four years—I've never seen him angry. He is the most even-tempered person I've ever known. He doesn't have an enemy in the world. He didn't know about Captain Mader and the others!"

She looked from face to face. For a fleeting moment her eyes met those of Captain Kunze. She seemed to detect a compassion in them, even encouragement. She took a deep breath and went on, hurling her words at him. "But even if my husband had known about them, he would've been hurt—terribly hurt—but he'd never have harmed anyone."

She was disappointed when she realized that Kunze was no longer looking at her. He appeared to be examining the green felt of the conference table for possible moth holes. General Wencel had resumed his seat and was thumbing through his portfolio.

"I hope you're right, Frau Gabriel," he mumbled. "I really do. For your and your husband's sake."

"So do I," General Kutschera added, and the chief of police nodded.

At one o'clock the gentlemen of the commission adjourned to the dining room of the Hotel Bristol, where a corner table had been reserved for them. General Kutschera and Inspector Weinberger ordered *Tafelspitz,* while Captain Kunze and Chief of Police Brezovsky decided on partridge *chasseur.* General Wencel, on a bland diet because of his ulcers, ordered *blanquette de veau* with rice. Two bottles of Gumpoldskirchner, a light Austrian wine, vintage 1905, accompanied the entrées. The captain mixed it with seltzer; the others, with the exception of General Wencel, who ordered Vichy water, drank it straight. They finished the meal with cheese and fruit. General Kutschera had a double Courvoisier. He suggested a round, but the men declined in view of their heavy schedule for the afternoon.

When they reconvened at three o'clock, they agreed that Inspector Weinberger should conduct the interrogation of Friedrich Gabriel. The suggestion came from Chief of Police Brezovsky, but it had been Captain Kunze's idea. On the walk back to the Presidium he had had a few minutes alone with Brezovsky, convincing him that it would be more practical if they kept General Wencel from acting as investigator and avenging angel. Kunze didn't exactly look forward to the questioning of Anna's husband. He had never met the man; all he knew about him was that Gabriel had exchanged a promising army career for love of a nymphomaniac. He had been in Kunze's opinion either sick or unbelievably naïve—in either case a man to be pitied rather than condemned. There was a fair chance that he *was* the fake Charles Francis, and if so, his attempt at mass murder was an act that elevated him from cuckold to tragic figure. A man like that would no doubt crumble under General Wencel's verbal flagellations, and this was a performance Captain Kunze did not wish to observe. The general's technique was to strip a man of his dignity before punishing him. In the course of his army career, Kunze had occasionally witnessed the degradation of a fellowman. He felt each time as though his own dignity had been lessened.

Friedrich Gabriel did not have the vaguest idea why he had been subpoenaed to appear at the Presidium. The writ commanded him to report there "immediately upon receipt of same." The commission had already left for the Bristol when he arrived shortly after one o'clock, and he was told to wait. When he suggested he go home and return after lunch, the detective on duty informed him gruffly that he was not to leave the building. Hungry, indignant, but otherwise untroubled, he had no choice but to bide his time till three in the afternoon.

A few weeks earlier there had been an attempt by persons unknown to break into the post office during the night. The police had instigated a routine investigation which had led nowhere. When Friedrich Gabriel entered Chief Brezovsky's office and recognized Generals Wencel and Kutschera, he concluded that the presence of the uniforms meant that the unknown postal burglar had been after military documents.

During the next half hour Inspector Weinberger managed to destroy Friedrich Gabriel as man, husband, citizen, even public servant. His first questions pertained to motives behind his resignation from the army. Then he switched to financial affairs: how much Gabriel earned; what his expenditures were; whether or not he had any pressing debts. Gradually, Gabriel felt the blood rise to his head. Still under the impression that the subject of the inquiry was burglary, he failed to understand why he was being treated not as a witness, but as a suspect.

"Will you come to the point, Inspector?" he demanded finally. "What do you want from me? What is this all about? Ask me a straight question, and I'll give you a straight answer."

The inspector took a deep breath.

"Very well, Herr Gabriel. I'll ask you a straight question. Did you send to the late Captain Richard Mader a circular signed Charles Francis, the envelope containing two capsules each filled with a gram of potassium cyanide?"

For several seconds Gabriel stared motionless at the inspector. Then he blinked a few times as though bothered by a sudden flash of light.

"Did I what?" he asked in a low, incredulous voice.

"Did you or didn't you send Richard Mader a lethal dose of cyanide in a letter addressed to his office at the Ministry of War?"

At last, the meaning of the question penetrated Gabriel's mind.

"Hell, no!" he replied. His voice was even, and he displayed no sign of outraged innocence. "What makes you think such rot? Why me? What on earth could I have had against the poor fellow?!"

"Wasn't he your wife's lover?" The session was not progressing according to Inspector Weinberger's expectations. Gabriel was either the best actor in the Austro-Hungarian monarchy or an unsuspecting, innocent victim of circumstances. The inspector was an experienced enough policeman to know that the latter interpretation was the more plausible. He longed to terminate the inquiry and dismiss the man before some irreparable harm was done. Unfortunately, the army demanded this man's hide. The targets of a bizarre murder plot had been four distinguished members of the General Staff Corps. One was dead; three had escaped. At the moment the motives of the murderer were a puzzle. They could range from a political plot to espionage to personal revenge. Blackmail, treason, homosexuality, money could be involved, aspects that could compromise the army, expose it to suspicion, even dishonor. However, if the murderer turned out to be a jealous husband, the shining image of the army would remain unblemished. Young, good-looking officers weren't supposed to lead the lives of monks. If Captains Mader, Moll or Hohenstein cuckolded a postal clerk, more power to the captains and shame on the postal clerk.

"No! He was not my wife's lover!" His face white, Gabriel addressed the entire commission. "And if you, gentlemen, think that your rank and position give you the right to fling dirt at my wife, you are very much mistaken. We don't live under a military dictatorship; we live in a constitutional monarchy. I intend to defend our good name and to hit back at anyone who tries to blacken it and that bloody well includes you!"

General Wencel stared at him, his face a marble slab with the Ten Commandments engraved on it. General Kutschera, a weighty but silent presence throughout the investigation, sat with closed eyes, either deep in thought or simply dozing. Brezovsky appeared slightly bored, having heard the same tirade many times as police officer. Captain Kunze squirmed uncomfortably in his seat. He had expected Gabriel to be a weakling or a fool, but he appeared to be neither. He seemed more a trusting and honorable man damned with faulty vision; he had looked at a whore and seen a saint. Now he was going to have his vision corrected through an extremely painful operation.

Inspector Weinberger sighed unhappily. Rising, he handed Gabriel one of the police reports, written in neat longhand, that lay on the table.

"Read this, young man," he ordered.

Kunze could not bear to watch the man. From where he sat he was able to see the Ring through the window and beyond it the park. His eyes followed a gray whirlpool of clouds on the autumnal sky. A drizzle was falling, and the naked branches of the trees glistened as though they had been coated with wax. A stray dog scurried along the park wall, its tail between its legs. Captain Kunze kept his eyes on the dog until it was lost from view, for it gave him an excuse for ignoring the man who was reading the police report on his wife's indiscretions.

"What do you say, Gabriel?" General Wencel's shrill voice broke the silence.

There was no doubt in anyone's mind that the report written in awkward German told Gabriel facts about his wife he had never known or even suspected. He looked like someone who had suffered a heavy blow or drunk himself into a stupor. He did not answer the general's question, apparently hadn't even understood it.

The inspector waited another moment.

"Well, what is your reaction, Herr Gabriel?"

Although his voice was low-pitched, Gabriel reacted as if a bullet had smashed through the window. His head jerked up and he gave the inspector a look of utter bewilderment. His face flushed with anger.

"Why did she do it? Who says all this is true? Just because you have it on paper, that's no proof! You're trying to trick me into something. That's why you want me to believe that she— What are you after? Tell me, and I'll help you any way I can. There is something I can tell you right now. It wasn't me who sent that—

whatever it was—to Mader. Don't waste time on me and let the guilty man slip through your fingers!"

"Prince Hohenstein and Captain Moll and Gersten were also sent circulars containing poison. Of the three, the prince and Moll had been your wife's lovers. Gersten, as far as we know, was not. Here"—the inspector proffered another sheet to Gabriel— "read this."

Gabriel did not reach for it.

"No!" He shook his head. "You can bring false charges against me, but you can't force me to read that filth."

Weinberger replaced the sheet with a shrug.

"Have Frau Gabriel brought in!" he instructed the clerk, who rose and left the room.

"Sit down, Herr Gabriel." The inspector motioned to a chair. He himself dropped his heavy bulk into his seat behind the table. Captain Kunze's stomach was churning with the same kind of nauseating discomfort he felt whenever he had to witness an execution.

Anna Gabriel was ushered into the room by the clerk. Kunze noticed with surprise that whereas a day of interrogation usually aged people, she now looked younger and more fragile than she had in the morning. Her green wool suit was rumpled and her once-neat chignon a tousled mass. When she caught sight of her husband, she halted for a second, her hand moving up to her face and brushing away a stray wisp of hair. There was a faint smile on her face.

"Have they told you?" she asked, looking straight into his eyes.

"Told me what?"

He stood erect and motionless. In his well-pressed gray suit —she took good care of his clothes—spotless white shirt with the starched collar and cuffs, he resembled a mannequin in a store window.

"About Mader and me." She paused to take a deep breath. "And the rest," she added.

He stared at her impassively.

"So it is true." It was a statement, not a question.

She merely nodded.

"All of it?"

"Yes."

Captain Kunze watched them not with the judge advocate's detachment, but the voyeur's fascination.

"What now?" Gabriel turned to Weinberger.

"We'll have to keep you here for the time being, Herr Gabriel," the inspector told him. "But don't worry. You have nothing to fear. That is if you didn't send the poison. You can trust us to find the murderer. Our men are very capable and conscientious. They seldom make mistakes. And I'm here to see that they don't in this case."

"Thank you," Gabriel's reply was mechanical.

"Could I talk to my husband alone?" Anna turned to Weinberger. "Just for a few minutes!"

The inspector contemplated an answer, but Gabriel didn't wait for it.

"I'd rather she wouldn't," he said.

For the first time, Anna seemed in danger of losing her composure. She placed a trembling hand on her husband's shoulder. He threw a glance at the hand, then found something more worthy of his attention in the far corner of the room.

"I know how you must feel," she pleaded with him. "But—but let me explain. Listen to me!" She turned to the commission. "Please, please, give me two minutes with him!"

"That won't be necessary," Gabriel shook his head. "With your permission, Inspector, if you have no more questions, I'd rather you had me locked up." He spoke in the curt and precise manner of the officer he had been before meeting Anna von Campanini, addressing himself solely to Weinberger as if there were no one else in the room.

"As you wish." The inspector nodded. He turned for confirmation to the members of the commission, then ordered the clerk to have Gabriel taken to one of the special cells reserved for more distinguished suspects. "He may have bedding sent in from his home, and supper, too," he added. "You needn't suffer any discomfort," he told Gabriel. "However, the lights must be on all night. Regulations, you know."

Gabriel bowed stiffly from the waist; then he nodded his head to the rest of the commission.

The clerk motioned to him, and he started for the door. He had almost reached it when his wife barred the way.

"I love you," she whispered to him. "I've never loved anyone but you. Don't ever forget it. Don't ever—"

He reached out for her, but only to push her aside. She stared after him as he followed the clerk from the room.

"You may leave now, Frau Gabriel," Chief of Police Brezovsky told her. "Unless there is anything you want to tell us, anything that hasn't already been discussed."

"I don't think there is," she said. She seemed composed and almost carefree once more. "You said I could send in bedding for him." She turned to Weinberger. "I think he'd like a cup of coffee right now. May I order it from the café across the street? And his supper and breakfast, too, in case he is not released before tomorrow morning. I mean, that isn't against regulations, is it?"

"Certainly not, Frau Gabriel."

"Well, then, I'd better be going. Thank you, gentlemen, and good-bye."

"Good-bye, Frau Gabriel," the inspector answered. The others mumbled their farewells. Only Captain Kunze rose as she left the room.

The commission agreed to reconvene at eight the following morning, but it was nearly ten by the time the last ones, Generals Wencel and Kutschera, arrived. On this fourth day after Captain Mader's death, new and important facts had been brought to light by the Security Bureau.

In addition to Captains Mader, Moll, von Gersten and Prince Hohenstein, four more officers had received the Charles Francis circulars, with their cyanide capsules. They subsequently responded to the inquiry sent out to all garrisons. Three men turned in their envelopes; the fourth, who had destroyed his, merely reported its receipt. Of the four, one was stationed in Galicia, one was in Budapest, and two were on leaves of absence. All the envelopes in the hands of the authorities bore the stamp of Post Office No. 59 in Mittelgasse, a narrow street near Vienna's Western Railroad Station.

"A strong enough clue to hang Friedrich Gabriel," General Wencel pointed out. "That's the place where he works."

The connection—or was it a coincidence?—had already been noted when the commission examined the envelope addressed to Captain Moll.

"In my opinion, a strong enough clue to acquit him," Inspector Weinberger commented. "That is, if he is ever indicted, which I doubt. If he had sent the Charles Francis letters, he would certainly not have mailed them from the office where he is employed. The man has nothing to do with the damn letters. Let's suppose he did know about his wife's affairs with Mader, Moll and Hohenstein. But what about the other five? Did she sleep with them, too? One in Galicia, the other in Budapest?"

"That's the crux of the matter." Wencel chuckled. "She could have. Because all recipients had one thing in common: They all were graduates of the War College, class of 1905, the same as Gabriel. Baron von Campanini, Frau Gabriel's father, was once their riding instructor. That was his last year in the service. He resigned the following summer, and his daughter was known to have been on very intimate terms with a number of his students. Friedrich Gabriel married her despite her reputation, which doesn't exactly speak for his character. In my opinion, Inspector, the fellow has no moral standards. He himself must have recognized this; otherwise he wouldn't have resigned from the service. He realized that he didn't belong in the Officers' Corps."

Officers' Corps! The synonym for honor. Loyalty. Courage. And the very heart of the austere body, the General Staff, was the supreme Brotherhood of Knights, the League of Warriors, the Kingdom of Heaven, residing on Mount Olympus, frequenting Valhalla. Any man who turned his back on its glory was considered a deserter, a defrocked priest, an outcast, a coward or a poisoner. In the Mader case, the army had one major objective: to find the culprit among the lower strata of humanity—the civilian population. The victim and the intended victims were officers—that could not be helped or kept a secret—but in order to preserve the shining reputation of the army, the murderer had to be a civilian.

Later in the morning, Captain Kunze dictated the compilation of the facts uncovered by the police, the Security Bureau and the Military Command of the Vienna garrison to his assistant, Lieutenant Heinrich. The report read:

1. All eight recipients of the Charles Francis circular were graduates of the War College, class of 1905, seven of them re-

cently promoted to captains and subsequently assigned to the General Staff Corps and one first lieutenant, presently stationed in Galicia. The circulars were mailed to their addresses as printed in the Military Ordinance Bulletin. All missives were of the same format and content: plain gray business envelopes, the circulars 23-by-15-centimeter sheets, the small boxes containing two capsules each wrapped and sealed in red tissue paper. The capsules had been filled and sealed by hand. The addresses, too, were hectographed with only the name filled in in a calligraphy executed by a drawing pen dipped in purple ink, the kind used in military mapping and charting. Since the missives were no heavier than ordinary first class letters, ten-heller stamps sufficed for each.

2. The text of the circular was as follows:

CONFIDENTIAL

CHARLES FRANCIS, P. O. Box 430   Date of the postal stamp
SIXTH DISTRICT
VIENNA

DEAR SIR:
The premature weakening of the male's sexual powers is one of the banes of our new century. To determine its causes and to find its cure are the most urgent tasks of modern medicine.

After years of research, a stimulant has been found which—without endangering the patient's health—is capable of considerably augmenting his sexual potency.

We are taking the liberty of enclosing a sample of this extraordinary stimulant.

Your approval will be our best publicity.

INSTRUCTIONS: After the opening of the box, the wrapping is to be torn off without damaging the capsules, which are to be taken with a glass of cold water thirty minutes before coitus.

CAUTION: Exposure of the capsules to air may cause deterioration of their contents.

EFFECTS STUPEFYING!!!

Orders mailed to the above printed address will be filled COD.

May we assure you, dear sir, of our discretion and sincere concern for your personal privacy.

In expectation of your kind orders, I remain

Your obedient servant,
CHARLES FRANCIS
Pharmacist

"Effects stupefying!" Lieutenant Heinrich grunted. "The understatement of the century."

Captain Kunze continued:

3. The police have ascertained that there *is* a Post Office Box No. 430 in the Sixth District. However, for years it has been rented by the Catholic parish on Barnabitenstrasse.

4. Each capsule contained one gram of potassium cyanide, ten times the lethal dose. Potassium cyanide serves no medical purpose; its main commercial use is in photography. In the monarchy only persons in possession of a permit may buy it, and stores are required to record all sales.

5. The police have questioned all druggists in metropolitan Vienna, as well as the provinces, so far without result.

6. The Military Command has not ruled out the possibility of a political conspiracy. The victim and the intended victims are highly talented young officers. There could be a hostile power behind the crime, trying to drain off the young blood in the K. and K. Army. At this stage of the investigation no guess is too absurd.

7. The Ministry of War has offered a two-thousand-kronen reward for any information leading to the whereabouts of Charles Francis.

Captain Richard Mader was buried with full military honors. The entire General Staff Corps, including Chief of Staff Franz Conrad von Hötzendorf, attended his funeral. The emperor was represented by Archduke Josef Ferdinand. Several funeral carriages were required to transport the wreaths and sprays. Mader's parents, two small elderly people, stared at the flamboyant floral display with empty, unseeing eyes. Atrophied by grief, their faces reminded one of shrunken Papuan heads.

Ingrid Fiala had arrived from Frankfurt the day before. Chief Brezovsky had sent her a round-trip train ticket and instructed a plainclothesman to chaperon her during the trip and settle her in a private home for the duration of her stay in Vienna. She was forbidden to speak to anyone, especially the press, or to leave the flat without police escort. After her arrival she was subjected to a thorough questioning but was unable to furnish any fresh clues. She appeared to be a nice, uninteresting girl, completely crushed by the tragedy. Chief Brezovsky's opinion was that he had wasted the taxpayers' money by purchasing her train ticket.

Before the funeral, waiting in vain for the police escort to call
for her, she finally decided to disregard their warning and sneaked
from the house through the rear entrance. Having arrived late at
the church, she sat in the last row among housewives, school-
girls, retired government clerks and other strangers, the uninvited
cortege that is always found at the funerals of celebrities and
murder victims.

She was much too miserable to pay any attention to the woman
in the very elegant sable-trimmed suit, with a heavy veil over her
face, who squeezed into the pew beside her. Neither had the
woman, who was Lily Wencel, any inkling of Ingrid's identity.
These two women, one the dead man's lover, the other his
fiancée, sat side by side, their bodies touching, their lips murmur-
ing the same prayers. After the service, General Wencel's wife
scurried out through a side exit to a waiting hack. Timidly Ingrid
went up to Mrs. Mader to express her sympathy, but was put off
by the Hecuban torment written on the older woman's face.

Anna Gabriel did not attend the funeral. During the four days
following Mader's death she thought of him infrequently. On the
few occasions she did it was not with compassion, but with an
odd kind of envy, the student's envy of a classmate who had suc-
cessfully passed an exam that still confronted her.

Friedrich Gabriel was still being held at the Presidium. Anna
had made several attempts to see him. Inspector Weinberger personally issued the necessary permission, had even talked to her
husband on her behalf, but Gabriel categorically refused to see
her. Once she tried to accost him in the corridor as he was being
escorted to the washroom, but he passed her without a word.

Now she lay stretched out on the bed they had shared in happier days and tried to imagine a future without him. There would
be men, the same as before, she decided. Sex was an addiction she
had unsuccessfully tried to cure over the years but failed to con-
quer even for her husband's sake. Without him her chances for a
victory were much slimmer. An only child, she had never felt at
ease with her parents, nor they with her. While the new century
had brought immense social changes, jobs and independence for
women, she had no education, no training and, in all honesty, no
desire to toil in a workshop or even an office. So that led her back
to men. From now on she would charge them for what in the past

she had given away. Perhaps she could even make a career of it, become one of the great cocottes, a *Dame aux Camélias*, Vienna style.

She reached out for the pillow on Fritz's side of the bed and hugged it to herself. "Don't cast me adrift, my darling," she admonished the pillow. "All I'm asking is one more chance. Let's start over. Forget what happened. I'll change. You'll see. I'll change. I promise, you won't regret it—"

Suddenly she let go of the pillow. The sound of her own voice brought her back to reality. Reality was the empty bedroom, Fritz in police custody, her marriage in a shambles, she herself beyond redemption. Rising, she walked briskly to the Baroque cupboard in the sitting room where they kept their liquor. Among the domestic products there was an elegant bottle of Napoleon brandy, almost full, which they had saved for special occasions. Deeming the present occasion special enough, she took the bottle to bed with her. She had almost emptied it before she felt sufficiently drunk. Then she staggered to the nightstand on Fritz's side of the bed, took his old service revolver from the drawer, and shot herself through the heart.

Between the twentieth and twenty-fifth of November the Vienna police interrogated three additional suspects in the Charles Francis case.

One was a Serb long known for his antimonarchist activities. When a hectograph and the same type of purple ink used in the circulars were found in his apartment, he was taken into custody.

An ex-corporal who had been given a dishonorable discharge by a court-martial at which Prince Hohenstein had been a member produced a foolproof alibi and had to be released.

The very promising third suspect was a bricklayer. He had boasted to his landlady of having sent the cyanide letters because he hated every goddamn officer from lieutenant to commander in chief and the emperor himself. After a short spell of elation the police were forced to admit that once again they had been mistaken. The bricklayer couldn't have written the circular for the simple reason that he was illiterate. A medical examination pronounced him unbalanced, and he was moved from the Presidium to the psychiatric ward of the Municipal Hospital.

* * *

On the evening of the twenty-first of November, Captain Kunze dined at home, in Rose's Gothic dining room with the high windows, reddish-brown velvet drapes and enormous silver candelabra. It was like eating in a mortuary.

Frequently, when he brought work home from the office or simply preferred solitude, he had his dinner on a tray in his study. Rose would respect his wishes and, if she had no plans for the evening, retired to bed. Her love for her lodger was so overpowering that the mere knowledge of his being under the same roof with her, even though rooms away, would ensure a sound sleep.

She was a big woman, tall and broadly built. Her dark-blond hair was lightly streaked with gray, and there were a few laugh lines around her eyes, together with wrinkles of petulance and suspicion. She had been a great beauty in her youth and at thirty-seven still had a handsome face and a well-proportioned body. Though no intellectual, she was not stupid and possessed an earthy sense of humor, except when the topic was herself. She was intolerant of criticism and changed her friends as frequently as her boldly stylish hats. Her cook had been with her for a number of years, but no maid remained in her service for more than a few months. Viennese employment agencies steadfastly refused to send her girls since one had leaped to her death from the kitchen window. Both Rose and the cook had insisted that the maid was the victim of an unfortunate love affair, which the police verified, but the stigma remained: Rose von Siebert had driven her maid to suicide. Kunze knew it to be untrue, although he was fully aware of the rough edges of Rose's character. He accepted her as she was: rash, passionate, vital, witty and loyal, a woman with the physical strength and the raucous, often blasphemous speech of the peasant.

They were just finishing dinner when Kunze was called to the telephone and Inspector Weinberger informed him of Anna Gabriel's suicide. She had been dead for hours when her maid found her stretched out on the bed, her eyes open, one hand on the empty cognac bottle, the other still clutching the revolver.

"I'd like to believe that Charles Francis killed Anna Gabriel as he killed Mader," Weinberger said, "but it's not so. We killed her, poor soul. We decided to produce a suspect acceptable to the army and didn't care how many innocents were destroyed in the process."

The bitter self-recrimination emanating from the inspector failed to surprise Kunze. He knew Weinberger to be an unusually sensitive and humane person, especially for a policeman.

"I guessed that you didn't think Gabriel was our man. Neither do I. We ought to let him go."

"Not for a few days," Weinberger protested. "I want him to get over his wife's death. I took it upon myself to tell him. Gently. That is, if you can tell a husband gently that his wife has just put a bullet through her heart. She was a trollop, but obviously she loved him, and I'm afraid he still loves her, despite her whoring. Things aren't as black and white as General Wencel would have us believe."

After Weinberger hung up, Kunze excused himself to Rose and retired to his study. A certain suspicion had plagued him ever since his assignment to the case. He had refrained from giving voice to it, because he knew the result would be an outburst of indignation from General Wencel. Now Anna Gabriel's suicide changed all that. He shared Weinberger's feeling of guilt, resolving to prevent the offering of another human sacrifice on the altar of military prestige.

The plan for the mass poisoning had been conceived by a person of intelligence and self-discipline. If the man was mad, there was uncanny method in his madness. Obtaining the cyanide, composing the circular, hectographing it, finding the right size boxes for the capsules, so the envelopes could easily be slid through the mailbox slot, watching their weight so they wouldn't require added postage, thereby arousing a postal clerk's curiosity, were a series of operations painstakingly thought out and flawlessly executed.

The key to the mystery was the man's motive. If he wanted to deliver a crippling blow to the General Staff, why select freshly appointed staffers for extermination instead of irreplaceable senior officers? No matter how one looked at it, there could be only one answer to the question of motive: personal gain.

Kunze slept restlessly, wakened earlier than usual, and spent two hours watching the clock till it was time for him to leave. He went straight to Inspector Weinberger's office in the Presidium, beating him there by a few minutes.

"I'll need the best handwriting expert you have," he told the inspector. "I have a certain suspicion but want to be sure before taking any action. Also, I'd like to keep it confidential, for I'd hate to hurt innocent people."

"You suspect a definite person."

"Strictly speaking, no. I suspect one of a group."

"An army group." It was a statement, not a question. When the captain nodded, he continued. "I knew that sooner or later you'd reach that conclusion."

"It's the only logical one. We've explored all sorts of motives, except who could have profited by the death of eight high-ranking graduates of the same War College class. The answer: the men who ranked immediately below them. The class originally numbered ninety-four. Two died, and Gabriel quit the army—that left ninety-one. After graduation, the men, all first lieutenants, were apportioned among the various arms of the monarchy to serve four years with the troops. On November first, the highest-ranking fifteen in the class were promoted to captains and assigned to the General Staff, while the rest were left to wait for their promotion according to seniority. Unless war breaks out, they'll have rather uneventful careers, probably retiring as full colonels—provided they reach that rank. None will ever make general." He paused for a moment to take a deep breath. "Now Mader's death has already rendered number sixteen eligible for promotion and the General Staff. If one more of the eight had died, number seventeen would also be eligible; if two more, number eighteen. So on and so forth."

"I see," Weinberger nodded. "You suspect number sixteen and the men ranking below him."

"That's right, except number sixteen was lucky or unlucky enough to undergo an appendectomy in the Brünn Military Hospital on the thirtieth of October. On the fourteenth of November, the day the circulars were mailed, he was still in the hospital, recuperating."

"Just for argument's sake, couldn't he have left the circulars with an accomplice before entering the hospital?"

"Not likely, because up to November first he had every reason to take his promotion for granted. Up to now, the first thirty in each graduating class became permanently assigned to the General Staff after the obligatory tour of duty in the field. This year, however, General Conrad unexpectedly revised the system and selected only the highest-ranking fifteen of the 1905 graduates. I don't know his reasons; he might have wanted to raise the standard of the Field Officers' Corps by larding it with more highly qualified men, or he might have wished to reduce the number of the general staffers. Anyway, his decision dealt a shattering blow to the fifteen men who for four years had taken the bottle-green uniform for granted."

"According to your theory, Charles Francis might be number seventeen."

"Possibly. Although number seventeen is stationed in Zagreb and hasn't been away from his command post since September."

"It seems you've already done some reconnoitering."

"Not enough. For instance, all I know about number eighteen is that he is stationed in Linz. As for number nineteen, he presents a rather interesting problem. He is the only one of the eight recipients who has not been promoted. His being stationed in Galicia more or less excludes him as a suspect, though. The same goes for number twenty, garrisoned in Cracow. Of course, either could have had an accomplice posting the circulars."

"So you're concentrating on these four."

"I might take a look at others, too, merely for safety's sake"— the captain nodded—"but right now these four—seventeen, eighteen, nineteen and twenty—are my major suspects."

"Let me warn you, Captain"—Weinberger chuckled—"you won't be very popular with your fellow officers for trying to find Charles Francis in their ranks."

"I know"—Kunze shrugged—"but I have no alternative."

"I'll find Johann Pobuda for you. He is the best handwriting expert I've ever worked with. Last time he helped us solve a very ingenious spy case."

Despite the inspector's best efforts, it was two o'clock in the afternoon by the time Johann Pobuda greeted the captain in front of the Getreidemarkt Caserne where the War College was located. The handwriting expert was an elegant little man of indeterminable age, with the porcelain skin and perfect posture of a shopwindow dummy. He wore a stylish fur-lined overcoat and carried the kind of black leather satchel favored by midwives on house calls.

The two entered the building and headed straight for the archives. The custodian, an old colonel past retirement age, was dozing peacefully in his office. He awakened with a start when the captain was announced.

"I'd like to take a look at the dissertations of the 1905 graduating class, sir," Kunze told him.

"Come back day after tomorrow," the colonel muttered gruffly. Still half-asleep, he was visibly annoyed at the disruption of his afternoon siesta.

"I can't wait that long, sir," Kunze insisted. "I must see them now."

"Always in such a goddamn hurry," the old man bristled. "You young people think a person is a magician. Supposing I locate the bloody papers. I'll need help to get them out."

"Just show me, sir, where they are and leave the rest to me," Kunze replied, wanting as little commotion as possible. "We'll go over them, then put them back in their places."

The solution satisfied the old man. He didn't even ask Kunze why he wanted to see the papers, which suited the captain. Mumbling to himself about the impatience of the young, the colonel led them to a small room where leather-bound dissertations, sweated out by generations of War College graduates, filled the shelves; then he shuffled back to his office to continue his interrupted siesta. Kunze had no trouble locating the output of the 1905 class. He took two Charles Francis envelopes from his briefcase, handing them to Pobuda.

"I'm expecting the impossible from you," he told him. "I'll show you a number of manuscripts in the hope that you'll find the hand that also wrote these addresses. The trouble is, the addresses aren't in the sender's regular longhand, but in the stereotyped calligraphy used by the army for mapping and charting."

Pobuda gave him an arch look. "If they were in the sender's regular longhand you wouldn't need me, would you?" Picking up the envelope bearing Captain Moll's name, he examined it for a moment, then took a magnifying glass from his satchel and held it above the lettering. "The mysterious Charles Francis," he mumbled. Being a faithful reader of the *Neue Freie Presse*, he guessed that his services had been drafted in connection with the poison case.

"That's right." Kunze nodded. Taking at random seven thin volumes from the shelf, he placed them on the table before Pobuda. "Let's start with these." He opened each script to a page bearing no indication of the writer's identity.

Johann Pobuda peeled off his left doeskin glove—he'd removed the right one earlier, when he had shaken the captain's hand—and examined the papers one by one. "They all were written under stress," he commented, "by young men. I'd say, by individuals in their middle twenties."

Kunze was not impressed. Any newspaper reader could have made the same observation.

"Is one the sender of the envelope?" Kunze asked. Somehow, the man's spinsterish primness irritated him. He'd never before seen fingernails—male or female—buffed to such a mother-of-pearl luster.

"No," Pobuda answered, promptly and with authority.

His tone reassured the captain. Of the seven papers, three were written by men of the promoted group and the rest by graduates ranking among the last fifty. He handed Pobuda another batch. Once again, the authors were lieutenants above suspicion. Pobuda examined the pages with deep concentration. "There is a slight similarity here," he mumbled, pointing at one of the spread-out manuscripts. He lined up the two envelopes with the open page, shifting his magnifying glass back and forth over them. "No," he finally said, "this isn't your man. His R's fooled me for a moment, but there the similarity ends."

Kunze selected the volumes bearing the names of the men ranking sixteenth, seventeenth, eighteenth, nineteenth and twentieth. "What about these?"

Pobuda grinned at him. "Are you still testing me, or have you decided to get to the heart of the matter?"

"You've been at it all the time," Kunze snapped.

"Don't tell me you have twenty suspects."

"I have ninety-one. Since you've eliminated fifteen, we still have a long way to go." This, of course, was not true, but he preferred to keep the man somewhat in the dark.

Pobuda lingered for a while on the longhand of number sixteen, the lieutenant who had had his appendix removed. Number seventeen seemed to offer him no problem, as he slid the magnifying glass only once across his writing.

"No, not this one, definitely not," he mumbled.

Number nineteen, First Lieutenant Josef von Hedry, stationed in Grodek, Galicia, was the passed-over recipient of the circular. Pobuda spent ten minutes examining his writing. "I might have to take this one with me to photograph it. Enlarged photos show more than the best magnifying glass or microscope. The L's and I's in this script look suspicious, but I'd hate to say that this *is* the man."

The handwriting of number eighteen, the officer stationed in Linz, was next. Pobuda leaned over it for a long time, his milky skin turning a faint pink. "This is it!" he exclaimed hoarsely.

Kunze grabbed the volume and read the name on the cover: First Lieutenant Peter Dorfrichter.

"This *is* the man," Pobuda repeated, firm conviction in his tone. "However, to be absolutely sure, I'd like to take the paper and the two envelopes home with me. I could have the answer for you by tomorrow morning."

Kunze thought for a moment. "All right. I must ask you, however, to keep the matter strictly confidential."

After clearing the last obstacle, the colonel-custodian's permission to have the dissertation removed from the files and taken from the building, Kunze parted from Pobuda. The same evening, shortly before he left his office to return home, an important message reached him. Two more newly promoted General Staff captains had received Charles Francis circulars and subsequently handed them in to their respective command posts. Both had been on leave and found the circulars in their accumulated mail when they reported for duty.

With these two, the number of the recipients had risen to ten.

On the following morning, Johann Pobuda reported the result of his night's work on the Dorfrichter paper to the captain: a thorough and scientific examination confirmed that the dissertation and the addresses had been written by the same hand.

By then Kunze was in possession of certain data on Lieutenant

Dorfrichter's private life and his service record. The image that emerged from them didn't correspond with that of a ruthless poisoner. The lieutenant's reputation both as officer and as gentleman was impeccable. Since his transfer to the Fourteenth Infantry Regiment in May, 1909, he had been stationed in Linz, a good five-hour train ride from Vienna. He had been married for two years, and his wife was expecting their first child. According to his précis of career, he was an ideal subordinate, loyal, well balanced, hardworking and dependable.

In the course of the morning, Kunze called in two more handwriting experts. To his surprise, they failed to corroborate Pobuda's opinion. The first man found unusual similarities between the writing on the envelopes and the term paper, the second expert similarities that could be detected in dozens of longhands. Neither answered with an unequivocal yes to the question of whether all could have been the penmanship of the same person.

The latter two reports were a blow to Kunze. He studied them for a long time, then reread Pobuda's opinion. Of the three, he found Pobuda's the most thorough and authoritative, while the wording of the others seemed ambiguous in spots, leaving a wide margin for error. The investigation, Kunze realized, had reached the stage where one couldn't afford to disregard a suspicion, no matter how vague. With sudden decision, he shoved the two controversial reports into his desk drawer and put in a request for an urgent meeting with General Wencel at the latter's office.

An hour later he addressed the general across an enormous desk cluttered with framed and dedicated archducal photos.

"I respectfully request, sir, that ten graduates of the War College, class of 1905—from the sixteenth ranking to the twenty-fifth ranking—be investigated in connection with the Charles Francis case. I also request that First Lieutenant Peter Dorfrichter, number eighteen in the class, be interrogated first."

Wencel reacted as though the captain had asked permission to blow up the Military Lawcourt.

"You know damn well that I won't permit that! How dare you suggest such a fool idea? I always thought you were a sensible man." The large blue eyes under the bushy but carefully trimmed eyebrows shot arrows of indignation at him, but Kunze's trained ear could tell the difference between real resistance and mere show and he refused to give ground. An editorial in that morning's *Arbeiterzeitung*, a Socialist daily, had accused the police of incompetence, the military of withholding information, the Security Bureau of shielding the culprit. Kunze had brought the paper along and now handed it to the general. Wencel took it, holding it gingerly with two fingers, as if it had come from a plague-ridden house.

"Don't tell me you agree with the damned Socialists. Maybe you yourself are one. I wouldn't be surprised."

Not being the product of a military academy, Kunze had never been accepted by men like the general for their very own. This, however, failed to disturb him. From childhood on, he'd been used to being if not precisely an outcast, at least an outsider—and had learned to live with it. Ignoring the gibe, he showed Pobuda's report to Wencel.

"I feel, sir, that Lieutenant Peter Dorfrichter is our most likely suspect. Nevertheless, at this point, we must proceed with caution. Arrange for his interrogation in a way that no one—including him—should know that he personally is under suspicion. This way, if he is cleared, he won't be hurt. His commandant alone must be told, but that cannot be avoided."

With ill grace, Wencel finally gave his consent. It was decided that a commission, consisting of Inspector Weinberger, Captain Kunze and the general, would board the train for Linz on the following morning. Two agents of the state police were assigned to accompany them.

When General Wencel arrived home that evening, he found his household aflutter. Madame Charlotte, the *friseuse*, was there, along with Berta, the little woman who did minor dress alterations, taking in and letting out seams according to his wife's fluctuating weight. Berta's employment was full time.

"What's going on?" He stuck his head in at the door of his wife's boudoir.

She stood in front of the three-way mirror while Berta sewed her into a new dress, a magnificent creation by the House of Worth. The abandoning of hooks and buttons was a device followed by the late Empress Elisabeth as it made a woman's waist several centimeters slimmer. It also had the disadvantage of restricting one's appetite which was no hardship for the empress, who had had little interest in food. But for Lily Wencel it was medieval torture.

"We're invited to the Auffenbergs for supper, don't you remember? You burned me, stupid!" she shouted at Madame Charlotte, who was attempting to curl the stubborn locks at the back of her head with a curling iron.

A half hour later she entered the general's study. "How do I look?" she asked.

"Splendid," he answered mechanically, then threw a glance at her and found that, indeed, she looked—he searched for the right word. "You look ravishing."

Since the beginning of the Mader investigation he had spent little time with her. Now he was surprised to see her resembling her old buoyant self. Gone were the gloom, the lethargy, the incriminatory and resentful expressions.

"So the poor bastard was impotent," she said.

Puzzled, he stared at her. Then, as the cyanide case was foremost in his mind, he realized she had referred to Mader.

"What makes you think he was?" he asked.

"He wouldn't have taken those cyanide pills, would he?"

"Capsules," he corrected her. General Wencel was a stickler for precision.

"Whatever they were, he took them. It means he needed an aphrodisiac."

Lily Wencel called herself modern, but quarrels had erupted occasionally between them over the subject of her frankness with regard to sex and other subjects, and her husband had called her lewd, shameless, and foulmouthed.

He rose, although he knew they were a good fifteen minutes early. "Shall we start?"

"Not yet. I don't want to get there while Ida is still putting on the war paint." She referred to her hostess, Frau Auffenberg.

Obediently he resumed his seat.

"The paper said Mader had an affair with Anna Gabriel."

"Yes, he had."

"It follows. He was impotent and needed someone like her to —to make a man out of him. But even she couldn't do the trick. That's why he took the pills—excuse me—the capsules."

"All right, he was impotent. So what?" He was tiring of the subject.

"I think it is terribly funny. All you gorgeous knights-errant, great Casanovas, glorious Gentiles! How you dazzle and flirt and strut, but when it comes to the essentials, you fizzle out like damp firecrackers." She spoke in the loud, shrill voice he knew so well and loathed.

He stared at her nonplussed. By a tacit agreement neither of them ever touched on the difference in their ethnic backgrounds. She was a devout Catholic, and so was he, and one of the few functions they attended together was Sunday mass at the garrison church. The sudden venom in her voice disturbed him. Was her attack aimed at him or the dead Mader? He rose again.

"Let's go," he said in the coldest judicial tone that had sent a chill through many an accused man. "I'd rather be early than late. Besides, tomorrow I have to get up at the crack of dawn to go to Linz to serve on a commission, goddamn it!"

He neglected telling her that the trip was in connection with the Mader case. It would have been her cue to return to the subject of the dead captain and his impotence.

The city of Linz lay shrouded in thick autumnal mist. The temperature had fallen to minus three degrees centigrade and continued falling. Trees and shrubs swayed in skeletal nakedness in a wind too lethargic to blow the fog away. The Danube was still free of ice, its mud-gray surface the mirror of a cheerless sky. It was the kind of day when summer seemed like a drunken poet's dream. How could the sun ever emerge from behind the thick layer of clouds that covered the entire countryside like a pitched tent?

Despite all their precautions, the commission's journey failed to remain a secret. The same train that brought them to Linz discharged a flock of reporters who followed their fiacres from station to town like hungry sparrows hoping for horse droppings.

Colonel von Instadt, receiving the commission in his office at the regimental command post, reacted to the charges against First Lieutenant Dorfrichter as he had done before: He refused to believe them.

"No, gentlemen," he told them. "First, I cannot accept the notion that any officer of this army could be the perpetrator of such a heinous crime. Second, Peter Dorfrichter, in my opinion, is the least likely to be involved. You speak of frustrated ambition, jealousy, paranoia. Nothing could be more alien to Dorfrichter's character. I happen to know him rather well. When my regiment took part in the annexation of Bosnia and Herzegovina, he was assigned as liaison to the Fifteenth Brigade. It was during that time that because of an incident I don't want to elaborate on now, I was temporarily relieved of my command. Many of my fellow officers felt that I was the victim of certain circumstances beyond my control, but only Dorfrichter risked sending a written report to the Ministry of War about it. Such an action is against regulations and could easily have cost him his career. That he knew. Now if Dorfrichter had been the paranoiac you say he is, he wouldn't have championed my cause and antagonized the ministry. Third, he is an exceptionally gifted man who could always find a place for himself in civilian life. Of course, up to now he has concentrated on an army career. He is better read and better informed than any of my subaltern officers. He speaks and writes six languages—German, French, English, Italian, Hungarian and Czech. I personally feel that his not being assigned to the General Staff is a great mistake and the army's loss."

"I hope with all my heart that you are right, my dear Instadt," General Wencel replied. "Nevertheless, our job is to continue with the investigation. Of course, the bywords are tact and caution. At this point, neither Dorfrichter nor anyone else should know that he is considered a suspect. We don't want to brand an innocent man. The interrogation should be conducted in a rather informal manner, in the spirit of camaraderie, and officers should report for interrogation in alphabetical order."

Inspector Weinberger lunched with the Linz chief of police, and General Wencel accepted Colonel von Instadt's invitation to be his guest at the officers' mess. Captain Kunze was included in the invitation but declined, explaining that there was much work to be done. Before returning to Vienna, he intended to familiarize himself with the local scene. He lunched at the Hotel Herrenhaus, which was not a bad choice—the food there was far superior to the cuisine at the officers' mess.

Built in the 1770's, during the reign of Empress Maria Theresa, the hotel had originally been a family mansion and boasted the charm and intimacy of a country house: with wide porte cochere, wood paneling in the lobby, a low-ceilinged dining room, with chairs designed to accommodate crinolines, and a cobblestoned yard, shaded by fine old oaks. The waiters matched the decor; they were elderly and dignified. Service was slow, but that disturbed neither guests nor staff. They all understood that good eating, like good lovemaking, should be undertaken slowly, with deep concentration and sincere appreciation.

Captain Kunze had his choice of tables, since not many were occupied on this gloomy November day. He chose one in the bay window, and spent a long time studying the menu, unable to decide between the hare *chasseur* and the *Wiener Rostbraten*. Finally he asked the headwaiter, who suggested the boiled beef. It was delicious, lean and succulent, and he expressed his satisfaction to the man who hovered over his table like an Altomonte angel over the crèche at the local Franciscan church.

"Incidentally"—Kunze's tone was easy and casual—"a friend of mine asked me to look up a First Lieutenant Peter Dorfrichter here in town. Do you, by any chance, know the lieutenant?"

For a fraction of a second the man's face froze, then softened slightly. Only a jurist with Kunze's experience would detect such a fleeting change.

"We're not popular with infantry officers," the headwaiter told him. "They prefer the Hotel zur Post. We're patronized mostly by the gentlemen of the Second Dragoon Regiment."

"I see. Nevertheless, you have heard of the lieutenant?"

"I'm afraid I haven't, sir." The headwaiter's voice was cool. He was ready to leave Kunze's table.

"But you knew he was an *infantry* officer," the captain insisted.

"That was just a guess, sir. As I don't know him, it was an assumption he was. I know practically all the cavalry officers in the area. May I suggest that the captain ask the concierge? Although I doubt that he can tell you any more."

After lunch, Kunze stopped at the desk in the lobby. He didn't identify himself to the concierge, but the man knew who he was and that he had arrived with the commission from Vienna. Kunze knew that news traveled faster by word of mouth in provincial towns than through the telegraph wires of big cities, especially when a concierge was at the receiving end.

"First Lieutenant Dorfrichter?" the concierge answered with a much too blank expression. "I don't think the gentleman has ever stayed at our hotel."

Kunze didn't press the issue, but made a mental note of the reactions of the two men.

Of the ninety-one graduates in the class of 1905, nine were stationed in the area of the Fourteenth Infantry Regiment with headquarters in Innsbruck. Of the nine, only three served in Linz: Dorfrichter and two others. In order to conceal the purpose of the investigation, not only these men, but twenty other subaltern officers in the area, were interrogated at their command posts.

Dorfrichter's turn came around midmorning on the day following the commission's arrival. By then the commission was in possession of some fairly startling clues amassed by the Viennese police agents in conjunction with their local colleagues. They had discovered that the Kirchhammer bookstore near the garrison command post carried the same stationery as that used by Charles Francis and that another Linz firm, owned by a man named Karl Ploy, manufactured, among other paper goods, the small boxes that had contained the cyanide capsules.

Peter Dorfrichter was the third officer to be interrogated. Like the others, he was ordered to report to Colonel von Instadt's office. He was deliberately kept waiting for an hour in the anteroom, Inspector Weinberger's idea being to unnerve the lieutenant.

General Wencel didn't care for the stratagem, but when Captain Kunze suggested that it might speed things up, he agreed to it. Colonel von Instadt was also present, but only as an observer.

The long wait in the anteroom didn't appear to have disconcerted First Lieutenant Peter Dorfrichter in the least. When finally called, he entered the room with even steps, clicked his heels, bowed smartly, and reported to his colonel in the proper military manner. The men rose and shook hands with him, discovering his palm to be cold, but dry, and his grasp firm.

He was taller than medium height with a slim body that appeared to contain only bones and muscle. His posture was faultless, and his movements indicated a ballet dancer's elegance. But there was no effeminacy. He was rather handsome, his face having retained some of the innocent prettiness of the once-small boy. Smooth dark-brown hair, a pale and clear complexion, a well-trimmed mustache over full lips, the intelligent eyes of a hunting dog reminded Captain Kunze of the Irish setter that had once been his faithful companion.

Wencel offered the lieutenant a seat.

"We're investigating a very unfortunate case," he began, "and will have to ask you a few routine questions. Please answer to the best of your ability."

"I shall, sir." Dorfrichter nodded. He had a surprisingly young voice for a man of thirty.

The voice had a strange effect on Kunze. The tone irritated him, along with the lieutenant's relaxed and unworried attitude. He felt a very strong resentment against the young man, then immediately rebuked himself. As a jurist, he had always tried to adhere to the axiom that a person is innocent until proved guilty, but now he allowed himself to be annoyed by a suspect's refusal to act or even to look like a suspect.

"Where were you on the thirteenth of November between eleven at night and eight on the following morning?" Wencel asked.

Dorfrichter frowned. He appeared to be concentrating.

"In my apartment here in Linz, sir." Then he tapped his forehead as if hit by a new recollection. "No, I am wrong. You said the thirteenth, didn't you, sir? At midnight, I boarded the train for Vienna and arrived at the Western Railroad Station at six thirty in the morning."

The general's expression changed from official solicitude to petulance. The answer did not fit his preconceived idea that the commission was investigating the wrong man. He threw an annoyed glance at Kunze, as though the captain's meddling had been responsible for this new circumstantial evidence. With a peremptory flip of his hand indicating that Kunze was to take over the questioning, he folded his arms and leaned back in his chair, a stern but noncommittal presence.

"What did you do after your arrival in Vienna?" Kunze asked. The pendulum had swung his way, yet this failed to lessen his inexplicable aversion to the man. The hint of a smile on the lieutenant's face disconcerted him.

"I took the first omnibus to town and went straight to my mother-in-law's apartment in Hahngasse."

"But on the eleventh of November, when you asked for a leave of absence, didn't you indicate that you planned to visit your parents in Salzburg?"

Kunze had spent the best part of the previous afternoon studying regimental records. Before leaving for Linz, he had collected all data concerning Dorfrichter: his grades at the War College, his physical description and fitness record contained in the army personnel register, and his service background recorded in the army qualification list. They blended into the image of a highly talented, conscientious but conventional officer. The man who now faced him did not fit this image. Lieutenant Peter Dorfrichter was anything but conventional.

"That's right, sir," he answered. He sounded flattered by the captain's interest in his activities. "That was my original plan. But my wife, who had been staying with her mother in Vienna, wrote to me that she wasn't feeling well enough to make the journey back home alone. That's why I went to fetch her. She is in— a certain condition, sir."

"Expecting?" General Wencel asked. His tone was friendly, almost warm, suggesting that a man whose wife was expecting couldn't be a poisoner.

"Yes, General."

"When is the child due?"

"The end of this month, sir."

There was a moment's silence. Then Kunze continued.

"Lieutenant, do you have any knowledge of the case this commission is investigating?"

"I do, sir. Just like anyone else who reads the newspapers."

"Then you must have read that the poison letters—all ten of them—were mailed in the vicinity of Post Office Number Fifty-nine in Vienna's Mariahilf district. They were collected between seven and seven fifty and stamped at eight o'clock in the morning. You have just told us you arrived in Vienna at six thirty on the morning of November fourteenth. One of the mailboxes handled by Post Office Number Fifty-nine is in front of One Twenty-eight

Mariahilferstrasse, a three-minute walk from the Western Railroad Station. The first omnibus after six thirty departs at six forty-two, which means that between the arrival of the train and the departure of the omnibus you had twelve minutes' time during which you could easily have walked to One Twenty-eight Mariahilferstrasse, posted the letters, and walked back to board the omnibus. What is your answer to this?"

Dorfrichter had listened with polite attention, his eyes never leaving Kunze's face. Now a light, almost apologetic smile played around his lips.

"I don't know what you expect me to answer, Captain."

"Just the facts."

"The fact is, sir, that I didn't walk to One Twenty-eight Mariahilferstrasse; neither did I post any letters or walk back to the omnibus stop."

"Just what did you do after leaving the station?"

"I descended the steps to the street, walked to the nearest lamppost, then back to the omnibus stop and boarded the vehicle."

"The nearest lamppost? What for?" The moment the question slipped out, Kunze knew he should not have asked it.

"I had my dog with me, Captain."

Someone laughed. Kunze, looking up, saw that Weinberger was the guilty party.

"No one in his right mind takes a dog along when he wants to mail a bunch of letters containing poison!" Colonel von Instadt muttered angrily.

Kunze ignored the remark.

"How long did you stay in Vienna, Lieutenant?"

"Only two days. I returned on the sixteenth of November and reported for duty on the seventeenth."

"But you failed to inform your commanding officer that you'd spent your leave in Vienna and not in Salzburg!"

"That's right, Captain."

"Can you explain why?"

"This is a garrison, Captain, not a prison camp!" Colonel von Instadt interrupted. "As long as my officers perform their duties to my satisfaction, their private lives don't concern me. Provided that they conduct themselves as gentlemen."

Dorfrichter acknowledged his commander's intercession with

a warm, reverent glance. Kunze felt the return of his initial aggravation.

"Thank you, sir." He nodded to the colonel, then returned to the lieutenant. "As I recall, you've just told us that you'd asked for and were granted a leave of absence on the thirteenth of November. According to regimental records you were on leave from the twelfth to the seventeenth."

Dorfrichter thought for a second.

"That's right, sir. I'm sorry. I was wrong about the date."

"Does that mean that you left for Vienna on the twelfth?"

"No, I left on the thirteenth, arriving there on the fourteenth, just as I stated before."

"What did you do on the twelfth?"

"Nothing much. I puttered around the house."

"You mean you stayed in all day?"

"Practically all day, Captain. Except when I walked my dog. I walked him three times."

"Look here, Dorfrichter." General Wencel suddenly spoke up. "In case you don't know, your handwriting has been compared with that on the Charles Francis envelopes and an expert found that the two were identical!" The general seemed annoyed, but whether at Dorfrichter or at Kunze, it was difficult to tell.

Dorfrichter reacted with a wide-eyed stare. For the first time he looked a little concerned.

"You cannot mean, sir, that you suspect me of having tried to kill ten of my fellow officers! Of having actually poisoned Richard Mader! You can't be serious, sir. Whoever said that I wrote the poison letters must be out of his mind."

"But you were in Vienna at the time the letters were mailed?"

"So were another two million other people! No, sir—on my word of honor, I had nothing to do with the Charles Francis case."

General Wencel rose, the others following his example. He turned to Kunze, indicating that the next move was the captain's.

Kunze said, "I respectfully suggest, sir, that we ask the lieutenant's consent to visit his home."

"All right." The general sighed. "If we've gone this far, we might as well go farther."

Dorfrichter answered without waiting for a direct question. "You have my consent, sir."

A wave of frustration swept through Emil Kunze. He looked at the young officer, eight years his junior, at the boyish, hurt face, and felt a sudden urge to dismiss him with an apology, thereby burying the whole distasteful matter. The temptation was great, but simultaneously he envisioned front-page newspaper articles and sessions with meddling civilians, reporters, bureaucrats and the police, and he knew that since the avalanche of the investigation had begun rolling, it could no longer be stopped, certainly not without a scandal.

"Look here, Dorfrichter," he heard Wencel speaking in a tone that once again implied comradeship, "we believe you because we want to believe you. There are, however, certain unhappy facts which might make some people skeptical. The Charles Francis crime has cast a hell of a shadow over the Officers' Corps at a time when the survival of the monarchy may depend on the reputation of the corps. We all know war is inevitable. It may break out tomorrow or not for ten years, but whenever it comes, the degree of loyalty and respect of the troops for their officers will mean the difference between victory and defeat." He paused for a moment and took a deep breath. "In case you *are* guilty, Dorfrichter, you must make it your duty to pass judgment on yourself and carry out the sentence without waiting for the military tribunal to do it. You understand me, don't you, Dorfrichter?"

The lieutenant snapped to attention.

"I do, General," he said, his voice loud and clear.

Wencel heaved a deep sigh.

"Do you want to go ahead to your house?" He pulled out his watch and glanced at it. "It is eleven forty-eight now. We want to give you time"—he hesitated—"for whatever you consider necessary."

"Such as, sir?" Dorfrichter asked.

"Hell—" For a moment Wencel was at a loss for words. "Like— like warning your household, damn it!"

Dorfrichter smiled for the third time during the interrogation, this time almost mischievously.

"I'd rather we went together, sir. I don't consider it necessary to warn my household. My wife is a very neat housekeeper. I'm quite certain the apartment will be in perfect order."

Once again it was obvious that Dorfrichter's attitude both confused and annoyed Wencel.

"Damn it, Dorfrichter!" he burst out. "There is too much evidence against you! You have a hell of a lot to worry about. I wouldn't be so goddamn frivolous in your place!"

The young officer's face froze.

"With the general's permission, I don't have anything to worry about, and I'm sure if the general were in my place, he wouldn't act any differently."

He looked Wencel straight in the eye. The general was the first to drop his gaze.

"Well." He started to say something, then stopped. Clearing his throat, he pulled out his handkerchief and began cleaning his reading glasses. The silence in the room was like the lull between the first thunder of a summer storm and the final outbreak.

"May I respectfully make a suggestion, sir?" Captain Kunze's voice filled the void. "Let us ask Lieutenant Dorfrichter to remain here while the searching party goes to his house. I think—"

"But why?" For the first time since the interrogation began, Dorfrichter seemed to lose his calm. In an irritated tone he interrupted his superior. "I see no reason why I shouldn't be present. It would only upset my wife if suddenly her home were turned upside down by a group of strangers. In her present condition any excitement could be harmful."

"I beg your pardon, Lieutenant," Inspector Weinberger said. Up to now he had followed the proceedings in silence. "The entire Linz garrison, including your wife, must know about the investigation. Several of your fellow officers have been questioned and their homes visited."

"Visited, but not searched!" Dorfrichter flared.

"That's true. However, I doubt that Frau Dorfrichter can tell the difference. This whole affair has been conducted with great consideration by the military authorities—some say with too much consideration. So leave it to the searchers on how to handle Frau Dorfrichter."

"At this point you may still withdraw your consent, Dorfrichter," General Wencel pointed out. He clearly disapproved of the interference since the inspector was only a civilian. "After all, no charges have been preferred against you."

"Thank you, sir." Dorfrichter, composed again, bowed stiffly. "I won't withdraw my consent." He faced Kunze. "Where do you want me to wait for the result of the search, Captain?" he asked.

Colonel von Instadt answered, "Find something to do here at the post. Look busy, damn it! I don't want any snooping reporter to jump to the conclusion that an officer of my regiment is a suspect in this goddamn murder!"

Marianne Dorfrichter was indeed pregnant. Before her pregnancy, she had been slim and delicate, with a waist that her husband could encircle with two hands. Now she felt heavy and grotesque and refused to appear in public or even to take a walk before dark. She wore a voluminous loden cape when walking and would not allow her husband to accompany her, only her maid and Troll, their dog. She refused even to visit close friends. She felt that anyone seeing her with him now would visualize them naked in bed, performing the act that had caused her condition. Appearing with him would be like deliberately exposing herself to the prurient curiosity of voyeurs.

She was stretched out on the bedroom sofa when Aloisia, the maid, a peasant girl with the build of a Japanese wrestler and the brains of a pigeon, burst in to announce that five army gentlemen wanted to see her.

"Something must've happened to the lieutenant," she added and began sobbing. "Something terrible! When Major Dallmayr was thrown by his horse, only three officers came to tell Frau Dallmayr that he was dead."

Marianne struggled to her feet, then crossed to the dressing table. Taking a brush and comb from a drawer she straightened her disheveled coiffure.

"Offer seats to the gentlemen. I'll be with them in a minute," she said evenly, then added: "And stop making a fool of yourself."

"Yes, madam," the girl said in a hurt tone and flounced from the room.

Marianne Dorfrichter put the brush down and stared at her reflection in the mirror. Her face hadn't changed, hadn't become bloated or its smooth *trecento* beauty marred with liver spots, the curse of pregnancy. Her body, of course, looked hideous, and she dreaded letting the five strangers see it. She was, however, an army wife and had learned that one never argued with the army. She rose, draped a knitted shawl around her shoulders, and walked into the "salon" to meet the visitors.

Of the five she considered only three to be "gentlemen": General Wencel, Captain Kunze and Major Schultz, judge advocate assigned to the Linz garrison. They were accompanied by two corporals, who were to do the actual searching under Captain Kunze's direction.

"Forgive us for inconveniencing you, madam," Wencel said after the introductions. She had offered them seats while the two corporals stood in the doorway. "I'm sure you've heard or read about the so-called Charles Francis case."

"I have." Marianne nodded.

"Unfortunately, some information indicates that the letters originated in the Linz garrison. We must investigate practically all subaltern officers at the post. Your husband, like the others, has given us permission to search his house. Let me assure you, it is a routine procedure. Our men will be very careful not to cause any damage. They'll put everything back in its place."

She listened without comment, then asked if the gentlemen would care for sherry. Wencel answered for them. "Yes, we would love it."

The crystal decanter with eight matching glasses was kept on an open shelf of the credenza in the dining room, and she ordered Aloisia to bring it. She also asked her to offer the corporals wine or beer, whatever they preferred, in the kitchen. They sought the eyes of Major Schultz, and when he nodded, they, too, accepted.

"May we begin now?" Captain Kunze asked when the two visibly refreshed corporals returned from the kitchen.

"Please do," Marianne said and pulled the shawl over her bulging abdomen.

Wencel and Major Schultz remained seated on the fragile chairs flanking a matching settee, while Captain Kunze followed the men, directing the search. They started in the salon and went over it quickly and efficiently. The room was furnished neatly and without much imagination, all pieces part of one set, bastardized Adam style, much too dainty for comfort, the wood dark mahogany, the upholstery pale-green silk moiré. There was also a vitrine with figurines, well-tended aspidistras in large cache pots and, on a stand, the small marble replica of the "Capitol Venus," one of her hands minus a finger. A machine-made French rug with a floral Baroque pattern covered the waxed and polished parquet floor and starched net curtains hung in the windows. It was a room used by the Dorfrichters only to receive in.

"You have a very lovely home, madam," General Wencel commented. He sensed her nervousness under the discipline-enforced calm and sought to create the mood of a friendly visit, to make her forget she was actually being interrogated. "While we were waiting for you, I said to Major Schultz, one can tell two happy people live in this home. Didn't I, Major?"

"Yes, sir, that's exactly what you said, sir." Schultz nodded, remembering no such remark.

She acknowledged the compliment with a faint smile.

Captain Kunze and the corporals had moved to the dining room. It conveyed the cozy inelegance of a place furnished with pieces selected for their usefulness, not for style or appearance. The richly carved credenza was Gothic, the long table in the center a heavy slab on four sturdy legs. Six leather-upholstered chairs were placed around it, four more set against the wall, flanking a large bookcase. Marianne heard the men open the glass door. They were going over the top row first, she decided, the dictionaries, the big volumes on tactics, strategy and gunnery her husband had pored over night after night.

"Did your husband ever mention Captain Richard Mader to you? I mean before the tragedy?" Wencel asked.

"I don't really remember. He might have. He spoke of several classmates, but as I didn't know them, the names didn't mean much to me."

"And after the tragedy?"

"He told me he ordered a funeral wreath. That was on the day the papers first wrote about Captain Mader's death."

"What was your husband's reaction to the news?"

"He ordered a funeral wreath."

"Yes, yes—but did he seem shocked or grief-stricken?"

"More grief-stricken than shocked. He felt sorry for the captain. Mader died so young, he said. He also said that the captain was the only one who'd remained a good comrade throughout his two years at the War College. He never acted like a competitor. That's what my husband said."

She spoke mechanically while her ears were tuned to the noises coming from the dining room. One man was still busy with books, probably shaking out every volume in search of God knows what. The other corporal rummaged among the dishes. *Have the glasses been dusted lately?* she wondered. *And the cups?* Some were chipped. She should have thrown them away—and the cracked plates and the soup tureen with the broken base. While in Vienna, she had planned to replace the damaged pieces, but by the time she got there her condition was too noticeable and she had remained indoors.

At one thirty, General Wencel and Major Schultz left to have lunch. Captain Kunze and the corporals remained. They were starting on the bedroom. Marianne wished she could watch them, but her pride forced her to remain stiffly seated on the settee as if she were having her picture taken. She picked up a magazine, pretending to read, while Aloisia kept dashing in from the kitchen, complaining as if the unscheduled visit had had only one purpose, to upset her workday. She wailed loudly about the disorder the men left behind, despite General Wencel's promise that they would put everything back where it belonged. Finally, Marianne lost her patience, ordering Aloisia to stay out of her sight.

She heard the men in the bedroom, pulling out drawers and opening wardrobe doors. They were looking over her dresses and would certainly find the skirt with the jelly stain she had forgotten to send to the cleaner's, Peter's shirts with the frayed cuffs, the mended sheets, the hand-me-down baby clothes outgrown by her sister's children, her husband's letters with their intimately sexual comments written to her during last year's maneuvers.

The door of the nightstand squeaked. Someone was lifting out the chamber pot. Good God, that, too? Wasn't there any limit to this humiliation, any respect for the privacy of a couple's life? Next, the beds would be turned down, the sheets pulled back and examined for semen stains.

The searchers moved to the kitchen. Aloisia, her face red and sullen, came in to ask for the key to the larder. Marianne felt that it was foolish to keep it locked, but all good housewives did, and she was no innovator to defy old customs. Ten minutes later Aloisia returned the key.

"They broke three eggs," she reported triumphantly. "And a jar of pickles. I wonder what they were looking for. I let the dog lick the eggs off the floor, but he didn't care for the pickles. Do you want me to wash them and put them into the jar?"

"Throw them away," Marianne ordered, covering her face with her hands. She was afraid the murderous rage she felt would show.

A period of her life it seemed had come to an end. She had loved the apartment; after two years of marriage it had become her first real home. But now that the hands and eyes of three strangers had probed into its every nook, she knew that her love affair with it was over forever.

It was three o'clock in the afternoon by the time Captain Kunze and the men finished their inspection. Dorfrichter had been right, Kunze thought. The searchers found no untidy cupboards, no filth under the carpets, no dirty dishes, no motheaten garments. Neither did they find any stationery of the Charles Francis variety, purple ink, cyanide or a hectograph. The only thing that could possibly have been linked with the poisonings was a small package of wafer capsules in the medicine cabinet of the bathroom.

Captain Kunze asked the question. "Do you know, Frau Dorfrichter, what your husband needed these capsules for?"

Still huddled on the settee, she looked frightened and demoralized. A few minutes earlier she had heard Aloisia leaving the apartment and knew that by now she was spreading the indignity of the official visit all over the neighborhood. Marianne no longer believed that the search had been a routine matter conducted the same way as in other subaltern households.

"The capsules?" she repeated. She understood there was a connection with whatever the men were looking for. She also remembered having read that Captain Mader's death was attributed to some poison-filled capsules mailed to him. How and why her husband could be linked with the case was a complete mystery to her. She tried desperately to decide what the least incriminating answer should be.

"I imagine he was taking some medicine. Yes, he had a bad cold recently. With complications," she added.

"Did you see him fill the capsules?"

"No!"

"Do you mind if I take these capsules with me?"

She wanted to tell them: "Go, get the hell out of here! You and your two oafs reeking of hair pomade and horse manure!" But she was an officer's lady, so she nodded quietly, even mustering a smile. "No, not at all, Captain."

The brave smile didn't escape Kunze's attention. He understood the considerable effort it had cost her.

When he examined Dorfrichter's background, he learned about Marianne's as well. Dorfrichter's father, a fairly successful businessman, was an exporter; hers, a Viennese bank clerk, was a few rungs below on the social ladder. Marianne was ten when her father, a passionate mountain climber, fell to his death in the Tyrolean Alps. Left without support, her mother had taken over the management of a kitchenware store in a lower-middle-class neighborhood, later buying the store from the invalid owner. Marianne, the youngest of her four daughters, was only twelve when she became afflicted with a touch of tuberculosis and eighteen by the time the doctors declared her completely cured. For six years she lay flat on her back either in sanatoriums or at home, bedded down near open windows and never allowed to engage in sports or attend school.

The fact that Dorfrichter married her spoke against his being a man of fanatical ambition. Such men usually married daughters of generals or millionaires, for obscure infantry lieutenants were seldom wealthy. Marianne was, however, exceptionally beautiful with an air of gracious elegance about her. She was also extremely adaptable; otherwise, it would have been impossible to become a perfect "officer's lady" in two short years of marriage.

"I understand you have just returned from Vienna," Kunze made conversation while wrapping the box with the capsules in tissue paper. His hands worked slowly and rather clumsily. Only later did it occur to Marianne that he had deliberately lingered over the chore.

"Oh, that was quite some time ago. At least two weeks."

"Do you often go to Vienna?"

"Fairly often. My mother lives there. We're Viennese. My family, I mean."

"Too bad that traveling has become so difficult nowadays. Everyone seems to be on the go. Our train was simply packed yesterday. Wasn't it unpleasant for you traveling alone?" His tone was casual, even remote. He didn't say "in your condition," but she knew what he meant and blushed.

"I wasn't alone. Peter—I mean my husband—came to Vienna to get me."

"Had you asked him to, or was it a gallant gesture on his part?"
This time she smiled.

"I suppose it was a gallant gesture. I didn't even know he had been granted a leave."

"Did he surprise you?"

"I should say he did. He arrived at the crack of dawn, around seven. I was still asleep, but he didn't wake me. I was finally awakened by the dog scratching at the door."

"That was on the fourteenth of November?"

She gave him a startled look. It dawned on her suddenly that she was being interrogated.

"Yes," she said in a low voice, "on the fourteenth."

After Captain Kunze and the corporals left, she waited five minutes, then threw on her loden cape and scurried to the house next door where there was a telephone and called her husband. There was a long wait, then the switchboard operator informed her that the lieutenant could not be reached.

She returned to their violated apartment. Despite Captain Kunze's efforts, the rooms looked ransacked. Crumpled spreads on the beds, linen haphazardly stuffed back into the drawers, doors left open, a box of powder spilled in front of the dresser. Marianne turned down her bed and, fully dressed, crawled under the comforter. She hoped for a good cry, but the tears failed to come. She fell asleep and was awakened by the squeak of the bedroom door. Looking up, she saw her husband in the doorway.

"Peter!" Jumping from bed, she rushed to him and clung as if he were a safe rock in a sea of raging floodwaters. "Peter, what do they want from us? They turned the house inside out, looked into every corner, searched for hours! Where were you? I tried to phone you, but they said you couldn't be reached."

He extricated himself gently from her tight embrace.

"Calm down, sweet." His tone was even, and he seemed his

usual unruffled self. "Remember, you're not supposed to become excited. It's bad for you."

"But, Peter, what is this all about?"

"Nothing that concerns us. There was a murder, and the clues are pointing to Linz, so there is an investigation. Unfortunately, it seems that the culprit is from the local garrison. We'll just have to put up with certain inconveniences until the man is found or the case is forgotten."

"They asked a lot of strange questions."

"What kinds of questions?" His voice seemed a shade livelier.

"All sorts. Did you go to Vienna on your own accord, or did I write you to come?"

"Of course, you wrote me."

She gave him a startled look.

"No, I didn't."

"You wrote me that you were not feeling well. Don't you remember?"

His tone, firm and slightly irritated, confused her.

"Did I really?"

"Certainly. I still have the letter somewhere."

"I wrote you several times. But I don't recall having—"

"That's why I went to Vienna instead of Salzburg!" He cut her short. "I couldn't let you travel alone." He paused. "What did you tell them?"

"I told them—I mean, the captain—that I hadn't asked you to come. I'm sorry, Peter, that's how I remembered it. I still do." Her spirits sank. "Was it bad that I told him that?"

"Can't be helped now." He shrugged.

"I could say I was mistaken."

"That would make things worse."

His strangely hollow tone disturbed her.

"Peter, I have an awful feeling that something is wrong. Don't look at me now. I want to say this: If you for any reason are involved in this terrible thing, let's put an end to it all. I'm willing to die with you—I am not afraid—" She found she couldn't bear the condemnation in his eye and averted hers. "Shoot me first and—"

"Then shoot myself?" He grinned. "The second similar suggestion today! Except the other charitable soul didn't offer to die with me. No, sweet. I won't shoot you or Troll or myself—"

"Troll?"

"I hope you didn't plan to leave him behind. It would make a much better news story with a dog in the suicide pact."

"You're horrid!"

"No, just sensible. I don't panic. Incidentally, did you tell the captain what you said when you and I read the November first promotion list together?"

"The promotion list?"

"Don't you remember? I read the promotion list and showed it to you, and you said you had known Captain von Gersten and that he was quite smitten with you and if you had encouraged him, you might be the wife of a general staffer now instead of an ordinary field officer's."

"I didn't say that!" she protested.

"Oh, yes, you did."

"I was just teasing you."

"I know. However, if anyone asks you, *it never happened!* Do you understand? Never! I didn't show you the promotion list, and we never discussed it. You don't know whether or not I ever read it. And if I did, I've never mentioned it to you!"

"Why is that so important?"

"It isn't. Not really. But they have this unfortunate case on their hands and are trying desperately to solve it in order to satisfy the public and the press. They are willing to pick an innocent man and sacrifice him for the sake of good relations between the civilian establishment and the military. It so happens that I refuse to be the sacrificial lamb!"

She was beginning to feel a little better, but still not completely at ease.

"I told them you bought a wreath for Mader's grave. They won't hold that against you, will they?"

"Of course not. Mader was a comrade. A nice chap. A good officer. No genius, but bright enough to be good company. Everyone liked him. Besides"—he paused for a moment—"besides I had a special reason for being fond of him. He once saved my life."

"He did?" She looked at him, surprised. "You never told me that."

"No, I haven't."

"How did he save your life?"

"It's a long story. I'll tell you some other time. Let's have supper now, shall we?"

II

THE morning after Dorfrichter's interrogation in Linz, a short, plump woman about forty, accompanied by a dignified man in a well-pressed but somewhat shiny black suit, appeared at the Vienna Presidium and asked to see Chief of Police Brezovsky. The two were led to the office of Captain Kubelik, the chief's first assistant. There the man introduced himself as Postal Inspector Blosch.

"Fräulein Anna Posselt is a clerk at Post Office Number Fifty-nine," he told Kubelik. "I think she has important information regarding the Charles Francis case."

When asked for details, he replied that Fräulein Posselt would speak only to the chief. At this point Captain Kubelik was beginning to doubt whether Fräulein Posselt could speak at all, since she hadn't uttered a single sound during the discussion. She was a stocky woman with a moon face and coal-black eyes and hair. In her floor-length winter coat she looked like a tumbler, a children's toy, her body carved from one solid chunk of wood and weighted down with lead.

After a short wait Fräulein Posselt and her escort were received by Chief Brezovsky. Brezovsky was polite, but to Blosch's disappointment, not overly eager to hear Fräulein Posselt's revelations. During the past few days there had been a great number of urgent tips confided by cranks and showoffs. Besides, he had been convinced from the very beginning that the culprit was an army man. Now General Wencel and his party were in Linz investigating a certain first lieutenant, and according to rumors, an arrest was imminent. Nevertheless, a shorthand clerk was called in to take down Fräulein Posselt's testimony.

"She is one of our most dependable employees," Inspector Blosch reported, reading the chief's thoughts. "More than twenty years in the postal service." He turned to the woman. "Now tell Chief Brezovsky about the Polish Jew and the letters!"

Fräulein Posselt took a deep breath.

"It was on the fourteenth of November, a few minutes before eight. There was a short line in front of my window, registered mail and stamps, and this Polish Jew was second in the line and craning his neck to see what was taking me so long when actually I was working fast. When his turn came he handed me a batch of letters. They were regular mail, the ten-heller postage already on them, so I told him to drop them in the box. He said the box had just been emptied, which was true—two colleagues were already sorting the mail—and asked me to give the batch to my colleagues so it would go out with the next delivery. He was very insistent, kind of a nuisance really. I asked him what the big hurry was, and he said that a lieutenant had sent him with the letters from Galicia and that it was very important that they be dispatched without any delay. To get rid of him, I told him to go behind the counter and put the letters on the sorting table, which he did."

She recounted the incident without emotion, her tone dull, monotonous, with neither pauses nor inflection.

"You didn't tell him about the address," Inspector Blosch prompted her.

"Oh, yes," she added, her manner somewhat livelier. "When he pushed the letters through the window, I got a glimpse of one address. The letter was going to a *captain*. No street was given, only General Staff Corps, Ministry of War, Vienna."

Brezovsky eyed her pensively. "Why did you read the address?" he asked.

Her pale face took on a pink hue.

"I didn't actually read it, just glanced at it, only because he made such a fuss about the letters. I wondered why the lieutenant didn't mail them himself. Why would he send a man from

Galicia to Vienna when an added postage of five hellers would have done just as well? It seemed very odd to me. It still does."

"You said the man was a Polish Jew. How could you tell?"

"He looked like one. He wore a caftan and had a thick reddish beard and spoke with a Jewish-Polish accent. He wasn't the first one I've seen in my life."

"When Fräulein Posselt told me about the letters," Blosch interrupted, "I immediately realized that there had to be a connection between them and the Charles Francis case and insisted that she come directly to you, sir. I consider helping the police a civic duty."

"We appreciate that," Brezovsky told him, adding to himself, *You also know about the two-thousand-kronen award posted by the Ministry of War.*

Brezovsky asked them to sign the transcript of the testimony before dismissing them, after which he ordered detectives to call on all captains assigned to the General Staff Corps to ask if they had received any letters mailed on the fourteenth from a fellow officer stationed in Galicia. One man went to Captain Mader's sealed apartment and searched through his papers. Brezovsky still considered the Dorfrichter clue the most promising one, but as the new tip also pointed at the army, he decided to discover its worth.

The man sent to Mader's flat returned with an envelope bearing the November 14 postmark of Post Office No. 59. The letter itself was missing, but the sender's name and address were scribbled on the back of the envelope. The sender's identity gave it special significance: First Lieutenant Josef von Hedry—also a War College graduate. He ranked nineteenth in the class of 1905, in which Dorfrichter was eighteen. Hedry's name had already popped up once during the investigation as one of the recipients of the Charles Francis circulars. The circumstance that he alone of the ten had *not* been promoted to the rank of captain was noted, but dismissed as insignificant. Hedry was stationed in faraway Grodek in Galicia and, according to his commanding officer on the long-distance phone, had not been to Vienna for more than six months.

Now, however, there was an envelope addressed to the late Richard Mader postmarked the same time: 8 A.M. November 14, at the same Vienna post office, No. 59, as the fateful Charles Francis circulars.

Chief of Police Brezovsky immediately telephoned the new development to General Wencel in Linz. After some deliberation the members of the commission decided that Captain Kunze should slip away quietly from Linz and take the first train to Grodek.

First Lieutenant Josef von Hedry galloped through the main allée of the Schönbrunn Palace park on a fox hunt. But then, why was he alone, and where had the pack gone? A second later he was no longer on horseback, but walking with a Budapest actress he had had an affair with the summer before. He was trying to remember her name, and could not, when a splash of icy water hit his face. He coughed, gasped for air, choking. The realization that he was drowning flashed through his mind, causing him to thrash out wildly with his arms and hit something soft and warm. Suddenly he knew where he was and where the water had come from. He was in Grodek, Galicia, and the water had been thrown at him by Natasha, a fat Ruthenian whore.

"Goddamn it, you stupid cow! Why the hell did you do that?"

He stared angrily at her sullen face. Polish whores were bad enough, but Ruthenian whores were the worst. A man had to be rolling drunk to copulate with them. Even so, the act left a horrible aftertaste. It was as dirty and degrading as everything else in Galicia. The Bible had been wrong when it described hell as a lake of fire and brimstone. Hell was a barren province, with swirling dust clouds and the ubiquitous stink of manure during the summer and bone-chilling winds, fog and knee-deep muck from September on. It had one sole redeeming feature. In the coming war—and Hedry prayed it would come soon—Galicia was expected to become a battlefield and razed thereafter from the face of the earth.

"Because you told me to," Natasha cried. "You said I had to wake you at six sharp, no matter what. If nothing else helped, pour water on you. So get up now! You'll be late for the *Vergatterung*."

Her name was not Natasha, but Hedry called her that. To have called her by her real name would have bred intimacy, and an officer had to keep his distance with the civilian population, especially in Galicia.

He sat up with difficulty. His head felt as if someone had split it with a hatchet. He remembered very little of the night before: the dinner at Jablonsky's with fellow hussars, followed by some drinking in one of the boxes of the Grille Parisienne, a miserable fleabag of a nightclub. By then three uhlans had joined them. As a rule, hussars, as well as uhlans, kept to themselves. Only the deepest boredom and frustration occasionally brought them together. The uhlans, however, were less miserable as an outfit. Most were Polish aristocrats, and Galicia was part of their country. The problem was, socializing with them led to drinking competitions and sometimes duels. Duels were strictly against regulations, but since they relieved the monotony, commanding officers condoned them—except when they resulted in death.

Hedry looked around the cluttered room and felt as if all the insects of Galicia were suddenly crawling over him. He jumped out of bed and began dressing with a haste that minutes earlier he hadn't thought himself capable of. He found his wallet with a considerably depleted wad of bills in it. He had no way of telling how much of the missing money he had spent during the night and how much Natasha had helped herself to. He peeled off a ten-kronen bill and gave it to her the way one gives a bone to a stray dog: holding it with two fingers so one's skin should not come in contact with the dirty mouth.

Ten kronen must have been a surprisingly generous compensation for services rendered because a wide grin spread over the girl's face. She threw her hamlike arms around the lieutenant's narrow shoulders and pressed his lanky body against her soft flesh. The unexpected gesture made him lose his balance, and for a moment he felt as though he were falling into a tub of dough. His nostrils filled with the smell of greasy hair, perspiration and sex, and a wave of nausea surged up from his stomach. He gave her a wild push that hurled her—all hundred kilos of her—against the bed where she remained, sprawling obscenely on top of mussed sheets of questionable cleanliness.

"Don't you ever touch me again!" he screamed while buckling on his sword belt. "And don't you ever drag me to your pigsty when I'm drunk because I'll kill you the moment I sober up."

He struggled into his greatcoat. How he loathed all of them, he thought. Male and female. How he hated spending the best years of his life in this godforsaken hellhole! How many more would he be able to stand? How soon would he crack? Nothing short of war could possibly save him!

It was still dark outside and the street deserted, except for a woman here and there, sweeping the sidewalk in front of her house. As he strode by, his spurs jingling, the red of his pants and the powder blue of his jacket splashes of beauty inside the shell of the open greatcoat, his handsome profile with the cocky little mustache tilted against the gray sky, the brooms came to rest for a moment. Bundled up against the November chill, the women looked like animated potato sacks. He didn't waste a single glance on them.

The Grodek he knew had only two kinds of inhabitants: comatose, ill-smelling peasants and swarms of small, black-clad, complaisant Jews. Of the two, he preferred the Jews. Without their helpfulness and ingenuity, the place would have been even worse. They transformed it from the completely unbearable into the almost bearable, could conjure up living quarters, French champagne, catered food, insecticides and loans. They were amazing; living in as dismal a poverty as the peasants, they possessed an inborn understanding of the basic needs of an entirely foreign culture. In the past, he had had anti-Semitic leanings, but here in Grodek he had come to like the Jews. What was more, he depended on them.

Before reporting to the barracks, he planned to go home, take a hot bath and change. He lived in another part of town but decided to walk. It would clear his head, he thought.

After a few minutes he was already feeling better. At least, physically he did. Nothing could help him emotionally. Ever since the discovery that his name was missing from the November 1 promotion list, his spirits had been hopelessly low. He had ranked number nineteen in the War College class of 1905. The year before, the thirty ranking highest in the class of 1904 had been—after an obligatory four-year tour of duty in the field—assigned to the General Staff Corps. Now, for some odd reason, probably the whim of the new chief of staff, Franz Conrad von Hötzendorf, only the first fifteen of the class of 1905 were thus advanced.

This slight alone would not have embittered him. Not overly ambitious, he always felt happier with the troops than behind a desk in an office. He loved the cavalry; it was his home, his country, his past, his future. What he loathed was Galicia.

The government, trying desperately to weld the population of a racially heterogeneous monarchy into one nation, had stationed Hungarian regiments, among other places, in Galicia, Austrians in Sarajevo, Slovenes in Salzburg, Bosnians in Budapest, Ruthenians in Graz, Czechs in Debreczen, all presumably busy fostering brotherly understanding, but in reality pining for home and hating every square inch of the alien soil and every member—young females possibly excepted—of its population. To know that—in a sense—he was taking part in a crusade did nothing to ease Lieutenant von Hedry's despair. To make his misery bottomless, he had also lost Lebovitz.

Lebovitz had been his house Jew, the best ever. A wisp of a man of indeterminable age, bright, understanding, tireless. Their association had begun when Hedry first stepped off the Vienna–Grodek–Tarnopol train and found no porter to carry his luggage and no hack to take him into town. Lebovitz had been on the same train, third class, returning from a nearby town where he had attended a funeral. Noticing the young officer's predicament, he immediately took charge. In no time there was a carriage for the lieutenant, a farm cart for his bags, a room in the town's best hotel, a box of insecticide to provide for undisturbed sleep, and the next day a flat with a bath and private entrance and letters of introduction to the most exclusive brothels in Tarnopol and Przemysl.

This gem, however, had decided to leave his native Galicia and emigrate to the United States. The move was a surprise to Lieutenant von Hedry, but for Lebovitz and a large group of his fellow Jews, it was the result of careful preparations. Twenty-three adult men, some with their families, had cast their lots with a young rabbi who organized the mass exodus. Most of them had relatives in the United States, so felt they were not taking too much of a risk. Lebovitz did not know a single soul in that faraway land but was one of the first to join the party. When Hedry tried to intimidate him by telling horror tales about Indian massacres and Wild West badmen, Lebovitz merely laughed.

"Lieutenant, sir, for a poor wretch who for twenty years has had to eke out a living by catering to military gentlemen, the Indians will seem like cherubim!" He added quickly: "Of course, I meant the uhlans, not the hussars. The uhlans are Polish gentlemen and bear no love for us Jews. The Hungarian gentlemen are a lot kinder. They never beat us up when they are sober."

Lebovitz had now been gone for ten days. Although he had assigned a nephew as his replacement, Hedry still felt like an orphaned calf. The nephew was a lanky young man suffering from a chronic runny nose. In the ten days he had not once changed his shirt, polished his boots, or used a handkerchief.

When Hedry reached home, he learned to his dismay that his plans for a hot bath had to be postponed indefinitely. A corporal was waiting for him with orders to report immediately to his commanding officer. His horse, Ideges, already saddled and covered with a blanket, was waiting for him in the yard. The lieutenant thought he detected the reflection of his own disgust in the animal's eyes. *Ideges* was Hungarian for "nervous," and the horse fully deserved his name. Any moving apparition, a piece of artillery, a bicycle, a motorcar or even a black-caftaned Jew on horseback made him rear and bolt. That is, unless he felt Lieutenant von Hedry's thighs pressing against his flanks. Then he became a lamb, although the lieutenant never punished him or handled him roughly. Hedry seemed to have a special gift for making friends with animals, less so with men.

It began to drizzle, and darkness thinned to a foggy gray by the time he reached the barracks. The commandant's office was on the first floor of a grim two-story structure near the gates. The master sergeant on duty announced him immediately.

Count Peterfy was tall and lordly, with probably the straightest back and the most boldly aquiline nose in the entire Austro-Hungarian Army. The stare of his steel-blue eyes was capable of sending shivers of fear through the boldest hussar. Hedry assumed that he was in for a thorough dressing down for some prank committed during last night's lost hours. It was almost a letdown when he realized that the steel-blue eyes held paternal kindness. *Jesus Christ!* he thought. *Someone in the family has died! Mama? God, don't let it be Mama! I haven't written her in six weeks.*

Then he noticed that the colonel was not alone. A captain he had never seen before rose from a chair beside the desk. His insignia indicated the Judge Advocate Corps. During the introductions Hedry learned his name was Emil Kunze.

"The captain has been assigned by the Military Lawcourt of the Vienna garrison to investigate a criminal case. He will ask you a few questions. Answer them to the best of your ability," the colonel instructed him. "Should you feel in need of my help, don't hesitate to ask. I've told the captain that you are one of my best officers and that I am ready to vouch for your integrity."

How strange, Kunze thought, that an Austrian colonel in Linz and a Hungarian colonel in Grodek reacted the very same way when one of their men was suspected of conduct unbecoming an officer. Was this equality a hopeful sign? Did it indicate that the monarchy was *one* country, after all, not a mosaic of many small ones? That she was no longer doomed to a slow death by erosion or a blowup caused by chemical reaction of various races living together? That the army was the very force to hold her together and help her survive, if not into eternity, at least for another hundred years?

He removed an envelope from his briefcase and handed it to Hedry.

"Do you recognize this envelope, Lieutenant?"

Hedry looked at it, puzzled.

"Yes, sir, I do. That's my letter to the late Captain Mader."

"Why did you write him?" Kunze asked.

"We were friends. When I read that he'd been promoted, I congratulated him."

"Despite the fact that you yourself were passed over?"

The blood rushed to the lieutenant's face. "I don't see what that had to do with it, sir."

Kunze closed his eyes for a moment. He had never been able to sleep on trains, and the trip to Grodek had been a long and tiring one.

"Have you been away from Grodek at all since the thirteenth of November?"

"No, sir."

"In that case, how is it possible that your letter to Captain Mader was posted in Vienna on the morning of the fourteenth?"

"My house Jew posted it when he passed through Vienna on his way to America."

Kunze's eyebrows shot up. "House Jew?"

"A local institution, Captain," the colonel explained. "As garrisons are rated, Grodek isn't exactly paradise. Especially for our younger officers. Even finding decent living quarters is a problem. And that's where these Jewish fellows come in. They're fantastically resourceful. It must have something to do with their religion. They are even better than Moses because they can bring not only cold but hot running water out of a rock!"

Captain Kunze acknowledged the joke with a polite smile, turning back to Hedry.

"Why did you have the man post your letter? Why didn't you mail it yourself in Grodek?"

"I thought, sir, it would reach its destination faster. The postal service is rather lax around here, to say the least."

"Was that the only mail you gave your man?"

"No, sir. I gave him three, perhaps four more letters. All addressed to friends in Vienna."

"Three or four?"

Hedry reflected for a moment. "Three."

"Friends in the army?"

"No, sir. Civilians."

"You mean to say the recipients were not fellow officers?"

"No, sir. Only Captain Mader was. The others were—well—ladies."

"All three?"

"Yes, sir."

Captain Kunze asked for their names and jotted them down.

"And the name of the",—he hesitated for a second—"of your house Jew?"

"Lebovitz."

"First name?"

"I don't know, sir. That's all I ever called him. But I can find out. His nephew substitutes for him. Sort of. I can ask him if you consider it necessary."

"It would be very helpful." Kunze nodded.

Their discussion had been conducted in a low, relaxed monotone. Though still somewhat baffled, Lieutenant von Hedry was proving cooperative.

"On the nineteenth of November you received a circular signed by a certain Charles Francis and promptly handed it over to your commanding officer. Is that true?"

"Yes, sir."

"You never opened the envelope?"

"No, sir."

"Why didn't you?"

The blood rising to Hedry's face turned his suntanned skin the reddish color of autumn leaves.

"I never opened it because all officers of the garrison were ordered to hand over the circular if and when they received it!" For the first time during the interrogation Hedry's face and tone betrayed irritation.

Captain Kunze gave him a long, inquisitive look. This young man puzzled him. Before starting out for Grodek, Kunze had familiarized himself with his background. He came from a very old and very wealthy family. The fact that he had managed not only to enroll in the War College, but to graduate from it, showed that he was much more gifted than the average cavalry officer. Right now, however, he was badly hung over, eyes red-rimmed, mouth kept from yawning with great self-discipline. In the properly clipped and outwardly respectful tone of his answers Kunze sensed a touch of condescension. A *von* Hedry was speaking to a Kunze. Once again, the captain marveled at the magnetic power of the army. Why would a man of Hedry's physical and mental superiority choose the army as a career when it offered nothing but boredom, dull company and cumbersome obedience?

"What are your plans for the future, Lieutenant?" he asked.

The young man frowned. The question didn't make sense to him. "May I ask in what way?"

"Do you intend to remain in the service?"

"But of course, sir."

"Despite the disappointment of your not having been assigned to the General Staff?"

The lieutenant no longer looked sleepy. He took a deep breath.

"Yes, sir, despite the disappointment of my not having been

assigned to the General Staff." His voice, though quiet, was bit-
ingly contemptuous. A prince reprimanding the court jester. It
suddenly became clear to Kunze why Charles Francis had added
the lieutenant's name to the list of his intended victims. *If he
ever used that tone to Charles Francis*—

"Do you remember a First Lieutenant Dorfrichter? He was a
classmate of yours at the War College."

The lieutenant shook his head like a man trying to dislodge
water from his ears. The change of topic was too abrupt.

"I cannot follow you, sir," he said with an almost mutinous
truculence.

"First Lieutenant Peter Dorfrichter." Kunze enunciated the
name slowly and clearly. "Do you remember him?"

"I do, sir."

"What was your relationship to him?"

Hedry shrugged lightly. "He was a comrade. A classmate."

"Were you friends?"

The answer came quickly. "No, sir." Then with the hint of an
apologetic smile: "Dorfrichter wasn't the kind to make friends
easily. Neither am I."

"Did you two ever have an argument? You were number nineteen and he eighteen. That means you were competitors."

"We all were, sir. The whole class. That's how it is at the War
College. No camaraderie. The road to success over the dead bodies of the men ahead of you. You certainly must know, sir. At
least, that's how it was when I attended the college. Perhaps today they have a more lofty-minded student body, but I doubt it."

How right you are, Kunze thought.

"You must have had an impression of Dorfrichter, though,"
he prodded.

"Well"—Hedry was thinking hard—"he was intelligent, talented. As a matter of fact, he was more capable than many who
outranked him. His trouble was nerves: He lost his head under
pressure. At examinations he didn't do as well as he should have.
And then his fear of horses!" He quickly corrected himself. "I
didn't mean fear, just dislike. He was no athlete. Unfortunately,
Major von Campanini insisted on making one out of him. He
would always assign him the most fractious horse. Dorfrichter

was thrown many, many times. Sometimes you had to feel sorry for the poor chap." He smiled. "And the horse!"

"You have the reputation of being one of the best horsemen in the monarchy, Lieutenant," Kunze told him.

Hedry shrugged. "That I wouldn't know, sir. Let me put it this way. I can ride. But that's no great accomplishment, considering that I was practically raised on horseback. It was an advantage Dorfrichter never had."

Kunze rose. "Thank you, Lieutenant. That'll be all for now. I'd be much obliged if you would give me the full name and last address of this man Lebovitz. Also the names of the group he traveled with."

"When do you want them, sir?"

Kunze paused as if the question had taken him by surprise.

"Now!" he said in a flat voice that nevertheless carried unquestionable authority.

Lieutenant von Hedry bowed stiffly to his superior officers, clicked his heels, and marched from the room. Outside, in the barracks yard, he barked at the first hussar lounging on the porch to bring his horse. With one powerful motion of his lean body he flung himself into the saddle and galloped off in the direction of the local ghetto.

A few hours later at the boardinghouse in the Leopoldstadt district of Vienna where he and his traveling companions had been waiting for their clearance papers, Moses Lebovitz received a summons. He was to go immediately to Chief of Police Brezovsky's office at the Presidium. The summons arrived at the worst possible moment. All the obstacles which had beset their journey had been surmounted, and the group's departure was planned for that same evening.

Although Lebovitz had met with no hostility during his two weeks in Vienna, he considered it safer to take a lawyer along. The lawyer had been an ex-schoolmate of the young rabbi, their travel guide, now a resident of Vienna. The big city had fashioned him into a suave, sophisticated man who didn't appear Jewish at all, at least not to Lebovitz.

The chief received them immediately. After a few cordial words which were intended to relax the nervous Lebovitz, Brezovsky asked him about his connection with Lieutenant von Hedry. Because it was so unexpected, the question stupefied Lebovitz. His body became bathed in cold sweat under the heavy caftan, and his fingers, curved like eagle's talons, dug feverishly into the upholstery of his chair. Perhaps the lieutenant had been robbed or even killed, he thought. And he, Lebovitz, was suspected of the crime. As a child and young man he had lived through several pogroms, but they had failed to frighten him as much as the chief's seemingly solicitous attitude. Lebovitz had understood the pogroms, but he did not understand the chief and his motives.

Yes, he had done favors for the lieutenant, he told him. Yes, he accepted small remunerations, but that was all he could tell. The gentleman assured him repeatedly that his services were most satisfactory.

"Lieutenant von Hedry gave you several letters to be mailed in Vienna. How many?" the chief asked.

Lebovitz stared at him wide-eyed.

Why the letters? Lebovitz fretted. Had there been anything of importance in them? Money perhaps?

"There were four, Herr Brezovsky," he stuttered.

"Are you sure there weren't more?"

"Yes, sir. I counted them when the lieutenant gave them to me and again at the post office."

"Did you drop them into a box?"

"No, sir. I wanted to make sure they wouldn't get lost, so I put them on the table where the mail was being sorted." He raised his voice. "If they got lost, blame the post office, sir, not me!"

"Did the lieutenant instruct you to mail them that way?"

"No, sir. As I've told you, I wanted to see that they'd be safe. And that they'd go out fast. I always try to give the best service to my gentlemen."

"Did you read the addresses?"

"No, sir."

"Why not?"

"Because I cannot read, sir. German writing, that is. I can read Hebrew. But you gentlemen don't address your letters in Hebrew."

"No, as a rule we don't," Brezovsky said, his lips twitching.

The interrogation lasted an hour. The chief informed Lebovitz that he must remain at the Police Presidium to be available for questioning by Captain Kunze, who was expected back from Grodek the following day.

"But, gnädiger Herr, I'm supposed to leave for Hamburg to-night!" Lebovitz cried. Fumbling in his pocket, he pulled out a carefully folded paper on which the young rabbi had jotted down the group's itinerary. "We change trains in Prague and Leipzig and arrive in Hamburg tomorrow noon. We sail from there on board the *Kriemhilde,* on the morning of the twenty-ninth. If I have to stay in Vienna, sir, I'll miss the sailing."

"So you'll take the next boat to America, Herr Lebovitz," Brezovsky told him.

Lebovitz had never been addressed as "Herr" in Galicia. The unusual honor added to his discomfort.

"But I cannot risk such a long trip all by myself! Alone, I wouldn't have come even this far. I was born in Grodek, lived there all my life,—I was once in Przemysl and twice in Cracow. That's all the traveling I've ever done. I cannot be separated from my group!"

Brezovsky rose and turned to the lawyer.

"I'm afraid we'll have to detain Herr Lebovitz. He may be a very important witness, and we can't risk losing him."

When Lebovitz cried out in agony, the chief patted his back reassuringly, continuing in the same kind, though authoritative, manner.

"I'll see to it that he's well treated," he assured the lawyer. "You may make arrangements to have food sent in for him from a kosher restaurant. And we won't keep him an hour longer than absolutely necessary. I want to emphasize once more that he is a witness, not a suspect."

The chief and the lawyer shook hands, and Moses Lebovitz was led away. That evening, as scheduled, the group of Galician *émigrées* left for Hamburg.

Three days later Lebovitz was released without ever having been questioned by Captain Kunze. The fact was that the police had clearly forgotten about him. Certain developments in the Charles Francis case had distracted them. If it hadn't been for his lawyer's inquiry, he might have been kept in his small, uncomfortable cell for several more days. There are disadvantages to being a guest, not a suspect, of the Police Presidium, the embarrassed lawyer explained to him.

After his release, Lebovitz paid the lawyer, then collected the tickets and passport the young rabbi had left for him and walked to the Northern Railroad Station.

He spent the hours till the departure of the Prague train seated in a corner of the third-class waiting room. At boarding time, he rushed out to the platform. It was a fast train with a number of coaches, wagons and sleeping cars. He moved alongside it, scanning the faces of the people behind its freshly washed windows. He found none of his own kind among them; they all—even the third-class passengers—looked frighteningly alien. When the whistle blew, signaling departure, he still stood on the platform, staring motionlessly as the train picked up speed and carried its load of wood and steel and human flesh from his sight.

He walked back to town to the travel agency which had arranged for the group's journey, to redeem his train tickets. Only his train fare to Hamburg was refunded. The agent said Lebovitz should have changed his mind before the ship sailed, after which Lebovitz picked up the ship ticket from the counter and calmly tore it to shreds.

In the evening, he boarded the Vienna–Grodek train. Even its much-used hardwood seats had a familiar feel. An old woman in the far corner lived on his street, and two men were from neighboring Winniki. Sleet began to fall when they passed the outskirts of Vienna. A rough wind beat against the already-frosted windows. Lebovitz stretched out and rested his head on the back of the seat. For the first time in days he felt peaceful and unafraid. He wondered what mad notion had ever made him want to leave for America.

Captain Kunze returned to Vienna on November 28 after another long, sleepless night on the train. From the station, he went to his office and put in a call to General Wencel, who was still in Linz.

"I'm convinced, sir," he told Wencel, "that Lieutenant von Hedry had no part in the Charles Francis poison plot. The Jew who mailed his letters—four to be exact—was some sort of employee of his. After questioning the lieutenant, I asked my assistant to call on the recipients of the letters. Three women. They all corroborated Hedry's statement. The fourth letter went to Mader. I have no reason to doubt that it contained just what Hedry said it did, congratulations on Mader's promotion."

General Wencel listened without comment.

"You'd better take the first train up here," he said finally. "There have been some interesting developments. At least, Inspector Weinberger thinks so. I, personally, don't want to make a move without you. You've started this mess; you finish it."

Kunze heaved a sigh that was loud enough to be heard at the other end of the wire. His head was spinning with fatigue; he'd hoped to go home at last, crawl into bed and sleep. He knew, however, that it would have been a wasted effort to argue with the order, for it was an order.

"Yes, sir, I'll do just that," he replied, not even asking about the important development.

It was that same morning on which Linz pharmacist Ritzberger awoke earlier than usual. Despite his fifty-six years, he felt well rested and vigorous and decided to fill the half hour till his customary getting-up time making love to his young bride, who was still asleep. He was about to reach out and shake her awake when the sudden recollection of a two-week-old incident hit him. Deciding to forgo conjugal pleasures, he jumped from bed, dressed hastily, rushed over to the residence of the Linz chief of police, his tarot partner of the night before, and roused him.

The urgent recollection concerned a private of the Fourteenth Infantry Regiment who had come to his pharmacy late one evening to ask for potassium cyanide, a rather large dose, as he recalled. The soldier's explanation was that his officer wanted it for a photographic experiment. The pharmacist told him, first, that he did not carry the poison and, second, that even if he did, he couldn't sell it without a permit. He advised the private to obtain one from the Municipal Health Office and take it to the garrison pharmacy, the only one in Linz to carry potassium cyanide. The soldier thanked him for the information and left. That was the last Ritzberger saw of him.

Captain Kunze boarded the eleven o'clock train. For a two-kronen tip to the conductor he got a compartment all to himself, took a nap, and arrived in Linz more or less refreshed. From the station he rode in a fiacre to the regimental command post, where General Wencel and Inspector Weinberger were waiting for him.

The session did not start promisingly. The Ritzberger clue, which in the morning seemed to point to strong evidence against Lieutenant Peter Dorfrichter, fizzled out in the afternoon. Ritzberger, confronted with Dorfrichter's orderly, declared that the private did not even resemble the man who had asked for potassium cyanide. The orderly was dismissed, but Ritzberger lingered on.

"Come to think of it, Lieutenant Dorfrichter's man looked familiar to me," he told them. "I must have seen him at the pharmacy more than once. I'm sure I waited on him not too long ago."

"Can you recall what he bought?" Kunze asked.

"What did he now? It must have been something without a prescription because I would remember that." The pharmacist thought hard; then suddenly his face lit up. "Capsules! Wafer capsules! That's what he bought! Several dozen wafer capsules!"

He described them, the same as those accompanying the Charles Francis circular. General Wencel moodily gave his consent to have Lieutenant Dorfrichter ordered to the command post for a second interrogation.

During this second questioning Dorfrichter seemed as carefree and relaxed as he had during the first. Yes, he had sent his orderly for the capsules. His dog, Troll, had worms but refused to swallow the medicine prescribed by the vet, so, he, Dorfrichter, had to feed it to the dog in capsules. In no time, Troll became blissfully worm-free.

The vet at the Fourteenth Infantry Regiment corroborated Dorfrichter's explanation, and the commission had no choice but to thank Dorfrichter for his cooperation and dismiss him.

During the evening all orderlies in the regiment were questioned in connection with the attempted cyanide purchase. When the man was not found, the search was extended over the entire garrison. General Wencel and Inspector Weinberger returned to Vienna, but Kunze remained in Linz. He spent the morning of the twenty-ninth reexamining all the testimony. At midday he accepted Colonel von Instadt's invitation to have lunch at the officers' mess.

During lunch he sensed in his host, as well as his table companions, a feeling of resentment under the thin veneer of hospitality. This failed to disturb him. Since his arrival in Linz he had been well aware of the garrison's opposition to the investigation. He deliberately ignored the coolness of the reception and pretended to enjoy the meal and—above all—the company.

The conversation centered on the latest accomplishments in aeronautics. One of the lieutenants at the table had been dispatched by the army's Aviation Committee to France to observe Blériot's takeoff on his historic Channel-crossing flight. The young officer glowingly declared it was the greatest experience of his life.

"I don't think airplanes will ever play a significant part in warfare, though," the colonel commented. "They might be used for reconnaissance, but the trouble is, they're too damned noisy. They'll be heard long before they reach the terrain to be surveyed. Nothing can beat the cavalry for that."

After seven years in the army, Kunze was still amazed at the one-track-mindedness of the military. For them nothing beyond the realm of warfare had any significance. Progress had no meaning, unless its aim was destruction. Every human plus had to be counterbalanced with its minus equivalent, so the ultimate result would be zero.

"The British are supposed to be experimenting with machine guns mounted on planes," the lieutenant told them.

"I've heard about that, too, but it doesn't seem likely. One plane butting against another, fighting it out like two medieval horsemen? Never! For one thing, planes cost too much. No government could afford the expense."

"They could be used for aerial bombardment."

"Never. At least not as long as we have armies commanded by officers. The enemy might differ from us in every respect, except one: Its high command, too, is made up of gentlemen. War is bloody hell, but certain rules going back to more chivalrous times still prevail. A bomb aimed at a munition depot might miss its mark and kill unarmed civilians. No military commander—I don't care which side he's on—would be willing to take the responsibility for an act as barbaric as that!"

Kunze didn't want to contradict the colonel by reminding him that the Germans were making impressive progress with their practice bombing from aircraft. Anyway, he had not attended the lunch to talk about aviation.

The conversation switched from airplanes to France and her army. There were rumors, the young lieutenant said, that the French uniforms might be changed, the French General Staff suggesting that they do away with the gleaming cuirasses of the cavalry and the red pants of the infantry, both excellent targets for modern, long-range field guns, but the majority felt that drab uniforms would take the glamor out of soldiering and would lower the troops' morale.

The discussion of the French led to the Sergeant Faraco case, recently on the front pages. He had tried to kill eighty of his comrades by mixing poison in their mess hall food at the Verdun garrison because he owed two hundred and fifty francs to one of them. Captain Kunze felt the timing perfect in which to bring up the Charles Francis circulars. He took a small box from his pocket and handed it to Colonel von Instadt.

"This is one of the boxes the cyanide capsules were sent in. It shows how shrewdly the man planned the whole plot. If the boxes had been a few millimeters higher, the envelopes couldn't have been pushed through the mail slots."

The box, made of thin cardboard with a green and white leaf design, passed from hand to hand. It reached a blond second lieutenant at the far end of the table. He stared at it for a long moment, then quickly, as if it were burning his palms, passed it on to the next man.

Kunze pounced. "Have you seen a similar one somewhere, Lieutenant?"

The officer gave him a bewildered look. There was a long pause. The answer came in a thick, low voice. "Well, I was given some pen points in a similar box. They were a birthday present."

"Pen points for your birthday?"

"It was a joke, sir. I once borrowed a pen from a fellow officer and liked its point. My birthday fell on the following day, and he sent me a dozen."

"What is your friend's name?"

"I'd rather not answer that, sir." The lieutenant's tone was politely firm.

"Why not?"

"Because we've been living under a cloud of suspicion, sir. The whole garrison. I wouldn't want to cause any embarrassment to a comrade."

There was dead silence around the table. Kunze scanned the faces. They resembled statues, sightless eyes and ears deaf to reason.

Colonel von Instadt broke the silence. "I have a suggestion, Dielmann." His slightly nasal, aristocratic voice held a touch of petulance. "After lunch you tell the captain the name of your friend in private. The problem seems much too insignificant to waste time on."

Although he awarded the victory to Kunze, he did it begrudgingly. The captain realized this, but a successful investigator, he knew, had to be like an alley cat: taking kicks in his stride, never passing up a garbage pail just because it smelled foul.

"Now the name!" Kunze said to Lieutenant Dielmann in the cloakroom as the young officer buckled on his sword belt.

Dielmann looked unhappy.

"Must I?" When his tormentor nodded, he sighed. "All right, sir. It was First Lieutenant Peter Dorfrichter."

Kunze failed to react because he had been prepared for the answer. If Dielmann had named someone else, it would have been a great disappointment.

"I must see that box, Lieutenant!"

"I might have discarded it."

"Find it! You will help the investigation and Lieutenant Dorfrichter, too, by finding it."

"I wish he'd never sent me the goddamned pen points!" Dielmann groaned. "All right, sir, let's go over to my place. I'll see if I can find the bloody box."

He lived not far from the command post. The box with the pen points in it was in the top drawer of a chest and the birthday note that had come with it in a pile of letters under a paperweight. Kunze pocketed them both, as well as a group photo which showed a party of officers—among them Dielmann and Dorfrichter—at a picnic in the nearby woods.

The box was identical to those sent by Charles Francis. The local police had already ascertained that the only shop selling them in town was the Moller General Store on Beethovenstrasse, not far from the railroad station.

The Mollers, father, mother and four daughters, lived in a small apartment behind the store. Whoever was not busy cooking, cleaning, sleeping, eating or gossiping waited on the customers.

"Do you remember having sold a dozen or more of these boxes to an officer during the early part of November?" Captain Kunze showed Moller Lieutenant Dielmann's sample.

Neither Moller nor his wife remembered the sale.

"There's usually no demand for them before Christmas," Moller told him, "when people use them for small gifts. We had a carton delivered on November first and expect it to last us till next fall."

All four daughters were questioned, and the freckle-faced fourteen-year-old turned out to be the one who had made the sale.

She remembered the customer clearly. He was a first lieutenant, not tall but not short either, had a mustache and needed the boxes to keep buttons in. She found this odd because why would an officer have twelve kinds of small buttons that would fit into such tiny boxes. She showed him larger ones first, but he didn't want them and was ready to leave when she remembered the new shipment. He looked at the boxes, said they were exactly right, and bought a dozen. He would not let her put them in a bag but slipped them into the pockets of his greatcoat. This was not unusual, though. She knew that officers carried only small packages wrapped in white paper and tied with gold string so people would know they contained candy, perfume or jewelry.

She didn't reveal the real reason why she remembered this particular customer. He was the only person who'd ever told her that she had beautiful hands. She was taking the boxes from the carton and lining them up on the counter when he complimented her. Up to then she had never paid any attention to her hands, but from that day on she used a lotion on them and slept in cotton gloves, haughtily ignoring her sisters' teasing.

Kunze showed the picnic picture to the girl, and she immediately pointed out Lieutenant Dorfrichter as the one who had bought the boxes.

From the store the captain went straight to his room at the Hotel Herrenhof and put in a call to General Wencel in Vienna.

*   *   *

November 30 brought no change in the weather. From the top of Römer Hill, where Lieutenant Dorfrichter lived, only outlines of nearby buildings were visible. The rest of the city lay enveloped in what seemed like miles of beer foam.

He was reading the morning paper at the breakfast table. Once again there was a front-page report on the Charles Francis case. Like previous stories, this, too, contained mere speculations. The army was still refusing to release any substantial information to the press.

On the day before, Baron von Mühlwert, a member of Parliament, had questioned the Ministry of War concerning the case. Why the secrecy? the baron demanded to know. Was the ministry trying to withhold the truth forever from the public? Or was it possible that the culprit had already been arrested, court-martialed and perhaps even executed?

"What's new in the paper?" Marianne asked. She had gotten up with him despite his insistence that she stay in bed and rest. Ever since Captain Kunze's visit she seemed to burst into tears over the most unimportant matter.

"Not much," Dorfrichter told her. "King Leopold of Belgium has been taken ill. He wants to disinherit his daughter Louise. Doesn't seem to have much luck with his daughters, does he? One marries against his will; the other runs away with an adventurer."

"What else?"

"The King of Denmark is coming to Vienna. The czarina is still suffering. I wonder what the papers would find to write about if monarchies were abolished? Oh, this is interesting! The Serbian Army has recently been outfitted with ninety-thousand repeating rifles, ten howitzer batteries, one hundred and fifty mitrailleuses, one hundred and twenty million bullets and belts for two hundred thousand men! They are officially denying that King Peter is visiting the czar. Which means that he is in St. Petersburg right now and being briefed by the Russian high command on their planned campaign against the monarchy." He dropped the paper angrily. "And we are dawdling and wasting precious time thinking peace will last forever!"

"What about the Charles Francis case?" she asked. "Have they found the man?"

"What man?"

"The man who sent the poison."

Dorfrichter rose.

"No, they haven't. And if you ask me, they never will. But before they give up, they will have wrecked a few more lives."

"Among them—ours," she said, her eyes filling with tears.

He laughed. "Not ours! They cannot hurt us. They can hurt only weaklings and cowards, but not us."

"I am a weakling and a coward," she said, sighing.

"You're a woman in the ninth month of pregnancy. Once you're your normal self again, you'll laugh about the whole thing. Until then, leave everything to me, sweet. I can be strong for both of us."

As usual, he walked to the barracks. His company was undergoing bayonet practice under the supervision of a top sergeant. To Dorfrichter the emphasis put on hand-to-hand combat by the high command seemed outmoded, even harmful. A believer in firepower, he defended his stand often and loudly, even to his superiors. It was no secret around the post that he performed the duties of a field officer correctly and conscientiously but with little enthusiasm. He functioned at his best during maneuvers, especially if he was permitted to act on his own initiative. During last summer's war games he had been assigned to Archduke Josef Ferdinand's staff. The archduke's unexpectedly impressive performance was attributed to Dorfrichter's presence in his entourage.

His company was composed of men from Upper Austria, sturdy sons of farmers and mountaineers. A few among them were from Dorfrichter's hometown, Salzburg, and the mountains surrounding it. He knew the families of some and had established easy rapport with the others as well, winning the respect and loyalty of his men. His commanding officers realized that if he were to lead troops into combat, his men would follow him blindly and devotedly.

Around eleven o'clock he received an order to report to Major Schultz's office at the command post. This time he was not kept waiting but ushered in immediately. He found the entire commission assembled: General Wencel, Inspector Weinberger—both had arrived from Vienna earlier in the morning—and Captain Kunze. Major Schultz, the head of the Linz garrison's military judiciary, was also present. A young lieutenant acted as recorder, and he alone rose as Dorfrichter entered. The others remained seated, and Dorfrichter was not offered a chair.

Captain Kunze began the interrogation. Without preamble, he held up one of the three green-and-white-patterned boxes lying on the table.

"Have you ever seen this box before?" His eyes fixed on the young man's face, he expected to observe a flutter of alarm and was slightly disconcerted to find none. The lieutenant's perfect composure evoked in him resentment mixed with awe.

Dorfrichter stepped nearer and looked closely at the box.

"Yes, sir," he nodded, then corrected himself: "Rather one exactly like it, when I sent Lieutenant Dielmann a dozen pen points."

"Did you buy it especially for that purpose?"

"No, sir. I had quite a few of them at the house."

"How many?"

"I don't know, sir. It would be hard to keep inventory of all the items that accumulate in a household."

"Did you ever shop at the Moller General Store on Beethoven-strasse?"

Dorfrichter shrugged lightly.

"I may have, although I don't recall the store. Beethoven-strasse?" he asked himself. "That's near the station. It is quite possible I bought something there. A ruler. I remember having bought a ruler in one of the small shops in that neighborhood."

"It wasn't a ruler! It was a dozen of these boxes!"

Dorfrichter shook his head. He seemed puzzled. "It must have been quite a long time ago, because I don't remember it."

"It was not so long ago," Kunze said. "Shortly after the first of November."

Dorfrichter answered with a gesture expressing bewilderment.

Kunze whispered something to the young lieutenant who rose, left the room, and returned with the youngest Moller daughter.

She was dressed in a brown wool skirt and a mutton-sleeved taffeta blouse borrowed from an elder sister for the occasion. A bizarre hat trimmed with what looked like a raccoon tail was perched on top of her hair. As she faced the group of solemn men, her lips trembled and she blushed. Her impersonation of an adult would sooner or later, she felt sure, be uncovered.

"Fräulein Moller." Captain Kunze stood up, moved closer to her, and gestured toward Dorfrichter. "Would you kindly look at the lieutenant and tell me whether or not you have seen him before?"

Silence filled the room. Dorfrichter standing erect looked straight into the girl's eyes, a half-smile on his lips. His was the only cheerful face in the room. The girl stared back at him, her gaze traveling up and down his figure, hesitating on his hair, his collar, even his shoes. She took Kunze's instruction literally and weighed her answer.

"Yes," she whispered finally.

"Speak more loudly, please," General Wencel ordered. "I can't hear you."

She raised her voice. "Yes."

"You mean you have seen the lieutenant before?" Kunze asked.

"I have." She nodded. Now she was no longer looking at Dorfrichter but, as though deliberately evading his eyes, stared fixedly at the floor.

"Where did you see him?"

"At our store."

"Tell us about the incident. What took place while the lieutenant was in your father's store? What did he say to you?"

"Well"—she still stared at the floor as though cuing herself from the parquetry pattern—"he came in and asked if we carried any small boxes. Like matchboxes, he said. I showed him some, but he said they were too big, and then I showed him others. We'd just gotten them in and he said they were fine and he would buy them. A dozen." She heaved a sigh, adding: "That was all he said."

"Oh, no, that was not!" Dorfrichter, smiling, shook a finger at her. "I also told you that you had beautiful hands, don't you remember?"

Her mouth fell open, and she gaped at him, then at her white-gloved hands, then again at the handsome face which mocked her. Too embarrassed to realize that the others in the room were as surprised as she, she blushed while they were merely perplexed.

After a long pause Kunze asked, "Did the lieutenant say that to you?"

Too confused to speak, she merely nodded.

"I also bought a small box of marzipan," Dorfrichter addressed her. "You had two kinds: plain squares and an assortment shaped like fruit. I bought the berries."

The girl shrugged.

"Did you sell the marzipan to the lieutenant?" General Wencel asked.

"I don't know. I might have."

"Does your father's store carry such candy?"

"Oh, yes, we certainly do! People usually trim the Christmas trees with it. We also have some in the shapes of animals. Little bears and lions and tigers." She was suddenly all business. "They look very pretty on the tree, and they're practical, too, because you can eat them."

The commission evinced no interest in marzipan bears and dismissed the witness. She curtsied to them, then to Dorfrichter, and scurried from the office like a cat that had knocked an inkstand over and wished to be off before the spot on the rug betrayed her.

"If I understood you correctly, Lieutenant," Captain Kunze continued, "you admit having bought these boxes"—he pointed at them—"at the Moller store."

"Not these, sir," Dorfrichter corrected him. "Similar ones."

"Goddamn it, Dorfrichter," General Wencel flared, "a few minutes ago you said you'd never been to that store and never bought any boxes there! What do you think we are here for? To play games?"

"With the general's permission, I merely said I did not recall the purchase."

"But you do now?"

"When I saw the little girl, it all came back to me."

"How do you explain your amnesia and its sudden cure?"

"The whole matter slipped my mind because it was so unimportant. Since we moved to Linz and rented our apartment, I've done a lot of shopping. In her present condition, my wife doesn't like to go out, so I had to shop for things like yard goods and linens and pots and pans that otherwise would have been her responsibility. I couldn't possibly remember every purchase, General."

"All right," Captain Kunze said. "You bought a dozen little boxes. Where are they?"

"I sent one to Lieutenant Dielmann."

"And the rest? The other eleven?"

"They should be at the house."

"They are not! Two men and I turned your house upside down, but didn't see any."

Dorfrichter frowned, pursing his lips. His left hand moved upward as if he were going to scratch his head, then dropped to his side.

"You're right, Captain." He nodded. "They are not there. Because I burned them."

Five pairs of eyes stared. For a while no one spoke; then General Wencel's voice, much too thin for his height and weight, cut shrilly through the silence.

"Why?"

"I used the boxes to make a sewing kit for my wife. It was to have movable compartments for different size buttons and thimbles. I bungled the first job. I tried a second time and bungled again. Finally, I bought larger boxes and managed to fit them into a square basket which my wife has been using ever since. I burned the boxes wasted on the unsuccessful attempts."

"I searched your apartment thoroughly, Lieutenant," Kunze told him, "but I don't recall having come across a sewing kit."

"You must have, sir. My wife usually keeps it on her nightstand."

General Wencel rose suddenly, causing the officers to jump to their feet. A few angry steps put him face-to-face with Dorfrichter.

"You want us to believe that the very existence of the damn boxes slipped your mind until you were confronted with the Moller girl, when, according to your own words, you had spent hours working with the boxes, assembling, pasting, fitting them? Come on, Dorfrichter, you're an intelligent fellow. If you want to mislead us, you'll have to invent a better lie!"

"I would, too, if I were lying, sir. Unfortunately, I am telling the truth, and the truth doesn't always make a believable story."

"Why didn't you mention the sewing kit when Captain Kunze first asked you about the boxes?"

"It slipped my mind. I've done a lot of work in the apartment. Put up shelves, made window boxes, painted walls, hung curtains. Jobs that, I admit, were beneath my station as an officer. But I'm not a rich man, General, and I thought as long as I performed them in the privacy of my home, I was not disgracing the army."

"Let's not digress, Lieutenant," Captain Kunze added lamely, annoyed at the general's taking over the interrogation.

"I have to be very careful to make both ends meet," Dorfrichter went on addressing Wencel as if Kunze had not spoken. "I didn't marry money—our families had literally to scrape together the thirty-thousand-kronen marriage bond—so I wouldn't have to leave the service. To be a member of the Officers' Corps has meant more than my life to me. For this privilege I'm willing to do without luxuries, hobbies, travel, leisure. And I demand the same sacrifice from my wife. I don't know, General, if you ever had to ask a woman to share poverty with you! But allow me to tell you, sir, it is not an easy thing to do."

"That'll do, Dorfrichter," Wencel burst out, venom in his voice. "We don't give a damn about how many shelves and window boxes you put up! That's not the charge! You are accused of having tried to poison ten fellow officers and killing one."

The blood left Dorfrichter's face.

"With your permission, sir, did you say—*accused?*"

Wencel glared at him. "That's exactly what I said." Then he turned to the members of the commission. "We're in agreement on that, aren't we, gentlemen?"

His eyes traveled from face to face collecting nods like a tramway conductor collecting fares.

"May I make a suggestion, General?" Inspector Weinberger asked. "Let us have a look at the sewing kit the lieutenant says he made for his wife."

Wencel thought it a good idea, and the young lieutenant was sent to fetch the kit. He took along a scribbled note from Dorfrichter in which his wife was asked to hand it over to the bearer.

While the man was gone, Dorfrichter was ordered to wait alone in the adjoining office. Its regular occupant, a captain on Major Schultz's staff, was absent from the room. He had left the front drawer of his desk pulled out halfway with its contents exposed to view. Alongside batches of stationery and printed forms, there lay—dark, shiny and loaded—his service revolver.

The office was on the ground floor, and whoever passed the curtainless window on the walk outside could see Dorfrichter seated in the desk chair, his spine parallel to the back of the chair, but not touching it, his arms folded. At one point he rose and started pacing the floor. A soldier walking by saw him stop at the desk, reach out for the drawer, and push it shut.

The messenger returned with the kit, which wasn't really a kit —this explained why Kunze hadn't remembered it—but a small wicker basket topped with a hinged lid, the inside, by means of nine square boxes, divided into compartments.

"Quite clever," Inspector Weinberger observed. He lived with his wife and three daughters in a house in Hietzing where every room looked as if a poltergeist had romped through it. His wife kept buttons in a tortoiseshell box, but when needed, the box could never be found.

"Frankly, I don't see what bearing this basket has on the case," General Wencel said.

He was getting impatient with the investigation. Now that the blame could not be shifted from the army, he felt the sooner the suspect was indicted, the better. There would be another big splash on the front pages, then the gradual diminishing of the uproar, and finally silence. Besides, he was anxious to return to Vienna. He had called his mistress on the phone and was told by her maid—his paid spy—that she had not slept at home.

"It's time we reached a decision, gentlemen," he told them. "I personally think the man is guilty as hell!"

All he wanted now was to have the others confirm his judgment without wasting too much time. Since he was in a hurry, he considered Dorfrichter's unshaken calm an affront and his speech about not having married money a deliberate jab. Wencel was not the only general with a rich, Jewish-born wife, but certainly the most sensitive one about it. An innocent remark could make him blister and become the sworn enemy of the man who uttered it. Right now he found it convenient to direct his anger at Dorfrichter.

"We have three very strong facts against him." Captain Kunze summed up the investigation. "One, he was in Vienna at the exact hour when, and at a short distance from the place where, the poison capsules were mailed. Two, the deaths of the recipients would have helped his career immeasurably. Three, he bought a dozen small boxes like the ones Charles Francis used. We also have one expert opinion positively identifying the handwriting as his, one opinion that is *à cheval*, and one admitting only a strong similarity. We still have no proof that he ever had any potassium cyanide in his possession or that he ever bought, owned or borrowed a hectograph. No Charles Francis-type stationery, purple ink, red tissue paper or glue was found in his apartment. No witness saw him at the mailbox on Mariahilferstrasse, although, wearing a uniform and walking a large dog, he would have been a rather conspicuous figure among early risers on their way to work." He took a deep breath. "Despite these circumstances, but in view of the substantial evidence against him, I consider his arrest advisable."

Wencel turned to Weinberger. "What about you, Inspector?"

"As a policeman, I am convinced of his guilt. As a fellow human being, I have my doubts."

"And you, Major?" The question was a tactful gesture toward Major Schultz, for he was attending the interrogation merely as an observer representing the local military judiciary.

"In view of the contradictory findings, may I respectfully ask permission to abstain, sir?"

"Are you on friendly terms with the accused?" Wencel asked. His voice, slightly falsetto, betrayed the fact that he was disgruntled.

"Not exactly, General, but I know him socially. There is a very strong bond of camaraderie among the officers of this garrison, sir."

"Very commendable," Wencel murmured, not looking as if he meant it. "Permission granted."

He now focused his blue eyes under the thick graying eyebrows on Captain Kunze.

"We're in for a hell of a scandal, but go ahead and arrest the man. That's what you've wanted—haven't you?—from the very beginning." His petulance implied the captain was to blame for the positive outcome of the investigation.

"I shall carry out the order, sir." Kunze failed to respond to the gibe.

Wencel rose briskly. "Well, then, gentlemen, let's consider the session closed."

Accompanied by the recording officer, Kunze entered the room where Dorfrichter had been waiting and informed him of their decision. Dorfrichter listened at stiff attention and offered no comment. He was asked to surrender his sword and his revolver—the latter in case he carried one. He said he did not, and he was not searched. He was still an officer, and his word was considered sufficient proof.

Escorted by Captain Kunze and the young lieutenant, Dorfrichter was taken by fiacre to the barrack's guardhouse, a grim thick-walled building in the far corner of a forbidding cobble-stoned court. Three of its cells were reserved for officers, and Dorfrichter was ushered into the first.

During the ride he had sat stiffly and silently. Now, as Kunze was ready to leave him, he suddenly stirred.

"My wife, Captain! Could she come to see me? What will she be told? I must speak to her!" The words shot from his lips like pebbles hurled against a wall.

"I'm afraid she won't be allowed to see you. No one will, except us."

"She is nine months pregnant. This may kill her. Captain, sir, I am a man—I am strong enough to take whatever is coming—but she is not!"

Kunze felt his earlier irritation turning to pity. His sudden and inexplicable compassion toward the man disturbed him more than his previous enmity had. He must watch himself in his contacts with Dorfrichter, he warned himself, and ward off the spell of the man's undeniable attraction.

They were alone in the cell. Outside, the provost waited behind the heavy oak door with the grille-covered peephole.

"I'm not supposed to tell you this," Kunze said, keeping his voice emotionless, "but right now Colonel von Instadt and his wife are at your home. The colonel took it upon himself to break the news of your arrest to your wife. And Frau von Instadt is planning to stay with her till a member of the family arrives so she won't be left alone."

"Thank God, there's still charity in this world!" The color was returning to Dorfrichter's face. "I know one is not supposed to send messages from this place," he added, "but in case you see my wife, please tell her not to lose faith in me. Tell her nothing really bad can happen to us as long as she stands by me."

Kunze gave no indication that he had heard the prisoner. As he left, the heavy door slammed shut behind him.

III

GENERAL WENCEL and Inspector Weinberger took the afternoon train back to Vienna, but Captain Kunze remained until that evening in order to arrange for the transfer of documents and transcripts from regimental command posts in Linz and Innsbruck to the Military Lawcourt in Vienna. He was about to leave for the station when the sergeant on duty stopped him in the corridor.

"What about the dog, Captain?"

"What dog?"

"Lieutenant Dorfrichter's Troll. General Wencel had him brought here. He's been in my room all afternoon. I gave him water and two frankfurters, but he won't eat or drink."

It had been agreed upon earlier that the Veterinary Clinic at the University of Vienna would examine the dog for worms and establish its willingness to take medicine with or without capsules.

"What kind of dog is it?" Kunze asked.

"I don't know, sir. He looks like a bit of everything. His wasn't a very class-conscious mother, that is certain."

Kunze followed the sergeant to his room. The muzzled dog lay in a corner. As big as a six-week-old calf, it appeared to be a mixture of all the breeds known in Austria and of some as yet unknown, in a way rather beautiful, but at the moment utterly miserable.

"Lieutenant Dorfrichter said he was training Troll to be a war dog," the sergeant explained. "He used an odd method, though.

Never whipped him, never shouted at him, just talked to him as if he was a child. I've never seen a man love a dog more. The lieutenant ordered one of his orderlies sent to the post stockade for six days because the man hit Troll with a riding crop. The charge was insubordination and disobeying a direct order. If it had been any other officer, there would've been a lot of grumbling in the company."

"Is Lieutenant Dorfrichter well liked?"

"Yes, sir. He is a very fine officer. The finest."

Kunze sensed a touch of reproach in the man's tone.

"What shall we do with the dog, Captain?"

The animal had flipped its ears back and watched the two men from the corner of its eye.

"Someone's got to take him to Vienna."

"That has to be done tomorrow, sir, as the office is closed. There is no one to write out travel orders for whoever goes with him. So I'll lock him up here for the night. The worst thing he can do is mess up the place."

"I can take him." Kunze had no idea what made him say it. Since the Irish setter of his childhood, he had not had any contact with a dog. Traveling with one of Troll's size could be a troublesome undertaking. "You think I could handle him?"

"I don't know, Captain. The two soldiers who brought him here had quite a time. That's why they muzzled him. I don't think he likes it. Lieutenant Dorfrichter never made him wear one."

"Well, let's find out," Kunze said.

The sergeant hooked a leash onto the dog collar and tried pulling the animal to its feet. Troll growled and remained curled up in the corner.

"Let's take the muzzle off!" Kunze suggested.

"He might bite you, sir."

Kunze unfastened the muzzle and pulled it off. He kept speaking steadily in a low voice. Holding onto the leash, he started for the door. The dog rose and followed him.

The train was crowded, and the conductor opened a reserved compartment for Kunze, remarking, "I've seen this dog before, Captain. He was with a lieutenant then. Oh, about a couple of weeks ago. The train was packed, and I had trouble finding a seat for the lieutenant. Most people object to dogs in the compartment. Especially to big ones like this here."

The man wished Kunze a good-night and left. The captain pushed up the armrest and stretched out on the seat but couldn't fall asleep. The last remark of the conductor troubled him. If Dorfrichter had really gone to Vienna to post the Charles Francis letters, why had he taken along a dog that could be identified from among a hundred other dogs? A man on a criminal mission would have wanted to blend into the scenery. Was it possible that despite the series of incriminating facts against him, Dorfrichter was innocent?

The dog became restless. It had boarded the train willingly enough, but whenever a uniform passed the compartment, it emitted short, shrill barks. *Poor bastard*, Kunze thought, *he misses his master*. He began talking to the animal, and the dog sat down at his feet and put its big, bushy head on his knees, its brown eyes full of trust. Troll reminded him more and more of his boyhood friend, the Irish setter at the Hartmann house, and conjured up ghosts of a seemingly dead past.

The young Emil Kunze's first memories were of other houses —two or three—where he had been the housekeeper's son, either fussed over or merely tolerated, but never a member of the family. He recalled that he had been ten when his mother went to work for the Hartmanns, and he had grown up with the three Hartmann children—Paula, his own age; Martin, one year younger; and Rudolf, three years older than he. Their relationship was one of total equality. They played and studied together and were separated only by the dinner hour, Frau Kunze insisting that her son eat with her in her room while the three Hartmann children ate with their parents or their governess.

From the first day, Emil Kunze had nurtured a worshiping admiration for Rudolf, who treated him with the august condescension of a thirteen-year-old for a boy of ten. Emil, the entire Hartmann household and the whole neighborhood fell under Rudolf's rule. He was tall for his age, strong, handsome, intelligent and tough. A word of praise from him was a medal of valor pinned on a boy's chest, his disapproval exile to Siberia. Under his leadership the group occasionally embarked on childish pranks, picking a neighbor's apple crop or sneaking a tame otter into a goldfish pond. When he entered the Wiener Neustadt Military Academy to follow in the footsteps of his ancestors, everyone predicted a brilliant military career for him.

From the day he entered the academy, Rudolf no longer engaged in pranks with the children. He looked incredibly handsome and grown-up in his cadet's uniform, played tennis with adults, and was often seen walking ladies twice his age home in the twilight after the matches. To Emil's great distress, he showed practically no interest in him, except to tease him occasionally. Then late one afternoon, when Emil was collecting the deck chairs from the garden, Rudolf followed him to the shed, bolted the door and, in his usual condescending manner, ordered Emil to take off his clothes. The boy, hypnotized, obeyed. What followed was an experience he could never eradicate from his mind. Although he knew what was happening to him, the rapture he felt made him unable to resist. In losing his halo, his idol had gained a much greater, more irresistible power over him.

The incident in the shed was repeated several times during the summer. Despite their secret encounters, however, Rudolf's attitude toward him never changed, adding to Emil's agony. Rudolf continued to ignore him, remaining nonchalant on the rare occasions when they spoke.

The following winter Rudolf, stricken with appendicitis, was taken to the Military Hospital in Vienna and underwent a successful operation.

Because Frau Hartmann felt indisposed on the day her son was to be released from the hospital—she spent two days in bed every month, as did all the women of her circle, with the exception of housekeepers, cooks and maids—she sent Frau Kunze to bring Rudolf home. Emil asked for permission to accompany his mother. At the hospital they went straight to Rudolf's room. The corridor was empty, and they entered the room without meeting anyone. The windows were open and Rudolf—they assumed it was Rudolf—lay on the cot under a white sheet, only his bare feet uncovered. Frau Kunze lifted the sheet from his face.

It was not in her nature to scream. She re-covered the dead boy's face, crossed herself, murmured a short prayer, and went to look for a doctor.

Emil remained beside the body, his first reaction one of black horror, his second an unmistakable sense of relief and deliverance. Immediately, he was shaken by a feeling of guilt, which remained with him for weeks, months, even years. At times it grew into the throbbing pain of a migraine headache.

After Rudolf's death, the creature closest to Emil's heart became the Irish setter. The dog repaid his affection in kind, playing with the other children, honoring the adults with token wags of his tail, but belonging only to Emil.

When Kunze was nineteen, the dog died of old age. With the animal gone, Emil's home became merely the house where, among other people, his mother happened to live.

It was after one in the morning when Kunze arrived in Vienna. From the station he took a taxi to Zaunergasse. The driver was not enthusiastic about having Troll for a fare. He drove a 1907 Panhard, upholstered in wine-red plush, which only a few weeks before he had bought secondhand from a count. He asked cautiously if the dog shed.

"Never had any complaints about that," Captain Kunze answered truthfully.

Kunze had wired Rose the hour of his arrival, and the entire household was waiting up for him. He hadn't been home for almost a week. The cook produced a platter of freshly fried chicken, and there was a chocolate soufflé rising in the oven. The moment Rose heard his key in the front-door lock she flew to the entrance hall to help him out of his greatcoat and relieve him of his sword and briefcase.

"Angel, I missed you so!" she cried, engulfing him in the soft, sweet-smelling warmth of her embrace. Then suddenly she spotted Troll. "What's that?" she asked shrilly.

"That is a dog," he answered. Sometimes it gave him a hellish pleasure to tease her.

"Is he housebroken?"

"I hope so. He was trained to be a war dog." He unhooked Troll's leash. "We had a nice walk in front of the house. Unless he has bladder trouble, your rugs are in no danger."

He started for his study, the woman and the dog following. Rose rang for the maid to serve the captain's dinner. Unbuttoning the high choke collar of his tunic, he sat down at the oblong Biedermeier table where he always took his meals when dining alone. The dog stretched out on Rose's antique Bokhara. She threw a pained look at him.

"Does he shed?"

"You're the second person to ask me that question tonight." He grinned. "To tell you the truth, I don't know."

"Where did you get him?"

"That's a long story."

He told her in a few words, and she seemed relieved.

"You gave me such a fright. I thought you wanted to keep him." Now that the danger was over, she became bold. "He'll be better off if he sleeps in the hall tonight."

"It is not heated."

"Dogs prefer to sleep in a cold place."

For some inexplicable reason he became annoyed. "How do you know?" he asked. "You've never been a dog."

"I don't care. I'll tell cook to find an old blanket, and we'll spread it in a corner for him."

The blanket was brought in, but Troll chose to sleep on Kunze's bed, curling up at the captain's feet. By morning the question of Troll's shedding was answered. He did—and profusely.

On his way to the Military Lawcourt Kunze delivered Troll to the Veterinary Clinic at the university. He explained to the professor in charge what the dog was to be tested for, saw to it that Troll was given a large enough kennel and, tipping the hospital orderly, asked him to take good care of the dog.

The morning papers reported Dorfrichter's arrest in front-page stories filled with speculations but few facts. Since the Ministry of War had issued nothing but a short statement, the reporters relied on their imaginations. In some articles, Dorfrichter was depicted as a monster, in others a sacrificial lamb. They all deplored the secrecy in which the army chose to shroud the case.

On his way to the lawcourt Kunze noticed long lines in front of newspaper kiosks. In the cafés people lingered over their breakfasts, waiting for additional bulletins in the midmorning editions. Rumors spread about Dorfrichter's being a spy, an anarchist, a sadist, part of an antimonarchist conspiracy. It appeared that no other murder case had caused such turmoil in the capital.

Late in the afternoon, Captain Kunze received an order to report to Schönbrunn Palace at six o'clock the following morning for an audience with Emperor Franz Josef. The order was delivered by a major from the emperor's Military Chancery.

"His Majesty most considerately thought you might be a late riser. That's why he didn't wish you to report at an earlier hour," the major told him. There was no hint of a smile on his face sporting a dark-blond replica of the imperial beard. Kunze wondered what was considered "early morning" at Schönbrunn.

The command read: "Full dress and decorations." He was able to comply with the first, but not the second. He rose long before daybreak and, as he put on his uniform, hoped the emperor would not be shocked at the sight of a medalless chest.

The taxi he had ordered the previous evening awaited him in front of the house. He was taking a chance by riding to Schönbrunn in an automobile. There was always the danger of a flat tire, a mechanical defect or a driver who simply forgot to have the tank filled. Horses were slower, but more dependable. Nevertheless, Kunze chose the motorcar. The nights were becoming colder, and he didn't want to arrive in Schönbrunn red-nosed and chilled to the bone.

The long journey along Mariahilferstrasse was uneventful. Traffic consisted primarily of peasant carts laden with provisions for the city's human and equine population. In the thick fog they constituted a definite navigational hazard for the streets were only dimly lit, the gas lamps pale-yellow daubs in the all-concealing blackness of the early dawn.

At 5:20 A.M. the taxi rolled through the majestic gates to the palace park. The lieutenant on duty directed the chauffeur to a side entrance, where a staircase led to the emperor's apartment.

Because he was almost an hour early, Kunze was led by one of the adjutants to a small room next to an aide-de-camp's office, where he found two men seated on frail Rococo chairs upholstered in imperial red damask: a doctor of the Medical Corps and a civilian in tails and white tie, both scheduled to be received before him.

The doctor, as he told Kunze in hushed tones, was ordered to

Vienna from Mostar to give the emperor a firsthand report on the alarming spread of VD among the occupying forces in Bosnia. The civilian was a headmaster from Prague and was to give his views on the success of the German language courses in Bohemian schools. Despite the full-dress uniforms and white tie and tails, the morning audiences were strictly business.

The doctor was summoned first. When he emerged again, his eyes shone as though they had just witnessed the Messiah's descent from the Jewish heaven. The fact that the "Messiah" had restricted himself to questions about the percentage of occurrence of syphilis among enlisted personnel failed to lessen his elation. The headmaster followed him into the "Presence" and returned a few minutes later with all the starch gone from the collar of his shirt and beads of perspiration running down his cheeks. Wholly oblivious of his physical discomfort, he beamed at Kunze like a boy who had received an unexpectedly good report card.

"His Majesty was most gracious to me," he announced as he walked from the room.

The adjutant announced Captain Kunze and held the door open to the emperor's study. It was a room every Austrian knew from description or pictures—too homely and unpretentious for the hub of an empire, its desk uncluttered except for writing implements, a stack of documents and a few family photographs in simple frames. On a small table, another large pile of papers lay waiting to be signed. Kunze wondered whether the old man really believed that it was his examination of every single dropping from the empire's bureaucratic bowels that kept the establishment from falling apart. At seventy-nine, the old man's memory was still amazing, no detail escaped him, be it the change of braiding on the dragoons' uniforms or the alteration of the language law in Hungary. Opposed to constitutional rule, but scrupulously adhering to it since granting it to his people, he resembled a conscientious lookout guarding against fire, looters and vandals from a watchtower built of state papers and memorandums.

Captain Kunze saluted stiffly; the door closed behind him, and he was alone with the sovereign.

As usual, Franz Josef had risen that morning at 3:30 A.M., looking forward to his bath. His private suite, decorated with priceless furniture, tapestry and rugs, lacked the convenience that had become part of most middle-class apartments in Vienna— namely, a bathroom. So each morning a large wooden tub filled with lukewarm water was carried in by two husky servants and a man, called *Badwascherl*, who gave the emperor his sponge bath. This *Badwascherl*, unfortunately, had grown both old and complacent on the job, the main reason being that no one, no matter how powerful and majestic fully clothed, could be the least awe-inspiring when stark naked. Morning after morning the *Badwascherl* reported for duty, slightly intoxicated, to regale the emperor with rambling lectures on the ills of the monarchy and the grievances of the population. Franz Josef, who under ordinary circumstances would never tolerate the slightest *lèse-majesté* from his entourage, listened spellbound to the man's discourses, to the mystification of the court. Some of them, however, astutely reasoned that the truth may have been that the *Badwascherl* represented a stratum of society with whom the emperor otherwise would never have come in contact. The man offered information none of the papers piled high on the imperial desk contained.

This morning the *Badwascherl* had staggered in totally drunk. The fire having gone out in the big tile stove in his room, he had had to fortify himself against the freezing cold with a double dose of his usual stimulant. Realizing that His Majesty would never accept a substitute, Kitterl, the emperor's valet, set about sobering the man up. The procedure took longer than expected, and the delay had made Franz Josef slightly testy.

He was still standing in the tub when Kitterl announced that Colonel Bardolff, Archduke Franz Ferdinand's aide-de-camp, was waiting outside with an urgent message. An envoy sent by the heir to the throne at this early hour portended even greater gloom for the emperor's day. From the beginning of the Charles Francis investigation the archduke had insisted that the army be spared all embarrassment. When he heard that the suspect was an officer, his wish was to have the case suppressed. Despite his feelings, Dorfrichter was arrested. Franz Ferdinand then felt it his duty to intervene and sent Colonel Bardolff to Schönbrunn with a request for an audience. Reluctantly, though, the emperor agreed to see Franz Ferdinand later in the day. He did not tell the aide-de-camp that by then he would have spoken to the judge advocate assigned to the case and made his decision.

Franz Josef stepped from behind his desk, acknowledged the salute, and proffered his hand. His handshake was firm and soldierly. Kunze had seen him once before during the maneuvers of 1902, but this was the first time they stood face-to-face. Since the maneuvers the emperor had aged but little. His shoulders more noticeably curved, his hair thinner, the pouches under his eyes more pronounced, still the blue eyes under the heavy Habsburg lids remained clear and alert, and at six in the morning he had already put three audiences and more than an hour's work behind him.

The emperor got straight to the point. "I understand, Captain, that you're in charge of the investigation against First Lieutenant Peter Dorfrichter suspected of one murder and nine attempted murders."

"Yes, Your Majesty." Kunze nodded. Looking at the careworn old man, he tried to analyze his own reactions. He knew he should have been awed, impressed, exhilarated, yet he was not. What he felt for his emperor was pity, rather than veneration. During his law career he had seen the same lines furrowing a commoner's forehead. The imperial face reminded him of other faces, marked by the same grief, disappointment, hopelessness. There was, he thought, nothing majestic about the old age of kings.

"I received Colonel von Instadt yesterday," the emperor went on. "He expressed high regard for Lieutenant Dorfrichter. He does not consider him capable of the crime. What is your opinion? As a jurist, do you have sufficient grounds for an indictment?"

Franz Josef waited, concentrating deeply, for the captain's reply. At that particular moment the guilt or innocence of one man held priority over all of Austria's problems, claiming their ruler's undivided attention. Once again, the emperor's infinite sense of duty was at work, as he endeavored to grasp, with average intellect, the essence of a question which might have defied the wisdom of gods. It was only now that Kunze understood why he had been summoned. Franz Josef had taken it upon himself to decide on the advisability of the investigation. He understood fully the harm an officer's conviction could do to army morale. He functioned, however, not only as supreme commander of the army, but as guardian and conscience of forty-three million men and women as well. Moreover, he was old, and the old, he knew, could ill afford to make mistakes. It was so simple for the young, he reflected wistfully. They could find refuge from the ghosts of their own blunders in drinking, lovemaking or a good night's sleep, but the old—they lay awake in their lonely beds, their mistakes crowding around them, taunting, provoking like a lynch mob.

The captain hesitated. He knew the answer the emperor secretly hoped for. A simple *no* would have freed Peter Dorfrichter and buried his case forever under mountains of affidavits, depositions, transcripts and records. The press, primarily the leftist newspapers, would pose a few embarrassing questions, but the next dissected body found in a wicker trunk or the next princess who eloped with a gypsy bandleader would push the Charles Francis case from the front pages and into oblivion. The emperor knew this, and were he not the man he was, he would have been satisfied with Colonel von Instadt's testimonial.

Kunze's thoughts turned to Peter Dorfrichter, the handsome young man whose smile seemed to have been built into his features. The image momentarily reawakened the nervous resentment he had felt in Linz. It was a fleeting sensation, too abrupt, too irrational to be fully explicable.

He gave a summary of the investigation, recounting the evidence both for and against the suspect. He depicted him as an able and talented officer, but also as a man sufficiently cold-blooded and sure of himself to be capable of murder.

"I'm afraid, Your Majesty," he concluded, "in my modest opinion, the facts of the case definitely warrant the lieutenant's indictment."

The emperor pondered the facts for several moments.

"Well then, Captain," he said finally, "continue your work and see to it that justice is done." He heaved a sigh; his face became empty of all expression, as though his mind, closed to the disheartening realities of the present, had escaped to a problemless void to rest and gather strength for the remaining duties of the day. He shook his head. "One wonders what the world is coming to."

It was no imperial pronouncement, but the complaint of an

old man who had fallen out of step with the new generation. The small clock which served to indicate the time allotted to each audience rang shrilly on the desk. Franz Josef thanked the captain, wished him luck, and dismissed him.

IV

LIEUTENANT DORFRICHTER had been in the regimental prison for two days without a single word having been said to him. Breakfast, lunch and supper were brought on trays by a guard and the empty dishes removed when he had finished his meal. The first few times he had tried to start a conversation with the guard, his questions were met with stubborn silence. The food obviously came from a restaurant and, he assumed, had been ordered by his wife. No other visible sign of anyone's caring about his predicament reached him.

His complete isolation came as no surprise. *The military criminal procedure established in 1768, during the reign of Empress Maria Theresa, under which an officer suspected of a capital crime was, after his arrest, handed over to a judge advocate, who was investigator, prosecutor and defense attorney and later member of the court-martial, was familiar to him.* Until the verdict the prisoner was not to communicate with anyone except the judge advocate—in Dorfrichter's case, Captain Emil Kunze.

At four o'clock in the morning on the third day of his imprisonment he was awakened by the provost and ordered to dress. His clothing had been removed the night before, clean underwear was produced, his uniform and greatcoat were returned freshly pressed, and his boots were polished to a high gloss. When he was dressed, he was escorted to the provost's office and handed over to three officers—two lieutenants and a captain—he had never met before.

They were from the Fifty-first Infantry Regiment stationed in Vienna. The captain alone spoke to him, introducing himself and his two subordinates. He then informed Dorfrichter that they were to escort him to the capital. He asked for Dorfrichter's cooperation, adding that they were armed and had orders to shoot in case he tried to escape.

It was a cheerless trip for them all. The past two days had helped Dorfrichter adjust to the vacuum surrounding him, and when his lame attempts at conversation met with no response, he gave up with a shrug. The officers, on the other hand, seemed visibly disturbed. Their prisoner, after all, was a comrade, and it pained them to treat him with discourtesy. Avoiding his eyes, they kept their conversation to a minimum.

They took a landau to the station, which at this early hour was almost completely deserted. When the train pulled in, they boarded the last coach, where a compartment had been reserved for them. Of the few people who saw them, only the sharpest observers noticed that only three of the four officers wore the obligatory sidearms, while the fourth was swordless and kept his hands deep in the pockets of his greatcoat.

They had been traveling for more than an hour when Dorfrichter suddenly broke the oppressive silence.

"I know you're under order to avoid all communications with me, sir"—he addressed the captain—"but you three gentlemen are probably the last unbiased people I'll have a chance to talk to and—"

"Spare us, Lieutenant." The captain tried to cut him short. "Nothing you may say is of—"

"Any interest to you. That's what you were going to say, sir. But you're wrong. The unjust imprisonment of an innocent person is of interest to every man, woman and child in this land! Because if it can happen to him, it can also happen to you."

"Spare us, Lieutenant! That's an order!" The captain raised his voice.

"I most respectfully defy the order, sir."

The captain squirmed uncomfortably. Normally a mild-mannered man, he was helplessly abashed by the prisoner's aggressiveness.

"Don't force me to reach for harsher measures." His threat failed to sound at all menacing.

"You may have me gagged, sir, but that'll be the only way to stop me! I am innocent. Judge Advocate Kunze has collected bits of disjointed facts against me and, by trimming them here and there, has made them fit into a large pattern. He may drag me before a court-martial, too, but will never have me convicted, unless he produces false witnesses who—"

"That's goddamn cheeky, Dorfrichter!" The captain was red in the face. "Accusing a man of perjury!"

"I said—unless! Otherwise, he'll never be able to prove that I had access to any cyanide or that I mailed the circulars. Or even wrote them. He can't prove something that never happened!"

"For Christ's sake, Dorfrichter, save your breath! We're not your judges! Let's suppose you get us on your side. What difference will that make? I mean to the outcome of your case?"

"I'll leave that to you, sir, and to the lieutenants. Three comrades convinced of my innocence might be a hopeful beginning. Don't forget, sir, I am in a hell of a spot. I need every bit of goodwill I can muster!"

The captain groaned and turned his head away. The two younger officers stared at the passing landscape through the window, remaining noncommittal. Nothing more was said until the train rolled into the Western Railroad Station in Vienna.

The news of Dorfrichter's arrival had spread through the city. A group of reporters gathered at the station was soon joined by a curious and excited crowd. There was much jostling and maneuvering for position for a close look at the antihero of the day. The reward, as in all such cases, was hardly worth the long wait on the drafty platform, the near fisticuffs and the wallets stolen in the melee. What the crowd saw was a pale young officer hustled to a waiting fiacre. The action was so fast that one newspaper photographer mistook one of the escorts for Dorfrichter. His picture appeared later under the caption "The Monster in Officer's Clothing," which led to a series of protests, corrections, apologies and the ridicule of the competition.

The cell of the military prison—one of the eight reserved for officers—was small but bright, containing a narrow bed, a table, two chairs and a wardrobe. Its grilled window overlooked a cobble-stoned courtyard, and the heavy door leading to the corridor had a peephole through which the guards could observe Dorfrichter's every move. When he was booked, he asked for a pen and paper to write his wife, but his request was denied. Next, he demanded reading matter but was told that, too, was against regulations. So were visitors or mail. Provost Tuttman, who at the time was present in the prison commandant's office, had the distinct feeling that Dorfrichter was about to lose his composure and bodily attack the commandant. He had seen it happen before, and he knew the signs: eyes clouding over, muscles twitching at the temples, fists balled. His long service as provost had convinced Tuttman that the very aim of the regulations was to drive prisoners to acts of open rebellion, which in turn would call for even more severe restrictions. This time, however, the prisoner regained his composure. He clicked his heels, bowed stiffly and apologized for having burdened the commandant with unnecessary demands, leading Provost Tuttman to surmise that they were dealing with an unusually shrewd prisoner.

Nor did Dorfrichter have any way of knowing that his father, mother and sister had arrived in Vienna the night before and now sat in the adjoining office, waiting to be received by the commandant.

Dorfrichter senior was a glass importer from Salzburg, short, compact, with the strutting temper of a fighting cock. The mother, a sad, obese woman, had features which bore a vague puffy resemblance to those of her handsome son. The sister had inherited the father's ruddy complexion and firm, bowling-pin silhouette. Her breasts resembled two tennis balls playfully slipped under the lace-trimmed bodice of her dress.

After Lieutenant Dorfrichter had been led to his cell, the family was admitted to the commandant's office. The father immediately gave voice to his indignation over his son's arrest in a rather incoherent but highly dramatic speech. Bringing up his son to become an officer had called for great sacrifices on his part. Anyone else would have groomed the boy to help him in his business. He had also given his daughter to the army, when he consented to her marrying a penniless captain in the dragoons. The marriage bond alone had cost a small fortune—this in addition to the large sum he had contributed when his son had chosen a wife of modest means. Despite the financial burdens, he considered having a son and son-in-law in His Majesty's service a great privilege. Wasn't it inconceivable that the offspring of such a loyal and patriotic citizen could be suspected of the most heinous crime of the century? He demanded the immediate release of the lieutenant or—at least—permission to see him alone.

When he was refused politely, but categorically, he broke down in sobs. His tears, mingling with those of his wife, left their daughter alone dry-eyed and coldly aloof. The commandant, a good, patient man grown impervious to tears during his long years in the prison, sent them off with the promise to make Lieutenant Dorfrichter's stay in his establishment as pleasant as could be expected under the circumstances.

During the next three days Dorfrichter remained in complete isolation. As in Linz, he was served three meals a day sent in from a nearby café. On the first day he refused to touch the food, but boredom and misery were hard enough to bear, and he evidently realized that it would be foolish to add to them the pangs of hunger. After the second day he ate heartily and devised a regimen for himself to break the horrible monotony of his idle days. He rose late in the morning—officers were not bound to the prison timetable—lingered over breakfast, then did calisthenics for thirty minutes. One of the guards who watched him through the peephole was a gymnast and could tell by the awkwardness of Dorfrichter's movements that the exercises were a newly acquired habit. They were followed by a sponge bath and a shave administered by the prison barber. He then spent the rest of the morning standing at the window, talking to himself. At least, so it seemed to the guards. They were able to catch a word or two, usually names of places like Ulm, Friedland, Wagram, Borodino, Leipzig. When this was reported to Captain Kunze, he deduced correctly that Dorfrichter was reciting the main battles of the Napoleonic Wars, evidently to keep his mind as nimble as his body.

On December 3, the same day Dorfrichter was transferred to Vienna, Captain Kunze obtained a search warrant from the chief prosecutor's office authorizing an official visit to the apartment of Frau Josephine Gruber, of 32 Hahngasse, Dorfrichter's mother-in-law.

The present search was the second one, the first having been conducted shortly after Dorfrichter's arrest. When in Vienna, the lieutenant always stopped at the Gruber home. The police had hoped to find the hectograph on which the circulars had been copied, writing implements, perhaps even some leftover cyanide hidden in the flat, but nothing of the sort turned up, and the searchers were forced to leave emptyhanded.

This time the search was merely a pretext. Kunze knew that Marianne Dorfrichter had come up from Linz, and he wanted to have a talk with her before she could be coached and prepared for the questioning. Since the apartment was civilian territory, Kunze was accompanied by Inspector Weinberger and two detectives.

The door was answered by a young peasant maid. Frau Gruber was in her housewares store on the ground floor of the same building, and the four men had to wait in the entrance hall while the girl went to fetch her.

Dorfrichter's mother-in-law entered breathing heavily and aglow with indignation. She was a pleasantly plump woman with short legs, and ample bosom, and as she faced Kunze, she reminded him of the legendary geese of the Capitol, the wing-flapping and hissing defenders of endangered Rome.

Frau Gruber led the four men through the narrow hallway to the dining room which also served as parlor, study and—during family reunions—as extra guest room. Representing elegance and culture amid all the utilitarian clutter were a vitrine holding a few heirloom pieces of silver and Meissen porcelain and a bookcase with the collected works of Lessing, Goethe, Schiller, Grillparzer and Shakespeare.

The men found four young women in the dining room, the four Gruber daughters. Marianne Dorfrichter, her protruding belly covered with a lap robe, sat in an overstuffed armchair at the window, her sisters around the table. They didn't move when the men entered, merely turned their well-coiffed heads toward them, and nodded curtly. To Kunze the scene resembled a tableau, a Vermeer painting conceivably entitled "The Visit." Her sisters had obviously come to commiserate with Marianne, to soothe and shelter her with family solidarity.

The two detectives began a systematic search. They had been instructed to look for letters and notes from Dorfrichter and correspondence concerning his person. Frau Gruber trailed them through the apartment, as if afraid they might steal the family silver. The daughters remained seated in stiff silence, pointedly ignoring the presence of the search party.

For Marianne, the youngest and most beautiful of the four Gruber daughters—as well as for her three sisters—marriage had been a step up the social ladder. Frau Gruber had insisted that virginity was a girl's most priceless asset to be sold to the highest bidder. Alma, the eldest, had married a manufacturer of kitchen equipment in Graz, Tilda an architect in Baden bei Wien, Liesl the owner of a department store in Klagenfurt. The husbands had two things in common: they were rich and much older than their wives. Marianne alone had married for love, becoming an officer's lady and moving up in the world the least of her considerations.

She had met Dorfrichter shortly before his graduation from the War College. During the six years of her illness she had been alone a great deal, dreaming, reading, watching the smoke curl from the chimneys of neighboring houses. She tried to imagine what life would be once she was allowed to go out into the world. Her thoughts centered on the man who would take her away from the confinement of the cluttered Hahngasse apartment, the four-times-a-day temperature taking, the constant fussing of her mother. She knew Peter Dorfrichter was the man the moment she first laid eyes on him.

Completely recovered from her spell of TB, but not from the loneliness of her adolescence, she longed to meet people but felt at ease with strangers only if her husband was beside her. He was the bridge connecting her storybook world with that of the flesh and blood. Now her bridge lay demolished at the bottom of an abyss, and she found herself once again the shut-in of the Hahngasse flat.

What made her days bearable was the fierce loyalty of her mother and sisters. They had come to her aid once before in a crisis, when Dorfrichter could not scrape together the thirty-thousand-kronen marriage bond, and they had come up with twenty thousand kronen. The rest had been contributed rather ungraciously by his family, because they were opposed to the marriage, the old Dorfrichters hoping for a more impressive match for their son.

Anyone with less character than Frau Gruber, now that her son-in-law had turned out to be a bad investment, would have changed her attitude. But Frau Gruber had only admiration for him. Marianne felt a touch of envy as she watched her confront the terrible captain, wishing she could display the same emotional indignation, but each time she tried to speak, her throat constricted.

"As long as we're here, Frau Gruber," she heard the captain say to her mother, "I'd like to ask you a few questions."

Frau Gruber folded her arms.

"Go ahead, Captain. I'm waiting."

"On the morning of November fourteenth, when Lieutenant Dorfrichter arrived from Linz, at exactly what time did he reach this apartment?"

Frau Gruber puffed contemptuously.

"I've been asked this question before. First by the detectives, then by the inspector himself. Why don't you ask them?"

Kunze spoke in a low tone, but it had the force of a volley. "I am asking *you!*"

"The answer is still the same. At seven sharp. I know because my alarm clock rang just as the maid let him in." Her voice grew a shade less pugnacious.

"Can you recall what he said and did on that morning?"

"When I heard his voice, I put on a robe and went to greet him. He had the dog along and a small suitcase. We hadn't known he was coming, and I was surprised to see him. I told him Marianne was still asleep in the red bedroom—we call it that because of the red drapes. He said not to wake her. Then he played with the children."

"What children?"

"My daughter Tilda's." She indicated the snub-nosed blonde in the black-and-white taffeta shirtwaist. "They were staying with me because my daughter had the painters at her house. They live in Baden bei Wien."

"What did he play with them? Games?"

"I wouldn't call them games. Whenever he comes, he always brings them presents. Toy soldiers and little cannons and such. He was setting them up on the floor. Then I had to leave to open the store."

"They were still playing when I woke up," Marianne broke in. She threw off the lap robe, rose, and turned to face the captain. Her cheeks were flushed, and she could not control the trembling of her lips; nevertheless, she forced herself to speak up in defense of her husband. Since their first meeting she had considered Captain Kunze a demon bent on destroying their lives, loathing him with a ferocity she had not known herself capable of. There had to be an explanation for the tragedy that had wrecked her life. She held the army too much in awe to blame, and so her bitter resentment was concentrated on one person, Captain Kunze.

"I heard the children laugh," she went on, "and my husband's voice. I found him stretched out on the floor with the children. The boy is six, and the girl is four, and they were on their stomachs, and so was he . . . and they were moving the toy soldiers about . . . and he was talking to the children about tactics and outflanking the enemy . . . and the children were having a wonderful time—and so was he." Suddenly her voice broke, and for a moment she looked as though she might faint. Her mother ran to her and cradled her in her arms.

"For God's sake, calm down, Marianne!"

"Leave me alone," she said, disengaging herself from the protective embrace. Her gaze remained fixed on Kunze, who stared back at her, surprised at the unexpected outbreak of fury. She was a grotesque sight, the fragile upper part of her torso, slim neck and small head sprouting from her puffed-up belly like a daffodil from its bulb. *She must be very close to delivery,* he thought.

"Do you think it possible for a man to be playing and laughing with two small children after having mailed ten death sentences?" she asked. "Because that's what those circulars were— death sentences. Only one was carried out, but that was a mere coincidence. A man would have to be mad or a monster to do such a thing. And my husband is neither—he is good and kind. You won't find a speck of evidence against him, because there is none! And he had nothing to do with the horror you're trying to hang him for—"

Marianne's outburst had a varied effect on the people in the room. Frau Gruber looked as though she were ready to scratch out the captain's eyes, her daughters sniffled, but Kunze felt annoyance. For some inexplicable reason Marianne Dorfrichter repelled him, possibly because of her pregnancy; he, the bachelor, the man without a family, found pregnant women unattractive, deformed, even monstrous.

"We don't hang innocent people, Frau Dorfrichter," he told her wryly.

The search was concluded shortly thereafter and, just as Marianne had predicted, yielded no evidence. As a gesture of appeasement, Inspector Weinberger apologized to the family for having inconvenienced them, to which they responded with a haughty silence. Kunze was almost at the door when Marianne stopped him.

"Captain Kunze," she said, managing to sound neither righteous nor insulting, "how is he? How is my husband bearing up under this dreadful thing?"

"I haven't seen him since Linz," Kunze said. "But I understand he is well. I expect to see him around the end of the week." Remembering the message Dorfrichter had given him, he decided against delivering it.

Marianne sighed. "Please tell him that I miss him very much. And that I believe in him. He shouldn't worry about me. I'll be all right." When Kunze didn't answer, she moved closer to him, their bodies almost touching. "Will you tell him? Or is that, too, against regulations?"

Kunze nodded. "It is, but I will tell him just the same."

Provost Tuttman ordered the guard to open the cell door. It was ten past ten, and Dorfrichter had already performed his calisthenics and now—fully dressed—was staring out the window, mumbling his mysterious litanies. At the creak of the heavy door he wheeled about to face the provost.

The provost saluted. "Sergeant Tuttman respectfully wishes to report." Dorfrichter, though a prisoner, was still an officer—only a verdict of guilty would deprive him of his rank. "I have orders, sir, to escort you to Judge Advocate Captain Kunze's office."

"At last!" Dorfrichter seemed almost cheerful, although looking pale and drawn.

The military prison adjoined the Military Lawcourt Building. If the prisoner were an officer, regulations prescribed that the provost march at his side and a guard with fixed bayonet behind.

Kunze's office was on the third floor, a high-ceilinged puritanically simple room with two windows overlooking the street, bookshelves lining the walls, a large tile stove and desks for the captain and his staff. Military law demanded that two members of the garrison judiciary be present during interrogations of accused and witnesses. Assigned to the case were Lieutenants Stoklaska and Heinrich, the latter acting as recorder.

After they had disposed of the formal salutes and the provost and escort had left the room, Kunze said to Dorfrichter, "Before we begin our talks, I want you to understand that I am conducting this investigation with an open mind. I have no prejudice against you. All I want to discover is the truth."

"That sounds noble, sir," Dorfrichter said. "I only wish I could believe it."

Despite his better judgment, Kunze bristled. The man was obviously not as smart as he had thought. Would anyone with an ounce of brains antagonize the person responsible for deciding his fate? Courage was one thing, bravado something else. Kunze wondered if the lieutenant had come to the conclusion that his case was hopeless. Defiance, he knew, was very often a sure sign of guilt. A man who knew he was to be executed had nothing to lose by kicking the hangman in the crotch.

"Be sensible, Dorfrichter. We're going to see a lot of each other during the next weeks, and it would make it much easier for both of us to have these meetings in a temperate climate. If I took the evidence against you at its face value, I'd say you're guilty as hell, but I don't want to do that."

"Why not?" Dorfrichter cut in, omitting the "sir."

"I've just told you why not. I don't want a conviction based on circumstantial evidence. There must be either absolute proof of your guilt or a confession from you."

"You'd prefer a confession, wouldn't you?" After a pause, he added the "sir."

"Not necessarily."

"But without it you couldn't have me condemned to death. That's the law, isn't it? If a man isn't caught *flagrante delicto*, he can be condemned to death only if he confesses. Isn't that so?"

Kunze was determined not to lose his temper.

"Let me remind you, Lieutenant, that in this room I am the one to ask the questions." His tone was that of a weary schoolmaster.

"Oh, but we must understand each other, sir. I must know what you are after, what your strategy is. So I can plan my defense."

"Dorfrichter, I have here the psychiatrist's report. It states that you possess an unusually high intelligence quotient. Near genius. So don't talk nonsense. It'll make me doubt the report."

Dorfrichter went on stubbornly. "Captain, sir, allow me to make my point. We are engaged in a kind of duel here. You're accusing me of having murdered a comrade, and I'm accusing you of intending to murder me."

"How was that again?" Kunze asked sharply.

"And the irony of it is," the lieutenant continued, "that if your charge is proved true, mine will be, too. By the process of proving me a murderer, you'll be a murderer yourself. So in that case there won't be much difference between the two of us, will there?"

Kunze gave him a half-ironic, half-exasperated look, wondering what Stoklaska and Heinrich were thinking of this debate. Both maintained an attitude of complete uninvolvement, Heinrich jotting down every word that was being said, Stoklaska staring through the window at the roof of a house on Hernalser Gürtel.

"Let's get to the point, Dorfrichter," Kunze said. "The psychiatric report indicates that you are a man of not only extraordinary qualities, but extraordinary ambitions."

"They usually go together, don't they?" The lieutenant grinned, beginning to look more and more as though he were enjoying himself.

"What was your first reaction when you read the promotion

list on November first and found that you had not been assigned
to the General Staff? Were you disappointed?"

Dorfrichter thought for a moment.

"No, sir," he said sharply. "I was not disappointed. I was livid.
Furious. I thought of my two years at the War College and before
that the general examination and the cramming and sweating for
the finals and became more and more outraged when I realized
that all that had been for nothing—for assignments in one lousy
stinking hick-town garrison after the other, for trying to make
soldiers out of a mob of oafs, for performing duties that any pig-
headed sergeant could perform. Yes, I was outraged over the stu-
pidity of a system that could waste talent and knowledge with
such extravagance!"

"And then you decided to do something about it."

"No, sir. I had a glass of wine. It stimulates most people, but
it calms me. So I had a second glass. And then I started thinking.
War is inevitable. It has to come. Now, in a year, or in five years.
The chief of staff is for it; the heir to the throne is for it; the emperor is against it. But he is seventy-nine years old. How long can
he last? Once war breaks out, men like me will be needed. The
decision of 1909 will be reversed in favor of common sense. So I
decided all I had to do was to swallow my anger, do my duty, and
wait for my time to come."

"What makes you so sure there will be a war?"

"It is a question of 'to be or not to be?' There is a lovely young
princess. Her name is Hegemony. Four knights—Russia, Germany, France and the monarchy—are in love with her. She herself
is not in love with anybody, because she is a sadist bitch, unin-
terested in normal sex, aroused only by the sight of spilled blood.
If one of the knights wants to win her, he must present her with
the severed head of his rivals. To make things more complicated,
there are also Great Britain and the Ottoman Empire. But the
Turk has pernicious anemia, and England is attracted by princes,
as well as princesses. So it is possible that both will stay out of the
tournament."

"Your reasoning is wrong. If there is a war, we'll fight on Germany's side. And Italy's. Let's suppose our alliance wins. That'll
result in a much stronger Germany. And Italy. Where does that
leave us?"

"That's it! That's why I'm telling you that people of my caliber are needed! The Germans have great advantages. More troops, more and better arms, a more homogeneous population. But we have the brains. Our War College is the best in the world. I know because I've been through it. Good God, Captain, have you read Bloch's *Is War Now Impossible?*" He took a deep breath. "The gist of his predictions is that after a first assault in which millions will perish, the war will become a kind of stalemate in which neither army will be able to get to the other. Everyone will be entrenched like moles, and the spade will be as indispensable as the rifle."

Kunze nodded. "Yes, I've read it. He might be right."

"Certainly. And this is what is going to happen if we don't wake up. There have been two inventions lately that'll change the face of the earth. The internal-combustion engine and the wireless telegraph. We have weapons of annihilating power, provided we can move them where we need them. Nevertheless, both the German and French training manuals—and ours, too—consider the bayonet assault the weapon of the offensive! They still depend on cavalry for reconnaissance. And horses for transportation! Our sole salvation is to revise our thinking, discard all those antiquated ideas forced on us by allies and enemy alike, and go our own way. The French General Staff is politically rotten. The Germans are stupid. Their chief of staff, General von Moltke, flunked out of *their* War College, which is a nursery school compared to ours. He was named to his post because he is the Kaiser's pet and bears an illustrious name. The Kaiser won't allow anyone with a milligram of talent on his staff, has filled all important army appointments with princes and toy soldiers who haven't the faintest idea of what war is. If we go along with them, we'll perish. If we go our own way, we may become a world power. But to gain that, you can't have me and men like me waste our time on drill grounds teaching troops to keep their buttons polished and their latrines clean. Not to mention the idiocy of my being here in this room, defending myself against an impossible charge!"

Kunze had been sitting motionless, his eyes never leaving Dorfrichter's face, hollow-cheeked with deep rings under the eyes. Not even the inner fire that hurled words like hot rocks from a seething volcano at the captain could color it. The prison pallor, hardly a week old, seemed to have coated it with the thickness of a rubber mask.

"I'm glad you have finally remembered the purpose of this meeting," Kunze snapped. "There is indeed a murder charge against you. It is my duty to remind you that all you've said up to now strengthens the prosecution's case!"

Dorfrichter chuckled. "For Christ's sake, Captain, don't waste any legal sophistry on me. Have some regard for my mental properties. Don't treat me as if I were some green recruit fresh from the woods!"

"No. You're certainly no green recruit! And I respect your intelligence. However, you've revealed yourself to be a fanatic. Ambition alone might not drive a man like you to murder. But ambition combined with fanaticism might!"

Dorfrichter leaped to his feet.

"I respectfully ask for permission to smoke, sir," he said.

"Permission granted."

Kunze pulled out his silver case—a gift from Rose—snapped it open and held it out to Dorfrichter. Heinrich lighted the cigarette. Thanking the lieutenant, Dorfrichter inhaled deeply, apparently relaxed.

"Fanatic or no fanatic, I have nothing to do with the goddamn circulars," he said.

Kunze let the profanity pass.

"Your wife sends you her love," he reported.

Dorfrichter's face turned a shade paler, a sickly greenish white. The hand which held the cigarette dropped to his side.

"You saw her, sir?" he asked in a muffled voice.

"Yes. About five days ago."

"How is she?"

"She is well—and believes in you. She doesn't want you to worry—and misses you."

"She hasn't had the baby yet?"

"Not when I saw her."

"That was five days ago."

"I'd have been informed if she'd had it."

"Why can't she visit me?"

"You're familiar with the regulations."

"But can't an exception be made? This is a hell of a way to treat an officer! What do you expect to accomplish by it? If you think you can crush me, you're very much mistaken. I'm not crushable, Captain. And no matter what medieval methods you may try, I'll walk out of here a free man. That I promise you, sir."

Kunze observed him coldly. The mention of his wife had caused Dorfrichter to let down his guard slightly. For the first time his hand had trembled as he smoked. There was still a show of defiance, but his tone had betrayed more panic than conviction. The separation from Marianne Dorfrichter was clearly the most disturbing aspect of his imprisonment. Guilty or not, the murder charge was an enemy he could fight. He could win the battle by using his wits and imagination, but there was nothing he could do about his wife. Beyond the wall separating them, she could fall ill or in love with another man or simply become estranged from him, and he had no way of reaching her. In his confrontation with Kunze he was invulnerable, except through her. She was the leaf that had fallen between his shoulders when he had bathed like Siegfried in the dragon's blood.

Kunze pulled out his watch and glanced at it.

"We may as well finish for today," he said. "We haven't accomplished much, but there is still time."

Lieutenant Stoklaska sent a messenger for the provost, and the ritual of salutes and respectfully asking permissions was repeated.

"First Lieutenant Dorfrichter is hereby dismissed. Staff Provost Tuttman, escort the prisoner to his cell!"

More salutes and more heel clicking, the sound of heavy footsteps marching through the corridors, and finally the heavy oak door, with the numeral 6 painted on it, falling shut.

Years later, looking back at that scene, Kunze often wondered whether it could ever have taken place in any country other than Austria. It was impossible to imagine, for instance, a Prussian judge advocate and an officer accused of a capital crime engaged in an informal dialogue that bordered on facetiousness. The German language itself as spoken by the Prussians was not appropriate. Certain basic ingredients were needed to make it work, ingredients that were strictly Viennese. Liberalism and humanism were still not passé in Vienna, and every Austrian nurtured a small flame of the 1848 rebellion in his soul while still unconditionally devoted to the emperor who had put it down. Archdukes were promoted to second lieutenants when they were fourteen, but a laborer's son could become an officer, even a general. The army constituted an empire within an empire, an enormous fetus embedded in the womb of the motherland, flesh of her flesh and blood of her blood. *Gemütlichkeit* penetrated every organ of the army and made life in its ranks, if not always a delight, at least bearable.

V

THE office of Dr. Paul Goldschmiedt was located in the midtown Kohlmarkt, the narrow street which led to the massive complex of the Imperial Burg. The building, one of the luxurious new apartment houses erected during the last decade of the nineteenth century, contained a marble-floored entrance hall and elevators in ornate grille cages with mirrored walls and morocco leather upholstery. Dr. Goldschmiedt rented two apartments on the second floor, had his offices in one, and lived with his wife and four servants in the other. His horses and carriages—a landau, a calash and two gigs—were stabled in a nearby side street alongside his Daimler automobile, the chauffeur of which cost him a hundred and fifty kronen a month.

It had been Frau Gruber's idea to approach Dr. Goldschmiedt because he was not only the most successful, but the most expensive, attorney in Vienna. The family refused to consider her suggestion at first. A cousin in the Gruber clan was a lawyer, and he was their first choice, but Frau Gruber wouldn't hear of him. The Dorfrichter case had become a *cause célèbre*. There had already been two interpellations in Parliament, both attacking the procedure by which the army investigation was conducted. Peter Dorfrichter's name appeared day after day in the papers, was discussed at tea parties, in clubs, in cafés and in the streets. Frau Gruber finally persuaded the family that a man like Dr. Goldschmiedt, who had achieved his reputation on the sensational criminal cases he had won, could not resist the publicity he would receive as Dorfrichter's defense attorney.

With an unfailing sense of the dramatic she assigned the task of approaching Goldschmiedt to Marianne. Her daughter protested violently. Since the first of December, after her husband's arrest her mother had brought her to Vienna, she had not left the Gruber apartment. She even avoided the windows because strangers, either reporters or plainclothes policemen, loitered across the street.

"I won't, Mama! I won't see Dr. Goldschmiedt. Not in my condition. I'll kill myself first," she said sobbing.

Frau Gruber remained unmoved by her daughter's tears.

"Your condition? You act as if you were the only pregnant woman in the world. When I carried you, I took part with your father and sisters in the famous folk festival of Princess Pauline Metternich. You were born five days later. No one found it objectionable. Your husband is locked up in a dank jail cell, where he can't even see a speck of sky, and his wife is not going to lift a finger to help him!"

Frau Gruber wrote to Dr. Goldschmiedt—holders of a law degree were addressed as such—and his office replied that the doctor would see Frau Dorfrichter the following afternoon. To make sure that Marianne did not change her mind, Frau Gruber accompanied her to Kohlmarkt. Both women wore black, the mother because of her age, the daughter to camouflage her bulk.

The waiting room of the Goldschmiedt law firm was impressive—the primary color was a discreet taupe; the paintings on the walls were somber landscapes. A row of offices opened off a long corridor, where the hum of work filtered through their closed doors. People continuously moved about, always on tiptoe, and speaking in hushed tones as if they were engaged in illegal activities.

The man who received Marianne—Frau Gruber remained in the anteroom—was of medium height, balding, more stocky than corpulent, his small dark eyes like two darting searchlights. He was conservatively dressed, but wore a red carnation in his lapel, a plain gold wedding ring and a heavy emerald one on his immaculately groomed hands. Marianne suspected that his short black mustache and his thinning hair had been touched up. Around fifty or fifty-five, he moved about with the self-conscious youthfulness of an aging prima donna playing an ingenue. Like aging prima donnas, he, too, possessed stage presence and an air of authority.

Marianne proffered her hand, and he lifted it to his lips. The hand kiss, a mere social gesture, had no significance. She was an officer's wife.

"What can I do for you, my dear?" His tone was kind, a trifle patronizing, and his piercing gaze combed her figure with embarrassing intensity. Marianne's face became flushed and her body moist with sudden perspiration. She knew she was going to cry, loathing herself for weakness and lack of self-discipline.

"Dr. Goldschmiedt, would you undertake the defense of my husband?" She felt the stinging tears bathe her eyes.

He took her by the elbow and led her to a group of fauteuils.

"Sit down, my dear." He took the chair facing her. "I've guessed that was what you wanted to see me about, so I've looked into the matter. I'm afraid—"

She cut in. "He didn't do it! He is innocent!"

"He may be, but at the moment that is a secondary question. The immediate problem is to get him out of the clutches of the military and have him tried by a civilian court."

"Please, Dr. Goldschmiedt, help him. I'm sure you can."

Her tears had dried, and she was composed again. He stared at her fixedly, becoming more and more conscious of her beauty. Hers was the kind of perfection that revealed itself only to a connoisseur. Some men might have passed her in the street without throwing a second glance at her, especially now with her grotesque silhouette. But to him, even her pregnancy was an attraction. Paul Goldschmiedt's interests in sex were wide-ranging. A born explorer, he always searched but never quite found. He could afford the best, which included whatever was considered novel and rare. A model husband and father, he usually did his more adventurous exploring abroad, where all he had to lose was money. On his own hunting grounds he restricted himself to liaisons with well-known actresses and expensive cocottes, though possessing them gave him less of a thrill than riding down Kärtnerstrasse in his Daimler. He was no fool, interpreting his lack of sexual appetite as a sign of approaching old age and resigning himself to the fact that only the unusual could arouse him. This young woman with the face of Botticelli's Flora and a protuberant belly attracted him as no one had since his affair with a Sudanese Negress in Paris the year before.

"My dear Frau Dorfrichter"—he shook his head—"I'd hate to raise false hopes in you."

"They won't let me see my husband or even write him. I went to the military prison on Hernalser Gürtel—I read in the paper that's where they keep him—and wanted to send him some clothing—socks and underwear and such. They wouldn't accept the package. They told me he would have to wear government issue. This is terrible. He must think I don't care about him, that I have deserted him."

"I'm sure he doesn't."

"I don't even know whether he is still alive!"

Gently Dr. Goldschmiedt petted her arm. "Of course, he is alive. This isn't the Middle Ages, my dear, but the twentieth century."

The touch of his soft, pudgy hand somehow reassured her. She felt strangely drawn to him, probably, she thought, because of his age. That was how old her father would have been if he had been alive.

Although Dr. Goldschmiedt didn't in the least resemble her father, sitting beside him made her feel less vulnerable than at any time during the previous terrible weeks.

"Will you take the case?" she asked. Her mother had instructed her to discuss the fee as well. Business matters must be settled beforehand to avoid disagreements later. Now she was at a loss about how to approach the question. "We're not rich," she floundered, "but we—I mean the family—we know how valuable your time is, and we're willing to—"

"That is not important, my dear." His tone was brisk, almost harsh. "If I take this case—*if* I take it"—the emphasis was clear—"I shall do it because I consider it my civic duty to fight for the abolition of an outdated and inhuman law, rather than for the man who is its victim."

He appeared firm and sincere. Marianne experienced a warm surge of gratitude.

Dr. Paul Goldschmiedt, considered by many a lecher and a cynic, could also be, when he wished, an idealist and a good Samaritan. Many things to many people, he was even more things to himself. With a brilliant, well-informed, incisive mind and excellent taste, he was also an amateur botanist. In the greenhouse on his estate on the Wörthersee he grew exotic foreign plants. His library contained, among first editions and works on history, philosophy, anthropology and psychiatry, the largest and most valuable collection of pornography in Austria, possibly in the entire monarchy. His most prominent trait, however, was a burning curiosity. He undertook challenge after challenge, experiment after experiment; life was an inexhaustible territory wherein every square inch had to be surveyed, analyzed and charted. No *nouveau riche*—the Goldschmiedt fortune had been amassed by his great-grandfather with each generation contributing to it—he had nevertheless an almost theatrical flair for ostentation, a love of luxury befitting an Oriental potentate. Proudly he traced his ancestry back to Isaac Abrabanel, the last of the great Jewish scholar-statesmen of fifteenth-century Spain, at the same time being spiritually attracted to the baroque splendor of the Catholic Church. He never became a convert but was often seen attending mass in the cathedrals of foreign cities. When he spoke to Marianne Dorfrichter of trying to right a hundred-and-fifty-year-old wrong, he meant every word.

"Give me a day or two, my dear," he told her. "I'll do some investigating and let you know the result. In the meantime, don't despair. You're much too young to give in to gloom. Troubles at your age are part of growing up. They have a role in forming your character, but their memory will pass sooner than you think. Right now, in your condition, you need all your strength. Save it. And let me do the worrying."

He had mentioned "her condition," yet oddly, it failed to make Marianne self-conscious. The terrible weight that had pressed down on her chest and pulled her belly groundward suddenly seemed bearable. She thanked him, and he beamed at her benevolently, laugh wrinkles radiating from his unhandsome face.

It was a rather awkward and time-wasting operation, but that was what the law prescribed. First the witness was called in, and name and data were taken down in longhand by Lieutenant Heinrich. Captain Kunze administered the oath, then began the questioning. Only after the witness had been dismissed was Lieutenant Dorfrichter brought in. The testimony was read to him and his reaction to it faithfully recorded. If there was a disturbing discrepancy between his and the witness' versions, the latter was recalled and confronted with the testimony of the accused.

Aloisia Prechtel, wearing her best dirndl under the heavy loden coat, a green felt hat with a jaunty feather and high-buttoned boots, sat on the very edge of the witness chair. She felt important, vengeful, yet wary. Her mistress had left Linz without telling her how long she would be gone. She took some comfort in her newly acquired prominence: Strangers accosted her in the street to ask about Dorfrichter's private life; reporters interviewed her; even Father Kolb of the Minorites' Church had invited her into the sacristy after mass.

Now she had been summoned to Vienna to testify under oath. She had never been in the capital before but fortunately had a cousin living in Vienna who met her train and escorted her straight to Captain Kunze's door, through which door she had to walk alone.

"Fräulein Prechtel," Kunze said after they had confirmed name, address, and how long she had been with the Dorfrichters, "I want you to go back to November thirteenth. Late that night Lieutenant Dorfrichter left for Vienna. Were you at the Dorfrichters' apartment that day?"

"Where else? I live there. I'm not the kind to go gallivanting just because the lady isn't home!"

"I didn't think you were," the captain replied patiently. "We understand that the lieutenant was on leave from the twelfth on. Can you remember whether he was at home on the thirteenth and, if so, what he was doing?"

"He was home, but I don't know what he was doing because he stayed in his room. Locked himself in."

Kunze remembered the apartment.

"What do you mean by *his* room? There is the salon, the dining room and the bedroom."

"The bedroom, of course. That's where his desk is."

"And he didn't let you get in all day?"

"No!"

"Did you find that unusual or had it happened before?"

"No. It never happened before. It kind of struck me as strange, but now I know why he stayed locked in! He was writing the letters to all those officers and filling the capsules with poison!"

The three men looked at her in surprise.

"How do you know that?" Kunze asked sharply.

"Everybody does." She shrugged. "It was in the papers, too."

"But did you see the letters and the capsules? Or find any dust or powder that looked like poison to you?"

"Dust is always poison to me. It makes people think I don't clean properly."

"What about the letters and the capsules?"

"I might have seen them. I don't know."

"Did the lieutenant keep himself locked in on the twelfth of November, too?" Kunze asked.

"Except when he took the dog for a walk."

"And who walked the dog on the thirteenth?"

"The lieutenant, who else? I have enough to do without having to chase after the dog!"

"You said the lieutenant walked the dog on both the twelfth and the thirteenth. That means he didn't stay locked up in his room all the time."

"No. He just kept the room locked. Took the key with him when he went out."

"So you couldn't get into the bedroom either on the twelfth or the thirteenth."

"Only on the morning after. By then the lieutenant was in Vienna."

Kunze leaned back in his chair and for a moment stared at the empty air before him.

"Thank you, Fräulein Prechtel, that'll be all for the time being."

Aloisia rose reluctantly. Having lost the initial nervousness that had constricted her throat during the first few minutes of questioning, she was just getting warmed up. "I gave notice on the third of November," she said suddenly to the three aloof men, who up to then hadn't seemed aware of her importance as a witness for the prosecution. "I wanted to leave immediately. On account of the lieutenant. He called me an idiot. Frau Dorfrichter begged me to forget it and stay. The lieutenant was very nervous, she said, because he was disappointed about not having gotten a promotion."

She offered the information as a bribe, hoping the captain would prolong the session. Kunze swallowed the bait.

"What promotion?" he asked.

"Promotion to captain, of course. They both were looking forward to it and to being transferred to Vienna. Then suddenly nothing more was said about it. When I asked her, she told me to mind my own business. And he went stomping all over the house, cursing everybody and slamming doors."

"When did you first notice the change in the lieutenant?" Kunze asked.

Aloisia lowered her fat, pear-shaped rump into the chair. "After the first of November." Stingy with her information, she hoped again to be prodded and cajoled.

"Did Frau Dorfrichter seem to be disappointed about not moving to Vienna?"

"That's hard to tell. She'd been kind of nervous before, too. She wasn't feeling too well. Besides, she hated getting big. She worried that he—I mean the lieutenant—would lose interest in her because of her condition." Aloisia giggled. "She is more the jealous type. She liked to keep tabs on him. Where he'd been, whom he'd seen and all that—"

"Did he give her reason to be jealous?"

"Heavens, no! He worshiped the ground she walked on. Some evenings I had to keep the supper on the stove for an hour before they were ready to eat. He couldn't wait till after supper, if you know what I mean. It used to make me mad. I could never plan anything like a soufflé because I knew that by the time they crawled out of bed it would be flat as a pancake. Of course, that was eight or ten weeks ago. Now she was getting too close to her time for that. Besides, her doctor told him to stay away from her since she was not too strong."

After her final piece of information Kunze dismissed her with such finality that she no longer thought of lingering. He had Dorfrichter brought up immediately after for questioning.

It had been two days since their last meeting. The lieutenant seemed to be in a more relaxed mood. Kunze was aware that he had adhered religiously to his self-imposed schedule: the calisthenics, the sponge bath and the endless soliloquies. And a new form of diversion had been added: a stroll on the Ring. At least that was what the stupefied provost called it. Dorfrichter would pace the floor of his cell and after a certain number of steps call out, like a tramway conductor, the name of a cross street. He would stop for a moment as if waiting for the traffic to roll by, then continue toward the next cross street. On the first day he covered the distance between the Opera and Weisskirchnerstrasse. The following day he walked as far as the Urania.

Aloisia's testimony was read to Dorfrichter, primarily the part concerning his, Dorfrichter's activities on November 12 and 13. The prisoner listened stony-faced and without interrupting.

"Any comment?" Kunze asked.

Dorfrichter shrugged. "What do you expect me to say? That I locked myself in to print the circulars and fill the capsules with poison?"

"Didn't you?"

"No! I was working and wanted to keep Aloisia from barging in on me. I was writing a treatise on the importance of the eighteen-cm howitzer up to now overlooked by the high command and had my manuscript and my research material spread all over the place. If I left the door open, she would've dashed in, collecting them into one neat pile, only to prove to me that she'd been cleaning." He paused for a moment, embarrassed. "I'm sorry, sir. I sound like a petty housewife. I never thought I'd discuss Aloisia's *modus operandi* with a fellow officer!"

"You said you worked on the treatise on the twelfth and the thirteenth of November. By then you knew you would *not* be assigned to the General Staff. What did you hope to accomplish? We both know the army, Dorfrichter. How the hell could you hope that your suggestions would influence the high command to revise their war plans?"

"I don't know what you're driving at, sir."

"I'll tell you, damn it!" Kunze raised his voice. The discussion was beginning to grate on his nerves. "You were determined to break through the wall that stood between you and the staff. You could achieve this only by eliminating three men who were ahead of you. There was no other way! You didn't want to remain a field officer, moving up grade by grade to the rank of colonel, pensioned off to die in comfortable and inglorious retirement. You did—"

Dorfrichter's shrill, angry laughter cut him short.

"You're certainly blessed with a creative imagination if I may say so, sir. When you can find no evidence against me, you simply dream up some. I am guilty because I wrote a treatise on the usefulness of the eighteen-centimeter howitzer. I'm the wicked Charles Francis because my longhand is similar to his, because I was in Vienna on the day his circulars were posted, because I bought a dozen small boxes in a general store. I don't think you can have me convicted, sir, unless you find more proof against me. The court-martial will consist of seven officers who will have eight votes while you'll have only one. I have faith in my comrades, whoever they may be. Their verdict will be not guilty no matter what pressure you will exert upon them!"

"I will not need further evidence. You will have confessed by then," Kunze told him in his flat, even voice.

His calmness seemed to anger Dorfrichter.

"Is that what you are counting on?" he asked heatedly. "My confession? I'd better tell you right now, sir, *don't!* I shall walk out of here a free man, and your promotion to major will have to wait according to your seniority!"

He rose and took a few nervous steps. Kunze, observing him pensively, could not help admiring the man's stamina. Two weeks had passed since his arrest, and instead of weakening, Dorfrichter seemed more self-possessed and secure than before. Guilty or not, he believed he would emerge the winner from the duel. Determination was written all over his handsome face, obvious by his balled fists, the spring in his step.

"What do you think of him?" Kunze asked Stoklaska and Heinrich after Dorfrichter had been led away. It was unusual for him to discuss a suspect with subordinates. A hundred-and-fifty-year-old law had made him judge, prosecutor and defense attorney, and right or wrong, he alone was burdened with the moral consequences of his decision. Now he had broken that rule. The two lieutenants assumed he had done it because he was confused.

"Looking at him, I'd never think he could hurt a fly," Stoklaska said. "But there is a hell of a lot of evidence against him. I'd hate to be in your shoes, Emil." When among themselves, they dispensed with formalities.

"There is still no proof that he could lay his hands on any cyanide. Without that you have no case, Emil," Heinrich pointed out.

The captain nodded. "That I know. But what is your impression of the man?"

"I'm afraid he is a damn good officer. The best. Guilty or not guilty—I'd let him go. He won't be of much use rotting in a prison cell when war comes. We're not so well off that we can afford to waste a man like Peter Dorfrichter."

VI

GENERAL WENCEL and his wife were giving a supper party at their house in Hietzing. For the first time in his army career Captain Kunze was also invited. The gold-engraved invitation was as impressive a sign of distinction in Vienna as an entrée to the Asquiths' circle in London.

Kunze was pulling on his new patent-leather boots—custom-made, but a bit tight—when Rose, after a token knock on the door, burst into the room.

"Paul is dying!" she reported in a tone much too cheerful for the subject matter.

"Paul who?"

"Uncle Paul." Her voice became appropriately mournful. The dying man was her favorite uncle. "He had a stroke. His doctor thinks it's a matter of a few days at the most. Poor dear. He is only sixty. Too young to die."

Kunze succeeded in squeezing his feet into the boots, and after rising, walked to the wardrobe and removed his tunic from its hanger.

"Next year you'll be taking me along to the Wencels' party," she told him.

His hand froze on the top button.

"I may not be invited next year."

Her expression indicated she had expected a different answer.

"But if you are, I will be, too." Leaning close, she kissed the gold braid on his shoulder. He pulled away, irritated. He felt at their age any such childish display of affection was uncalled for and embarrassing. He knew she was waiting for a question from him, but he refused to comply.

"When I last saw Uncle Paul, he told me he had made a new will, leaving his house and some stocks to me." She spoke breathlessly, her eyes fixed on his face. "If he dies, we can get married."

"He is not dead yet, is he?" His voice sounded more brusque than he had intended. "He may recover and live happily ever after."

"I can dream, can't I?" she asked. Her lips trembled, and her eyes were moist.

"You always told me you loved him. How can you wish him dead?"

"Because I love you more than him! More than anyone. And because it is not the best life for a woman, left behind all the time, invisible, never able to say: 'This is my man!' We belong together. I call you my lodger—you call me your landlady. That would be all right if the only thing holding us together was a lease!"

Suddenly he felt deeply ashamed. Here was a woman who had given him tenderness and understanding and, above all, a home, without demanding anything in return. When he was ill, she nursed him; when he felt lonely, she kept him company; when he needed solitude, she stayed out of his sight; and when he wanted sex, she took him into her bed. Without her he would have remained a drifter, engaged in a few fleeting and meaningless affairs, returning evening after evening to some empty flat where the only cheerful sound came from the horn of his gramophone. After crossing to her, he pulled her into a tight and, for him, loving embrace.

"Don't be such a child. Of course, I want to marry you. I never look at another woman, you must know that." He pushed her away gently. "And now please don't cry on my full-dress uniform. Every tear stains this damned fabric!"

She laughed as he wiped her face with his handkerchief, adding wistfully, "I only wish I could go with you tonight. I have a new dress I haven't even shown you yet. It's white lace with a band of black velvet at the bottom. It's stunning! You'd be proud of me!"

This was one of her good days. Her hair, freshly washed, was soft and shiny, despite the gray streaks at her temples, and her skin the soft pink of the Renoir girls. She wore a velvet housedress with a flounce down the front and a train which barely touched the floor. Remembering the opulence of the well-shaped body encased in the tightly laced corset, he suddenly realized that it had been weeks since he'd last held her in his arms.

The Wencel party was an army affair with a mere sprinkling of civilians. The green of the General Staff uniforms was the prevailing color; the entire war clique was present headed by Conrad von Hötzendorf, a trim, slight man with the nervous energy of a fox terrier and the firm bite of a bulldog. He and his colleagues opened their newspapers to the court bulletins each morning hoping to read that Emperor Franz Josef had been ordered to bed by his physician, an indication that the imperial health—at last —was failing. A headline reporting a stroke or a heart attack would have cheered them even more. Had they resided in Serbia or Turkey and served in armies of lower moral and cultural standards, they would long ago have banded together to plot the monarch's assassination, but no matter how much they wished Franz Josef out of the way, no such radical solution had ever entered their minds. They fretted and seethed, and the top men paid frequent visits to Belvedere Palace, the Viennese residence of Franz Ferdinand, the heir to the throne, or to his country estate in Konopischt in Bohemia. General Conrad had even gone so far as to bang his fist on the emperor's desk during an argument, incensing the old man, but failing to move him one step closer to war. The only concession the chief of staff could extract from him was support for a thorough reorganization and modernization of the army. The general had achieved wonders during the three years of his tenure, but like a boy who had been given a dream toy for Christmas, he was not allowed to play with it.

Emil Kunze was not gregarious at parties. More an observer than a participant, he was intrigued by the small comedies and dramas played out at army affairs, the friendships made or renewed, the intentional or unintentional snubs meted out, the careers bolstered or aborted, the love affairs dissolved, and the harmless bantering which often ended in duels and utterly meaningless deaths.

As usual, a contingent of subaltern officers had been invited —preferably cavalry, nice boys who refrained from getting boisterously drunk and waltzed diligently through the night with army wives and daughters regardless of looks, weight or sense of rhythm. The hussars were the most magnificent-looking and the least comfortable. Dragoons and uhlans sported narrow black trousers and soft, light footwear, but the hussars' full-dress uniform consisted of tight-fitting vermilion pants, a heavily gold-braided powder-blue tunic and knee-high patent-leather riding boots. After a night's dancing, piercing pain shot up their legs. Spurs were *de rigueur*, and their discreet jingle was a haunting counterpoint to the voluptuous swell of the music. The damage done to dress hems and trains was in most cases irreparable.

The women—on the whole—were better-looking and better-gowned than at most army occasions, when the evening dresses were the creations of staunch little dressmakers handed down from generation to generation who materialized before every social season to convert grandmother's damask draperies into a copy of a Poiret or Worth. This evening the ladies were clothed by *haute couturiers,* and their jewels were real: The necklace adorning a décolletage was, in some cases, worth more than the husband's army pay for a year.

Lily Wencel's dress had the new Directoire silhouette, its fabric pale-green satin overlaid with gold-yellow tulle. She wore her famous emeralds and looked striking. Only one set of jewelry outglittered hers: Frau Goldschmiedt's diamonds. The Goldschmiedts were one of the few nonarmy couples invited to the party. The wife was Lily's cousin twice removed, though Dr. Goldschmiedt needed no family ties to be included. He was a member of the Jockey Club; rumors persisted that he was soon to be elevated to the baronage by the emperor.

Earlier in the evening Goldschmiedt had sought out Captain Kunze amid the galaxy of uniforms. His acquaintance with Kunze stemmed from his employment by the venerable law firm of Teller and Bauer.

"What a pleasant surprise to see you, Captain!" Goldschmiedt beamed. "Had I known I'd meet you here, I could have saved writing a letter. You'll find it tomorrow in your mail." When Kunze failed to ask what the letter was about, he went on. "I'd like to see you about Lieutenant Dorfrichter. I have been appointed by his family to represent him."

This was news to Kunze.

"I'm afraid there isn't much you can do for him, Doctor," he said. "As you know, he is subject to military law, which excludes the participation of a civilian defense attorney."

"It would be up to the Ministry of War to transfer the case from the military to civilian courts, wouldn't it?"

"Not exactly. It would be up to the crown."

"But if Minister von Schönaich supported it? As you must know, public opinion is against the secrecy of the investigation."

"Is it now?"

"Don't you read the papers, Captain?"

"Public opinion has also been against the trimming of the trees on Opernring and the ordinance requiring all dogs to be muzzled and leashed. Nevertheless, the trees are being trimmed and the dogs muzzled."

"There have been two interpellations in the Parliament during the past week. You were called the Unholy Trinity, one person representing investigator, prosecutor and defense attorney, and the Dorfrichter case is being referred to as Austria's Dreyfus affair!"

"As for the Unholy Trinity, Dr. Goldschmiedt, each of my aims is truth and justice, in that order," Kunze said. He knew he sounded pompous but could not help it. People like Paul Goldschmiedt always made him say things he regretted later.

"Don't misunderstand me, Captain, there is nothing personal in my criticism, but you're human, too. You can make mistakes."

"I hope you don't think, Dr. Goldschmiedt, that all our efforts are concentrated on Lieutenant Dorfrichter. Because it's not so. We're searching in several directions. Up to now more than half the troops garrisoned in Linz have been interrogated about an attempted purchase of cyanide at the Ritzberger pharmacy. Another clue came from Baden. It concerned a blond young man who bought a quantity of wafer capsules and acted rather suspiciously. Ten or twelve persons who might be linked with the case are being kept under surveillance. Whenever civilians are involved, the police cooperate with us. You may know Inspector Weinberger. He is our liaison."

"That's all very reassuring, Captain. Nevertheless, Dorfrichter is still locked up like a mad dog."

"He is in a very comfortable, well-heated cell and is in good health. The most competent members of our Medical Corps see to it that he stays that way. His food is sent in by the family, and I left special orders with the provost to have the hot dishes served hot and the cold ones cold. He gets no reading matter and cannot communicate with the outside world, but that may change later."

"And the lights never go out in his cell, and he is watched day and night," Dr. Goldschmiedt snorted.

"That's true, but let me tell you something: You might do more harm than good to the man if you delivered him to civilian jurisdiction. Our military laws permit a death sentence only in case of a full confession or direct evidence against an accused officer. However, a civilian court might become convinced of his guilt and sentence him to death. By trying to free him from my clutches, you may be leading him straight to the gallows, Dr. Goldschmiedt."

"May I assume, Captain, that you won't second my plea to the Ministry of War?"

Kunze felt anger rising from his stomach to his throat. He wouldn't have been surprised if flame had leaped from his mouth into Dr. Goldschmiedt's face.

"No, I won't." Somehow he managed to keep his fury under control. "I consider the present procedure to be in the best interests of both the accused and the public."

Afterward, they made small talk, but merely to observe decorum, then carefully avoided each other for the rest of the evening. In truth, Kunze felt more disturbed about his own reaction to Dr. Goldschmiedt's proposition than about the proposition itself.

To divert his thoughts from Paul Goldschmiedt, he crossed to the large reception room, where the carpet had been rolled up and the furniture moved to the wall to make room for dancing. A Hungarian gypsy band from the Grand Hotel was playing a waltz. It was a lovely picture: skirts whipped into whirlpools of color, jewels catching the light of the chandeliers, heads undulating to the rhythm of the music like a field of poppies in bloom, tail-coated swallows and penguins dotting the mosaic of gold-braided tunics and, along the wall, the chaperones, with their ample bosoms pushed up by the much too tight corsets and their wide skirts charitably hiding the rest of their anatomy.

Lily Wencel was dancing with a General Staff captain named Dugonich. Kunze knew him. He had been a recipient of a Charles Francis circular. When a young uhlan cut in on him, he kissed his hostess' hand, then walked straight to Kunze.

"How is our friend Dorfrichter?" he asked. His pronunciation of the word "friend" lacked amity.

Of medium height with a body that seemed all muscle and no fat, dark skin, and an aquiline face, he looked like a gypsy, though no one would dare take him for one. The son of an immensely wealthy landowner, descendant of Serbian chieftains, settled in the south of Hungary, he possessed the aloof ease of the invulnerably rich.

"He was all right when I last saw him," Kunze replied. He disliked discussing the investigation outside the courthouse, for both judicial and ethical reasons. This time, however, the tone of Captain Dugonich's question aroused his curiosity. "You sound as if you don't like him."

"I hate the bastard," Dugonich told him. "Not because he wanted to kill me—"

"That hasn't been proved yet."

"As far as I'm concerned, it has! He is the kind that would do a thing like that. I spent two years in the same classroom with him. Two years is a long time when you're twenty-five and twenty-six. I imagine it doesn't seem so long after a man has reached forty or fifty, but at twenty-five, two years amount to a century. He sat at the desk next to mine. Hohenstein to my left, Mader behind me. Now don't tell me I'm a snob, but if I hate anything, it is an upstart, a climber. I know I've been damn lucky, had great advantages over chaps who've come from the petit bourgeoisie. But just because a man doesn't have my background, money—or Hohenstein's background, title—he doesn't have to be a son of a bitch! Mader wasn't, Gersten wasn't, but Dorfrichter was! The ambition to be number one was written all over him. He didn't succeed because he tried too hard. Before examinations he became so tense that when you spoke to him, you got a blank stare for an answer. If you had stuck a pin in him, he wouldn't have felt it. No doubt, he had brains. But teachers resent a student who is always ahead of them. He also antagonized some of his classmates. Everyone knows that there is no real camaraderie at the War College. It's dog eat dog. You have to go through three different eliminating processes before you're accepted. More than fifty percent of the class gets kicked out before graduation, but even so, no matter how madly ambitious you are, you ought to hide your eagerness and, if you don't make the grade, try to be a good loser. Well, even then, Dorfrichter was willing to walk over dead bodies."

"What do you mean?"

"There was a man ahead of him. At the end of the first year Dorfrichter was number twelve and this man, Hoffer, eleven. During the summer of 1904 we three were assigned to the command post of the Fourteenth Infantry Regiment in Innsbruck. It isn't a very exciting garrison, except for mountain climbers, so there was a lot of drinking and card games. Hoffer was a passionate but rather bad gambler, who lost most of the time. Dorfrichter drank with moderation and very seldom gambled. On that particular night at a *chemin de fer* party he sat in for a comrade who had to leave early and caught Hoffer cheating—at least, Dorfrichter called it that. The circumstances were never quite clear, because everyone was drunk—everyone except Dorfrichter. They weren't playing for high stakes, so the matter was not deadly serious. Also, there were no outsiders in the group. It would have been easy to accept Hoffer's explanation that when he called seven, he mistook a two of hearts for a three. He had been dealt a queen, a four and the disputed two and threw his hand down without letting the other players have a look at it. Dorfrichter picked up the cards and spread them out on the table. 'Your seven is only six!' he said. As I told you, Hoffer was cockeyed drunk and let a few uncomplimentary remarks fly. The matter reached the regimental council of honor, and Dorfrichter repeated the accusation that Hoffer had been cheating. A few unpleasant facts about Hoffer, debts, a paternity suit, his connection with a prostitute were brought to light before the council. After the session, Hoffer shot himself, and Dorfrichter started the second year at the War College as number eleven. After Hoffer's funeral I looked up Dorfrichter in his quarters, and I told him what I thought of him as officer, comrade and human being. Frankly, I wanted him to hit me or challenge me, so I could carve him up, but he wasn't going to oblige. He waited for me to finish and all he said was: 'I'll remember this!' When I first heard his name mentioned in connection with the Charles Francis circulars, I wanted to report the episode, but then I thought perhaps he was innocent, after all, and in that case I'd be the same kind of a bastard he was in poor Hoffer's affair. But now I've run into you and decided to let you draw whatever conclusion you like from it."

"He started the second year ranking number eleven. Why did he slip?"

"Well, some of the professors disliked him. Besides, he wasn't as physically fit as the majority of the class. The rigors of the field trips wore him out. His horsemanship was deplorable. In the beginning he was thrown during every riding drill. I think he never got over his fear of horses. Old Campanini decided that Dorfrichter's failure reflected badly on his prowess as instructor and retaliated by assigning him the most fractious horses. He was going to teach him to ride or break every bone in his body."

"Do you know of anyone else in the class who was on bad terms with Dorfrichter?"

"I don't. But that doesn't mean anything. The War College wasn't like the rest of the army. Partly because there was no time for friendships and partly because we all were competitors. Few men were liked by the whole class—Mader was one. There was no better comrade in that whole class than Mader."

Supper was about to be served, and the hostess came over to them, inviting them to her table. It seemed to Kunze she had been paying special attention to Captain Dugonich all evening. She had danced the cotillion with the guest of honor, General Conrad, but before that, whenever her emeralds had twinkled, they had done so against the background of Dugonich's bottle-green tunic.

Supper was a great success. The year before, Lily Wencel had scored a decisive victory over rival hostesses: She had hired the late Johann Strauss' cook. The fat little woman, Hungarian by birth, but blessed with Viennese taste buds, was as great a talent in her own metier as her late master had been in his. The guests, seated at midnight, rose from the table—having put away six courses and four different wines, beginning with a local Gumpoldskirchner and ending with vintage Veuve Clicquot—at two in the morning. Everyone had eaten too much and was either slightly, pleasantly or very drunk.

Toward the end of the meal, Lily Wencel upset her glass, spilling champagne down the front of her dress. Since the spot was large, she decided to go upstairs and change. Entering her dressing room, she found her personal maid fast asleep. The maid was expected to wait up for her mistress no matter how late to help her undress. This time, however, Lily shook the girl awake and sent her to her room. The girl left hastily before her mistress could change her mind.

Captain Dugonich, having been briefed by his hostess on the floor plan of the house, still managed to open the wrong door twice before discovering her dressing room. Lily stood in front of the floor-length mirror in her petticoat, with her voluptuous, white-skinned torso encased from bust to hip in a heavily boned silk corset. Dugonich closed the door softly, his eye on her while his hand searched for a key. Finding none, he threw a glance at the door and saw there was no lock.

"Can't you lock this door?" he asked. "It warps my style to know that the husband may walk in any minute."

She laughed. "Not in this house. We've found the secret formula for a happy marriage. Each respects the other's privacy. Karl is much too civilized to barge in here without being asked."

"Do you ever ask him?"

"Once in a while. I must let him prove to himself that he didn't marry me for my money. It helps him keep his self-respect."

"Quite a psychologist, aren't you?"

"No. Just cautious. I've learned that a man without self-respect can be dangerous. Self-respect, like a chain, keeps the wild animal from going for the jugular vein."

He pulled her in his arms and pressed his lips on the side of her neck where a vein throbbed. His right hand glided over her body, exploring.

"I'd hate to be your husband," he told her.

"You couldn't be my husband. I'd never marry you."

"Why not? I'm rich, well bred, handsome."

He was trying to untie the knotted lace of her corset. She threw back her head, and her eyes were misty under their heavy Oriental lids. Her breathing was heavy.

"I'd never marry a man I could fall in love with."

His hand became still. The word "love" had the effect of cold water on him. There was nothing he dreaded more than emotional involvement.

"Don't you think we're taking a terrible chance?" he asked. "Wouldn't it be better if we met in town tomorrow? I have a flat on Himmelpfortgasse—"

"No!" she fumbled with the buttons of his tunic. "Now!"

She clung to him with such force that he fell backward, pulling her with him onto the satin-covered chaise longue. The flames raging in her smothered his defenses, engulfing him. For a second he glimpsed the reflection of their entwined bodies in the mirror, his buttocks naked above the loosened vermilion pants, half-buried in yellow ruffles of petticoat, and chuckled. *What a sight for a person entering the room,* he thought. The unexpected sound of laughter cut through her enchantment, and she flashed a look of cold suspicion; then, closing her eyes again, she sank back into the oblivion of pleasure.

Later he asked her, "Do you play this game every time you throw a party?"

She had changed into a blue chiffon evening gown, and he was struggling with the intricate hooks at the back. She turned abruptly, and for a moment he thought she was going to slap his face.

"No," she said. "I can't always find a partner."

"With all these young bucks around? I'm sure each one would give an eyetooth."

"An eyetooth—yes. Then afterward he'd ask me to put in a word for him with the general. What I've told you about self-respect, in other ways, goes for women, too. I won't be used. At least, not yet. In a few years perhaps, but not yet. Now I want to be taken as I am with my partner risking as much as I do."

Now he understood. No lock on the door!

He laughed. "You bitch." But he found himself feeling suddenly chilled.

Captain Kunze spent the morning poring over the service records of the recipients of Charles Francis circulars, still trying to find a common denominator which would explain why *these* ten had been marked for death. His exchange with Captain Dugonich had given him the idea of questioning each about his relationship to the accused.

"This is strange," he pointed out to Lieutenant Stoklaska. "Nine out of the ten are top horsemen—good at other sports, too. Their physical fitness is especially evident in their career résumés. Moll is the only exception. He was graded 'barely satisfactory' by Major von Campanini, the same as Dorfrichter."

"Maybe Dorfrichter had some personal grudge against Moll."

Kunze nodded. "We'll have to find out about that—and about a lot of things," he added with a groan.

Dorfrichter was escorted in for interrogation. He appeared to have gained weight. The deep rings under his eyes and the lines of fatigue around his mouth were gone. He did not appear as pale as before, no doubt because he took his daily "walks" with the window of his cell wide open. The weather had turned cold, and the temperature in his cell was allowed to drop near the freezing point before he closed the window, but he insisted he preferred pneumonia to suffocation. When asked how he felt, he replied that he was bored but otherwise had no complaints.

"What was the relationship between you and Captain Karl Moll?" Kunze began.

If he expected a revealing reaction, he was disappointed. Dorfrichter answered with a blank stare.

"Captain Moll? I don't think I know a Captain Moll."

"All right—First Lieutenant Moll. He was one of your classmates at the War College."

Dorfrichter rubbed his forehead pensively.

"Moll— Oh, that Moll! Now I remember him vaguely. After all, our graduating class numbered about one hundred men. I don't believe I can name more than ten offhand."

"Why did you say *ten?*"

"Why did I say ten?" Grinning, Dorfrichter mimicked him. "Because that's how many circulars I mailed. It was a bad slip, I admit. More proof of my guilt!"

"Let's stop playing games! Just answer the question."

"I hardly knew him. I cannot even recall what he looked like. I don't think I've seen him once since graduation."

* * *

Later that afternoon Captain Karl Moll sat in the same chair facing Kunze's desk. At present he was assigned to the Railroad Bureau of the General Staff and looked very much like a man whose main concern was that of keeping trains running on schedule. His face was clean-shaven, as was his head. His speech had a touch of the Prussian to it, and he used expressions that were not common to Austrian Army vernacular. The Prussian showed in his bearing as well. He was stiff, very correct, lacking the grace and geniality of the Viennese.

"My relation to Lieutenant Dorfrichter," he reported, "was not exactly harmonious. I'm afraid he disliked me, and I reciprocated his feelings."

"What was the reason? Was there some conflict?"

"I wouldn't call it a conflict. Quarrel is a better definition. Well—"

Not interested in semantics, Kunze cut in. "What were your quarrels about?"

"Mainly military problems. First, may I tell you something about myself? My father emigrated from Germany to Austria as a young man. I was born here, but the rest of the Moll family still live in Breslau. Two of my uncles and six of my cousins are officers in the Prussian Army. Professional soldiers. Through them I've learned what true discipline means. I'm afraid our Austro-Hungarian Army is a bit too—too *gemütlich* for its own sake. Dorfrichter refused to admit this!"

Moll's long-windedness began to grate on Kunze's nerves. "You mean to say you argued solely about abstract concepts and there was no personal conflict between you?"

"Of course not," Moll said, seemingly amazed at the captain's lack of perception. "We also disagreed on the importance of the quick-firing field gun."

"Think hard," Kunze insisted. "Can you remember any incident of a more personal nature?"

"I'm sorry, I can't."

"Have you had any contact with Dorfrichter directly or indirectly since your graduation?"

"No contact whatsoever. There is one thing, though. Now it comes back to me. You said 'indirectly.' In 1907 I was assigned to the Twenty-eighth Infantry in Kecskemét, Hungary. I rented two rooms from a certain Frau Varga. A few months before, the rooms had been occupied by Dorfrichter. He left Kecskemét when he transferred to the Thirteenth Brigade in Sarajevo."

"And?"

"Last year I ran into Dorfrichter at the ministry. I told him about it. 'Small world, isn't it?' I said. He turned very red in the face and left in a hurry. I was sort of puzzled. I still am."

"Did your landlady speak of him?"

Moll thought hard, pursing his lips and wrinkling his forehead. Kunze suddenly wondered why an attractive young woman like Anna Gabriel had slept with such a thoroughly charmless man. Kunze thought often of Anna Gabriel, never quite able to rid himself of the feeling that he had been partly responsible for her tragedy. A man who liked to keep his conscience as clean and tidy as his desk drawers, he found even his partial guilt to be a stubborn and ineradicable speck on it.

"All I can recall is something Frau Varga once mentioned," Moll said finally. "Dorfrichter had a love affair with an actress in Kecskemét. I hope I'm not confusing him with someone else. You know these small-town garrisons. Not much for a bachelor to do except sleep around and drink. There were a lot of spicy stories about other officers, too."

"Who was the actress? Did you know her?"

"No. She left town with Dorfrichter. There was some scandal about her disappearance."

"You wouldn't know her name, would you?"

"I'm afraid not. But I can write Frau Varga and ask her. She'll be more than glad to give the information. Ever since the office of town crier was abolished, she's filled it on a voluntary basis."

Kunze told him he would appreciate the information, and Captain Moll departed. Since the first suspicion had fallen on Dorfrichter, his past, particularly his activities in each of his garrisons, had been investigated, but returns were meager. He had been well liked, appraised as a fine officer by his superiors, and respected by the troops. His sex life—as far as the investigators could ascertain—was normal: innocent courtships, affairs with married women of easy morals, visits to highly commendable brothels and, from the day of his marriage to Marianne Gruber, blessed domesticity.

Peter Dorfrichter was brought back in the afternoon, his cheeks flushed, his nose and ears almost purple. He had been in the middle of his "walk" when summoned by Provost Tuttman.

"You'll catch your death one of these days," Kunze commented.

He chuckled. "Wouldn't that be too bad, leaving you with an unsolved case on your hands? But don't worry. I want to live and walk out of here a rehabilitated man. Whether you like it or not."

Kunze felt oddly perturbed by the cocky, schoolboy tone.

"Don't be an ass, Dorfrichter. You can't possibly believe that I want an innocent man condemned. I never asked for this god-damned job and don't for a moment think that I'm enjoying it. So let's dispense with the quips and see to it that we finish this unpleasant business one way or another."

Dorfrichter pulled himself erect in his chair.

"I'm sorry, sir," he said. Kunze thumbed through the notes he had jotted down earlier. He was still disturbed, more deeply, he knew, than the incident warranted. Dorfrichter broke the silence. "May I ask you a question, sir?" When Kunze nodded, he asked, "Have you had any news about my wife? How is she? Has the child been born?"

"No, the child has not been born, and she is well. She has retained an attorney to do whatever he can for you."

"Thank you, sir." Dorfrichter's manner was stiff. If he felt reassurance, it did not show. "Will you allow me another question, sir?"

"Go ahead."

"Do you know what happened to my dog?"

"Troll is in Vienna at the Veterinary Clinic."

"What for?" Dorfrichter's alarm seemed genuine. "What are they doing to him?"

"You said you bought wafer capsules because your dog refused to swallow his medicine. We want to find out if that is true."

"Of course, it's true! But if I'd known that they'd vivisect him, I'd never have said it!" He sounded furious.

"He won't be harmed. I can vouch for that. He's well taken care of."

"How do you know?"

"Because I personally delivered him to the hospital and made sure that he would be well treated. I brought him with me from

Linz, then kept him at my place overnight. He chose to sleep on my silk comforter on my bed, in case you want to know."

The ordinarily stony-faced Lieutenant Stoklaska was the first to chuckle. Heinrich joined in.

Dorfrichter apologized with a sheepish grin. "I'm sorry, sir."

Kunze switched subjects. "Speaking of animals, you seem to be fond of dogs. What about *horses*?"

"What about them, sir?"

"I've seen your fitness report. Also your grades at the War College. Baron von Campanini didn't have a very high opinion of your horsemanship."

Dorfrichter remained still.

After a pause he asked, "What does that have to do with the Charles Francis circulars?"

"I didn't say it had anything to do with them. I was merely curious."

"Horsemanship." Dorfrichter pronounced the word as if it were a curse. "You go through hell to get into the damned college. First, the recommendation of your commanding officer. You break your neck to get it—one mistake and you're out! So you somehow manage to avoid the one mistake and are admitted to the general examinations. That's in January. About two-thirds make it; the rest are eliminated. In February, preliminary examinations; then in October eighteen days of tension and toil. At night you're so wrought up you can't fall asleep. In the morning before starting out for the casern, you throw up. Then you and about one hundred and fifty more manage to live through the final entry examinations. After two more years ninety-four are left to graduate. Your subjects are military geography, weapons, General Staff administration and operation, war history and strategy, tactics, army organization, terrain appreciation, natural science, fortresses and fortress warfare, cultural history, state and international law, French, Russian and finally—riding! In between there are field trips, mapping. In the field you live under warlike conditions—no meals from sunup till sundown, grueling marches or endless rides. Either your feet are so swollen you have to sleep in your boots or your ass looks like a fresh-cut beefsteak. Then after two years of ordeal—almost three with the examinations—you graduate. Your head is like an encyclopedia. You can rattle off the battles of the

Punic Wars, or Wellington's deployment of his cavalry at Waterloo, or the difference between the application of *habeas corpus cum causa* by the Napoleonic and the English laws, or the conjugation of the French irregular verbs. But all this knowledge won't help you if Baron von Campanini isn't satisfied with the way you lift your ass when you jump your horse across a ditch. There won't be horses in the next war. At the start, yes—because the first offensives will be under the command of senile old men who still live in the nineteenth century. Nevertheless, a bad mark from Baron von Campanini can put you back from number eleven to number eighteen—"

Kunze waited calmly for Dorfrichter to run out of breath. Patience was something he had learned during his years as the housekeeper's son.

"I thought you finished the first year as number twelve."

"I did." There was a slight pause. "The man ahead of me killed himself."

"What made him do it?"

"How should I know? He wasn't the only one. An uhlan hanged himself during the first year. The commander was dismayed because he considered the method unbecoming an officer. If I remember correctly, there was also an attempted suicide. The officer cut his wrists. Another example of *mauvais goût!* He lived but was advised to leave the army. A man died of exertion during a field trip. Yes, the emphasis was on physical fitness. Forced marches of forty kilometers a day. A man could be a genius at tactics, but marching out of step resulted in a demerit. Whoever dreamed up the curriculum didn't know that the internal-combustion engine had been invented."

Kunze suspected that the heat emanating from the well-stocked tile stove, plus his burning indignation, caused the flush on Dorfrichter's cheeks. He sat forward tensely on the edge of his chair as if readying himself for a leap across the desk at the man facing him. Suddenly Kunze realized that their parts were reversed, had been probably since their first meeting in Vienna, Kunze, the defendant, and Dorfrichter, the prosecutor. It was merely a passing sensation, but he knew he had to break the spell Peter Dorfrichter was casting over him or he would lose the contest. Then he asked himself, *What contest? What am I fighting for? A pro-*

motion to major, the life of this man, or something more impor-
tant, a prize so tremendous that it doesn't even have a name?

"Do you know that practically all recipients of the circulars were graded very good in horsemanship by Campanini?" Kunze asked.

Dorfrichter relaxed somewhat.

"I do not. Am I supposed to? Frankly, I can't follow you, sir. I imagine your questions are supposed to confuse me and involve me in contradictions, and I would gladly oblige if I knew what you were getting at. Are you suggesting that I wanted to kill ten men because they could stay in the goddamn saddle longer than I could?"

"Moll couldn't."

"Here we go again! Moll! You seem to have a fixation on that son of a bitch!"

"Why do you call him a son of a bitch? This morning you said you hardly remembered him."

"I'd forgotten the snotty little bastard; then you reminded me. I've been thinking. Lots of things that had slipped my mind come back to me now. Yes, we had a few disagreements. He was one of the stupidest men in the class."

"He ranked number twelve."

"That's possible. There were others like him. Photographic memory, no brains. Without the training manual they couldn't lead a squad out of the barracks latrine!"

"What about Captain Dugonich?"

"Is that another one on the list?"

"Never mind that! Have you forgotten him, too?"

"Hell, no! I mean, no, sir." He corrected himself with a grin. "Who can ever forget Titus Dugonich? Now there was a horseman for you! Attila the Hun, although he was a goddamn Serb. There wasn't a wild horse or a wild woman he couldn't mount."

"What was the relation between you?"

"None. We didn't belong to the same clique. Theoretically, there is supposed to be absolute equality in the Officers' Corps, but not in practice. If you were willing to kiss asses, you were invited to tag along on Dugonich's sorties, which usually ended in drunken brawls with café mirrors smashed and at least two policemen hospitalized, which, considering the generous hush money they got, in addition to the long rest, made them the envy of the entire Viennese police force. Anyway, he didn't socialize much with his classmates. Most of his friends were hussars and dragoons stationed in Vienna. They had either his kind of money or his capacity for whoring and drinking. These were the prerequisites of entrée to the Dugonich mansion on Herrengasse. I'm sure the rules are still valid today."

"Aren't you exaggerating?" Kunze suggested. "Why would a man with such low moral standards aim for the War College and the General Staff?"

"Because he could afford it. I don't mean financially. He had the brains. But he used them only to get by. He told me once that he was bored with field service, and that's why he tried for the college. After he'd made it, he merely let the current carry him."

"Did you like him?"

"I couldn't say that. Yet I didn't dislike him, either."

"Was Lieutenant Hoffer a friend of his?"

Dorfrichter frowned. "Hoffer? That was the chap who killed himself in Innsbruck. They might have been friends. I wouldn't know. I've told you I had not much contact with Dugonich."

Kunze sprang his trap. "Did you have any contact with Captain Ahrens?" Ahrens was not one of the recipients of the circulars.

For the first time that day, Dorfrichter seemed to have been caught unawares. He quite obviously did not know how to react to the name. Kunze imagined he could hear the wheels revolving in the lieutenant's head. He had no doubt been ready for the ten names on Charles Francis' mailing list, had planned his reaction to them, might even have rehearsed the answers, mumbling to himself in front of his cell window. Outwitting and outguessing an interrogator were part of defense strategy, a firmly and soundly devised part. On the Ahrens question, however, he had stumbled, if only for a split second. And this was how Kunze chose to interpret his hesitation.

The lieutenant spoke finally. "Ahrens was number one. Quite brilliant and very tough. I think one day he'll either be Chief of Staff or shot by a subaltern. I understand he is assigned to the Railroad Bureau now, though he ought to be in Intelligence."

Once he began talking, he became more and more voluble. "He was disliked by everyone, including his teachers. They made it damn hard for him, but they couldn't keep him down."

"How about his riding?"

"He was good. Don't think for a moment, sir, that old Campanini would have overlooked the slightest fault."

"You sound as if you liked him. Ahrens, I mean."

By now Dorfrichter appeared completely relaxed.

"Have it your way." He shrugged. "The fact is, I hated his guts."

"Then why didn't you send him one of your circulars?"

Dorfrichter threw him a quick, searching glance.

"How was that, sir?"

"Why did you leave him off your list? Mader was on it, Gersten, Prince Hohenstein, and seven others—but not Ahrens!"

"Oh, so there were actually ten. Thank you for the information."

"That's right. Ten. So why not eleven?"

Dorfrichter leaned back in his chair, apparently enjoying himself.

"I was number eighteen, wasn't I? With three out of the way, I'd have become number fifteen. Would have made the promotion roll. Three dead out of ten was a very conservative estimate. After all, I didn't want to commit mass murder."

Kunze pounced. "So you admit to having sent the circulars!"

Dorfrichter rose abruptly.

"Hell, no! I don't!" he said angrily. "I merely wanted to find out what you would say. And you said exactly what I'd expected you to." Taking a deep breath, he resumed his seat. "May I ask a question for a change, sir?" His voice sounded tired. "Why are you badgering me? Why not number sixteen, and seventeen, and nineteen, twenty, twenty-one, up to twenty-five? They would have profited by the elimination of the ten officers ahead of them!"

"We've investigated and found them to be above suspicion."

"Have you really? You're wrong as far as I'm concerned. You could be wrong about them, too. Take one more good look. You may find clues you've missed."

"You're a hard nut to crack, Lieutenant," Kunze said, weary of the sparring. "Let's call it a day, shall we?"

* * *

When Kunze left the Military Lawcourt it was still daylight. Not until he stepped into the street did he notice the snow, the first of the winter. It must have been falling for quite some time; a clean white carpet covered the pavement. A small boy, bundled up in a coat several sizes too big for him, rushed from a house, pulling a sleigh, although the snow wasn't deep enough for sleighing.

Emil Kunze tried to remember what he had been like at the boy's age, five or six. He had worn no hand-me-down coats, had never been alone on the street, and had never owned a sleigh. The memory of the house where his mother had been housekeeper flashed across his mind, fuzzy, distorted. High-ceilinged rooms; draperies constantly closed; the jingle of spurs echoing eerily through a long, narrow entrance hall; their own room, so small that when moving from table to dresser, one climbed across the bed; an enormous kitchen with stove tops polished a shining black; someone pale and unpleasant lying amid ballooned pillows and eiderdowns; orders to be quiet, Emil, don't raise your voice, Emil, walk on tiptoes, Emil. Madame has a sick headache, Emil! Jigsaw puzzles, erector sets, picture books, kaleidoscope, a magic lantern, but no sleigh. Oh, what a quiet little boy! Is he a relative? Heavens, no! That's Emil, the housekeeper's son.

That was the trouble with life. Every age had its desires. Unfulfilled wishes couldn't be stored and taken out at more propitious times. They dried up, turning to straw like cut roses. *So much for sleighs*, Kunze thought wistfully.

The air was crisp, and by the time he reached the Ring, the snow was thick enough to dull the clatter of the horses' hooves on the cobblestones. He could have taken a shortcut across the maze of crooked little streets between the Gürtel and the Ring, but suddenly felt a need to get away from the gray canyon of houses with no sky and no air above them.

He tried to shut Peter Dorfrichter from his mind, but the lieutenant kept returning like a shameless beggar, along with that disarming, infuriating grin. Kunze had decided long ago that Dorfrichter was guilty, yet two weeks had passed since his arrest, and he still had no evidence. He was beginning to suspect that his methods were at fault. In previous cases where there was no direct evidence, his procedure had been to dissect the suspect, turning him inside out, concentrating on what made him function and whether or not he was capable of the crime. In his multiple role of investigator, prosecutor and defender, the first step was to convince himself that the man *was* guilty; the second, to convince the court. In Dorfrichter's case, he had already passed this first stage and should have been ready to move on to the second. But there were too many questions without answers. Not one witness had come forward to admit that he had seen Dorfrichter and his dog near the mailbox on Mariahilferstrasse. Not one of the people who had ridden with him in the overheated compartment on the Linz–Vienna train had smelled the cyanide which even though enclosed in sealed envelopes should have given out a strong bitter-almond odor; none of the implements used in writing and manifolding the circulars had been found in his or his mother-in-law's apartment!

As Kunze neared the Hofburg, the bells of the Votive Church chimed three thirty. On a sudden impulse, he headed toward the gates. If he was lucky, he could catch Gersten in his office and get his questioning out of the way. They were old acquaintances, so Kunze wouldn't have to go through official channels to see him.

Hans von Gersten was General Hartmann's nephew. As a child, he had spent more time at the Hartmann house than at his own. His family had been army; his father, Colonel von Gersten, was still in the active service. It was a constant source of amazement to Kunze that the unruly, difficult little boy had developed into a paragon of an officer. Correct, conscientious, dutiful and intelligent, he was the best shot in the army, participating in the 1908 Olympics and winning a silver medal for Austria.

At the present time he was assigned to the Telegraph Bureau. He came rushing out when Kunze was announced, greeting the captain with an exuberant bear hug. A head taller than his visitor, he had put on weight. The lower part of his torso revealed a bulge which, together with his long neck and narrow shoulders, made him resemble a mother kangaroo.

"What a nice surprise!" he told Kunze as he led him into his office. "I heard that you'd been assigned to the Dorfrichter case and tried to telephone you, but it took central so long to make the connection that I gave up."

"That's exactly why I came to see you—the Dorfrichter case."

"Have you solved it? There isn't much about it in the papers."

"We have some very strong circumstantial evidence, but that's all. One of the things that puzzle me—supposing he *is* Charles Francis, why did he select ten officers out of fifteen—rather sixteen—as he included Hedry who was not one of the promoted men? Why did he spare the other six?"

"I could try a guess if you told me who the six were."

"Ahrens, Schönhals, Widder, Trautmannsdorf, Messemer and Einthofen."

"The war party!" Gersten cried. "They're in agreement with him or he with them that the sooner we attack the Balkans, the better." He frowned. "However there were others of the same opinion. Moll, for instance—and Hedry. So obviously, he had other reasons as well."

"What would be his reason in your case?" Kunze asked.

Gersten answered without hesitation, "His wife! I can't think of anything else. But remember, Emil, these are just conjectures. You yourself said you weren't absolutely sure that Dorfrichter was guilty."

"I give you my word, Hans, that anything you say will remain between us."

"I met Marianne Gruber through her brother-in-law, the contractor who did some work for my father," Gersten told him. "She made quite an impression on me, and I was determined to get her in the hay—without success, alas! This was in Vienna, during my second year at the college. One night there was a dance, organized by some merchants' association. Not my cup of tea. Nevertheless, I volunteered to be her escort—of course, with her mama in tow. Then for some reason I couldn't make it and asked Dorfrichter to fill in for me. And the bloody fool fell in love with her that very night. He lost his head completely, which was remarkable, considering what a self-disciplined, cool bastard he was. He'd been courting Moltke's niece. She was older than he and looked like a Valkyrie, but a connection with the chief of staff of the German Army would have been a big help to his career. He let all that slip through his fingers because of Marianne Gruber. I didn't know how mesmerized he was, so I kept chasing after her until she told me she'd become engaged to him. When I heard this, I tried to talk sense to him—in his own interest—because the girl wasn't so important to me. He told me to mind my own business and dropped me." Gersten paused, gathering his thoughts. "While he served a tour of duty in Kecskemét, I ran into Marianne again. From what she told me, I gathered that he'd been stalling. He must have realized that marrying her would hurt his chances and tried to get out of it. I'd heard that he had a girl in every garrison. Marianne seemed to be taking it very hard, and I was ready to console her. Of course, I never considered anything serious. I couldn't see myself telling my father that I wanted to marry Marianne Gruber, whose mother had the kitchenware store on Hahngasse. After a while Marianne began to warm up to me. She let me walk her home from church, even with a detour through Stadtpark. Word about us must have reached Dorfrichter, because he returned unexpectedly to Vienna. Two weeks later they were married. The families, his and hers, somehow scraped up the money for the marriage bond—thirty thousand kronen. When he was transferred to Bosnia, he couldn't take her along until he found suitable married quarters. Last year around this time I was shopping at Sirk's and she came into the store. When she spotted me, she made a quick about-face and walked out again. Evidently, she thought it would upset him if someone saw us together. She was still very beautiful."

"She still is. Although she is very pregnant right now."

"Yes, I know. It was in the papers. Poor Marianne. I wrote to her when Peter was arrested, but she never replied."

"Why do you think she married him? Was it love or merely a step up on the social ladder?"

"I'm sure she was madly in love with him. And jealous. During their estrangement any rumor about his women drove her out of her mind. She never admitted it to me—she's much too proud—but her sister, Tilda, the wife of the contractor, told me. I used to see a lot of her. She is not as pretty as Marianne, but—"

"More accommodating?"

"I didn't say that. She's married to a hard-drinking old buzzard —twice her age, just because in Mama Gruber's eyes he was a catch. At least, poor Marianne married for love—though now I'm sure she wishes she hadn't."

"I don't think so. She is very loyal, stands by him. How long —only time will tell."

"Probably to the bitter end. If you had female prison guards, it would be a different matter. But this way she can be sure of his fidelity. And that—if I know her—is of primary importance."

Kunze stayed a little while longer, reminiscing about mutual friends and things of the past. Of all the Hartmann children and cousins, Hans von Gersten had been Mrs. Kunze's favorite and, despite the eight years between them, Emil's, too. As a small boy, Hans had always turned to him for advice and protection and help with his schoolwork. The Hartmann children had been much too wild and self-centered for anything but fun. The strong, dependable refuge had been the quiet Emil Kunze. Now, as they faced each other, Gersten felt the same respectful affection for the older man that he had in his childhood. Kunze had not changed. The years had failed to mar either his face or his character. A born judge, Hans von Gersten thought, for he had never known a man less affected by the whims and prejudices of the society in which he lived.

The snow was falling in large, downy flakes as Kunze left through the Michaelerplatz gate. Whenever he was in the center of town, he took a detour through Josefsplatz. During his pre-army years he had been in Rome, Venice, Florence, Paris, even London, but to his eyes no architectural marvel could match the perfection of this square. He loved it with the warmth that—as a rule—only ownership can germinate in one for a piece of real estate. He stopped under the arcades and stared at the statue. His silhouette softened by the thickening snow, Josef II appeared timeless and lonely on his pedestal.

Kunze thought momentarily of the fools who couldn't wait to unleash a war, remembering the stories the Hartmanns' great-grandmother had narrated about the horrors of the Napoleonic Wars: the devastation, the refugees, the terrible insecurities in the wake of an enemy invasion. How could people be sure that a new war would not end with Cossacks ransacking the Hofburg, Serb cavalry horses grazing in the Stadtpark, and Montenegrin *komitajis* shooting out the window panes along the Ring? Would men still be able to plan for the futures of children and grandchildren with the confidence bred during the dull peaceful years?

* * *

Shortly after arriving home, Kunze received a call from Dr. Goldschmiedt. The phone had been installed in his study a few months before, but he was still not sure that he liked the idea of being available to anyone able to pay a few hellers for a call. It was a fine gadget for offices, he thought, for life was becoming complex in the new century, but to have it in one's home was a different matter.

"Forgive me for disturbing you after office hours," Dr. Goldschmiedt said, "but I thought you would want to know that Frau Dorfrichter had her baby. A boy! Four kilos!" For a jaded old roué, the voice sounded much too elated, Kunze thought.

"When did it happen?"

"At six this afternoon. The poor little woman had a very difficult time. She started having pains early last night. Around three in the morning I called Professor Hain. He saved her life and the baby's, too. The midwife would have killed them both."

"How did you know she was in labor?"

For a moment the line was still.

"I made her mother promise she would notify me when the time came. I really wanted Frau Dorfrichter to have the baby in a sanatorium, but she refused. She has a horror of strangers. When I received the message, I rushed over to the Grubers."

"Lucky for Frau Dorfrichter," Kunze said, unable to control the sarcasm. "To have you for her attorney. Service above and beyond the call of duty!"

At dinner Kunze told Rose about the Dorfrichter baby. She looked at him for a long time while her eyes slowly filled with tears.

"Don't start crying now," he told her irritably. "Everyone is so damn sorry for the man. Petitions, sob stories. There will be a deluge of them tomorrow. 'Baby's father imprisoned by monster judge advocate!' 'The agonies of a lonely wife!' National heartbreak, with nobody, but nobody, giving a goddamn about Richard Mader who died like a dog, twisted into a pretzel by the pain, choking on his own blood."

"I wasn't crying for Dorfrichter," she said, her voice sharp. "Or for his wife."

"Who else then?"

"Us." The look she gave him was the coldest, most indignant one he had ever seen on her face. "We'll never have a baby."

For a moment he didn't know what to say. The thought that she would want to start a family had never occurred to him. She was thirty-seven, in his opinion past childbearing age. Evidently, she did not feel that way, which disturbed him. He fervently hoped it was one of her fleeting, irrational moods.

"We are not married. Would you really want to bring a little bastard into the world?" he asked her.

"I wouldn't mind if you were willing to stand by me."

"All right. I'll keep that in mind. But before we start on the project, I have an important errand."

"Where are you going?"

"I must break the good news to the lucky father."

VII

THE lamp hanging from the ceiling with its twenty-five-watt bulb and white-enameled tin shade bathed Peter Dorfrichter's cell with a dim, depressing light. The prisoner lay on the narrow bed, his nightshirt open at the neck, his head resting on the single pillow with its coarse linen case, his body straight under the heavy blanket. Still awake, he sat up when he heard the key turning in the lock. The guard held the door for Kunze.

"With the captain's permission," the guard said, "wouldn't it be better if I stayed?"

"That won't be necessary," Kunze replied.

"Shall I remain at the peephole, sir?"

"Go back to the guardroom. I'll ring if I need you."

Dorfrichter's cell, one of eight reserved for officers, contained, among other conveniences, a bell so the inmate could summon the guard. At the moment Number 1 held a lieutenant accused of embezzling regimental funds. The other cells were vacant.

Dorfrichter's face looked gray against the whitewashed wall behind the iron headboard. "She is dead!" he said dully.

"Congratulations! You have a son," Kunze told him.

The news had no effect on Dorfrichter. He was motionless. Only his eyes moved, following Kunze across the room.

"She is dead, isn't she?"

"Of course not. She is perfectly well. It was not an easy birth, but both mother and son are doing fine."

Dorfrichter heaved a sigh and after a while murmured, "Thank you, sir." He started to rise.

Kunze stopped him. "Don't get up. I wouldn't have disturbed you this late, but I thought you had a right to know that you're the father of a son."

"It was most considerate of you. Won't you sit down?"

Kunze took the chair at the far side of the table. The lieutenant leaned against the headboard. With his hair tousled, he looked ten years younger than his age. Fatherhood had put him in a pensive mood, and for the first time since Kunze had been investigating his case, the smugness and insolence were gone from his face.

"It must have been hard on her."

Kunze nodded. "The baby weighed four kilos."

"That's rather large, isn't it? For a newborn child, I mean."

He is still more concerned for the mother than the child, Kunze thought, shrugging. "I wouldn't know," he said. "I've never had any experience in that line. I'm a bachelor."

Dorfrichter seemed oblivious to the answer.

"She is so frail. We should probably have waited to start a family." The grimness of the situation suddenly dawned on him. "What kind of future will my son have? In elementary school I had a classmate whose father was in jail—for robbery I think. I can't remember. No one spoke to that boy except to call him names—cruel names. Children can be monsters. Is that what's going to happen to my son? I wish he had died. It would be better. For his mother, too." He stopped, regarding Kunze with an embarrassed grin. "I'm sorry, sir. This goddamn jail will make a slobbering old woman out of me yet." For a moment his lips twitched with the old irony. "Of course, it would be too much for a new father to ask permission for a visit from his wife and son!"

"You know very well that I cannot change regulations."

"Isn't it against regulations for a judge advocate to see a suspect in his cell—at night and alone?" Dorfrichter asked angrily.

If he had hoped to shock the captain into a swift departure, he failed. Kunze remained seated and gazed at him calmly.

"You're a bastard, Dorfrichter. I personally think you're capable of anything if you're crossed. Right now, if you could, you would feed me a dose of cyanide and watch me die. Nevertheless, I still plan to do my best to make jail bearable for you. I will not, however, give your wife permission to visit you unless you confess. That is final." Ready to leave, he stood up. "Incidentally, I got the news from Dr. Goldschmiedt. He stayed at your mother-in-law's apartment during the delivery. When things were not going well, he called in Professor Hain."

Dorfrichter's dark eyes widened.

"Professor who?"

"Hain. An obstetrician. Very good and very expensive. There is no need to worry when you have a man like Dr. Goldschmiedt looking after your wife."

"What is he like?" Dorfrichter asked. "I don't know much about him. We've never met."

Kunze started for the door.

"Aging, very rich. Some say he is a lecher. A damn good lawyer, though."

"I apologize, sir," the captain heard Dorfrichter say. "I lost my head. I appreciate your coming here. I really do."

Kunze rang the bell summoning the guard. When the door finally opened, he left the cell without bidding good-night to its inmate.

Emil Kunze seldom dreamed.

The dream he had during the night following his call on the prisoner was frighteningly vivid, with images only slightly out of focus.

A crowd of men in uniform milled around him in a garden. A classmate from boarding school—or was it Rudolf Hartmann?—suddenly turned into Peter Dorfrichter. Now they were no longer in the garden, but indoors. Dorfrichter lay in bed as he had during their talk in the cell, shirt collar open at the neck, but the room dissolved into Richard Mader's bedroom. They were speaking Russian, which delighted Kunze, for he hadn't known he could speak it. Suddenly Dorfrichter reached out for him, pulling him down till their heads rested on the same pillow, a wonderfully simple gesture of friendship. Embracing Dorfrichter, he felt his skin tingle and glow as if exposed to the midsummer sun. A pleasure so intense throbbed in his loins that he cried out. His voice awakened him, and he sat up in bed, trembling and spent.

He switched on the light on his night table, and slowly, agoniz-ingly, the turmoil left his body. A long while later nothing re-mained but the memory of the climax and then finally cold panic. "Goddamn you, Dorfrichter." He cursed the empty room, failing to exorcise the demons and conjuring up instead the pale young face with the soft, smiling lips framed in silky hair the color of dark chestnuts. An aftershock of excitement vibrated through his body. He repeated his curse, "Goddamn you to hell," not really knowing whether it was intended for Peter Dorfrichter or himself.

Long-ago incidents now appeared in sharp flashes before him, as though thrown by a magic lantern on a screen of memory: The shed in the Hartmanns' garden, Rudolf's pale hands bolting the door, his tall, naked body outlined against the shuttered win-dow of the shed, night games at boarding school. At eighteen his first experience with a woman remembered as something low and dirty, because he had detected little black spots—unmistakable signs of bedbugs—on the whore's sheet. The girl's face was blank, but the little black spots were even now as distinct as they had been that night.

I won't ever see Dorfrichter again, he vowed. *I'll ask to be re-lieved from this case, which I should never have taken on in the first place. Let someone else wrestle with the bastard. Let some-one else wipe that smug, self-assured smile off his face. There's no doubt he's as guilty as hell. Sooner or later he'll be caught. Witnesses who saw him post the letters or sold him the cyanide will come forward. He'll hang, damn him, or if he's lucky, he'll be stood against a gray wall, blindfolded, unsmiling and scared.*

And then he was ashamed. Not since boarding school days had he indulged in daydreams of revenge and vindication. Even then, he had been embarrassed, learning early to control his emotions, to master his instincts. Now, at the supposedly mature age of thirty-eight and after a disturbing dream, he had to acknowledge the fact that uncontrollable urges were gaining command over his soul.

It was almost daylight when he fell asleep. At eight, the alarm clock awakened him, which was unusual. On most days he was up long before the bell rang.

*   *   *

That morning there was a message from Captain Moll on his desk suggesting lunch in the dining room of the Hotel Bristol.

Moll's Hungarian ex-landlady had done her detective work well. The actress' name was Klára Brassay and she had been a member of the Kecskemét stock company from January through September, 1907. The critics had agreed on her talent, and the public filled the theater whenever she played. Kecskemét was a garrison town in the middle of Bugac, a Hungarian steppe, where every young female star stirred up great excitement among the younger officers, and competition was keen for her favors. In Klára Brassay's case, however, these were not bestowed on the army, but on an elderly Budapest banker named Sándor Hodossy.

Kunze interrupted. "Sándor Hodossy! Is he related to Captain Zoltán Hodossy?"

Moll thumbed through Frau Varga's ten-page letter.

"Yes, he is." He pointed out a line. "She says here Hodossy's son was serving in Kecskemét with the Thirteenth Hussars at the time. Why?"

"Because Captain Zoltán Hodossy is one of the Charles Francis ten and was promoted to captain and permanently assigned to the General Staff on November first—the same time as you."

"Of course! I remember Zoli—that was Zoltán's pet name —from the college. He graduated number thirteen. One rank behind me. A rather likable chap. For a Hungarian, I mean."

"What else does your ex-landlady say?"

"This will interest you: For a long time no one could get close to Klára. Except Hodossy senior. She was driven to the theater in a big limousine and picked up again after the show. Then suddenly, toward the end of summer, she began to ride in a hack and was seen everywhere with Lieutenant Peter Dorfrichter. When Dorfrichter was transferred to Bosnia, Klára disappeared, too. She didn't even bother to give notice at the theater. The only one who remained in touch with her after her departure was the wardrobe mistress, who received two letters from her. One written on the stationery of the Grand Hotel in Vienna, the second giving a Pension Kralik, also in Vienna, as her address. When Klára stopped writing, the woman attributed it to the thoughtlessness of the young. Until a letter of hers was returned with 'Addressee Deceased' written on it."

Frau Varga had added some of her own conjectures on how and why Klára had died, but Kunze ignored them. Back in his office, he sent a wire to Captain Zoltán Hodossy, presently in charge of Pioneer and Infantry Troop Maneuver Planning at the headquarters of the Sixty-first Brigade in Budapest, asking him to set a time when they could meet. He then dispatched Lieutenant Stoklaska to the Grand Hotel. The lieutenant returned with the information that a certain Klára Brassay *had* been a guest there between the seventeenth and twenty-fifth of September, 1907, a quiet guest, however, for no one could remember anything noteworthy about her. She had left Pension Kralik as a forwarding address.

Kunze and Stoklaska found the house in one of the grim side streets of Ottakring, a working-class district.

The maid who answered the door looked like a badly put-together scarecrow, much too weird even to fool a sparrow. She stared at the officers with the glassy, expressionless eyes of the retarded. She let them in reluctantly, asking them to wait in the dank, cluttered hallway while she fetched the owner.

Frau Kralik was a large, fat woman, who smelled of perspiration and hyacinths. Her shock of coarse pitch-black hair gave Kunze the impression that she had been dipped headdown into a bucket of shoe polish. She led her visitors into a dirty parlor with fly-specked windowpanes, a smoking tile stove and an unmade cot.

"Yes, I remember the girl," she answered Kunze's question. She spoke cautiously, as though tasting each word, rolling it on her tongue before spitting it out. "She moved in here on Wednesday, and the following Tuesday she was dead."

"Had she been sick?"

She shrugged.

"I don't know. She spoke hardly any German, just a few words."

"How did she find your place?"

"Through a friend of mine who worked as a maid at the Grand Hotel. That's where the girl was staying. She must have run out of money and asked about a cheaper place. When Klára died, she had five kronen and a few hellers in her purse. She owed me fifteen kronen. So the young man paid."

"What young man?"

"The one who took care of the funeral."

"What was he like?"

"A fine gentleman. Good-looking, too."

"An officer?"

"No. A civilian."

"Was he a friend of hers?"

"I don't know. He was here only twice before she died. And never stayed long. The second time they must have quarreled because she was crying when he left and he slammed the door."

"What did they quarrel about?"

"How should I know? I never eavesdrop on my lodgers. Besides, the two quarreled in Hungarian, which I don't understand. I told you she couldn't speak German."

"Was the young man Hungarian?"

"No, he was as Viennese as I am. But he spoke Hungarian."

"You said he took care of the funeral."

"It was like this: After the quarrel the girl locked herself in her room. The next day I started wondering what she ate because I don't allow my lodgers to cook in their rooms. You've got to have house rules if you don't want your place burned down. I knocked on her door and asked if she needed anything. She wouldn't answer, so I thought she wasn't feeling well and didn't want to be disturbed. The following day there was still no sign of her, so I knocked, and when there was no answer, I got worried. So I opened the door with my master key. She didn't look good to me, so I called a doctor. He said she'd been dead for more than twenty-four hours."

"Do you have the doctor's name?"

"I do, but it won't help. Dr. Schnorr died last year."

"I want you to give it to me anyway. Now let's go back to the young man. Did you know his name?"

"No, but after she moved in, I mailed a letter for her, addressed to General Delivery, Main Post Office, Poste Restante, c/o Kornblume. I took a chance and wrote to the same address saying she'd died. I also found some papers among her things. Her father was a Calvinist clergyman in a village in Hungary. So I wrote him, too. When I didn't hear from him, I thought maybe he wasn't her father or didn't care about her. Then a week later the bell rang, and there he stood on the threshold, large as life. That's not quite right, though, because he was awfully puny, especially for a minister."

"What about the young man?"

"Oh, he came the day after I wrote to the address. He was the gentleman friend, just as I'd thought. By then she'd been taken to the morgue. He told me to pack her things and keep them for the family, paid what she owed me, then left to make arrangements for the funeral. I was hurt, because I would have liked to attend. She was a human being, wasn't she? But he had her buried without notifying me or anyone else. When her father came, I couldn't even tell him where to look for the grave. He found it, though, through the General Register Office. She'd been put to rest, poor soul, in the Central Cemetery."

Kunze took out a picture of Lieutenant Peter Dorfrichter. It showed him in dress uniform, with shako and sword.

"Do you know this man?"

She glanced at it. "That's him!"

"Klára Brassay's young man?"

"No. The lieutenant who poisoned all those officers. Dorfrichter! That's his name. He's been in all the papers."

Kunze handed her another photograph. It was an enlargement of a group picture taken of the Dorfrichter family six years earlier: son, daughter and parents. The lieutenant was bareheaded and wore a dark serge suit.

"What about this one?" he asked Frau Kralik.

She examined it thoroughly. "Jesus Maria! That *is* him!"

"Dorfrichter?"

"No! The young man!" She reached for the uniformed photo and held it next to the family portrait. "Jesus Maria! That is the same man!" She turned to the captain. "I guess the uniform and shako confused me." Her face flushed with excitement. "So that's who he was! A murderer!" She paused. "I am sure he killed her, too."

"Why do you say that?" Kunze asked.

"No one saw the girl alive after he left." Suddenly her mouth fell open and her eyes grew glassy as though she were having a vision. "Now I remember something else!" Spittle bubbled at the corners of her mouth. "I had another Hungarian boarder at the time, a palm reader who worked in the Prater amusement park.

Klára told this woman that she had trouble sleeping and asked her where she could get sleeping pills. A few days later the woman offered to give her the address of a pharmacist, but Klára said to forget it, she'd already gotten pills from her gentleman friend."

"Who told you about this?"

"The palm reader! After we found Klára dead. I was going to report it to the police, but the death certificate said heart failure, so I thought why get mixed up in a murder case? It's bad enough to have someone die in your boardinghouse."

Captain Kunze did not comment.

"When exactly did Klára Brassay live here?"

"The fall of 1907. Early fall because she complained of being cold and we never heat the rooms before the fifteenth of October, unless my boarders pay extra. Another house rule. But she didn't want to pay."

Kunze asked Frau Kralik to show them the room where Klára Brassay had died. It was a tiny cubicle at the end of the hallway, with a narrow window opening on an air shaft.

"What a place for an actress to make her final exit" was Lieutenant Stoklaska's comment.

That afternoon Kunze received confirmation from the General Register Office that Klára Brassay had indeed been buried in the Central Cemetery on October 4, 1907.

"Three days later, on the seventh, Dorfrichter married Marianne Gruber," he told Stoklaska. "Perhaps Frau Kralik's suspicion that he had killed her boarder wasn't so absurd after all."

The following day Inspector Weinberger's men tracked down the Hungarian palm reader, who corroborated Frau Kralik's statements. But by then Kunze had left for Budapest and a meeting with Captain Zoltán Hodossy.

In a way, he was grateful for the turn of events that put him aboard the Vienna–Budapest train. He hadn't seen Dorfrichter since the night he'd informed him of the birth of his son and decided later to refrain from seeing him for a while. He knew he had to find the answer to the question that had plagued him ever since his nightmare: whether his feeling for the man was the hunter's fascination with an elusive prey or a disturbing and dishonorable passion.

Captain Hodossy was waiting on the station platform when the train pulled in. Wide-shouldered, stocky, he was every inch the cavalry officer, even though clad in the bottle-green uniform of the General Staff. A polite and quiet man, he nevertheless moved through the crowd as if he owned every square inch of the ground beneath his feet.

He drove Kunze to the Hotel Pannonia in his own Daimler touring car, the cost of which Kunze estimated to be at least twenty thousand kronen. The two men had never met, but as both were members of the Officers' Corps and captains, neither outranking the other, they fell into an easy camaraderie, one of the blessings of army life.

"I assumed your inquiry was in connection with the Dorf-richter case," Hodossy said after Kunze told him his reason for coming. "I read in the papers that you'd been assigned to it. I don't envy you. It's a damn messy affair."

They drove along Váczi Boulevard. It was an unusual day for December, cold but sunny. Snow had fallen the day before, and the sidewalks had been cleared, but the roadbed was still covered with a thick carpet marred here and there by wheel marks and horse droppings. There were more sleighs and fewer automobiles than in Vienna. Horses shied frequently as the Daimler passed, and people darted panic-stricken across the street whenever Hodossy blew his horn.

"What was the relationship between you and Dorfrichter?" Kunze asked.

"At the college I considered him one of the most gifted men in the class, but we didn't have much personal contact. A year later, in 1906, I was serving a tour of duty as battalion adjutant with the Thirteenth Hussars in Kecskemét, and he transferred to the Twenty-fourth Infantry there. I was glad to see him again; he was a lot more interesting company than my field officer comrades. We became friends. I frequently took him with me to Budapest, even initiated him into the School."

"What *school?*"

"Of course. How would you, a Viennese, know about the Ho-dossy School?" He chuckled. "It's not really a school—it's more like a club, but without a membership fee or clubhouse. My fa-ther's caprice, or should I call it folly? It was founded by him when he was a young man, and when he goes, the school will go, too. His main purpose in life is to teach the golden youth of the city how to be gentlemen. He owns a bank and ten thousand acres near Kecskemét. But these are only important in as much as without them he couldn't be a modern-day Petronius."

Zoltán Hodossy's tone as he spoke of his father was facetious, rather than sarcastic. He may not have shared the old man's notions, but there was no doubt he was very fond of him. Kunze preferred to wait before bringing up Klára Brassay's name.

"Your father must be quite a remarkable person."

"He certainly is. No two people have the same opinion about him. Some think he is a pompous old egotist, which he is not. He doesn't really take himself or his eccentricities seriously. He feels that life stops being worth living when one can't take jokes seriously or serious things for jokes. Anyway, you'll meet him and his School tonight. They're having their usual Tuesday dinner. He told me to bring you—that is, if you have no other plans for the evening."

"No plans whatsoever. Thank you very much."

"Great! The dinner is at the Vadászkürt Hotel. I'll call for you at nine. Oh, yes—it's informal. He didn't know whether you'd bring a dress uniform."

Sándor Hodossy was a formidable old man, white-haired, taller than his son, with the noble profile of a Roman and the lynx eyes of a gypsy horse thief. He held himself very straight, and his bearing caused others, when addressed by him, to snap to attention, physically as well as mentally. His age was indeterminate, owing to his alertness. It was only later that evening that Kunze saw him slacken for a moment, revealing his seventy-odd years, but he caught himself immediately with a vigorous shake of his white-maned head.

The guests, impeccably dressed, well mannered, amusing and intelligent, were his son's age and younger. The only officers present were Kunze and the younger Hodossy. The other guests were writers, actors, college professors, painters, musicians and the wealthy sons of businessmen. In Kunze's honor they all spoke in German.

On earlier trips to Hungary, Kunze had always returned home with indigestion. This evening he had nothing to fear. The food, a blend of French and Hungarian cooking, was neither rich nor spicy, and the champagne was vintage French.

At eleven, Captain Hodossy and several of the young men disappeared, returning with an assortment of pretty young actresses and chorus girls who had appeared that night in local theaters and cabarets, none older than twenty-five, and all elegantly dressed and well mannered. The blonde Captain Hodossy had escorted was seated next to his father, and it was obvious to Kunze that she was the older man's date. The son had merely been delegated to fetch her because his father, as host, had not wanted to leave the party.

When the party broke up at two in the morning, no one was drunk, despite the amount of liquor consumed. Hodossy senior had proved to be a very sophisticated host. Nevertheless, Kunze could not rid himself of the feeling that he had participated in a ritualistic feast given by an Oriental potentate.

The following morning he took a fiacre to brigade headquarters, where Captain Hodossy was waiting for him. He looked fit and rested, which amazed Kunze, for he himself was definitely hung over, although he had drunk less than either Hodossy. *Those damned Hungarians,* he thought, *can drink rat poison spiked with hemlock and never feel it.*

Captain Hodossy spoke when they settled down in his office. "About Peter Dorfrichter. I left off yesterday telling you that he'd been accepted into the School. Last night you saw what the school was like—a group of young men intent on getting the most out of life without being too vulgar about it."

"Does the name Klára Brassay mean anything to you, Zoltán?" Kunze asked.

"It certainly does," Hodossy exclaimed. "At one time she damn near became my *stepmother!*"

"What was she like?"

"Before I answer your question, I'd better tell you one more thing about Father. Beside the School he has another hobby— probably his true vocation. To turn little whores into courtesans. Taking a chorus girl or a minor actress and making a *Dame aux Camélias* out of her, preferably without consumption. He usually keeps them for a year or two, teaches them how to speak, eat, dress and undress,—travels with them, and, when they've become sufficiently polished, releases them as simply as one releases a caged bird. Sometimes he has to shake the cage a little, because the bird doesn't want to leave. They usually don't fly far, and one can find them perched on the nearest rich man's shoulder. Father is awfully good to them, and when he detects any special talent in his protégées, he helps them develop it, opens doors for them and finds showcases where they can shine and be discovered. Klára Brassay was one of the girls. Not a great beauty, but she was witty, gay and talented. Father found her in Kecskemét when she appeared with the stock company there. I don't think she loved him, but she realized how much he could do for her career. I'm sure she was faithful to him, which was not easy because all the unmarried officers of the garrison were after her, and some of the married ones, too, not to mention the civilians. They sent her carloads of flowers and had a gypsy band serenade her night after night . . . They thought of bizarre pranks to get her attention. One drunken infantry lieutenant for instance stopped at her house and pissed 'I love you, Kl—' into the snow under her window. As the story goes, he ran out of special ink at the letter *l*, went home, woke his orderly, and told him to finish the word. The private just stood there. 'Can't you piss, damn you?' the lieutenant yelled at him. 'Piss I can, Lieutenant, sir,' the soldier said, 'only write I cannot!' Of course, I can't vouch for the story."

"*Si non e vero e ben trovato.*" Kunze grinned.

"Anyway, it gives you an idea to what desperation boredom in a small garrison can drive an otherwise normal adult. About once a week I took Klára to Budapest, so she could continue her graduate studies with Father, and whenever Peter Dorfrichter was free, he came along. I don't know when and how, but she fell in love with him. She was probably ripe for it, and he came along just in time. He has the kind of charm that irritates, but attracts. With a touch of menace," he added. "The fellow—"

Kunze stopped him. "Menace?"

"I may be wrong, but that's what I always felt about him. Long before his name became connected with those bloody capsules." He paused to light a cigarette. "He didn't give a goddamn about Klára but made a big play for her. I think it flattered his ego to take her away from Father and the garrison. They had a well-publicized affair and were seen night after night having supper at the Beretvás Hotel. Father took it hard. I think she was the only girl he's ever been serious about. If Dorfrichter hadn't come along, I'm sure he'd have married her. He wouldn't have done too badly. She was a very decent sort. For instance, though he didn't want her to, she returned all the presents Father ever gave her. By then Dorfrichter knew that he was going to be transferred, but she didn't. When his orders came, he left town without saying good-bye to her. At first, she couldn't believe that he was gone. A week later she, too, disappeared from Kecskemét. There were rumors she followed him to Bosnia."

"She followed him all right," Kunze said, "but not to Bosnia. To Vienna."

"Anyway, I heard sometime later that she died."

"Did you ever try to contact her after she left?"

"Never. It would've been awkward because of Father. I thought the sooner he forgot her, the better."

"Has it ever occurred to you that Dorfrichter could have been responsible for her death?"

Zoltán Hodossy looked shocked.

"No. Was he?"

"We don't know. What do you think?"

"She was insane about him. He might have considered her a nuisance by then. He had an off-and-on engagement with the girl he married later."

"Only *three days* later! Klára Brassay was buried on the fourth of October, and Dorfrichter married his wife on the seventh."

"I'll be damned. Nevertheless, he didn't have to kill her, to get rid of her. She wasn't the kind to use blackmail."

Kunze changed the subject. "Now what about the circular? Let's assume Dorfrichter was the sender. What reason would he have to kill *you*?"

"I can't think of any."

"Why you, and not—for instance—Ahrens?"

"Perhaps he left the choice to fate. Put fifteen names into a hat and pulled out ten. Incidentally, I once saw him do the same thing at the races. I'd studied the forms for hours; he closed his eyes and stabbed his finger at a horse on his program. I lost; he won."

"You were friends with him. Could he be Charles Francis?"

"That's hard to say. No doubt, he was ambitious. Probably dreaming of a meteoric career. After all, Napoleon has been dead less than a century. Many young officers feel if Napoleon could rise to the top, so could they. But imagine a Napoleon born in Austria and entering Franz Josef's army in 1898. He would still be a second lieutenant at the age when Napoleon conducted the Italian campaign and captain when he crowned himself emperor and—with luck—major when he married a Habsburg daughter and ruled Europe. I don't know what he'd have done in Dorfrichter's place. Grown fat placidly or poisoned the men who blocked his way!"

"Could Dorfrichter be Charles Francis?" Kunze repeated his question.

Captain Hodossy thought for a moment.

"I suppose he could. But you'll have a hell of a time proving it."

After Budapest, Vienna seemed more than ever the only place to be. Kunze, arriving home late in the afternoon, was told by the cook that Rose had left for Graz to attend her Uncle Paul's funeral.

The captain was just sitting down to dinner when Rose called.

"He died day before yesterday. We'll bury him tomorrow," she shouted. The long-distance phone was still a mysterious novelty to her, and she never believed she could be heard at the other end of the wire. "The attorney said it would take a few weeks about the will, but there won't be any complications. I'll probably have to stay here, though, till things get cleared up."

She hadn't even waited for *rigor mortis* to set in before talking to the attorney, Kunze mused, rebuking himself for the malicious thought.

"Take care of yourself," he told her, realizing with a pang of conscience that he didn't miss her. He was tired and glad to be alone to enjoy his dinner and a bottle of Burgundy. His sleep that night was dreamless.

For the first time in Kunze's memory the expression of defiance was gone from Dorfrichter's face. He must have continued his daily promenades because his skin had the pink-and-white frosted look of someone coming in from the cold. After the usual ceremony of salutes and the dismissal of the guards, he sank into the offered chair with a loud sigh.

"Those goddamn corridors," he said. "And stairs! I did the whole Ring today, including the quay. From the Opera to the Opera. I'm worn-out." He lighted the cigarette Kunze offered him. "Have you had any news about my wife, sir?" He exhaled the smoke slowly. "And the child?"

"No news. Anyway, I wasn't here. I was in Budapest seeing a friend of yours—Captain Zoltán Hodossy."

Kunze watched the prisoner closely. Outside of a few army men, no one knew that Hodossy was a recipient of one of the Charles Francis circulars. He had been among the last to receive one, and when he had handed it in to his commander, he was warned not to discuss it with anyone. The mention of Hodossy's name should surprise Dorfrichter—unless he was Charles Francis.

No reaction showed on his face. He returned Kunze's searching gaze with a blank stare. Taking a few puffs on his cigarette, he squashed it out.

"Am I expected to ask you why you saw Hodossy?" His tone had a raw edge to it.

"Not unless you wish to."

"In that case I won't. Why should I make it easy for you?" The mocking little smile was back. "You'll just have to think of the next question without me giving you the cue."

"I will, don't worry," Kunze snapped. "Were you friends with Captain Hodossy?"

"Very good friends. We still are, I hope. He is a decent sort. Especially for a Hungarian."

That was what Moll had said about Hodossy, Kunze remembered.

"You don't like Hungarians?"

"I have nothing against them except their goddamned red-white-green patriotism. I don't know how far they can be trusted once it comes to a war. I would not put it past them to extort certain privileges in exchange for their cooperation. God knows they've been intractable enough in peacetime, too."

"You always talk as if war were inevitable," Kunze pointed out.

"Don't you think we have a pretty good life as it is? And in a war we might lose more than we gain?"

"That depends on who will be in command, sir. Senile old arch-dukes or young men with modern, unorthodox ideas."

"Men like you?"

"Why not, sir?"

"I'm sure your first act would be to stand us—incorrigible pacifists—against the wall."

"That's right, sir." Dorfrichter grinned.

"Lucky for me that we're still at peace and you're not in command," Kunze said. He was having trouble controlling his irritation. He was angry, hopelessly excited. He hated the man for it, but more than that, he hated himself. "Let's get back to Hodossy. You said you were friends with him. How about his father?"

"That bloated old fool!"

"Nevertheless, you accepted his hospitality."

"For a while. There is a Hungarian saying: When the devil gets hungry, he eats flies! That's what happens to you when you're stationed in a place like Kecskemét. It's impossible for our kind to establish any rapport with the natives. They're full of goulash, gypsy music and chauvinism. You should see them night after night at the Beretvás, ordering the gypsies to play in their ears as if they were deaf and crying big fat tears into their wine. And when you ask them what the song was that made them weep, they tell you it went something like this: "*A csizmámban nincsen kéreg mert megette a patkány-féreg!*""

"I beg your pardon?"

"Translated literally: 'No lining in my boots—got chewed up by the vermin rat.'" He chuckled. "The sensation of the year is the new cashier at the café. To be the first to seduce her is like being decorated with the Distinguished Conduct Medal. Afterward she is passed from bed to bed! A blonde called Piroska held the record. She infected eleven men with the clap. There's nothing else to do in the whole goddamn place but drink and whore."

"Don't they have a theater?" Kunze asked.

"They have a building. It looks like a theater. But the performances! They use the same cast and sets for both the *Merry Widow* and *King Lear*."

"That reminds me, did you know an actress called Klára Brassay in Kecskemét?"

"I did, sir." Dorfrichter nodded. It was evident that he was expecting the question.

"What was your relation to her?"

"Exactly what Zoli Hodossy must have told you. I had an affair with her."

"I understand she followed you to Vienna. Did you continue seeing her here?"

"I did," Dorfrichter said after a moment's hesitation.

"Although you were engaged to be married. If I'm not mistaken, you married your wife soon after Klára Brassay arrived in Vienna."

"Exactly."

"Did you see Klára Brassay after your wedding?"

"I did not."

"Why not?"

"Because she was dead, that's why," the lieutenant snapped, losing a bit of his composure. As his nervousness grew, Kunze's subsided, as though they were seated on opposite ends of a seesaw.

"When did she die and of what?" Kunze asked.

"Around the first of October, 1907. Of heart failure."

"How do you know?"

"It was stated in her death certificate."

"You had this girl follow you to Vienna, although you were ready to marry your present wife. She came here, and in about two weeks' time she was dead and buried three days before your wedding. Very convenient timing, I should say."

"First of all, I didn't ask her to follow me. When I left Kecskemét, I told her we were finished. She seemed to accept it; then suddenly she appeared in Vienna, making a nuisance of herself."

"I understand she was old Hodossy's protégée and—"

Dorfrichter broke in sharply. "Protégée? She was his whore!"

"All right, she was his whore. Nevertheless, you started an affair with her, causing her to leave the old man. Didn't you feel responsible?"

"No! She was an adult. She knew what she was doing. Frankly, sir, I don't understand your reproof. If a thing like that ought to give one a guilty conscience, the entire Officers' Corps should be wearing sackcloth and ashes."

"I have testimony here from someone who spoke to Fräulein Brassay shortly before her death. She told this person that her friend—meaning you—would provide her with sleeping pills. Did you?"

Dorfrichter paled. "I did not!"

"The landlady at the pension testified that you arranged for her funeral," Kunze added. "Why did you?"

"Because I was the only person she knew in Vienna."

"She had a family. Her parents were alive. Did you try to contact them?"

"I did not."

"Why not?"

"I didn't consider it my duty."

"It seems to me you were in a great hurry to have her buried. Was an autopsy ordered?"

"No."

"Why not?"

Dorfrichter pulled a handkerchief from his pocket and wiped away tiny pearls of perspiration which glistened on his forehead.

"There was no need for it. The cause of death had been ascertained by a physician and recorded in the death certificate."

Kunze leaned forward, looking Dorfrichter straight in the eye. "Let me ask you, Lieutenant, were you personally convinced that she had died of heart failure?"

"I had no reason to doubt it."

"Couldn't she have died of something else? Like an overdose of the sleeping pills you never gave her?"

The lieutenant averted his eyes. Then he rolled his handkerchief into a ball with his nervous fingers. With a sudden movement, he stuffed it into his pocket as though ridding himself of embarrassing evidence. He switched his gaze back to the captain's expectant stare.

"Yes, she could've died of something else," he said, once more calm and sure of himself. "Like an overdose of sleeping pills— someone else gave her." He grinned. "Of piercing her heart with a hatpin. Of holding her breath till she collapsed for lack of oxygen. How should I know when the doctor didn't?"

"You think she could have committed suicide? Did she ever say she would?"

"Of course, she did. Suicide! That's their favorite means of extortion!"

"Why do you mention extortion? Was she in a position to cause you trouble?"

Dorfrichter threw an incredulous look at the captain. "But, sir," he said, his tone indicating he was speaking to a retarded child, "by now the picture must be absolutely clear to you. There I was ready to be married when up popped this girl I'd had a roll in the hay with making all sorts of demands on me. I had a damn hard time convincing her to be sensible and to go back where she'd come from. When I thought the matter'd been straightened out, instead of taking the train to Budapest, she died. I might have canceled my wedding, but even that wouldn't have brought her back. So all I could do was give her a decent Christian funeral, and hope that my fiancée wouldn't find out about her."

"You're a pretty cynical bastard, Dorfrichter, aren't you?"

"For Judas' sake, sir, do you want me to shed a bucketful of crocodile tears? It would show a lack of respect for your intelligence if I did. I felt no responsibility toward Klára. It's grossly unfair to call a man names for not loving a certain woman. The end of any affair is always the unloved's fault. He or she is unlovable. But if you say this out loud, you're a bastard. Some men are cowards enough to let themselves be cowed into lifelong slavery, just because a woman loves them. I prefer to be called a cynical bastard and retain my freedom."

"The question is how far you are willing to go to protect your freedom," Kunze told him.

"What do you mean, sir?"

"You know very well what I mean. Did you kill Klára Brassay? Did you feed her poison or pierce her heart with a hatpin or smother her?"

Dorfrichter laughed. "You're joking, sir."

"You know damn well that I am not!"

"I see. I poisoned Mader, tried to poison nine other officers, and also poisoned Klára!"

"Did you or didn't you?"

Dorfrichter shook his head indignantly. "Of course not! Neither Klára nor Mader. No, no, no!"

"All right," Kunze said curtly. "We'll have her disinterred. Luckily, forensic medicine has made great strides. Pathologists can now determine the cause of death, even though the corpse has been buried for years." He turned to Stoklaska. "Have the lieutenant escorted back to his cell."

Dorfrichter had risen and stood staring at the roofs visible through the windows.

"I've told you, sir, that she threatened to kill herself. Even in Kecskemét, she was given to strange moods. One day she was full of life; the next she couldn't stop crying. She may have taken poison, but I didn't give it to her."

Kunze didn't reply. The meeting had gone quite well, he thought. What he had feared—that inner doubts might hamper him in the conduct of the questioning—failed to materialize. He felt more relaxed now than at the beginning of the interrogation. After a lengthy stalk through the veldt the prey was within the range of the gun. He was convinced that Klára Brassay had died of poison and that Peter Dorfrichter had had a hand in her death. He telephoned Inspector Weinberger and asked him to arrange for the exhumation of Klára Brassay's corpse and an autopsy.

Meanwhile, two detectives were sent to the Hungarian village where the Reverend Brassay administered to the spiritual needs of his flock to question him about any significant item in his daughter's luggage, which had been left at Frau Kralik's pension.

Rose returned from Graz late one afternoon. When Kunze arrived home, she had already changed to her brightest and fluffiest negligee. She could not know that the captain disliked it on her because he rarely commented on the way she dressed. If she asked him what he thought of a new outfit, he invariably answered that it was becoming even if it didn't appeal to him.

"Uncle Paul left everything to me," she told him the moment he entered. "That is—almost everything. The estate will have to pay his housekeeper ten thousand kronen in cash. I suspect he also gave her some stocks. Perhaps she just took them. I don't plan to make an issue of it, though, mainly because I don't want to hold up things. The lawyer thinks he can wind up the whole matter in two months. Today is the twentieth of December—that would be the end of February, so we can plan on a March wedding. Wouldn't the ides of March be lovely?"

"Why the ides of March?"

"It sounds like such a perfect day."

"It didn't to Caesar."

She threw her arms about him. "Aren't you happy?" she asked.

He didn't feel happy at all, either about the prospect of marriage or the tight embrace in which she encircled him. Her negligee had slipped from one fleshy shoulder, and he was reminded of the fatted geese from Hungary, plucked clean, their plump breasts a pale yellow, as they hung from the rafters of the stalls in the open food market he had passed on his way home. He pushed her away gently. Her softness only seemed to make him long for slim, firm limbs, bony reassuring hands, the feel of a rib cage under taut, cool skin.

"You don't look happy," he heard her say. Her big blue eyes seemed full of reproach.

"I'm a little tired," he lied, kissing her lightly on the forehead.

He wondered what Lieutenant Peter Dorfrichter would have done in his place. Probably walked from the apartment never to return, regardless of the expression in those big blue eyes. He would have realized the moment had arrived for a clean break, that failing to make it meant—how had he put it?—lifelong slavery. Dorfrichter was indeed a bastard because he had had the guts to leave a woman he didn't love. Emil Kunze was a good man because he stayed with his own unlovable. What it really came down to, he thought wryly, was that he was good because he was weak and Dorfrichter was a bastard because he had the courage of his convictions. Rose loved him, and because she did, he was shackled to her for the rest of his days. From the beginning of their affair he had recognized her love for what it was, a large hungry octopus, eight arms reaching out for him, pulling him to its soft, sacklike body, yet he made no move to escape. He didn't even have the excuse of youth. *The wish to be loved*, he mused, *is the folly of the young. Maturity begins with the discovery that to love is far more difficult than being loved, and few*

*men are brave enough to admit it, preferring to deceive them-
selves by labeling superficial interests, perhaps even sexual attraction, love.*

"Irma and Alfred are delighted," Rose said.

"What about?" Kunze asked absentmindedly, then remembered
they were Rose's sister and brother-in-law.

She gave him a startled look. "About us getting married. What
else?"

She has told them already, Kunze thought. "That's nice," he
murmured.

"I hope the army won't have any objections," Rose went on.
"The apartment is in Alfred's name, of course. Still they might
find out that I've lived here, too. Do you think it'd be a good idea
if I moved in with Irma and Alfred, I mean until the wedding?"

"How about *me* moving out?" Kunze asked, intending it as
a joke. Then suddenly the idea began to appeal to him. "Yes,
that's it. I'll take a flat somewhere near here. A sublet will do. It
doesn't have to be anything fancy. Two rooms or a bed-sitting
room with a separate entrance and bath."

"What about your meals?"

"I can have breakfast in a café on my way to the office and
come here for dinner. After all, it's only for a short period."

The "short period" seemed to reassure her, and she said she
would start looking for a suitable flat. When the maid announced
dinner, he saw that the table had been set with Rose's best
Meissen china. A bottle of champagne was cooling in a silver
bucket.

"What's the occasion?" he asked, merely to tease her. Ever since
his moving out had been agreed on, he was feeling more cheerful. Not that he believed he could escape marriage; there was no
appeal against the sentence. Nevertheless, moving to new quarters
was a change—in his present condition, a real blessing.

After dinner they listened to phonograph records. Music always
put Rose in a romantic mood, and when she had played the
"Merry Widow Waltz" for the second time, Kunze rose and—with
the excuse that he'd had a very hard day—wished her good-night.
After he left, she allowed the machine to run down; then she,
too, went to bed, taking the almost full champagne bottle with
her.

* * *

The detectives returned from Hungary, and Inspector Weinberger called on Kunze at the Military Lawcourt to inform him of
the results of their investigation. During the past two days the
Viennese daily papers had published sensational stories about the
life and death of Klára Brassay. Enterprising reporters had
talked to members of her family, the manager of the Kecskemét
theater, her ex-colleagues, the concierge of the Grand Hotel and
Frau Kralik. One foolhardy young man had even tried to interview Hodossy senior but was thrown out bodily by the old man's
Senegalese masseur.

"My man had a hard time getting any information from the
Reverend Brassay," the inspector told Kunze. "He said he had
broken with his daughter when she ran away from home and
went on the stage. His wife was a little more cooperative. She told
the detectives that once she'd gone to Kecskemét after Klára and
tried to take her home, but when her daughter lighted a cigarette
right in front of her, she became convinced that Klára was beyond
redemption. She walked out without a word and never spoke to
her again. I'm sure she believes to this day that her daughter's
miserable end was God's way of punishing her for smoking."

"Sounds like typical Calvinist reasoning," Kunze observed.

"We have a more important bit of information—also from her
mother. At six, her daughter had scarlet fever which left her with
a weak heart. As an adult, though, she seemed to have gotten
over it. The death certificate mentioned heart failure, and that
seems to tie in with the mother's statement."

The autopsy results reached Kunze's desk a day later. Klára
Brassay's body had been buried for more than two years; consequently, it was impossible for the pathologists to find the exact
cause of death. They ascertained, however, that she had not been
strangled or suffered other injuries; neither had she been poisoned. The toxicological report was negative. The medical consensus read: death by *natural causes.*

Kunze was alone in his office when the sealed envelope was
delivered by Inspector Weinberger's messenger. His first reaction
was to send for Dorfrichter and tell him about the report. Then
he remembered that during the entire investigation Dorfrichter
had lost his composure only once when Klára Brassay's possible

death by poison was discussed. The girl had threatened to kill herself, and when she was found dead, Dorfrichter must have assumed that she had made good her threat. He arranged for a fast and quiet burial to avoid a scandal, which he, a General Staff hopeful, could ill afford. If poison were found in the girl's body now, no one would believe in his innocence. This Dorfrichter knew and the thought probably kept him awake nights. Kunze decided against sharing the report with the prisoner. If one wanted to break a man, there was no better method than to inflict insomnia on him.

He speculated also on the effect the newspaper reports would have on Marianne Dorfrichter. Shortly before marrying her, her husband had had a wild affair with an actress. Most probably he had never mentioned Klára Brassay to her, just as he never admitted having sent the ten circulars. Aside from wounding her pride, the story must have made her doubt his veracity. Dorfrichter, locked up in a cell at the Military Prison, had a great deal of time in which to think about his wife's reaction. He had no way of dispelling her doubts, of winning her back if she had drawn away. Another weight to add to the pressure on him. Another thorn in his flesh to prevent his sleeping soundly.

VIII

KUNZE had not seen General Wencel since the party at his house. When he received an order to report to the general's office, he knew it would not be a friendly chat.

Wencel began without any preliminaries. "You've been on the case more than one month now, kept an officer with impeccable reputation under arrest since the thirtieth of November. Today is the twenty-third of December, yet you've failed to produce any conclusive evidence against the man or obtain a confession. You even tried to make a sordid murder case out of some wretched chorus girl's death. It blew up in your face. How much longer are we supposed to wait for results?"

"With the general's permission, I didn't make a case out of that young woman's death. The press did. Incidentally, she was an actress, not a chorus girl."

"What the hell difference does that make?" Wencel said moodily, then added, "How are you planning to proceed?"

"Same as before. Questioning witnesses, looking for more clues."

"More? I didn't know you had any!"

Kunze remained silent.

"You don't advise that we release the man?" the general asked.

"Certainly not, sir."

"Well, then continue with the investigation, damn it! You're dismissed!"

The dismissal was unusually rude, but Kunze didn't mind. The session was over, and that was all he cared about. He was about to open the door when Wencel stopped him.

"I was called to Belvedere Palace yesterday. His Imperial Highness Archduke Franz Ferdinand expressed dissatisfaction with the way we've handled the case." When Kunze did not reply, he added: "I'm telling you this because I hope it'll make an impression on you."

Kunze remained at the door.

"Evidently it doesn't," Wencel muttered.

"Doesn't what, sir?"

"Make an impression on you!"

"No, sir. If the archduke becomes emperor tomorrow, he can let Dorfrichter go, even pin a medal on his chest if he wishes. But today the emperor is Franz Josef."

"Dr. Goldschmiedt has seen Baron von Schönaich. He is trying to have the Ministry of War hand the case over to civilian authorities."

Evidently, Wencel had decided to give out his news by the spoonful.

"He told me at your house that he would try it."

"And what did you tell him?"

"To save himself the effort. The ministry will refer the case to the Crown."

"He is no friend of yours, you know."

"Minister Schönaich?"

"No, Dr. Goldschmiedt!"

"I never expected him to be. As a matter of fact, sir, I prefer *not* to be listed among his friends."

Wencel reached out for a folder on his desk and began thumbing through it, indicating that the audience was at an end.

"That'll be all, Captain," he said, adding, "Merry Christmas!"

"Merry Christmas to you, General, and to Frau Wencel." Kunze's answer sounded much too cheerful, and he made his exit quickly.

He found Heinrich and Stoklaska waiting for him in his office and could tell by their expressions that they had news for him.

"They've found the man!" Stoklaska announced. Usually precise and to the point, he seemed much too excited now to make sense.

"What man?" Kunze asked.

"The private!" Heinrich answered.

"The orderly who wanted to buy cyanide at Ritzberger's!" Stoklaska exclaimed. "In Linz!"

At last Kunze understood. "That's interesting. Now will one of you tell me what happened?"

After every private at the Linz garrison had been interrogated, the search was extended over the entire monarchy. Every soldier transferred from Linz to another garrison was questioned. The man was finally located in Zagreb. He readily confirmed pharmacist Ritzberger's recollection. The lieutenant whose orderly he had been had sent him for cyanide. When he returned home and reported that the pharmacist had demanded a certificate, the lieutenant grew annoyed and made a suggestion about what Ritzberger could do with his cyanide. A few days earlier both officer and orderly had received their transfer orders; the private had since reported to the Seventeenth Infantry in Zagreb and the lieutenant to the Twenty-eighth in Nagykanizsa.

Kunze telephoned the regimental command post in Nagykanizsa, requesting the interrogation of Second Lieutenant Xavier Vanini regarding the attempted cyanide purchase. The same afternoon he received the answer in a telegram. It dispelled the mystery of the Ritzberger clue. A passionate amateur photographer, Lieutenant Vanini had needed the potassium of cyanide to develop pictures by wet-plate process. When Ritzberger refused to sell any to his orderly, Vanini was already busy packing. Soon after his arrival in Nagykanizsa on the twelfth of November, he obtained a permit from the Municipal Health Office there and subsequently bought the chemical at a local pharmacy.

Kunze reread the telegram.

"This puts us back where we started a month ago," he commented to Stoklaska, then after reflecting for a moment, ordered, "Get me all information available on this Vanini. Personal file, service background, précis of career, photo, everything!" He drummed nervously on the desk top with his fingers, then turned to Stoklaska. "I hate to do this to you, but I want you to take the next train to Linz. If I'm not mistaken, there is one leaving at five. You'll have the evening and tomorrow morning to collect all the documents and information. If you take the early-afternoon train back tomorrow, you'll still be in time to light the Christmas candles." He looked away. It was thoughtless of him to send a young man out of town the day before Christmas, and if the lieutenant made a wry face, he didn't want to see it.

To his relief, Stoklaska didn't question the order. A devoted reader of detective stories, he was probably amused by the Sherlock Holmesian aspect of the assignment. Also, he had just broken with his girl, was unattached at the moment with no definite plans for the holidays.

The Lawcourt Building had emptied early because most people failed to return after the midday recess. Stepping to the window, Kunze looked down at busy Hernalser Gürtel. It had been snowing all day, and the weather bureau promised a white Christmas. He loved Vienna in any season, but more than ever during the winter and on snowy Christmas Eves when the city became a hushed cathedral with the black sky as its dome. He could never understand how anyone could celebrate Christmas Eve with profane music and noisemakers as it was celebrated in Paris. It was to Kunze's mind an evening for family reunions, gift giving, and peace.

Now, at five in the afternoon, Vienna bustled with the last-minute rush of people anxiously trying to reach home before public transportation came to a halt, the exodus of children from the Opera after a special matinee of *Hänsel und Gretel*, the rumble of roller blinds being pulled down over shop doors, the swish of twig brooms sweeping the snow off sidewalks, the jingle of sleigh bells, and—at times—the twentieth-century sound of auto horns jarring the city's nineteenth-century harmony.

Stoklaska returned with a briefcase full of documents. The unknown Xavier Vanini's entire life lay spread out on Kunze's desk. There was nothing especially noteworthy about it. The picture that emerged from the various précis and qualification lists was that of an average field officer, born twenty-seven years before in Trieste, Roman Catholic, single, educated in Fiume, graduated from the Wiener Neustadt Military Academy, assigned to tours in Graz, Lemberg, Sarajevo, Linz and, finally, Nagykanizsa.

"Sarajevo from January, 1907 until November, 1908," Kunze

said. "Dorfrichter was in Sarajevo from October, 1907, until May, 1909. Both with the Eighteenth Infantry Brigade. Most likely they knew one another. Both transferred to the Fourteenth Infantry in Linz." He studied the man's latest career précis. "Suited for field service, shows limited initiative, not recommended for patrol duty, performs better under supervision."

"I don't think he is considered a very highly qualified officer," Stoklaska observed. "Well liked, especially among the younger set, but not taken too seriously. A heavy drinker, but carries his liquor well. Supposedly up to his neck in debts and in the hands of moneylenders, but somehow muddles through with the help of friends."

"Any connection between him and Dorfrichter?"

"Nothing apparent. Off duty, they moved in different circles. Vanini with a younger and less restrained crowd, the Dorfrichters with the elite. Dorfrichter was a General Staff candidate and had to watch his step. Vanini was second-rate, which, too, had its advantages."

"Then it's obvious that there could be no collusion between them. They weren't friends, and not even killing the entire General Staff would have helped Vanini's career. One more blind alley. Sorry to have sent you on a fool's errand," Kunze apologized.

Stoklaska smiled. "I didn't mind. I love train rides. Once, when I was five and we spent the summer in Strobl on the Wolfgangsee, I sneaked on board that toy train that runs along the lake and my parents had to go to Ischl to collect me. Besides, last night I had a very good dinner at the Hotel Herrenhaus. Incidentally, the maid—a chatty old crone—told me she'd once seen Peter Dorfrichter at the hotel. She sounded as if he'd been involved in some scandal."

Kunze suddenly remembered the reactions of the headwaiter and concierge to his questions about the lieutenant.

"What exactly did she say?" he asked.

"Nothing specific. Whetted my appetite, then shut up. Not even for five kronen would she say any more."

"You should've offered her ten," Kunze said.

He quickly scribbled a note on the memo pad before him: "Call Inspector Weinberger about Herrenhaus."

*   *   *

"Do you know a First Lieutenant Peter Dorfrichter?" Kunze asked the private who sat stiffly on the edge of the chair in front of his desk.

Boka gave him one of his dead-fish looks. The captain had offered him a seat, which made him suspicious. He felt much more at ease with officers who acted true to form. In other words, like bastards. He remembered, too, his previous experience with the captain and was wary.

"I respectfully report, sir, I know a First Lieutenant Peter Dorfrichter."

"How well do you know him?"

Boka weighed carefully all the possible consequences of his answer.

"I respectfully report, sir, I heard some people say he is the officer who sent the poison to Captain Mader."

"And to your knowledge what was the relationship between Captain Mader and the lieutenant?"

"I respectfully report, sir, I don't understand the question."

Kunze leaned forward in his chair as if trying to shorten the distance in meters, as well as attitudes, that separated him from the Hungarian.

"Look here, soldier, what I am trying to find out is: Did Lieutenant Dorfrichter have a grudge against your captain?" He spoke slowly, stressing each syllable. "It's hard to believe that an officer would want to kill a comrade, but if he did, he had to have a strong reason. You spent four years with Captain Mader and—"

"Five!" Boka cut in. There was pride in his tone, and for a quick moment his eyes filled with emotion.

The sentiment didn't escape Kunze.

"You and I—we both want the same thing. To find the man who killed Captain Mader. So think hard. Did your captain ever have a fight with Lieutenant Dorfrichter, a disagreement over a woman or money—drunk or sober?"

Slowly Boka shook his head, shifting his backside to a more comfortable position on the chair. The discovery that he knew something Captain Kunze didn't gave him an advantage over his interrogator.

"I respectfully report, sir," he said, cautiously doling out the information, "the lieutenant had no grudge. He had reason to be grateful to Captain Mader."

"Grateful for what?"

"For saving his life—what else?"

It took Kunze a few minutes to decipher Boka's German and understand who had saved whom. When the basic facts were established, he asked Boka to give him the full story of the life-saving.

"I respectfully report, sir, Lieutenant Dorfrichter waded into the water, and a big wave came and knocked him off his feet, and he started yelling, and Captain Mader jumped in and pulled him out."

"Damn it, Boka! Be a little more specific! What water? Was it a river, a lake? Where did all this happen and when?"

"In Castelnuovo, sir. June, 1904."

After the examinations at the end of the first year the entire War College class—rather, the survivors—was taken to Castelnuovo on the Adriatic for instruction in swimming, sailing and navigation. The training was strenuous and demanded a great deal of vigor and energy. The individual performances were graded, and the marks went into fitness reports.

It seemed that one warm evening Mader, Dorfrichter and three other lieutenants decided to treat themselves to a picnic on the beach. At least this was what Kunze gathered from Boka's erratic narrative.

"They took three girls with them," Boka went on, "and a big basket of food and ten bottles of champagne in a crate filled with ice. I was the only orderly along. It was still daylight when we got there, but we stayed after dark, so I lighted a campfire for them. Later some of the gentlemen took the girls to the cabanas. Captain Mader and Lieutenant Dorfrichter stayed at the fire, though. I was not far from them, lying on the sand. We were all drinking; the captain gave me a whole bottle—that's the kind of man he was. Then the lieutenant got up and ran into the water. I heard the captain tell him to watch out—Lieutenant Dorfrichter was not used to drinking, and that night he had more than he could handle. He said he wanted to cool off, and the next moment he was screaming for help. The captain was dressed except that he had his tunic off, but he jumped in anyway and went after the lieutenant. He was like that—always ready to help others. Once he climbed up on the roof of a four-story house in Cracow to rescue his landlady's cat; the damned cat crawled out through an attic window and—"

Kunze cut in. "Get back to Castelnuovo!"

"Yes, sir. Well, Captain Mader had trouble finding Lieutenant Dorfrichter in the dark. Like I was saying, a wave had swept him —I mean the lieutenant—off his feet, and the undertow was carrying him out. Finally, the captain did reach him and pulled him out. He was coughing and sputtering, the lieutenant was, and we stood him on his head and shook the water out of him. The other three officers—they heard the screaming—came running to see what happened, but Captain Mader told them the lieutenant had been fooling, so they believed him and went back to whatever they'd been doing with the girls in the cabanas. Lieutenant Dorfrichter was still in pretty bad shape. It took him a long time to get back on his feet."

"If you heard Captain Mader say that the lieutenant was joking, how do you know he wasn't?"

"I respectfully report, sir, Lieutenant Dorfrichter was scared out of his wits in the water. Screamed like a stuck pig. I also heard him ask the captain not to tell anyone that he almost drowned. And the captain gave his word he wouldn't. And he never did."

"Have you?"

"Have I what, sir?"

"Told about it?"

"No, sir. I didn't think it would be right as long as Captain Mader gave his word. That went for me, too."

"Did Captain Mader and Lieutenant Dorfrichter remain friends after this incident? Stay in contact?"

"I don't know, sir. We—I mean the captain and me—weren't stationed in the same garrisons with the lieutenant."

"Do you remember who the other three officers were on the beach that night?"

Boka was thinking hard.

"One was Lieutenant Gabriel—that's the one who later married Major von Campanini's daughter and left the army. One was from the Fourteenth Dragoons—that's where all the officers are clean-shaven. I don't remember his name. He was a baron, but

Jewish. And I don't know the third one's name, either. I heard
that he'd killed himself that same summer in Innsbruck."

"He must mean Hoffer," Kunze said to Stoklaska.

"That's right, sir!" Boka agreed. "Lieutenant Hoffer. It's hard
to believe he shot himself dead. He looked like a man who could
fall off his horse in front of the emperor and get up laughing."

Kunze had not seen Dorfrichter since he had questioned the
prisoner in connection with Klára Brassay's death. If he expected
to see him troubled, he was very much mistaken. The Dorfrichter
who was escorted in by Provost Tuttman and the armed guard
was bright-eyed, pink-cheeked, and appeared to be the most relaxed man in the Austro-Hungarian Army.

"What's the bad news today, sir?" he asked cheerfully after his
guards left the room.

"Nothing especially bad. I've just heard that Captain Mader
once pulled you out of the Adriatic. Why haven't you ever mentioned it?"

Dorfrichter's eyes clouded over. "Should I have?" he snapped
with annoyance. "You knew I was a bad horseman. Now I am
also a bad swimmer!"

"Goddamn it, Dorfrichter!" Kunze flared. "I'm not interested
in your physical fitness. I want to know whether or not you killed
the man who pulled you out of the sea, Richard Mader."

"I've told you I didn't! But you don't want to believe me. You
keep dragging in events that have nothing to do with the case. I
told you I didn't kill Klára Brassay, but you had her dug up,
ordered an autopsy, and where are you? It would've been simpler
and cheaper to take my word in the first place."

He knows we found no poison, Kunze thought. *Someone's told
him about the result of the postmortem and set his mind at ease,
which accounts for his looking relaxed and at peace with himself.
Six weeks of solitary confinement should have left their mark on
him, but obviously haven't and he hasn't asked about his wife and
child. Before, they were constantly on his mind. Doesn't he wonder what his wife's reaction is to the Brassay affair? He must
assume that the story has reached the papers. Is he in touch with
his wife? It wouldn't be the first time that messages were smug-
gled in and out of prison.*

Kunze returned to the business at hand. "I'm amazed at you, Lieutenant. Your vanity seems to be stronger than your instinct for self-preservation. If Mader really did save you from drowning, you'd be a monster to want to kill him. And I still don't believe you're a monster!"

"Frankly, sir, I've reached the point where I don't much care what you believe. I only wish you wouldn't try to solve this case by reading my palm. Find a witness who saw me mail the damned circulars or sold me the poison. But you won't, because there is no such person!"

"Perhaps. And perhaps we've already found him."

"Well, then, produce him and put me before a court-martial. Let's get it over with! How long do you want to drag out this cat-and-mouse game?"

Kunze rose to step closer to him. "I asked you: Did Mader pull you out of the water or didn't he?"

"None of your goddamn business!" Dorfrichter shouted. "Dig him up, too, and ask him yourself!"

Kunze paled. "That'll be all for today!"

Angrily he called in the guard and had Dorfrichter taken to the anteroom, where he remained until Provost Tuttman came puffing upstairs to escort him back to his cell.

"The bastard didn't ask about his wife!" Kunze reported to Stoklaska. "I have a feeling he's heard from her. They might be communicating." He lighted a cigarette. No matter how hard he tried, he couldn't keep his hand from shaking as he held the match. "I wouldn't put it beyond Dr. Goldschmiedt if he'd arranged it. He tried to have the case switched to a civilian court and didn't succeed. Now he'll try something else. He is not the kind to give up easily." While he talked he felt his aides' eyes on him. Lieutenant Dorfrichter wasn't the first suspect who had turned nasty during interrogation. However, they'd never known Captain Kunze to lose his calm.

On his way home he stopped at the Security Bureau to tell Inspector Weinberger about his suspicion and to have Marianne Dorfrichter put under police surveillance. Beginning the following morning, the Gruber apartment was to be closely watched and every person visiting Marianne quietly investigated.

"Incidentally," the inspector said, "if you hadn't come to see me, I'd have come to you tomorrow. After your telephone call about the Hotel Herrenhaus, I contacted the Linz police. They did speak to the concierge and the headwaiter at the hotel, but neither wanted to remember any incident in connection with Peter Dorfrichter. Then yesterday I had a letter from a detective on the Linz force. He wrote that he had some information that might interest us and would come to Vienna, but his chief wants us to pay his expenses. I answered in a telegram that we would, and he'll be here in the morning."

IX

THE detective, Johann Schiff, came originally from the Tyrol and looked as though he had never left his mountains for a city job in Linz. He wore a dark-green woolen suit with silver buttons, heavy boots and a rakish felt hat with a chamois brush. His skin was the weather-parched skin of a game warden, though the high color may also have resulted from the sunshine that comes in bottles. His chief had described him as one of his most intelligent and trustworthy men.

"Last fall I had some business in Vienna and was returning to Linz on the riverboat," he told Kunze. "It was the twenty-first of September, an unseasonably warm day. The Danube was very calm, but there are always some people who get seasick at the mere sight of a wave, and that's what happened to this young girl: Mitzi Haverda. I have two daughters, and when I saw her turn green and move to the rail, I asked the skipper for a glass of brandy, took it to her, and made her drink it. Then I talked her into stretching out on deck, and in no time she was feeling better. She told me that she was going to Linz in answer to a want ad. The ad had been placed in a Vienna paper by a couple looking for a young 'congenial' housekeeper. She had sent them her references and her photograph, to which the husband replied that he would meet her at the landing pier. The girl was unusually pretty, and I wondered why they didn't want her to go straight to their address. We'd had several cases of white slavery: young girls lured to hotel rooms, anesthetized, and shipped to a brothel in the

Orient, so I became suspicious. I told the girl to go along with whatever the man might suggest. I would follow them and step in at the right moment." The detective took a deep breath. "Well, it was just as I expected. Oh, yes, the husband had written her—quote, 'hold a rose between your pretty lips,' unquote—which, too, sounded rather strange. She'd bought the rose in Vienna the night before and it wasn't much of a rose by the time she disembarked with it clamped between her teeth. People stared at her, wondering what she was up to, but the rose served its purpose, for a young man immediately went up to her, took her by the arm, and led her to a waiting fiacre. She looked at me to see if I was following, and I signalled to her not to worry. I heard him give the address to the driver. It was the Herrenhaus, and that confirmed my suspicion. At the hotel, I followed them into the lobby. He must have rented a room earlier in the day, for he took her straight upstairs. I let them have a head start of half a flight, then went after them and watched them disappear into a third-floor room. A waiter saw me and notified the house detective and the manager. They thought they'd caught a sneak thief, but I identified myself and told them the nature of my business. They acted as though a male guest had never before entertained a female in one of their rooms since the reputation of their stately old barn was at stake. They wanted me to leave the matter to them, but I insisted that we break up the tête-à-tête. The door was locked, but we were let in without any trouble. We found them seated at the table with an almond *torte* and a bottle of sweet wine in front of them. The young man acted outraged, but I insisted that he come with me to the precinct station. This made him reconsider. He identified himself as First Lieutenant Dorf-richter. He admitted having lured the girl to the hotel under false pretenses. Nevertheless, all he had in mind was an 'innocent little adventure,' provided the girl was willing. Linz being a garrison town, we don't take the escapades of young officers too seriously, so I was inclined to forget the whole thing if his regimental command confirmed his identity. So we walked to the command post —it's only a few blocks from the hotel—and there the officer on duty corroborated his statements."

"Did you tell them at the command post why you wanted him identified?" Kunze asked.

"Yes, sir. I hoped he'd get a thorough dressing down."

"And did he?"

"No, sir. The officer on duty handled the whole thing as a capital joke. He even promised the lieutenant not to tell his wife. That's how I found out that Lieutenant Dorfrichter was married."

"Do you, by any chance, remember the name of the officer on duty?"

"I do, sir," the detective answered, producing a notebook. Glancing into it, he went on: "He was Second Lieutenant Xavier Vanini. I jotted it down because I didn't like his attitude. I've told you I have two daughters—I wouldn't find it a capital joke if a young man were taking *them* to a hotel."

"Vanini." For a moment Kunze had to think where he had heard the name before. Then he remembered. The officer whose orderly had tried to buy the cyanide at Ritzberger's. There was nothing unusual about the name's popping up again. Someone had to be on duty at the command post, any second lieutenant of the Fourteenth Infantry Regiment. On that evening it happened to be Vanini. A mere coincidence.

"What did you do about the girl?" Kunze asked the detective.

"I told her to wait in the hotel lobby. When I finished at the post, I took her to the railroad station, bought her a third-class ticket, and put her on the train to Vienna. I thought I was going to see the last of her. You can imagine my surprise, sir, when a week later I ran into her on Mozartstrasse. First, she tried to lie her way out: She was just passing through Linz, but when I threatened to arrest her for vagrancy, she broke down and admitted that she was living with Lieutenant Dorfrichter in Waldeck. That's one of our suburbs."

"Living with him? Didn't he live at home?"

"He rented a room for her in a private house and saw her every day. Sometimes at nights, too. I warned her to get out of town within twenty-four hours, or I'd arrest her for prostitution. That scared her and maybe scared the lieutenant even more, for the next day she was gone."

"Did you contact the lieutenant?"

"No, sir, I didn't. We have orders to show tact and understanding when dealing with officers, especially hot-blooded young gentlemen. Service in a peacetime army can be frustrating. They've

got to let steam off once in a while. But the girl, she was something else. Daughter of honest, God-fearing working people. So
when we come across a case like that, we do our best to bring the
girl in question back to her senses by whatever means we find
most effective."

Kunze eyed the man pensively. Detective, policeman, law en-
forcer in a city of sixty-five thousand souls. A man blessed with
an almost Biblical approach to duty and a blithe disregard for
laws and ordinances whenever they proved impractical. Always
muddling through with flying colors, just like all his superiors
and the entire Austrian bureaucracy. Young officers allowed to
let off steam for the good of the country and daughters of the
working class kept on the straight and narrow, also for the good
of the country.

"Have Dorfrichter brought up," Kunze ordered Stoklaska. When
the lieutenant left the office to send word to Provost Tuttman,
Kunze turned to the detective.

"Herr Schiff, I want you to take a good look at Lieutenant
Dorfrichter. I will ask you if you recognize him as the man you
found in the company of a young woman in a room at the Hotel
Herrenhaus in Linz on September twenty-first. If he is the same
man, merely answer in the affirmative. Nothing more or less.
That'll be all we want from you at this time. Afterward Lieutenant Heinrich will accompany you to the paymaster's window to
collect your fare and expense money. We appreciate your coming
here and giving us some very valuable information."

While they waited for Dorfrichter, Kunze pretended to pore
over documents on his desk. He tried to focus his attention on
the papers, but it strayed. The prospect of an encounter with
the lieutenant filled him with nervous tension. As always, he both
feared and desired it. He looked forward to each meeting expecting a miracle and felt spent and disappointed when it failed to
materialize. He could no longer fool himself with the explanation
that the development he so desperately wished for was the man's
confession. That he desired, too, as impatiently as ever, but there
had to be more. A wall coming down, a bridge built, a hand
proffered, a word spoken. He prided himself on the fact that all
his life he had been in control of his emotions. But now suddenly,
on the threshold of middle age, an infection grew inside him, an

illness no drug could suppress or cure. In calmer moments he clearly expected it to disappear much like a bout of hay fever. In his relationship with the man there was no direction and no hope. Nevertheless, of all his days and nights only the moments spent in the same room with Peter Dorfrichter contained significance. They were like green islands in the shallow, muddy river of wasted time.

As usual, Dorfrichter entered the room with Provost Tuttman at his side and a soldier with fixed bayonet behind. As he caught sight of Detective Schiff, he froze on the threshold. Throwing a hostile glance at Kunze, he then snapped to attention. Stoklaska and Heinrich arose and returned his salute; Kunze acknowledged it with a nod. Dorfrichter's presence made him feel as though the oxygen had been sucked from the air. It made breathing difficult. At the same time, the hunter in him noticed the prisoner's momentary shock at Detective Schiff's unexpected appearance. A more pronounced shock than the appearance of any other witness.

Kunze dismissed the escorts and turned to the detective. "Herr Schiff, will you please face the lieutenant! And tell me whether or not you have seen him before?"

Schiff's eyes had been on Dorfrichter ever since the lieutenant entered the room. "Yes, sir, I have seen the lieutenant before."

"Is he the individual you observed meeting a young girl named Mitzi Haverda at the Linz pier on the twenty-first of September and found an hour later with the same girl in a room of the Hotel Herrenhaus in Linz?"

"Yes, sir. He is the same individual."

"Thank you, Herr Schiff. You may leave now."

The detective bowed stiffly. Kunze and Stoklaska shook his hand, and Heinrich ushered him from the room. From the threshold he threw a parting glance at Dorfrichter, but the lieutenant ignored it.

When the door closed behind the two, Dorfrichter turned to the captain in mock exasperation.

"What the hell did you do that for? So I slept with the girl! Does that prove that I killed Richard Mader?"

The tone of banter caught Kunze unawares. This wasn't suspect talking to investigator, but comrade to comrade. It was more disconcerting than a display of hostility.

"Hell, Dorfrichter, you lured an unsuspecting young woman under false pretenses to Linz and led her straight to a hotel with the obvious intent of seducing her."

"What else? You don't take a girl to a hotel to play cribbage. As for luring her to Linz under false pretenses, that's how it appeared to that old buzzard of a detective. The fact is, when the girl answered our ad, she didn't seem like someone who wanted to work very hard. She wrote that she *wasn't* prepared to do any heavy work like washing windows and scrubbing floors and that she'd been employed only in male households before, homes of bachelors or widowers. That's why my wife immediately decided against hiring her. By then my wife was in her sixth month, and almost from the beginning of her pregnancy I'd been staying away from her on doctor's orders. The girl looked damn pretty on the picture she'd enclosed, so I thought I'd take a chance and write her. She came and had no objections when I took her to the hotel. We were having a pleasant chat when the detective burst in and dragged me to the police station and then the command post. When he put her on the train, I thought that was the end of the incident. A day later I got a letter from her apologizing for the inconveniences she'd caused me and offering to come back to Linz. I jumped at the offer—who wouldn't have?—and she came. The rest you know. You see, sir, I am not such a villain after all. Anyway, to dispel your misgivings: She was no virgin, so no irreparable damage was done."

Kunze found himself chuckling. "You're a bastard, Dorfrichter." He found it almost impossible to steel himself against the insolent charm that made even his brazen self-assurance seem appealing. He gave him a long searching look. What he now saw was an extremely handsome young man with the pale, delicate complexion of a Tiepolo angel, the warm, soulful eyes of a hunting dog and the lascivious lower lip of a Spanish Bourbon.

"Did your wife know about Mitzi Haverda?" he asked.

The Tiepolo skin took on a slightly chalky hue.

"No, of course not! May I ask you a question, sir?"

"Go ahead!"

"Are you married?"

The way the question was asked made Kunze uncomfortable.

"No, of course not."

Dorfrichter grinned. "That's what I thought! If you were married, you'd know that adultery is a misdemeanor, unless your wife finds out about it. Then it becomes a capital crime, and you're lucky if you get away with a life sentence." He fell silent for a moment. "I hope, sir, the press won't ferret this out. I mean the incident with Mitzi. My wife's had a lot to bear—with me here and the child. She wouldn't understand how insignificant such a thing is, how little the girl meant to me. Hell, sir, I don't have to defend myself before you—you're a man—but women simply refuse to accept the facts of life. Especially my wife. She'd be hurt—she's miserable enough as it is. There's a limit to what a person can stand."

"You should have thought of that in September!"

"For God's sake, Captain, September was in another life! We were an average couple, not the circus freaks we are now. I never cheated on her before and was not going to make a habit of it in the future. How could I know that within a few months every petty incident of my life would become common knowledge from Salzburg to Mostar?" He took a deep breath. "Sir, you can prevent the leakage of any information from this office. I'm respectfully asking you to keep the Haverda incident from the press. Not for my sake, but for my wife's. To protect her from a shock."

For the first time in the course of the investigation, Dorfrichter showed himself to be vulnerable. Like every man, he had his Achilles' heel. It was the woman with the indecently bulging body and the angel face. (Kunze had not seen her since the official visit to the Gruber apartment, and that was how he remembered her. And that, he thought, was how Dorfrichter must have remembered her, too.) What was her hold on him? Kunze wondered. Certainly not sex, because in that case Dorfrichter wouldn't have been able to make love to Mitzi Haverda with the ease and insouciance of a tomcat. Not her wit or intelligence; she didn't give the impression of being especially brilliant. Not her giving him a son, for he always seemed more concerned about her than the child. Whatever it was, though, his feeling for her seemed to be the strongest factor in helping him preserve his equilibrium during the lengthy investigation.

"I can't promise you anything," Kunze told him. "There are always a few reporters keeping watch in front of this building.

They may not have recognized Detective Schiff, but if they have, you can be sure they'll find out what business he had here."

Dorfrichter frowned. "He's such a righteous bastard, he'll be delighted to tell them!"

"I won't be able to help that. I personally release as little news as possible to reporters. For that, I've become the favorite target of press attacks and parliamentary criticism for my—as they put it —lack of cooperation. You'd be surprised what names I've been called."

Dorfrichter threw him a sly glance. "They're on my side." He didn't ask it; he stated it.

Kunze nodded. "So it seems."

"They'll be glad when, in the end, you have to let me go." The lieutenant grinned. "That will, of course, delay your promotion to major."

I'm not doing this for promotion, Kunze wanted to tell him but didn't. How could he explain his motives to a man who'd been willing to kill ten of his comrades for a *promotion?* Or had he really been able? the captain suddenly wondered. Wasn't he, Emil Kunze, the only person stubbornly believing in his guilt? Hadn't everyone else connected with the investigation doubted his guilt at one time or another? Hadn't that doubt appeared in Stoklaska's and Heinrich's eyes on several occasions? He looked at the face smiling at him across the desk, wishing fervently that he could read the thoughts behind the smooth forehead. In a century when man was to explore the depths of the oceans and the air masses of the atmosphere, the most limitless region was still another person's mind!

"You're a stubborn fellow, Dorfrichter," Kunze pointed out. "You don't want to admit that you could lose this game!"

"I might lose a hand or two, but not the game! I have great respect for your ingenuity, sir, but I have a feeling that you follow guidelines that are more or less obsolete. You go along with Joseph de Maistre when you say, 'A battle lost is a battle one thinks one has lost, for a battle cannot be lost physically.' So you try to break down my morale by keeping me in solitary confinement, conjuring up ghosts of my past, including some insignificant love affairs. Well, this kind of warfare was very effective in Napoleon's days, but today Skoda is building a three hundred five-mm mortar and Krupp a four hundred twenty-mm gun. So if you want to defeat me, bring on your big guns. Proof that I had the cyanide in my possession, that I hectographed the circulars—and mailed them! Without that, sir, you don't have a ghost of a chance against me." He paused. "And now that we've cleared that up, may I sit down, sir?"

"But of course." The captain consented, feeling embarrassed at having let the prisoner stand all this time. He took out his case. "Smoke?"

After Dorfrichter had helped himself to a cigarette, Kunze held out the case to Stoklaska. The latter struck a match and lighted the three cigarettes.

"They say it's bad luck to light three cigarettes with the same match," Dorfrichter observed. "But whatever it is, it can't affect me. I've reached bottom. The only way for me is up."

X

THE large, beefy man had been standing in the drafty doorway since noon when he'd relieved a colleague. It was almost four now, and his feet had turned numb long ago, and the temptation to sneak away to the taproom on the corner was strong. He figured he could step inside and watch the house across the street through the window. On the other hand, he just might miss the woman. He had followed her the day before and had had a hard time keeping up with her. She'd been like a weasel, swift, unpredictable, blending into the scenery. He had damn near lost her once on Franz Josefs-Kai and again on Schottenring.

He was still debating with himself over the advisability of a quick glass of wine when she emerged from the shadows of the porte cochere. In the foggy twilight, she looked even smaller than he remembered her. One meter and twenty-five centimeters, that's what he'd put down in his report, but now one fifteen seemed more likely. When Inspector Weinberger had asked him to describe her, he hadn't known whether to call her an undersized woman or an oversized midget. She wore the same dark gray winter coat with an astrakhan collar as the day before and held a muff of the same fur. She resembled a little girl dressed for a costume party.

This time, too, she headed for the quay, but not without stopping for a moment on the sidewalk and glancing up and down the street. Was it caution? the detective wondered. Did she know she would be followed? Evidently not, because she walked at an even pace, not looking back. He had to allow her a half a block start, which made keeping up with her difficult. She turned into Türkenstrasse, which convinced him she was headed for the Gruber apartment at 32 Hahngasse. On Deutchmeister Platz, instead of following her, he veered to the right, continuing along the Danube Canal at a fast gallop. Puffing and panting, he raced down Grünertorgasse and reached the Hahngasse entrance of the Gruber house half a minute before the woman. Looking back from the doorway, he detected the silhouette of a colleague in the shadows of an arch on the opposite side of the street. He started upstairs but slowed as he heard the clatter of her tiny boots on the stone steps. His heavy breathing echoed through the low tunnel of the stairway. As she was about to pass him, he reached out one hamlike hand and grabbed her by the arm. Through the heavy coat sleeve her bone felt as fragile as that of a bird's wing. For a split second, she was surprised; then screaming a wild curse, she tried to break free.

"Police, Frau Pausch," he panted. "You're under arrest!"

By then his colleague was coming up the steps. "Have you got her?" he asked. Reaching them, he took hold of her other arm, pulling her down the steps toward the light in the arched entranceway.

"You can't do this to me!" she screamed. "We're not in Russia! I'm a respectable woman! A citizen. I'll make you pay for this. There are courts in this country. Even if I have to go to the emperor!"

"He is a busy man, the emperor is, Frau Pausch," the detective muttered. He was often amazed at the nerve of people. One would catch a pickpocket in the act, and the first thing one heard from him was the emperor's name. "Let me have the letter, Frau Pausch!"

"What letter?" she asked.

"You know what letter. If you don't hand it over voluntarily, Frau Pausch, we'll have to search you."

"Not without a warrant—you can't!"

"Here is the warrant, Frau Pausch." The large detective showed it to her under the light. It had been issued by the attorney general's office that morning. It was written in neat, clerical hand, and there was no doubt about its legality.

She read it with a slight frown.

"All right," she told them, "you can have the letter. But not here. I have it tucked under my camisole." Her defiant look dared them to take it.

Inspector Weinberger's voice came from the other end of the wire. "I have news for you. Your instinct was correct. Dorfrichter has been in contact with his wife. For quite some time now. We've caught the carrier pigeon with his letter under her wing."

"A pigeon?" Kunze frowned.

"A woman."

"Who is she?"

"A seamstress named Sophie Pausch."

"Never heard of her."

"I didn't think you had. I'm holding her in my office. I'd rather not discuss it on the phone. Would it be too inconvenient for you to come over during the afternoon?"

Kunze glanced at the clock on his desk. "No, not at all. I can come right now."

At first glance, the person huddled in the worn leather armchair in Weinberger's office looked like a child. Then she lifted her head, and the lamplight revealed a parchment-yellow skin crisscrossed by fine lines of age. Only her eyes were young, dark and bright, the eyes of a trapped mouse. She wore a green wool dress under the gray winter coat and laced two-tone boots. Her feet did not quite reach the floor.

Weinberger had risen to greet Kunze. They shook hands; then the inspector addressed the woman. "This is Captain Kunze. He is a very kind man. Talk to him frankly and honestly, and he'll see to it that your punishment won't be too harsh."

"I don't care if he shoots me dead!" Her voice was shrill, that of a street urchin. "It's my brother I'm worried about. What will happen to him?" Sliding from the armchair, she faced Kunze with the belligerence of a fighting cock.

Puzzled, Kunze looked at Weinberger. "Her brother?"

The inspector grimaced unhappily. "This is something I didn't want to tell you over the phone. She is Provost Tuttman's sister."

Speechless, Kunze stared at him.

"No!" he said finally, his astonishment turning to anger. He couldn't tell at whom he was angry, Tuttman, Dorfrichter or this grotesque little woman. "Has he lost his mind?" He turned on her. "What made him do it? Money? Who bribed him? Frau Dorfrichter? Dr. Goldschmiedt?"

"Nobody bribed him," she shouted back. "There's no money in the world that could buy him. You may not know it, sir, because he is not an officer, so you never bothered to find out what kind of a man he was. You gentlemen look at the uniform, never the man who wears it."

It was a deluge of words. Both men tried to cut in, without success. At last, losing his patience, Inspector Weinberger raised his voice to a volume that Kunze thought caused the window-panes to shake.

"Shut your mouth, goddamn it! And you'd better answer the captain's questions truthfully, or your brother will rot in irons for the rest of his days."

The look she gave him was whimsical. "You don't scare me, Inspector. Nobody rots in irons nowadays. All right." She faced Kunze. "What do you want to know?"

"Who hired you?"

"Nobody hired me. I volunteered."

"I don't believe you."

"I didn't expect you to. You're not the kind of person who would understand someone like me."

"Get to the facts, damn you!" Inspector Weinberger barked.

"All right. The facts. I saw this poor dear woman's picture in a magazine, then read that she had just had a baby—and my brother kept telling me what a fine gentleman Lieutenant Dorfrichter was. He'd never had a better prisoner! So one evening I said to my brother—he is a widower and I keep house for him—'Johann,' I said, 'we've got to help these unfortunate people. It's our Christian duty, Johann.' He refused at first, but I kept after him, so in the end he said he'd talk to the lieutenant. In the meanwhile I went to see Frau Dorfrichter. It took me a long time to convince her that she could trust me. I told her: 'Try me, what have you got to lose?' So she gave me a short note, and I gave it to my brother, and he gave it to the lieutenant. And then my brother left a sheet of paper and pencil under the lieutenant's pillow. I took the letter to Frau Dorfrichter. I've never seen a more beautiful longhand. His every line is like a string of pearls!"

"How long has this been going on?" Kunze asked.

"About two weeks. Believe me, sir, my brother would never have done it if it hadn't been for Christmas. It's inhuman to keep an innocent man locked up like a wild animal, without as much as a Christmas greeting from his family."

"How do you know he is innocent?" The story was bizarre, but Kunze found himself believing it.

"He says he is. Besides, the people think so, too. Everyone does."

This Kunze had known for some time. Day after day there were anonymous letters in his mail, some pleading, some insulting, some threatening. Even if a few had been written by Dorfrichter's family or friends, all of them had not been. The pictures that appeared in the papers showed a young officer smiling innocently into the photographer's lens. There was nothing sinister about him. He exuded warmth and charm, and women cut out his photo and pinned it next to the pictures of matinee idols on their walls. In person, his charm was even more irresistible. Otherwise, a man like Provost Tuttman would not have risked his livelihood for him.

"You maintain that neither you nor your brother accepted money from the Dorfrichters?"

"I do," she said, pulling herself to her full height.

"Did they offer you any?"

"Frau Dorfrichter did, but I refused it."

Kunze shook his head. "How very noble." He flashed a half-amused, half-exasperated glance at the inspector. "What next?"

Weinberger handed him a folded paper. "Here is the letter we caught her with."

Both sides of the sheet were filled in a fine flowing hand. Indeed, the lines did look like pearls strung on a thread. Kunze let his eyes glide over them. They contained a man's avowal of his deep and undying affection for a woman. It surprised him that a man of Dorfrichter's brilliance would use the worn and slightly stilted phrases of a lovesick schoolboy. Evidently, Kunze mused, love had a very limited vocabulary; besides, one found another man's passion ludicrous unless one was uncontrollably attracted to the man, in which case one found it painful. One thought recurred throughout the letter: Peter Dorfrichter could not lose if Marianne Dorfrichter stood by him. He was an innocent fighting against overwhelming odds. However, with her love he could win the fight.

After Inspector Weinberger had Frau Pausch escorted from the room, he said, "I don't envy you, Captain. I've been a policeman for thirty-five years, but I've never come across a more trying case. Trying for the investigator, that is."

Kunze was still staring at the letter. "Do you think he is innocent? I mean, do you ever have doubts?"

Weinberger reflected for a moment. "I don't know. Sometimes I do. But of course, I'm not in as close contact with the man as you are. The fact that he had a simple soul like Provost Tuttman under his spell would not influence me. The most charming man I've ever met during my career was an embezzler. He was such delightful company that I felt robbed when I had to hand him over to the judge. He was guilty as hell, yet I'd rather have had him to dinner at my house than the judge. This is one of the dangers of our profession: Sometimes we find the criminal more fascinating than the solid citizen, mainly because he is the more fascinating individual. He presents a puzzle, a challenge. The solid citizen seldom does."

Weinberger had a feeling that Kunze was not listening. He seemed to be grappling with some problem, and the inspector fell silent to let him listen to his own thoughts.

"I'd like to try something if you agree, Inspector," Kunze finally said. "I'd like to let the correspondence continue between the Dorfrichters."

Weinberger nodded. "That could be arranged."

"How? I don't think the Pausch woman would cooperate. You can't talk sense to an idealist. They are a pain in the ass."

"I'm not thinking of her. I'd like to get a woman from the Security Bureau. She could deliver Dorfrichter's letters to his wife with the explanation that Sophie Pausch was taken ill."

Kunze nodded. "I'll have Provost Tuttman arrested today, but not while he's on duty. I'll wait until he gets home. His arrest must be kept a secret, especially from the press. I'll have an absolutely reliable man take Tuttman's place at the prison. He'll tell Dorfrichter that Tuttman, too, is ill. Let's hope Dorfrichter doesn't suspect the truth."

"What do you expect to gain?"

"Wait! I haven't finished! I want you to give all the details of the Mitzi Haverda incident to the press."

The inspector gave him a contemplative look. "When?"

"The sooner, the better."

"You're determined to break Dorfrichter, aren't you?"

"I am."

"And you think this will do the trick?"

"I hope so. His wife will be hurt and may even turn against him. That's what he fears, or he wouldn't have tried to wheedle a promise from me to keep the thing quiet."

The next day the *Neue Freie Presse* printed an exclusive report on the Mitzi Haverda incident. Marianne Dorfrichter slept late. Since her husband's arrest, sleep had been her sole refuge from the terrors of the days. She was awake twice during the night to nurse her child but fell asleep immediately afterward. Johann Ludwig, christened the day before—Johann for his paternal and Ludwig for his maternal grandfather—was an exceptionally good baby. Marianne had feared that he would show the effects of the shock she had suffered before his birth, but this had not happened.

Somehow, though, she had failed to experience the ecstasies of motherhood that new mothers were supposed to feel. It was hard to realize that this was her child and would remain her responsibility for the rest of his life or at least until he was grown. The future terrified her anyway, though her moments of black despondency, during which she could foresee no end to her separation from her husband, had been less frequent since the visits of Frau Pausch. At least she knew Peter still loved her. Before, she had often visualized him in his horrible cell, a man kept in agonizing solitary confinement, feeling himself forsaken by everyone and turning bitter against the world. At the same time that his letters reassured her they made her long for him more desperately. In the night she would dream and waken, her body aching with desire. This, too, frightened her because she had considered sexual appetite to be the man's prerogative; women were created to satisfy it, but not necessarily to draw pleasure from the act.

Despite her overpowering love for him, she had entered the room of the Baden bei Wien hotel where they were to spend their wedding night with the trepidation of a sacrificial lamb. She hadn't known what to expect, merely that she would be used and hurt. Her mother had sent her off with a few hasty and cryptic intimations: A woman might hate it and still become pregnant; she had better keep herself clean because men easily lost their bearings in the dark; she should never let the man know that intercourse bored her—otherwise, she would bore him.

She was used and hurt that night and for some time afterward lived in a daze. The transition from pedestal to mattress had been too swift. She had never before seen a man in underwear, much less a man in underwear urinating into a chamber pot beside her bed. Closing her eyes, she stuffed her fingers in her ears and would look at him again only when he was fully clothed in his uniform with its gold braid and shiny buttons. Even then, however, he seemed a total stranger, and she could summon not the slightest vestige of her former love for him. Numb and empty, she thought alternately of suicide or entering a convent. Then suddenly everything changed, and she could remember clearly just when the inexplicable change occurred. They were going to take a walk, and he went downstairs to wait for her. She stepped through the door of the hotel, and when she saw him standing in the street, his slim, graceful figure outlined against the autumnal garden hedge, her passion for him welled up in her with the force of a tidal wave. It seemed as though he had been away and—just when she was ready to give him up for lost—returned safely. She flew to him, taking his arm. The body that had disgusted her became as familiar as her own. She never told him about the agony of those early days. He had been too deeply immersed in the pleasure of possessing her, and if he had noticed it, he more than likely attributed it to a girl's natural reaction to losing her virginity. He was an experienced lover and, after her initial shock wore off, knew how to awaken the female in her. She adored every minute of her days spent with him but found their lovemaking their crowning glory. When they furnished their apartment, they chose a sedate bedroom set with twin beds, but she preferred to sleep with him in his. Jealous of his time spent with others, she made him shed his bachelor friends, shun their card games and stag parties. Her pregnancy caused the first interruption in the happy routine of their marriage. At the beginning of her fifth month, around the end of July, she began hemorrhaging and her doctor advised total abstinence from marital intercourse, and thereafter she and Peter slept in separate beds. She started hating pregnancy, considering her bloated body obscene. Peter remained unchanged, gentle and loving, assuring her that no sex was a minor privation in payment for the fabulous gift of their child. She believed him because she wanted to, but her ears were tuned with extra sharpness to the tone of his voice, her gaze searching his face whenever he returned home. His duty hours seemed longer, but he'd been transferred from Sarajevo to Linz only two months before, and she knew that every garrison made different demands on its personnel. Impatiently she counted the days until her delivery but before her time came, the sky had caved in on her.

On this January morning she glanced at her watch on the night table. It showed five past ten. Johann was asleep, and nothing stirred in the apartment. Her mother would be downstairs in the store, and the maid gone to do the marketing. Marianne rose, slipped on a pink flannel negligee and the new pantofles her sister Tilda had given her for Christmas, and went to fetch the morning paper. This was always the first thing she did after awakening, her secret hope being that one morning she'd read of Peter's release. For a short while after Dr. Goldschmiedt had entered the case, she had been in high spirits, then, when nothing happened, felt bitterly disappointed. Nevertheless, she had not lost faith in the attorney or in her husband's ultimate redemption.

The paper was not in the dining room, which she found odd, for her mother always left it on the buffet. She felt a touch of anger at the maid, who must have mislaid it when she cleaned the room. She was searching the kitchen when the maid, a straw shopping bag in each hand, struggled in from the corridor. As she opened the kitchen door, a gust of icy January wind hit Marianne in the face.

"Where is the morning paper?" she asked.

The girl shrugged. "How should I know?" After dropping the

bags, she blew on her hands, then turned her back on Marianne and began unpacking the groceries.

"Go down to the corner and get one!"

The girl didn't look up. "Now?"

"Now!"

"If I were you, I wouldn't read the paper today," she said, a touch of truculence in her voice.

Marianne felt her head swim. There was bad news in the paper; that's why her mother had hidden it. *Peter has confessed* flashed through her mind; then she reprimanded herself. Nevertheless, the thought refused to die.

"Bring me a paper! Right this minute!"

The maid shrugged, gave her a nasty look, then flounced out, slamming the door behind her.

Fifteen minutes passed before she returned. Marianne remained in the kitchen, slumped on a stool, her face cradled in her palms. She lifted her head when she heard the girl enter.

"What kept you so long?" she asked in a tortured voice.

The maid flung down the folded copy. "You'll read it soon enough. I had to run all the way to the news kiosk on Schotten-ring. No tobacco shop around here had a single copy left." Her gaze was fixed on Marianne, as she waited for her reaction.

Marianne picked up the *Presse* without looking at it and left the kitchen. In the privacy of her room, she spread it out on the bed. The Mitzi Haverda story was in the first column on the third page. The *Presse* had done a thorough job; its staff had already interviewed Mitzi, as well as Detective Schiff. The report, written as though the information had come from the Linz police, had been corroborated by Judge Advocate Captain Kunze's office.

Marianne reread the piece for the third time before the facts became clear in her mind. She remembered Mitzi Haverda as one of the applicants who'd answered their ad for a "mother's helper" in September. She even remembered her picture, a pretty girl dressed in a form-fitting dirndl, her braided hair coiled on her head in Empress Elisabeth fashion. Some instinct must have warned her, for Marianne was immediately opposed to hiring the girl. She had given the picture to Peter to be returned. Instead, he had written the slut to come to Linz, and they had become lovers while she was getting heavy and ugly with his child. She could never again believe a word of his! While pretending to be as much in love with her as ever, he had sneaked off to sleep with a cheap little bitch, who wanted forty kronen a month but wasn't willing to scrub floors or wash windows.

The pain was so sharp that it made her gasp. The baby woke and began to wail at the top of his healthy lungs. Marianne jumped to her feet. She was going to kill herself and her child. Throw herself out the window with him in her arms. She was at the crib reaching for him when the absurdity of the idea hit her. His small skull would surely crack open on the pavement while she might possibly survive! Her arms dropped, and falling to her knees, she buried her face in Johann's pretty pillow with the embroidered forget-me-nots, a gift from her sister Tilda. She sensed about her the emptiness of death. A cycle had come to its end, and she saw no reason to enter a new one. There were two kinds of people: suns and satellites. She was born a satellite, and now her sun had burned to ashes in a self-consuming fire, and she was left to revolve around a void. Strangely, her anger was directed not at her husband, but at herself, as if she had committed a grave misdeed. Her wish was to punish herself, inflict pain on herself, make herself bleed in retaliation for the undefinable crime she was burdened with. Looking around frantically, her eyes fell on the sharp scissors lying next to a half-finished baby shirt. Savagely she stabbed her left wrist with them. The pain was sharp, and blood trickled from the cut vein. She screamed and collapsed on the floor.

When she came to, she saw that the bleeding had stopped. Her negligee was spotted, and a few drops had fallen on the rug, but that was all the damage done. She washed the negligee in the bathroom, then bandaged her wrist loosely with a handkerchief. The spots on the Dokhara didn't show. This was the advantage of Persian rugs; they could absorb the soil of centuries without losing their beauty. Too bad, she mused, humans weren't made that way.

The bell rang, and she heard the maid answering the door and an unfamiliar female voice asking for Frau Dorfrichter. Before the maid could call her, Marianne stepped into the entrance hall.

The woman was middle-aged, wearing a shabby tweed suit and carrying a large purse.

"Frau Dorfrichter?" she asked.

Marianne answered with a nod.

"Frau Pausch sent me. Her brother was taken ill suddenly—the doctor thinks he has pneumonia—and she had to stay home to nurse him." The visitor threw a glance at the maid. "May I have a word with you alone, Frau Dorfrichter?"

Marianne led her into the dining room. When the door closed, the woman handed her a folded paper.

"This is from your husband. He gave it to Provost Tuttman yesterday." Her eyes spotted the handkerchief on Marianne's wrist. The wound must have opened, for there was a bright-red stain. "What happened to your wrist?"

"Nothing," Marianne said, her voice harsh and forbidding. Unfolding the letter, she read the avowals of eternal love. The woman's intense gaze suddenly irritated her.

"Frau Pausch said her brother would have one of his men deliver your answer to the lieutenant," the woman told her.

"There is no answer!" Marianne snapped.

"What do you want the man to tell the lieutenant if he asks why there's no answer?"

Marianne liked this woman less and less. Tiny Frau Pausch had been so wonderfully warm and concerned. Her friend in a coldly impersonal way seemed merely inquisitive.

"Just what I told you. There was no answer!"

The woman shrugged.

"And tell Provost Tuttman that he needn't bother forwarding the lieutenant's messages from now on."

"I shall tell him."

There was a moment of awkward silence.

"I imagine that's all then." The woman started for the door.

"Wait a minute!" Marianne called out to her. "I've changed my mind."

She went to her room, cut out the *Presse* report with the same scissors she'd used to slash her wrist and hastily scribbled on the margin of the page: "We're finished. I don't want to see you or hear from you again." Folding the paper, she slid it into an envelope and handed it to the woman. "Please have this delivered to the lieutenant." Then realizing she had behaved rather rudely to someone who was doing her a favor, she said quickly, "Thank you

for your troubles. I'm grateful, and if there is anything I can do—"
It occurred to her that Frau Pausch's friend might expect a tip
or at least carfare. "I am sure you had expenses and—" Her voice
trailed off when the woman shook her head briskly.

"No expenses whatsoever. Glad to have been of service, Frau
Dorfrichter. Good-bye."

As usual, Kunze arrived at his office before his staff. It was a
habit he had fallen into during the last years. He enjoyed having
a half hour to himself to be able to read the morning papers without having to listen to Rose's running commentary. Since the
second of January he'd been living in a sublease Rose had found
for him in Traungasse. It was only a block away from her house;
nevertheless, he came in just as early. He assumed he had reached
the age when it was too much of an effort to change the set routine of his life.

The apartment belonged to two elderly spinsters named Baldauf and Knoll. Their relationship remained a mystery to him,
primarily because he had never bothered to ask about it. He had
a large corner room for a study and next to it a small one which
contained a bed, a wardrobe and a washstand. The bathroom was
across the corridor. After years under the same roof with Rose,
he felt surprised and a little guilty at finding the peace and quiet
of his bachelor quarters so enjoyable.

That morning the news of the world was depressing. The Balkans were in turmoil. In Serbia the war fever, which had subsided
after Crown Prince George's abdication as heir to the throne,
had flared up again. In Crete the Greeks had decided to elect
deputies to the motherland's Parliament, and such an act would
most certainly result in conflict between Turkey and Greece.
Italy showed a renewed interest in Tripoli. There were rumors
that she was conducting secret negotiations with France and
England and offering to sever her alliance with the Central Powers in exchange for the Entente's support of her North African
claims. There were no further stories on the Mitzi Haverda affair.
The dignified *Neue Freie Presse* had evidently left the exploita-
tion of the lurid news to the boulevard papers.

Later in the morning, Stoklaska handed the captain a report
from the Veterinary Clinic concerning Dorfrichter's dog, Troll.

"High time," Kunze remarked. The report bore the letterhead "Veterinary Clinic of the University of Vienna." The dog Troll, it read, persistently refused to swallow tapeworm powder even when wrapped in a wet wafer. Filled in capsules and pressed down his throat was the only way it could be administered. So far Lieutenant Dorfrichter had told the truth. On the other hand, the clinic declared the dog to be completely free of tapeworm, and they had found no sign of any previous infestation.

"Incidentally," Stoklaska said, "the orderly who brought the report said that they were going to destroy the dog as soon as they heard from you that you considered the report satisfactory."

Kunze, still studying the paper, was slow to react to the impact of Stoklaska's words. Suddenly their meaning was clear. "Destroy the dog!" His voice sounded abnormally shrill. "Why? Who said they could destroy him?"

Puzzled, Stoklaska stared. "I don't know, Emil. That was all the orderly said."

"Call the damn fools! Tell them I don't want the animal killed or vivisected or harmed or whatever they do to the poor beasts that fall into their hands." Then after a pause: "Anyway, who the hell gave them permission to destroy him in the first place?"

Stoklaska called the clinic.

"The family did," he reported after replacing the receiver. "The university wrote to Frau Dorfrichter for instructions, and she wrote back that in her present situation she couldn't keep the dog, and would they find a good place for him? Obviously they couldn't. They say he takes up too much room and eats too much, so they must get rid of him one way or another."

"So she couldn't keep him? The bitch!"

The words had slipped out before Kunze could control his sudden anger at Marianne Dorfrichter. He was aware of Stoklaska's and Heinrich's surprised looks.

"I never knew you were such an animal lover." Stoklaska chuckled. It was an innocent remark; nevertheless, disturbing to Kunze. Pretending not to have heard it, he snapped, "Tell the bastards to send him here." Stoklaska's grin helped him recover his sense of humor. "Why not? Dorfrichter was training Troll to be a war dog, so he might as well join the army. He's got more brains than some first lieutenants I know around here."

So Troll was delivered to the office that same afternoon. He looked thin and bedraggled, holding his tail between his legs and flipping his ears back warily. When he caught sight of Kunze, however, he raced around Kunze in gradually narrowing circles, emitting short, shrill barks, then, flopped down at his feet.

"I'm afraid, Emil, you're stuck with the fellow," Stoklaska commented. "Unless you let the prisoner take the dog off your hands."

"Not on your life!" Kunze muttered, admitting to himself that the dog's performance was flattering him. The only problem was what to do with him. Finding decent people who'd keep him wouldn't be easy. So he had no choice but to take the dog along when he went home. He anticipated some trouble from the spinsters Baldauf and Knoll, but to his relief they didn't object to his having a dog.

Rose, on the other hand, showed much less understanding.

"Not again!" she greeted him as he arrived at her place with Troll in tow. Kunze had been expected for dinner, but Troll had not. "I hope you won't bring him every time you come. He sheds, you know. It took the maid three days to brush his hair off the rugs after you brought him here the last time!"

He grinned at her. "You shed pretty badly yourself. I always find your hair on my tunic. But I've never made an issue of it."

"That's not funny!" She sounded hurt. "Anyway you can't have such a big dog in an apartment. I personally could never understand why people kept pets. Parrots, maybe. They at least talk. But dogs?"

"Perhaps because they don't," Kunze told her.

The provost who'd taken Tuttman's place was a much younger man, with a friendly moon face, short-cropped blond hair and an impressive Kaiser Wilhelm mustache. He and the woman in the tweed suit had been summoned to Kunze's office. Her name was Paula Heinz, and she was on the payroll of the Security Bureau. She recounted her meeting with Marianne Dorfrichter in the clear flat tone of an impartial observer, precisely as it had taken place.

Kunze turned to the provost. "How did Lieutenant Dorfrichter react to his wife's letter?"

"He was mad as a hornet. Not at his wife, but at the newspaper report. He read the page twice, then tore it to shreds. After I left his cell, I could hear him pacing the floor slamming things around and cursing. With the captain's permission, unless I was mistaken, he mostly cursed the captain."

"You were not mistaken," Kunze said.

"He remained in a nasty mood all day yesterday," the provost went on. "Hardly touched his supper. Sent for me first thing in the morning—and gave me this letter."

He handed the paper to Kunze. Both sides of the page were filled with Dorfrichter's handwriting. Compared with the previous letter, the lines were uneven and straggly, words crossed out and punctuation haphazard, as though the writer had been in a hurry or under a strain. The Haverda affair was a concoction of the press, Dorfrichter insisted, begging his wife to believe in him and stand by him because he couldn't survive without her love.

Kunze read the letter with mixed feelings. It sounded ludicrous and at the same time pleaded for pity. Once again he wondered how a man of Dorfrichter's caliber could be so completely infatuated with a harebrained woman. Her reaction to the newspaper account of the Haverda story was exactly what Kunze had anticipated. Wasn't that proof enough that he'd judged her correctly?

"If the lieutenant asks you about this note," he said to the provost, "tell him you forwarded it to Frau Pausch. Don't tell him anything else. If he gives you more letters, hand them over to me."

"When shall I see Frau Dorfrichter?" Paula Heinz asked.

"You needn't see her again. At least not for the time being. You've been most helpful, Fräulein Heinz. I'll tell Inspector Weinberger how pleased we were with your performance."

Kunze dismissed the two and returned to what he had been occupying himself with for the past days: a thorough study of all photos, documents and correspondence collected at the Dorfrichter apartment. He concentrated on papers dating from 1908 and 1909, searching for some sign, clue or indication hitherto overlooked.

XI

BEFORE his transfer to Linz, Peter Dorfrichter had been assigned to the Thirteenth Brigade in Sarajevo, where he conducted demonstrations of artillery tactics. He had performed brilliantly as his commanding officer, Field Marshal Baron von Weigl, pointed out in his career précis. Kunze read the précis, his mind filled with resentment against the army for wasting such talent on field duty. Wasn't it understandable that frustration could drive such a man to a mad act?

Kunze knew that his feelings of leniency toward Dorfrichter were dangerous. They were beginning to blur his vision, and he had better suppress them, or his next move would be to conjure up evidence in the man's favor and, as a final step, release him. This must not happen. He could not let himself fall so dismally from grace. He must not follow the pattern set by fools like Provost Tuttman and the sentimental Frau Pausch.

He went on digging. He reread the letters Dorfrichter had written to Marianne from Sarajevo during the summer of 1908 when she was in Vienna, visiting her mother. When he had gone over the correspondence before, Kunze had been annoyed and disturbed by the constant allusions to the couple's lovemaking, past and future. It seemed as though Peter Dorfrichter considered having Marianne Gruber sharing his bed the crowning achievement of his life.

Here and there, Kunze came upon more prosaic bits of information: people Dorfrichter had seen, places he'd been to. The name Xavier appeared quite frequently.

"I had the chaps over last night, we played cards, but don't worry, not for Xavier's stakes."

Then again: "I spent the evening with Xavier. He is terribly depressed, seems to be in some trouble, as usual."

And: "Worried about Xavier. He's in bad shape. Drinks heavily, doesn't report in the mornings, lets his sergeant take the inspection."

And a few weeks later: "You're right about Xavier. But how can I turn my back on a drowning man?"

Xavier, Xavier, Xavier!

Xavier was of course Xavier Vanini. They had been close friends in Sarajevo, but not in Linz. That in itself, however, wasn't strange. Few friendships lasted forever. Young men drifted apart as they matured. Vanini seemed to be a rather unstable and inept officer, certainly not in Dorfrichter's class. They may have quarreled, or Dorfrichter may have heeded advice from Marianne, who evidently disapproved of Vanini. Yet Lieutenant Xavier Vanini was the only one among Dorfrichter's past or present friends who had had access to cyanide.

Kunze wondered if he shouldn't have Dorfrichter brought in for questioning, then immediately discarded the idea. He still didn't have enough proof. Dorfrichter would only laugh in his face again. Perhaps even create a scene. He must still be in a vile mood because of the Mitzi Haverda report. Good God, wasn't this a hopeless pursuit, a crooked Via Dolorosa they were traveling together, with two cyanide capsules at one end and a gallows at the other?

He went on digging and found another name that had special significance: Captain Baron Landsberg-Lövy, who had been one of the ten recipients of the Charles Francis circulars. That he had served a tour in Sarajevo at the same time as Dorfrichter was no news to Kunze. During the past weeks the private life and military career of each recipient had been examined and his relationship to Dorfrichter thoroughly investigated. Landsberg-Lövy, the son of an immensely rich Jewish industrialist, like many of his brethren, had entered the army during the sunny years of Austrian liberalism in the late 1890's. The army became a bighearted foster mother, once she accepted a man for her very own, and his race, creed, background, pocketbook made no difference. A rich

Jew was just as likely to succeed as a poor Gentile. After the turn of the century the threat of change lingered in the air; Franz Ferdinand was openly anti-Semitic, and with his ascendancy a trend away from liberalism was expected. However, Franz Josef was still very much alive, and with him the Austrian attitude of tolerance and enlightenment.

Kunze found two short notes written on Landsberg-Lövy's elegant stationery with the embossed crest among Dorfrichter's papers. In one, the baron expressed his dismay over X.'s lapse but promised to give the matter ample thought before taking any hasty steps. In the second, he wrote that he felt more sorry than shocked about X. and agreed to "dear Peter's" suggestion to meet him and discuss a solution satisfactory to all concerned.

X. could have been anyone, but why not Xavier Vanini?

The two notes linked three men: the suspect in a cyanide poisoning case, an intended victim, and a third person with access to cyanide! An odd triangle.

Kunze wondered why Dorfrichter, a methodical man, had considered the notes worth saving. Had the meeting mentioned in the second note ever taken place? And if so, what was the "solution satisfactory to all concerned"?

After a six-month tour of duty in Prague, Baron Landsberg-Lövy was once again stationed in Sarajevo, assigned as a staff officer to the Thirteenth Division. He had been on leave when the Charles Francis circular reached his address. By the time he returned to the division Richard Mader was dead, and warnings had been posted at all garrisons. This circumstance might have saved the baron's life, although he was a much too sophisticated man to have been tempted by capsules promising "stupefying results." But then, Kunze remembered, so was Mader, and he had succumbed to their temptation.

Kunze wrote Landsberg-Lövy a short note asking where and when they could meet in Vienna or, if this was inconvenient, in Sarajevo.

On the second of February, Provost Tuttman's case was tried by a court-martial. His plea was guilty, and he was sentenced to three years in the Mollersdorf Military Prison. His sister's case was heard by a civil court, and she was given a six months' jail sentence.

Kunze was depressed by the Tuttman judgment. He'd done all he could to help the man because he preferred a softhearted prison guard to a martinet, but General Wencel had given orders that Tuttman be made an example and Judge Advocate Szabó, in charge of the Tuttman case and recently promoted from candidate, complied.

Poor old asthmatic Tuttman. Kunze hoped he would not find prison unbearable. After all, he'd spent half his life in one. It didn't really matter on which side of the bars one lived.

The captain wondered what had possessed Tuttman to risk his livelihood for Peter Dorfrichter. Did the lieutenant hold the same outrageous attraction for the guard as he held for him? Did the fact of Tuttman's being a bachelor contain the answer to the question? Men of his class seldom remained unmarried, yet had Tuttman had any homosexual leanings, they would have become apparent, especially in the position he held. Or were they known in the guardroom, with the austere third floor of the lawcourt kept unaware of them? Poor old Tuttman, no matter how concupiscent his feelings might have been, the forfeiture of thirty years' loyal service was too severe a penalty. Another victim of the evil radiation that seemed to emanate from the man Dorfrichter.

After the ex-provost had been transferred to Mollersdorf, Kunze telephoned the prison commandant to put in a good word for the man. He was reassured to hear that the prisoner—in consideration of his experience in the same sphere of work—had already been made a trusty.

The captain had just hung up when the phone rang again.

He recognized Inspector Weinberger's voice. "I have news for you. Guess who boarded the Milan-Nice sleeping car at the Western Railroad Station last night?"

"Not the vaguest idea."

"Dr. Goldschmiedt."

"That's no news. Isn't the Côte d'Azur one of his favorite game preserves? I've heard that he has his own bed at the Hôtel de Paris in Monte Carlo and his personal linen, too."

"That he has. A trick he learned from the Russian grand

dukes. But this time he's taking a lady along to go with the bed. Evidently, he's decided not to depend on the local supply."

"That's interesting. Now I'm sure you want me to ask who the lady is. Consider yourself asked."

"Marianne Dorfrichter."

Kunze's hold on the receiver tightened. "I'll be damned. You must be mistaken."

"No. We kept her under surveillance even after Frau Pausch's arrest. For the past week, Dr. Goldschmiedt has seen her at least once a day. Then last night he drove to her house in a rented limousine, went upstairs, and returned with her and a small suitcase he carried himself. Something he's probably never done before. Carry a suitcase, I mean. Our man had enough sense to call all railway stations, so by the time the automobile reached the Western Railroad Station the police on duty there were alerted. Dr. Goldschmiedt was clever; he had a clerk take him and the lady to the train through the freight room, but he couldn't outwit us."

"It's hard to believe she'd go away with him. What about the child?"

"Some time ago her mother hired a wet nurse for the child."

"Poor bastard," Kunze said.

"The child?"

"No. Dorfrichter. We haven't left him much moral support, have we?"

"Wasn't that your idea? Not to leave him any?"

Kunze ignored the gibe. "In the unlikely case that he is innocent," he said, "where will he go? Not back home. He is not the kind who'd go back to her after this."

The inspector repeated the word. "Innocent?" He sounded somewhat incredulous. "I didn't think such a possibility had ever crossed your mind."

"Of course, it has!" Kunze was suddenly anxious to finish the conversation. "I'm no mind reader. How the hell can I be absolutely sure of a man's guilt when all I have is a few shreds of flimsy evidence?"

"It's a damn hard case," Weinberger agreed amiably. "And I don't envy you. Evidently, Frau Dorfrichter no longer shares your doubts. She's made up her mind, or she wouldn't have taken off with our friend Goldschmiedt!"

XII

COLD, bright February sunshine enveloped the huge glass dome of the Milan station. Marianne Dorfrichter stood in the corridor of the *wagon-lits* car, watching the turmoil on the platform. It reminded her of scenes in a huge kaleidoscope in which colored fragments formed a different pattern with each turn, yet somehow always managed to remain the same. There was a mother waving tearfully after a departing train, a family welcoming an arrival, lovers embracing, two little boys chasing each other in a tunnel burrowed through the dense crowd, a student lugging a heavy suitcase, passengers calling for porters and porters shouting their numbers, vendors hawking their wares, and newsboys shrieking the headlines as though they were announcing the Day of Judgment.

So this was Italy, Marianne thought. Peter had promised to show her Venice and Rome the following summer. It was to be the first of many vacations he had promised they would take together. Now she was in Italy, but not with Peter. During the night, whenever the rattle of the wheels woke her, she wondered if she shouldn't get off. She gave herself time until Milan, a long stopover while their sleeping car was coupled to the Marseilles train. One minute before they were to leave again she was still undecided.

Dr. Goldschmiedt had come to see her after he'd read the Mitzi Haverda story in the *Neue Freie Presse*. At first, she refused to see him. He insisted, and later she was glad that she had. Soothing and sympathetic, he was not at all like her mother, who had tried to convince her that what Peter had done was normal and to be expected from any husband, even the best. Frau Gruber considered her daughter foolish and self-centered, but Paul Goldschmiedt seemed to understand fully how deeply hurt she was. It was hard to recall just when he first mentioned the Riviera. He made it clear there were no demands or conditions attached to the invitation; she was not expected to do anything she didn't want to do. He was a rich man, and what was money good for if not to help one's friends? She had been through a terrible ordeal; she needed a change to preserve her health, not only for her own sake, but also for that of her child.

Marianne realized they were playing a game. And she chose to ignore the fact that she knew neither the rules nor how it would end.

A whistle blew, there was a sudden lurch when the wheels of the car began to turn, and then they were leaving Milan. She had her coat on and enough money in her purse for the fare back to Vienna, yet she didn't move. Just then, as if sensing the significance of the moment, Dr. Goldschmiedt stepped from his compartment. Tactfully he had kept his distance during the night but seemed surprised to find her dressed and in the corridor.

"I was just coming to see if you were awake and, if so, order breakfast for you," he told her.

She admitted that she was hungry, and they went to the dining car. She had had meals on trains before with efficient service and decent food, but nothing to what she experienced now. Traveling with Paul Goldschmiedt was like appearing in a well-directed play: each actor delivering a polished performance, entrances and exits on cue, nothing left to improvisation.

In Nice they were met by two limousines, a flock of footmen and a person wearing striped trousers and a black coat who looked dignified enough to be the mayor of the city.

To escape, as Dr. Goldschmiedt put it, the bloodhounds of the press, he had arranged for them to stay in a villa rented from a French aristocrat. The villa was in Èze, a good half hour's drive from Nice on a winding road that followed the capricious design of the coastline. Marianne was not to use her own name but registered with the police—this was the law for every foreigner, even those staying in private homes—as Albina Brammer, single, Catholic, Austrian national, born 1886 in Bad Gastein. She did not ask whether Albina was a real person or a figment of his imagination.

She had been looking forward to the ride, but by the time they left Nice she was too tired to keep her eyes open. She must have dozed off, for the first road sign she saw was that of ÈZE. The car was traveling on a straight stretch alongside the railway tracks, beyond which the terrain sloped gently downward to the sea. They passed the railway station and stopped in front of an ornate iron gate with the name Èze les Oeillets spelled out in grillwork letters on an arch above it. A footman opened the gate, and they entered a terraced park, passed a two-story coach house and several smaller buildings and stopped in front of the side entrance to a pink villa built in the Mediterranean style on a wide, esplanade-like projection overhanging the beach.

When Marianne stepped onto the balcony, the view staggered her. She had not known the world could be this beautiful, the sky melting into the sea and the outline of the Cap Ferrat peninsula enveloped in the mauve-colored gauze of approaching night. Mauve turned to dark gray, and the stars and the lights in the faraway houses shot out their beams simultaneously, as though switched on by the same hand.

Partir, c'est un peu mourir was one of the few French phrases she knew. But it wasn't true, she decided. To leave is not to die, but to be reborn. She was not the same person who had left the ugly Gruber apartment twenty-four hours before. She was no longer Marianne Dorfrichter, not even Albina Brammer. Perhaps she was once again the young girl who, wrapped in blankets near the open window, had watched the smoke swirl from the chimneys across the street and recognized the shadowy outlines of kings and castles and exotic flowers in it.

"Isn't it the most beautiful sight?" She heard Goldschmiedt's voice behind her.

He stepped to the railing, putting an arm on her shoulder. "Wouldn't it have been a pity to miss it?"

She nodded. "It would." But somehow the spell was broken, and she was again Marianne Dorfrichter.

Nevertheless, she found herself both distracted and amused by the business of getting settled. An elderly maid, resembling a dowager princess in exile, unpacked for her. Marianne wondered what the woman thought of the sensible dresses and underwear made by Fräulein Elsa, the twice-a-year outfitter of Frau Gruber's and her daughters' households from pillow slips to ball gowns. Her flannel panties certainly looked incongruous on the shelves of the magnificent armoire, the interior lined with quilted silk, the color of a cardinal's mantle.

Marianne's French was poor, but it didn't matter, for the maid anticipated all her needs, even those she herself hadn't been aware of. Her clothes were taken out and pressed, her shoes polished. A coiffeur materialized to comb her hair. The maid came back to assist her in dressing for dinner. This she found a nuisance, but it seemed to be part of the routine of the house.

She was grateful to Goldschmiedt for being patient and tactfully leaving her alone. They occupied two upstairs bedrooms, each with its bath, and a small salon between them. She'd never had her own private bath before. Certainly not one with marble floor and walls and a tub the size of a pond. She wondered what the villa rented for, probably more per week than the Linz apartment for a year.

They had supper at the Negresco in Nice. At first, she felt helplessly overpowered by its spaciousness and barbaric splendor and took Goldschmiedt's arm for reassurance. As they entered the dining room, the maître d' sighted them. Greeting Goldschmiedt with discreet exuberance, he led them to their reserved table, presenting it to Goldschmiedt as though it had been a fort defended at the risk of life and limb against an invading enemy.

When they were seated, Marianne dared look about. For a moment she felt distinctly ill at ease. The magnificently gowned and bejeweled women made her painfully conscious of the pongee party dress of Fräulein Elsa's she was wearing. Goldschmiedt must have guessed her thoughts because he reached out for her hand, patting it gently.

"You're the most beautiful woman in the room," he told her. "There isn't one who wouldn't exchange her face and figure for yours!"

"But they're so elegant."

"They're well dressed. They wouldn't be here if they didn't know how to dress well. It's a matter of money."

"But I've seen women with a lot of money who could never look elegant, no matter what they wore."

"Army wives in old Vienna."

Supper must have been ordered ahead of time, for a flock of waiters appeared to serve the hors d'oeuvres. Goldschmiedt cast an appraising glance at the selection, nodding his approval. "I love this hotel," he told Marianne. "Nice, and the Riviera are the result of God's and man's best joint effort, a new, much more sophisticated Garden of Eden, which already has its serpents. Look at that man in the corner! Middle-aged, graying. With the woman in the green dress wearing an aigrette in her hair. He's the biggest munitions dealer in the world. If it were up to him, the war between France and Germany would break out tomorrow. If I got up now and shot him, I'd be a greater benefactor to mankind than Marconi and Paul Ehrlich put together." Goldschmiedt smiled. "Too bad I'm such a coward!"

Marianne frowned. "But isn't war inevitable? Isn't it the only thing that will save the monarchy from becoming a second-class power?"

"Are you quoting your husband?"

The blood surged to Marianne's face. "Yes—in a way."

"Of course, that's what the army is itching for. To put their precious theories into practice. They won't rest until they have destroyed all the loveliness and beauty you see here. Nothing will remain, people, buildings, not even the palms on the Promenade des Anglais!" He went on. "Imagine what a missile from a twenty-two-cm field gun could do to the lobby of this hotel! But let's change the subject. I'm glad you're here and I can take you to my favorite places and rediscover them through your eyes. I consider myself a very lucky man, dear heart."

It was the best supper she had ever eaten in her life. She dared not ask what was on her plate, merely hoping it wouldn't be snails and clams or frog legs, delicacies which had never been staple fare at Hahngasse. A different wine accompanied each course, and by the end of the meal she felt pleasantly carefree. Goldschmiedt ate little and drank less. His eyes were fixed on her face with the deep concentration of an art collector who had bought a painting and wondered if it was worth the price. At first, she felt self-conscious, but as the room blurred into a beautiful, rainbow-hued prison, his face too dissolved, half-hidden as it was by the pink carnations on the table.

"You must be tired. I think we'd better go," she heard him call to her from miles beyond the table. As he rose and moved to her side, waiters materialized, pulling out her chair. She could not remember having risen. "Shall we go?" Goldschmiedt's voice held a note of urgency. The room revolved around her, and for a moment she feared she wasn't going to negotiate the frightening distance between the table and the exit. She took a step, realizing with great relief that she was able to walk. Freeing her arm from Goldschmiedt's grasp, she moved between the tables, feeling people's eyes on her, but they disturbed her no longer, for now she knew they stared because she was beautiful.

She was surprised to find the maid waiting in her room but didn't protest when she helped her undress. The woman drew her bath for her and later held out a warmed terry-cloth robe, slipping it around her with the professional solicitude of a nurse.

A silk nightgown and peignoir were laid out on her bed. She had never seen them before but accepted them as trappings of her reincarnation.

The next thing she remembered was a beautiful brocade dressing gown reaching to the floor, a bottle of champagne cooling in an ice-filled silver bucket, and then Goldschmiedt pouring from it into low-stemmed crystal glasses. He sipped at his, while she downed hers in one thirsty gulp.

And then she was naked on a bed. A lamp burned somewhere in the room, appearing so pale that it might have been a lighted window on the tip of Cap Ferrat or on board some distant ship. Arms embraced her, and gentle searching hands and lips made her sleepy. A voice asked if she were enjoying the caresses, and she told the voice politely that she did, very much indeed. She couldn't possibly tell it to stop and let her sleep. It would have been tactless.

She slept late the next morning and woke with a dizzy feeling and a piercing headache. Dr. Goldschmiedt gave her pills that dulled the pain, and they had breakfast in the upstairs salon, she in her new negligee and he in his fancy dressing gown. A little after eleven they were driven to Nice in one of the limousines.

A brisk wind was blowing, but the sky was as blue as that on the postcards displayed in the gift shop windows on the Rue de France. She would have liked to buy some and send them to people in Vienna but knew somehow she shouldn't. She tried to remember the reason but couldn't. Although the headache was gone, she felt as though all her thoughts were trying to filter through a slimy mass that clotted her brains.

They passed a store selling fine linens. Dr. Goldschmiedt took her arm.

"Let's buy something pretty for the baby," he said, guiding her toward the entrance.

Surprised, she looked at him.

"What baby?" she asked. His frown told her that her question made no sense.

"Your baby. Who else?"

"Of course. My baby—who else?" She smiled dutifully, so as not to annoy him.

Luckily he took charge of the proceedings in the store, explaining that the baby was a boy two months old, and settled for pants and jackets. They were adorable and very expensive, and Marianne thanked him exuberantly.

On the Ruhl terrace Marianne pretended to watch the passersby while desperately trying to dispel the fog that enveloped her thinking. Slowly, it dawned on her that she must have given birth to a child not long before. Her husband, Peter, was in jail, accused of a terrible murder, but it seemed as though he weren't really her husband. She found herself feeling sorry for the woman with the husband in jail but preferred not to think of her because such remembrances spoiled her sense of *joie de vivre* (another French expression she knew).

Paul bought her expensive gifts that day, followed by lunch in a tiny restaurant in the old town, ordering what he described as the best *bouillabaisse* on the Côte d'Azur. Afterward they were driven to an elegant mansion set back from the street by a grillwork fence and a narrow front yard on the Boulevard Victor Hugo. There they took an elevator to the second floor to a *salon de couture*, where he ordered several outfits for her, all to be delivered within four days. A lovely evening cloak trimmed with ermine fitted Marianne perfectly, and Dr. Goldschmiedt talked the manager into selling it although it was a model. Wrapped in layers of tissue paper, it was sent down to the waiting limousine.

When they returned to the villa, Goldschmiedt asked the maid to draw the drapes in his room and turn down the bed, after which he made love to Marianne, once again asking for her assurance that she enjoyed his embraces. Marianne decided that if the routine were to continue, she would have to have a few drinks before going to bed with him.

Later in her own room she dozed off and was awakened by the maid, who helped her dress for supper. She was followed by the hairdresser.

After they both left, Dr. Goldschmiedt stuck his head in at the doorway to see if she was ready. She said she was and started down the stairs.

"Won't you wear your new cloak?" he asked.

Puzzled, she stared at him. "What cloak?"

"The one we bought this afternoon," he said, and there was a frown again.

"Of course, the cloak!"

She returned to her wardrobe, and there it was, hanging in all its elegant splendor, with the beautiful ermine collar.

"It's beautiful!" she told him while he wrapped it around her. She smiled. "I'm afraid I haven't even thanked you for it."

"You *have* thanked me. Now let's go!"

His smile was gone, and he seemed preoccupied during the ride to Monte Carlo.

They dined at the Hôtel de Paris where the maître d'hôtel expressed his regret at not having *le docteur* stay with them this time. Discreetly Dr. Goldschmiedt pointed out some august personages to Marianne. Two grand dukes, each with his entourage, were seated at separate tables, and the very elegant, young-looking man dining with a party of bejeweled women and men in tails was Manuel, the King of Portugal. The atmosphere, even more awe-inspiring than that at the Negresco, caused Marianne to feel as though she had spent all her life in places that catered to kings and grand dukes.

During the ride home she fell asleep and upon reaching Èze les Oeillets was awakened by Goldschmiedt. They stepped onto the terrace, for Goldschmiedt wanted her to see the moonlit sea.

Obediently she admired it, suppressing a desire to ask how they
got there and what they were doing in a place where everything
seemed blurred, sparkling as though it were underwater. Seconds
later while climbing the steps to her bedroom, she was overcome
with dizziness. Not precisely a physical discomfort, it brought
with it a sensation of numbing anxiety. Feeling lost, she reached
out frantically to grab the arm of the man beside her, not so much
for support as to reassure herself that she was still in the world of
the living.

"We had a bit too much to drink, didn't we?" he asked, his
voice gruff and reprimanding.

The next day they returned to Nice for a fitting at the salon.
A fawning saleswoman in black asked her respectfully for her
name.

"Madame Dorfrichter," she replied, relieved that she had been
able to remember it. When she caught Dr. Goldschmiedt's angry
glance, she knew that she had committed a *faux pas*—another
French expression she understood well.

"Madame Brammer," he corrected her, but the saleswoman's
surprised expression told him the damage had already been done.

"Do you want to set the whole French press on our tracks?"
he asked Marianne after they had left the salon.

She shook her head. "Heavens, no, of course not."

The word "press" had conjured up a fleeting image of the over-
coated men leaning against lampposts on Hahngasse in Vienna,
ready to jump at her the moment she left her mother's house.

"Then kindly remember that your name here is Madame
Brammer!"

"I'll remember it," she promised meekly. She certainly didn't
want to annoy Paul, her only link with reality. How would she
ever find her way home if he should disappear and leave her
stranded in this weirdly beautiful vacuum? "I'll remember it from
now on," she repeated eagerly.

"I hope so," he mumbled, then finally smiled and gently stroked
her face.

The press found them the following day while they were having an *apéritif* on the Ruhl terrace.

Marianne had awakened late that morning, feeling restless and depressed. The wind had subsided, and the sea lay calm and serene below the esplanade.

For the first time, that day, the spectacle of the crowd moving past the Ruhl, the lovely corso of carriages and limousines, the wide ribbon of the palm-lined promenade following the curve of the bay and, to the far right, the hint of a peninsula—or was it just a cloud?—had brought her contentment. But then, a short, fox-terrier-faced man had stopped at their table and accosted her in rapid Viennese German.

"Good day, Frau Dorfrichter," he greeted her. "I heard you were here and couldn't miss the opportunity of bidding you welcome."

He spoke as though they'd known one another, but she couldn't remember having seen him before.

"Thank you." She could tell by Goldschmiedt's peeved expression that she'd done something wrong again.

"You're mistaken, young man," he barked at the stranger. "The lady is not Frau Dorfrichter!"

At last she recalled his instructions.

"You're mistaken." She tried to sound as stern as he had. "I am Madame—" But she couldn't remember the name.

The young man grinned. "Oh, but you *are* Frau Dorfrichter! And you sir, are her attorney, Dr. Goldschmiedt. May I introduce myself? Reinhard Lothar, at your service." He produced a press pass, which identified him as a staff member of a Viennese boulevard paper.

"Get the hell away from here," Goldschmiedt hissed, "or I'll call the headwaiter and have you thrown out!"

Instead, the man pulled up a chair and sat down.

"You're a smart man, sir, you know it wouldn't do you much good to make me mad, now that I've found you. Frau Dorfrichter had better talk to me. If she doesn't, I'll wire my report to Vienna anyway. I'll just use my imagination." He turned to Marianne. "Are you enjoying yourself, Frau Dorfrichter?"

"I am—very much." She looked at Goldschmiedt for direction, but his face was a cold, inscrutable mask.

"Dr. Goldschmiedt certainly takes good care of his clients. Does your husband know that you're vacationing with him?"

"I don't—" Marianne began, but Goldschmiedt rose abruptly and threw a few bills on the table.

"Let's go," he said to Marianne.

The reporter barred his way. "Just a minute, sir. You can't interrupt a lady in the middle of a sentence. What were you saying, Frau Dorfrichter?"

"I don't have a husband," she whispered, terrified.

Grabbing her arm, Goldschmiedt began to drag her away. The reporter clung to them.

"But you do, you do. While you're soaking up the Riviera sunshine, he is rotting in a dark jail cell in Vienna!"

The words pierced her consciousness with the sharpness of a spear, and tearing her arm from the attorney's grip, she wheeled about to face the young man.

"He is not in a dark cell! His cell is very bright—it has a big window. That's what Captain Kunze told Dr. Goldschmiedt. And he doesn't—"

She wanted to say that Captain Kunze didn't lie, because, after all, he was an officer, but Goldschmiedt's hand once again clamped on her arm, and he thundered rudely, "Hold your tongue!"

Their automobile was parked on the Albert I side with the chauffeur at the wheel and a footman watching the Ruhl terrace for Dr. Goldschmiedt's signal. When the pair reached the sidewalk—with the reporter at their heels—the car was already rounding the corner. The footman, throwing the door open, helped them in.

"Get moving, damn it!" Goldschmiedt shouted. The car immediately shot forward. The footman, on the running board, clung to the door handle. For a moment it seemed as though the reporter might join him there, but he evidently reconsidered, remaining on the sidewalk, grinning sheepishly as they drove away.

"Where to, sir?" the chauffeur asked. He didn't dare stop and let the footman climb inside.

"Just drive on!" Goldschmiedt shouted, turning to Marianne. "Have you lost your mind? Did you have to talk to the bastard?"

Trembling, Marianne withdrew to the far corner of the seat, her eyes on the footman. "He'll fall off," she whispered.

"Never mind him! What in damnation made you talk about the cell?"

She regarded him vacantly. "What cell?"

"Your husband's!"

"My husband's?"

"What's the matter with you? Are you sick?" Alarmed, Goldschmiedt pounded on the glass partition separating them from the driver. "Stop! Pull over to the curb! Stop!"

The car halted, and the footman climbed inside. Marianne heaved a sigh of relief.

"He could've fallen off and crushed his skull," she whispered.

Goldschmiedt stared at her. "Don't you remember what you said to the man?"

"What man?"

"The reporter."

"Was he a reporter?"

"I've told you not to talk to anybody!"

"I forgot," Marianne told him. She was feeling terribly tired and confused. "I'd like to go home."

"To Èze?"

"Èze?"

"Are you playing a game or—" He pounded on the partition again. "Back to Èze!" he ordered the chauffeur in a voice raucous with excitement.

They left for Vienna the following day. By then Marianne Dorfrichter had slumped into a state of complete apathy, interrupted only occasionally by periods of exhilaration. She accepted the decision to leave without any display of regret but became upset when she saw her suitcases being loaded into an automobile.

"I want to stay," she informed Goldschmiedt. "I like it here. I don't want to leave ever."

"But don't you want to get back to your baby?" he asked her.

She gave him the same glassy stare he'd become familiar with during the past few days.

"What baby?"

His panic produced beads of perspiration which rolled down his forehead.

"You had a baby—two months ago." He was careful to address

her in a soothing tone, the professionally sympathetic voice of the defender of the unjustly accused.

Smilingly, she shook her head. "Whoever told you such a lie? I've never had a baby."

The journey home proved uneventful. Dr. Goldschmiedt grew increasingly tense, though without cause, for Marianne remained friendly and docile. They got off in Baden bei Wien to avoid the reporters who would certainly be lying in ambush for them at the Western Railroad Station.

Reinhard Lothar had carried out his threat, sending a story to his paper that was published in an extra edition, under the flamboyant headline LOVE TRYST ON THE CÔTE D'AZUR. When their train halted in Salzburg, Goldschmiedt bought a copy and immediately wired his office to have a rented limousine meet them. His Daimler, well known in Vienna, would have led the pack of hounds to the Baden station.

They drove straight to Hahngasse. Recognizing the house, Marianne refused at first to leave the car. It was a gloomy, freezingly cold day, the sun hidden behind gray clouds and an acrid-smelling fog heavy to the lungs. Though her cheeks were burning, Marianne had shivered all the way from Baden. Goldschmiedt suspected she was running a high temperature but planned to deliver her to her mother first and make whatever arrangements were necessary afterward.

Cautiously he told Frau Gruber, who had been hastily summoned from the store, "I'm afraid Marianne is not well. It's nothing to cause alarm. A condition that often occurs after childbirth."

Frau Gruber's eyes were filled with accusations. When Marianne had told her of the attorney's invitation, she had violently opposed the trip. They had quarreled, but Marianne, usually sensible and obedient, had left with Dr. Goldschmiedt while her mother was away visiting friends.

"What have you done to my child?" Frau Gruber asked.

Goldschmiedt longed to leave without futher conversation, yet he knew that an abrupt exit would lead only to trouble. "No one's done anything to her," he snapped. "She's just tired. As a matter of fact, it's lucky she was with me when it happened."

"When what happened?"

"Her symptoms of—of emotional instability."

"Drop the fancy language! You mean she's out of her mind?"

"Heavens, no, Frau Gruber. I just told you, she's tired. She has had too much to bear. A few weeks' rest in a sanatorium, and she'll be herself again. Put her to bed, and stay with her. I'll contact a friend of mine, Dr. Josef Breuer, a wonderful man! He's had great successes with similar cases. You must have heard of him—he's an associate of Dr. Freud's."

She seemed unimpressed. "Never heard of either," she told him coldly.

"I'll have him consult Professor Hain, and together they'll decide on the right course."

"You took advantage of my daughter. Some defense attorney!"

He managed to control his annoyance. "Don't worry, Frau Gruber. Everything'll work out fine. I'll take care of the—the financial side."

He reached out to pat her shoulder, but stopped the gesture in midair as though afraid that she might bite him. After a half-hearted wave, he quickly left the apartment.

Throughout the discussion, Marianne had sat like a model schoolgirl, on a straight-backed chair.

Johann and his wet nurse were in the bedroom that had been Marianne's before her trip. At times the infant's shrill wails filtered through the wall, but Marianne didn't seem to hear them. In bed she lay staring at the ceiling, her eyes intently examining each crack and discoloration in the paint.

Frau Gruber, settling down in an armchair by the bed, watched her daughter, the youngest and most beautiful of the four, the one she'd had so much hope for and spent so many hours protecting and nursing, through scarlet fever, diphtheria and tuberculosis, only to lose her to a much more ravaging disease.

"*Mein Sorgenkind,*" she whispered. "My child of sorrow."

Kunze asked the provost with the Kaiser Wilhelm mustache, "Didn't Lieutenant Dorfrichter say anything? Not a word?"

"Not a word, sir. I handed the newspaper to him. He took it, glanced at it, then went to the window and remained there. Had his back turned to me. I could see his face in the glass, though. He looked normal. Like always."

"What did *you* say to him when you gave him the paper?"

"Something like he might find it interesting, that I thought he should see it—I don't exactly remember. I was rather embarrassed, sir."

"Were you?"

The provost took a deep breath. "Yes, sir. I knew it would make him feel bad. Being locked up, he can't get drunk or beat the hell out of the woman."

"That'll be all, Provost!" Kunze said curtly. The man was already at the door when he called after him, "I want Lieutenant Dorfrichter brought up for questioning!"

The man wheeled about. "You want him now, sir?"

Kunze raised his voice. "Damn right I want him now."

"Yes, sir." Saluting stiffly, he left the room.

Kunze rose and paced the floor awaiting the onset of the nerve-racking tension which appeared before every confrontation: anticipation, fear, longing, desire for a miracle, dread of God knows what! Torn between wanting to crush Peter Dorfrichter, destroy him, kill him, and hope of a redeeming word, a gesture of amity, a look of approbation from the man. *So this is love,* Kunze mused, *not just a word lightly and irresponsibly used by the young, but the essence, the desire mingled with torment that caused Medea to kill her children, Antonius to betray Rome, Ophelia to lose her sanity. How cruel of fate to burden a judge advocate on the threshold of middle age when he has begun to feel safe from the mistakes of youth.*

The drumbeat of triple footsteps approached the door. Kunze had purposely neglected to summon Lieutenants Stoklaska and Heinrich—witness and recorder—whose presence at all interrogations was obligatory. His plan was to call them in after he had a few minutes alone with Dorfrichter.

The three men—prisoner, provost and guard—entered. Kunze could tell by the expression on the provost's face that the man had noted the absence of the two lieutenants and drawn his own conclusions. He suspected, no doubt, that the captain was up to some new tricks to harass the prisoner. Goddamn it, what was there about Dorfrichter that made everyone root for him? A few more days, and the second provost would be smuggling messages, if he weren't already.

At last, they were alone. Dorfrichter, silent during the routine of salutes and dismissals, now stood at stony-faced attention in the middle of the room.

"At ease," Kunze said, fighting to keep his voice casual. "Sit down, Peter."

For the first time he used the lieutenant's Christian name. If he expected to create a climate of amity, he was disappointed.

"You bastard!" Dorfrichter murmured dully.

The insult did not surprise Kunze. Subconsciously, he had expected it, wondering later if this wasn't his reason for arranging for a meeting without witnesses.

"I could ration you to bread and water for that," he pointed out.

"Why don't you? Might be the straw to break the camel's back."

"Goddamn it, Lieutenant, don't you understand I am not the hangman? I'll let you go the instant I'm convinced of your innocence!"

"Yes, but by then you will have destroyed my marriage, my career and my integrity as a man and an officer." He took a deep breath. "You gave out the Haverda story to the press. You wanted to wreck my marriage. And you succeeded. Then you saw to it that I'd learn about my wife's affair!"

"What do you mean?"

Dorfrichter moved closer. "You caught Provost Tuttman and had him arrested. Then put your flunky in his place. Like a bloody fool, I gave him a letter to my wife. I bet my life that he's never delivered it, that it's somewhere in that stack of papers on your desk. Then you had him sneak that canard to me this morning. What were you trying to achieve by it? What kind of bloody monster are you? All right, you want me hanged—then hang me! But don't kill me little by little."

"Pull yourself together, Lieutenant. There is a limit to the abuse I'm willing to take from you."

"You wouldn't take any if you didn't feel guilty as hell."

"Guilty of what?"

"Don't have me spell it out for you. You're a pervert, Captain, a sadist bastard. You torture me because it gives you pleasure. You don't want justice done. You don't give a shit about justice. All you want is to see me under your heel, cringing and licking your boots."

Kunze pounded his fist furiously on the table. "That does it!" he shouted. "One more word, and I'll let you rot in jail for the rest of your life."

He felt a murderous hatred for the man. If he'd had a gun handy, he didn't doubt that he would've shot him unflinchingly between the insolent and much-too-knowing eyes. For a second the fierceness of his anger made him dizzy, and he had to hold onto a chair. Never before had he experienced an emotion of such intensity. It was a terrifying moment. Letting go of the chair, he stepped to the window, turning his back on Dorfrichter.

"You're insane," he pronounced.

He heard the lieutenant move behind him. "You released the Haverda incident to the press to break up my marriage, didn't you?"

"It didn't need much breaking up, did it?"

"What do you mean?"

Kunze still felt a need to hurt the man. "She might've been waiting for an excuse to wash her hands of you."

When Kunze turned to face the prisoner, the agony in the lieutenant's eyes melted his bitterness, producing a shameful longing to comfort and placate.

"Don't let it touch you. She isn't worth it. No woman is," he added lamely.

Dorfrichter, who had been staring vacantly into space, now focused his eyes on Kunze's face. "You said you weren't married."

"No. I am not."

"Then how do you know what they're worth?" He waited for an answer, but when none was forthcoming, he went on. "Why did you have the provost give me the paper?"

Kunze turned back. "I do the questioning around here, Lieutenant!"

"Then question me, goddamn you!"

"Did you send the circulars?"

Dorfrichter burst out laughing. "No! Jesus Christ, this is beginning to be like a children's game—dumb crambo. Only we don't do it with rhymes. May I give you a bit of advice, Captain, sir? Request to be taken off this case. You've had a slim chance of solving it, but from now on you'll have no chance at all."

Kunze rang the bell on his desk. "I want the lieutenant escorted back to his cell," he said when the sergeant on duty entered. He turned to Dorfrichter. "You may wait in the anteroom for the provost."

"Wouldn't that be against regulations, sir?" the lieutenant asked with a sarcastic smile. "I might try to escape."

Kunze felt his bones suddenly leaden.

"That was an order, Sergeant," he said in a voice hollow and dead.

XIII

TROLL had developed the habit of climbing up on the sill of the study window, where he could watch the street and recognize Kunze rounding the corner of Traungasse on his way home from the office. The captain would look up, and the sight of the big, bushy head would cause him to accelerate his steps. By the time he inserted his key in the front-door lock the dog would be there in the hallway, greeting him with exuberant tail wagging and a low, guttural sound strangers mistook for hostility. But Kunze knew it was the dog's way of telling him he had been missed. They would go to his bedroom, where the captain exchanged his shoes for an old pair of boots; then—rain or shine —they would head for the Stadtpark. Kunze would unleash Troll, and the dog would race up and down the graveled walk. A sign admonished owners to keep their dogs leashed, but that was observed only by civilians. The park guards, all war veterans, considered a captain's dog outranked all civilians; consequently the ordinance didn't apply to Troll. After the romp, they walked to a small restaurant in Weihburggasse for a simple but good meal, with the exception of Sundays, when they had midday dinner at Rose's. She had endeavored to make Kunze take all his meals at her home, but the captain had refused. She had never stopped fussing about the dog; Kunze was not willing to leave Troll behind, and so they had compromised on Sundays.

On Friday she called him at the office to tell him that her lawyer had cleared the matter of her uncle's legacy, and within a few days she would be in possession of the entire bequest. She made her announcement in the grave tone of a jury foreman; at least, that was how it sounded to Kunze. She wanted him to come over that evening, so now he and Troll were on their way to Zaunergasse. He to discuss wedding plans and the dog to be restricted to the corner of the salon, where an old potato sack was spread out for him.

The captain was somewhat surprised to find Rose's attorney, an old family friend, and also her sister and brother-in-law present, all flushed with excitement. There was so much simple, child-like joy in Rose's eyes that Kunze himself became infected with it. Giving up his freedom seemed a small sacrifice compared to the happiness their marriage meant to her. She was, he knew, passion-ately loyal and the only person in the world who really and truly loved him. He realized, with a pang of conscience, he had never been absolutely sure about his mother, about the ratio between love and duty in her feelings for him.

It was decided that he would immediately put in a request to the corps for the commandant's permission for the marriage. The bride-to-be being a lady of unblemished reputation and proper social standing and in a position to produce the required bond, they had no reason to expect any complications and therefore could safely plan on a March wedding. After some deliberation, they agreed on the fifth.

The party lasted until the early morning hours. Several bottles of champagne were consumed, with the result that everyone— the cook and the maid included—was glowing. Even Troll had a merry time. Rose fed him chunks of goose liver and roast beef, ob-viously intent on establishing more cordial relations. She inti-mated to Kunze that she wouldn't mind if he and Troll stayed for the night, but the captain, considering their engaged status, felt it wouldn't be proper if he failed to leave with the other guests.

The mood of contentment remained with him until the fol-lowing morning. Upon his arrival at the office, he found Captain Baron Landsberg-Lövy's reply to his letter on the desk. The baron apologized for being late in corresponding, but he had been on an inspection tour of the Bosnian bases and received Kunze's note only upon his return to the command post. He could be at Kunze's disposal any time in Sarajevo; however—unless the matter was of great urgency—he could save the captain the trip, for on February 25 he would be in Vienna. Kunze immediately wired back that the February 25 date would suit him perfectly. Then he sat down and began to compose his request for a marriage permit to the corps commandant.

Captain Landsberg-Lövy was a wiry, dark-haired man with the sharp, hook-nosed profile of an Assyrian warrior and the controlled ferocity of a well-trained Doberman pinscher. His lithe body moved with grace, but also with a certain wariness as though an ambush were constantly within the realm of possibility. Exceedingly well mannered, there was, however, a touch of provocation and condescension to his courtesy. The power and the wealth of an industrial empire stood behind him, and no one was allowed to forget it.

He arrived at Kunze's office exactly at the agreed time. They hadn't met before, yet their greeting was relaxed and cordial, in keeping with the tribal customs of the Austro-Hungarian Officers' Corps. Both being captains, first names were in order.

"I hope you don't consider this meeting an imposition," Kunze explained, "but I've come across two notes of yours to Peter Dorfrichter—one dated August nineteenth, 1908, the other September first, 1908. I found them in his files. I'd appreciate it if you would tell me exactly what they refer to."

He kept his eyes fixed on the baron and could tell by the slight stiffening of the man's facial muscles that the request was not welcome. He handed Landsberg-Lövy the note. After clamping a monocle on his left eye, the baron examined the two letters. At last, he placed them on the desk, and the monocle dropped from his eye, to dangle for a moment on its black ribbon.

"I'm afraid I can't tell you more than what is written there," he said with cool finality.

"You mean you don't remember who the person X. was and why you were dismayed over his lapse and why you felt sorry—more sorry than shocked—and what the meeting with Dorfrichter was going to be about?"

"Just as I've said, Emil, I can't tell you more," Landsberg-Lövy repeated.

"Why not?"

"I'd rather not explain that."

"My dear friend, we're conducting a criminal investigation. You could be ordered to cooperate, but I'd prefer you did it voluntarily. Isn't this mysterious X. Lieutenant Xavier Vanini?"

The baron thought for a moment. "Yes. It is Vanini."

"What did you mean by 'lapse'?"

Landsberg-Lövy jumped nervously to his feet. "You're investigating Dorfrichter, not Vanini! I assure you the matter referred to in my notes concerned only Vanini and myself. Dorfrichter was merely a sort of go-between."

"Why Peter Dorfrichter? Why not someone else?"

"Don't ask me. He was Vanini's choice. Or perhaps he volunteered. All I know is he approached me on Vanini's behalf. I assume they were close friends."

"What is your reason for not disclosing the nature of the dispute? It was a dispute, wasn't it?"

The baron wearily dropped into the chair. "Yes—in a way. A man's personal honor was involved! We settled the matter, and I gave my word I'd forget it. So I've forgotten it."

Taking a few letters from a pile on the desk, Kunze spread them out. He had already read them so often he could have recited them by heart.

"Dorfrichter wrote these to his wife during the summer of 1908. Vanini's name occurs in them quite frequently. It seems the young man was in constant trouble. Drinking and neglecting his duties. At one point Dorfrichter indicates that he had to help straighten out some unpleasant business for Vanini. That letter was dated September third—two days after your *second* note. In that you agreed to meet Dorfrichter on Vanini's behalf."

"Why ask me? Why not Dorfrichter and Vanini?"

Kunze wasn't going to let the baron's attitude disconcert him. "I will—in due time. Now a very harmless question. Was that meeting between you and Dorfrichter amicable? Was there any friction?"

"None whatsoever! We were in perfect rapport. A most likable chap—I mean Dorfrichter. Frankly, I'll never believe that he is the man behind that damned circular. A vile prank. And in bad taste, too. You must have some evidence against him, or you wouldn't keep him under arrest. However, I'm convinced you're wrong. For instance, why would he have sent me the poison? We were on the best of terms. Besides, he knew me: I'm not the kind to take patent medicine. If I have something wrong with me, I go to a doctor."

Kunze waited patiently for the baron to finish, then nodded.

"Dorfrichter might not be Charles Francis. Nevertheless, we must examine every clue. Going back to that meeting in Sarajevo—Dorfrichter went to you because Vanini'd gotten into hot water. How? My guess is money. You said, his honor was at stake. How? It means he committed a dishonorable act. You won't tell me what because it would hurt him even today. He might be kicked out of the army. Perhaps arrested. You were willing to cross out the debt or whatever it was—which placed him under a lifelong obligation to you. But there's a third person who knows about it, and that's Dorfrichter. For whatever service he rendered in the case, Vanini is indebted to him, too."

"According to your reasoning"—the baron grinned—"it could be Vanini who sent me the poison!"

"You might be right!" Kunze agreed, falling silent. Vanini himself had stated that he had had cyanide. He was stationed in Linz, where the boxes and the stationery were obtainable. According to information supplied by his regiment, he reported for duty in Nagykanizsa on the twelfth of November, having arrived there the previous night. That meant he could not have been in Vienna and dropped the circulars into the Mariahilferstrasse mailbox on the fourteenth. Nevertheless, he could have had someone else do it. But why? Why would he want to dispatch ten General Staff Officers to hell? Out of the ten he knew Baron Landsberg-Lövy personally and possibly one or two others. What grudge could he have had against the rest? Unless, like some field officers, he resented the General Staff *in toto*. Or was he a mental case? Good God, if Vanini were the man and not Dorfrichter!

"I can't say you're much help," he told Landsberg-Lövy. "You seem to forget that I'm conducting a criminal investigation, not a medieval tourney. Your bloody code of honor merely obstructs justice."

The baron rose. "There isn't anything I can do about that," he said stiffly. "Is that all you wished to discuss?"

"For the moment, yes. I may have to get back to you, though, after I've talked to the men involved."

The baron clicked his heels. "At your service."

Alone, Kunze pondered the possibility of Vanini's involvement as an accessory or even as the guilty party. It was a slim chance but couldn't be disregarded. This time he would not leave the fact-finding to others but, if necessary, go to Nagykanizsa himself.

There was a knock on the door, but, before Kunze could answer, the door opened, and Stoklaska stormed in, looking excited and waving a slip of paper.

"Captain Titus Dugonich was found seriously wounded by gunshot in a flat on Himmelpfortgasse."

The flat opened directly off the second-floor landing of an old house that stretched from Himmelpfort to Ballgasse, with entrances on both streets. It had an exit through the kitchen to the back staircase, making it strategically perfect for Dugonich, who used it as his home away from home. If a suspicious husband rang the front-door bell, his wife could safely slip out through the kitchen, dash down the stairs to Ballgasse, hail a fiacre, and be home long before him.

When Kunze reached the flat, he found the janitor of the house and a civilian in shirt sleeves at the wounded man's bedside. The latter turned out to be an obstetrician living on the third floor of the same house. Shortly after Kunze's arrival, Regimental Medical Officer Dr. Ruppert made his appearance, which gave the scene a touch of the *déjà vu*, with the difference that the victim, unlike Richard Mader, wasn't dead, but very much alive, emitting loud and violent curses. He lay in bed on his right side in a rather awkward position, nude, except for a shirt thrown over his shoulders. The bullet had entered the pectineus, emerging in back through the *vastus lateralis*, on its way nicking the thighbone. At least, this was the obstetrician's conclusion, which Dr. Ruppert, with his usual contempt for civilian medical opinion, refused to confirm.

Dugonich was in acute pain and still bleeding, although the bullet luckily had missed the main artery. The shooting had taken place in the drawing room that opened off the entrance hall and was furnished like an Arab sheik's tent with Oriental rugs, damask drapery, and hanging scimitars and a collection of antique firearms in glass cases. There was blood splashed on the wall and a large puddle on the floor where Dugonich must have lain before he had been carried to bed.

"I'd just gotten home from a case," the obstetrician reported, "when my phone rang. A female voice told me to go down to Two B—I might be needed. Then she hung up. First I thought someone was playing a prank; nevertheless, I went downstairs. The door was open, and I found the captain on the floor, wounded. He was wearing that silk dressing gown you see on the chair. And nothing else. I managed to control the bleeding, then had the janitor help me carry the captain to the bed. My wife phoned the police. Incidentally, I hadn't known he was an officer. I've seen him once or twice entering or leaving the house, but he was always in mufti."

Mufti was against regulations, but Kunze could understand that a man on his way to a secret rendezvous preferred to blend in with the scenery.

The picture was pretty clear in Kunze's mind. The flat was what the penny dreadfuls aptly described as a love nest. Here Dugonich had been meeting lady friends whose number and variety were the talk of the town. A jealous husband or discarded mistress had probably taken a potshot at him. The location of the wound indicated that the intention was not to kill, but to make the captain's future philanderings impossible. Luckily he or she wasn't a very good marksman.

While they waited for the ambulance, Kunze attempted to question Dugonich, but the victim's pain and outrage made him incoherent. He cursed "the bitch" but when Kunze asked her name, his answer was an outburst that would have silenced a drill sergeant.

Later that day, the same commission that had convened three months earlier to investigate Richard Mader's murder met in Chief Brezovsky's office at the Presidium.

"An attempt has been made on the life of the second man on the Charles Francis list," General Wencel told them. "Now I'm sure Captain Kunze will tell us that he sees no connection between Mader's murder and Dugonich's shooting."

Kunze nodded. "I won't, sir, at least not before I've talked to Captain Dugonich."

The commission had been in session for more than an hour. The obstetrician and the janitor were called as witnesses.

"How did the woman's voice sound to you?" General Wencel asked the doctor. "Did she have a foreign accent?"

"No, General. She sounded Viennese."

"Like a working-class person?"

"No, sir. I'd say upper-class."

"Can you recall what she said? The exact words?"

"I'll try, sir, but she was much too excited and at first hard to understand. I gathered that she wanted me to go down to apartment Two B and attend a sick person. She may have said 'wounded.' Then she added something that confused me."

"What was that?"

"She said, 'I hope I got his balls.'"

For a moment there was startled silence in the room. Inspector Weinberger's mustache quivered dangerously.

"You maintain, Doctor, that despite the vulgar expression, she was upper-class?"

"Certainly, sir. Cultured and ladylike."

Kunze went from the Presidium straight to the garrison hospital but was barred from Dugonich's sickroom. The captain's leg had been operated on, his broken thighbone set, and he was still under the influence of the anesthetic.

On the following morning he finally saw Dugonich. The captain was pale, and there were deep rings under his eyes, but he displayed a slightly more cheery disposition than the day before.

"How do you feel?" his visitor asked.

"Like a bloody fool."

"Who is she?"

"Who is who?"

"The woman who shot you?"

Dugonich's eyebrows went up.

"Who said it was a woman?"

"You did! You wouldn't call a man a bitch. You don't keep that sort of company."

Dugonich remained silent.

"Come on, who was she?" Kunze urged.

"Let's say, I was cleaning a gun and it went off."

"Damn it, Dugonich, stop being so bloody chivalrous. How can I investigate any damn case when you all turn knight in shining armor and deaf and dumb. Why do you have to make it so difficult for me?"

"You're making it difficult for yourself. All right, an enraged female tried to shoot off my balls. That's something between me and her. None of your goddamn business. It's my bloody leg that's in a bloody cast. The army will have to do without my services until it heals. Pretend that I fell off my bloody horse."

Kunze sighed. "Dugonich, General Wencel is obsessed with the idea that you were shot by whoever poisoned Mader. Possibly a political assassin. Serbain, Russian, Czech, Hungarian. Hell, he's never fully accepted the theory that Charles Francis might be an Austrian Army officer."

Dugonich burst into a fit of laughter which convulsed his whole body, causing his wounds to ache. His laughter was followed by groans and curses.

"Tell the old buzzard to keep his nose out of my affairs," he grunted. "Or he might find he's sticking it into his *own* shit."

Kunze nodded. "I see." Now he knew who the woman was. Lily Wencel. He was amazed he hadn't thought of her before.

"You don't see a bloody thing," Dugonich said angrily. "I merely meant—"

Kunze cut him short. "I know what you meant. I'd better tell you that we've found the bullet. It was fired from a twenty-two-caliber revolver, most likely a Browning. Was it yours?"

"No. She brought her own hardware."

"What happened to it?"

"How should I know? I was busy bleeding to death." He grinned. "One thing is sure: She's got a hell of a sense of humor. First trying to castrate me, then calling an obstetrician. The good man arrived equipped with forceps and all—I must be the laughingstock of Vienna." After a moment's pause, he went on. "You'd better do something about the general. He might feel obligated to take revenge for the blot on his escutcheon and, being a better shot than his wife, finish the job."

Kunze chuckled. "And he has no sense of humor. He'd aim at your head. No, the only solution is the accident story. No matter how unbelievable. You were cleaning a gun, and it went off. He'll have to understand that you're being discreet. Protecting some female's reputation. He knows you better than to think you'd protect a Russian spy."

"What about the rest of the commission?"

"No need to worry. They didn't seem too keen about an investigation yesterday. Must have had a pretty clear picture of the whole affair. Anyway they're not as sold on the infallibility of the Officers' Corps as Wencel is."

Once again General Wencel had been summoned to Belvedere Palace for a dressing down. Archduke Franz Ferdinand had read about the Dugonich shooting in the papers and was outraged at the corps command's failure to keep the affair a secret from the press. For a change he shared Kunze's opinion that the background of the shooting was an amorous entanglement. He found the whole case distasteful and damaging to the reputation of the General Staff and made it clear that once he became emperor, officers like Captain Dugonich would have no place in the army hierarchy. Then with his usual illogic, he demanded that—since the case had already been laid before the public—all the details be unveiled in order to put an end to speculations and rumors.

"I most respectfully disagree with His Imperial Highness," Kunze protested when told about the archducal command. "Captain Dugonich maintains that the shot was accidental and self-inflicted."

"Don't be an ass, Kunze," Wencel grunted. "You know that's a damn lie."

"Most likely, sir. But why would an honorable man like the captain tell a lie? For honorable reasons. You, sir, have had more social contact with the captain than I. You're familiar with the circle he moves in. What if the woman in question were of that circle? The wife of a highly respectable man? Wouldn't that cause even wider ripples?"

His eyes narrowed with suspicion, Wencel gave him a long, pensive look.

"What exactly do you know?" he asked sharply.

"Just what I've told you, sir."

"Has the gun been found?"

"No sir, not yet. The person might have taken it with her."

"The bullet?"

"Fired from a twenty-two-caliber revolver."

"Have the police found any witnesses who saw the person enter or leave the flat?"

"No, sir. But I'm in contact with Inspector Weinberger, and he promised to inform me the moment they have any new details. Nothing up to now, though."

"Damn inefficient," Wencel roared. "You're very much mistaken if you think that I'm satisfied with your handling of the case. Blunder after blunder. But let me know if anything develops." Then gruffly: "You're dismissed!"

Captain Kunze found the gun in the folds of the heavy silk damask that formed an Arab tent in Dugonich's drawing room. The police, searching the flat before, had somehow overlooked the drapery. Kunze had gone to the flat to make sure no personal belongings—a handkerchief, a scarf—were left to betray the identity of the woman. Then, to his surprise, he found the gun. It was a beautiful thing, a Browning, its side plate engraved with the line "Happy anniversary! Your loving husband, Karl."

After ascertaining that General Wencel was in the Lawcourt Building, Kunze went to the nearest post office and called the general's house, asking to speak to Frau Wencel.

"This is Captain Kunze," he told her, noting the startled silence at the other end. "I'm sorry to disturb you, but I have some property of yours which I'd like to return to you without much ado."

The silence lasted several seconds longer; then there came a whispered "Why?"

"Because I consider it to be in the best interest of all concerned."

"Oh, you dear man!" she cooed. There was a gurgling sound, which he could not identify as either laughter or tears.

"I have one condition, though," he said. "Promise me that you'll practice on inanimate targets from now on!"

"I promise," she whispered. "This kind of thing is a once only act."

"I'll take your word for it. Anyway, you'd better collect that gadget. It's not proper to throw away anniversary gifts."

They agreed to meet in the Schönbrunn Park behind the gate nearest the Wencel villa. Lily would be accompanied by her white Pomeranian, her alibi should anyone see her. Kunze would have Troll along for the same reason.

"Needless to say, I'm very grateful," she admitted after they had agreed on the time. Then: "How is he?"

"As well as could be expected under the circumstances," Kunze answered. "His leg is in a cast, but the doctors hope it'll heal completely."

"Is he very mad at me?"

"Rather. But that's understandable, don't you think?"

They met in the gray, wintry twilight, under naked trees, two dog lovers braving the bone-chilling mist. There was no one else close by. In the distance a bundled-up woman walked two shivering fox terriers on the frost-bitten lawn. While Troll inspected the coquettish blue ribbon tied on the Pomeranian, Kunze slipped the revolver to Lily Wencel in a handshake. She dropped it into the pocket of her seal coat.

"Thank you again, and tell him I'm sorry."

He nodded. "I will."

"Sorry that I missed," she added with a laugh. Then fastening the leash on the Pomeranian, she pulled her away from Troll.

XIV

LIEUTENANT Xavier Vanini was strolling on the footpath alongside the deep ravine at the bottom of which the railroad tracks ran. Something kept bringing him here, especially on days cursed with hangovers. It eased his depression somewhat to know there were trains leaving the damned place, that one wasn't completely and irrevocably shut off from the rest of the world.

A cold wind was blowing, and the lieutenant shivered. Come to think of it, he hadn't stopped shivering since last fall. He looked up at the grim February sky, hating it. During the past few days the temperature had risen above freezing point, and the snow of the week before had turned to slush. The Hungarian landscape lay flat and desolate, with its bare trees and stretches of gray-brown fields. The vision of sunny Quarnero Bay returned, and he felt a longing that almost choked him.

He had been born in Trieste, but when he was three, his father, a customs official, was transferred to Fiume. He grew up in a port, busy enough to be a constant source of excitement and friendly enough to be safe for a small boy. Summer and winter, the sea was his playground—the fishing boats, the steamers navigating along the lush coast dotted with unfashionable resorts, the freighters manned by the world's most colorful people from the blond giants of Scandinavia to the tiny Malayans.

When Xavier was thirteen, his father died. The following summer his mother met a retired infantry colonel from Graz who was vacationing in Abbazia and married him. The colonel did not approve of a young boy who could curse in ten languages, including Siamese, preferred mussels pried off sea rocks with penknives to *Wiener Schnitzel* and had a starfish tattooed in red, blue, and green on his upper left arm.

The only way to rescue such a wayward boy for society, the colonel decided, was to give him a strict military education. Xavier was sent off to Wiener Neustadt. Not a model student, he muddled through to a second lieutenancy because basically he was a good son and wished to please his mother.

However, if a man has to live with a gnawing pain, he is likely to use any available means to cure it. Vanini drank and gambled and became involved with the wrong kind of women. He was never able to make ends meet, remaining one step ahead of total financial and moral bankruptcy. It was easy for a young and handsome officer to run into debt because if everything else failed, usurers could always count on the prospect of a rich marriage. Vanini paid exorbitant interests, so each new garrison meant a breathing spell for him, old debts and threats left behind while as yet untapped sources offered themselves for new loans. It was a game, dangerous and disturbing, and he did not know how long he could remain afloat. Sooner or later he would have either to leave the army or to settle for an ugly girl with a wealthy father.

He had been in Nagykanizsa since the twelfth of November, already reaching the point of no return. His creditors in Linz had banded together against him, and there was a mere trickle from the new moneylenders in Nagykanizsa. In desperation, he wrote his stepfather, who answered with a four-page letter of recriminations and no money order.

Beneath him a train thundered through the ravine. It was headed southwest; he could read the sign on a sleeping car: "Budapest-Zagreb-Trieste." It was four o'clock in the afternoon; the train would reach its destination early in the morning. His state of hopelessness depressed him; why couldn't he be a man and extricate himself from the quagmire of his existence? Do it before its wet slime buried him completely. Graz, Wiener Neustadt, Sarajevo, Linz, Nagykanizsa—harsh, ugly-sounding foreign places; what was he, a goddamn dago, doing in them? What was the use of being an officer and a gentleman when he had to walk a tightrope?

He ate two frankfurters and drank a carafe of wine in a café on the market square. The wine made him feel better, and on his way home he stopped at a tavern and had a second carafe.

The house where he rented a furnished room was a five-minute walk from the market square. A yard ran the length of the property. Behind a screen of lilac bushes, now bare-branched and giving no camouflage, were the outhouses. Of the three, Vanini had exclusive use of the first with a private key, which he mislaid most of the time.

As he approached the house, he noticed with some surprise that his light was on and that there were two soldiers, bayonets fixed, flanking the entrance. He halted dumbfounded.

"What the hell—"

They snapped to attention, maintaining their silence. Moving to the door, he threw it open and entered the room. A man wearing a captain's uniform with the collar patch of the Judge Advocate Corps was seated on the ugly tapestry-covered sofa. He rose slowly, taking a step forward.

"Lieutenant Xavier Vanini?"

Vanini stared at him, blinking. "Yes, sir."

He was too surprised to salute or give his name in the proper manner.

"I'm Captain Emil Kunze, judge advocate with the Military Court of the Vienna garrison."

"Sir," Vanini said. The heat from the tile stove and the wine were making him dizzy.

"You're under arrest, Lieutenant," the captain said evenly.

It took Vanini several seconds to grasp the meaning of the words. Then he said, "I am what? On what charge?"

"For the time being, accessory before the fact. I hope it won't be anything more serious."

Kunze was facing a man of medium height, with silky black hair, olive skin, and eyes the color of hazelnuts. Vanini seemed younger than his twenty-seven years and was at the moment, Kunze observed, slightly intoxicated.

To have a warrant issued against Vanini, Kunze knew, was a bold gamble; General Wencel had at first categorically refused to give his consent, relenting only when Kunze promised to keep the lieutenant under arrest no longer than forty-eight hours, releasing him if nothing developed.

During the fiacre ride to the casern, Vanini repeatedly tried to converse with the captain, but met with an icy silence.

In the small office the light of a swag lamp hung from the ceiling illuminated Vanini but made of Kunze a blurred shadow behind the desk.

"Last December you were questioned by your regimental command about an attempted purchase of potassium cyanide at the Ritzberger pharmacy in Linz. You sent your orderly to make the purchase, but he was turned away. Is there anything you want to add to the explanation you offered at that time?" Kunze asked.

Vanini listened wide-eyed. His head cleared somewhat, but now his heart beat so loudly he was afraid the captain might hear the pounding. *That damned cyanide again*, he thought, wondering where the trap lay.

"I don't know what you want to hear, sir," he said cautiously.

"You know very well what I want to hear!" Kunze snapped. The young officer's genuinely puzzled look made him wonder if he weren't barking up the wrong tree. "What did you do with the cyanide?"

"What cyanide, sir? My orderly didn't get any!"

Kunze pulled a slip of paper from his pocket and leaned into the lighted circle beneath the lamp.

"I'm referring to the two sticks of cyanide you purchased at the garrison pharmacy in Sarajevo on the fifteenth of August, 1908. What did you need them for?"

Vanini blinked a few times, as if dazzled by the light. "August fifteenth, 1908? Oh, yes! I bought them because I was going to take pictures at General von Weigl's garden party to celebrate the emperor's birthday."

"And did you take the pictures?"

"No, sir."

"Why not?"

"I don't remember."

"So you didn't use the cyanide?"

"I did—later—for other photos."

"Taken in Sarajevo?"

"Yes, sir."

"Did you have a darkroom at your quarters in Sarajevo?"

"No, sir. I used the one at the command post."

"You did at the start of your tour in Sarajevo," Kunze pointed out. "But you soon lost interest in photography—"

"No, I must contradict you, sir. I still have the equipment and—"

"But you didn't take any more pictures in Sarajevo!"

Vanini's cheeks burned, and he tugged nervously at the stiff high collar of his tunic. "Is that why you arrested me, sir?" he asked hoarsely. "Because I stopped taking pictures?"

For a moment the only sound in the room was the fire crackling in the potbellied iron stove.

"I stopped doing a lot of things in Sarajevo," Vanini went on in the plaintive voice of an unjustly scolded child. "I gave up tennis, betting on horses, even chasing women. To substitute for my former hobbies, I switched to a local product that came in bottles and had an eighty percent alcohol content."

Kunze kept his eyes focused on the young man's flushed face.

"Let me refresh your memory, Vanini. On July twenty-first, 1908, a Sarajevo pawnbroker named Abraham Herrlich lent you two hundred kronen on your photographic equipment. The ticket was never redeemed, which explains why you lost interest in photography."

As though trying to massage away a headache, Vanini rubbed his forehead with both hands.

"Am I correct, Vanini?"

"Yes, sir."

There was a hurt look in his eyes and a defiant stiffness around his jaw, humiliation at having been caught in a lie.

Kunze had come to Nagykanizsa well prepared. He'd made several phone calls to Sarajevo, talked to, among others, the men at the division command post photographic laboratory, then taken the train to Linz and questioned more than a dozen people there.

"So you no longer had your camera and the rest of your equipment when you purchased two sticks of cyanide at the garrison pharmacy in Sarajevo. Am I right?"

"Yes, sir."

"What did you need them for?"

"I told you, sir. I wanted to take pictures at the garden party—"

"But you didn't have your equipment!"

"I was hoping to redeem it, sir. Unfortunately, I wasn't able to."

"Well then, what did you do with the cyanide?"

"Probably threw it away."

"Don't you know?"

Beads of perspiration appeared on the young officer's forehead. "How could I? How could anyone? After all this time!"

Kunze held his breath. Was the wild-goose chase turning into a tiger hunt? Had he stumbled on the solution to the Charles Francis puzzle? Was the vague guess of a few days before the key to Dorfrichter's cell door? Was Dorfrichter innocent and Vanini the culprit?

"You're not very fond of the army, are you, Vanini?" he asked.

The young man threw him a puzzled look. "Fond in what way? As a citizen or as an officer? I don't know what you mean, sir."

"While stationed in Linz, you were repeatedly heard to make derogatory remarks about your comrades in general and staff officers in particular."

"That's possible, sir. I'm not a saint who loves everybody."

It was getting late, and Kunze was beginning to tire. He had had a long train ride and several hours' wait on Vanini's rickety sofa with the broken springs. It was time to play his trump card. "What caused your animosity against staff officers?"

Vanini pulled himself erect in his chair. His eyelids drooped as though he were trying to screen his eyes from Kunze's penetrating glance.

"For your information, sir," he said in a high-pitched voice, "there's never been much love lost between the field army and the bottle greens! As far as I'm concerned, they make me puke."

He's losing his Italian temper, Kunze thought. *He'll grow reckless and give himself away out of sheer bravado.*

"Could it be, Vanini," the captain asked in a casual tone, "that you stuffed twenty wafer capsules with that cyanide and sent them to ten newly promoted staff officers?"

The combined effect of the wine consumed earlier that evening and the heat from the potbellied stove had slowed down the lieutenant's mental processes but failed to lessen the force of his reaction. He jumped to his feet as though bitten by a snake.

"No! No!" Then he froze and stared at Kunze. "Is that why you have me under arrest? This is insane! I had nothing to do with the bloody capsules!"

"You seem to know about them, though!"

"Of course, I know about them. I read the papers just like everyone else. You can't do this to me! Just because I bought two sticks of cyanide more than a year ago! There isn't a big enough jail to hold everyone who did. Are you going to arrest everyone?"

"No. Only you."

"Why me? Why single me out?" Vanini screamed. "I protest! I demand that you release me immediately!"

"Not unless you account for the cyanide. What did you do with it?"

Vanini slumped back into his chair. "Why would I want to kill those men? I didn't even know them!"

Kunze waited a moment, then dropped his bomb. "I had a talk with Captain Landsberg-Lövy before I left Vienna."

Vanini's face turned purple. "That goddamn Jew! I knew that he wouldn't keep his mouth shut!"

Kunze suddenly had a sinking feeling. This young officer's protest seemed much too spontaneous. Confused, unhappy, bitter perhaps, but certainly no psychopathic killer. Xavier Vanini lacked the slyness, the viciousness of a madman. Average intelligence, weak, no special talents; perhaps an accessory to, but not the perpetrator of a diabolic crime.

"Come now, Vanini. It wasn't Landsberg-Lövy who tried to fox you; it was the other way around." Kunze felt his way cautiously.

"He gave his word he wouldn't talk!"

This confirmed the captain's guess. The conflict was about money, most likely a debt Vanini had owed the baron.

"How do you know *he* talked?"

"Who else?" Vanini asked.

"Peter Dorfrichter."

"Not Dorfrichter!" he protested. "What would he have gained by it? No, not he!"

"You two used to be close friends in Sarajevo."

"That we were, sir," the lieutenant agreed. "And I am proud of having been his friend."

"Proud enough to cover up for him?"

"I don't know what you mean, sir."

Kunze refused to answer, moving back into the shadows to await Vanini's next move. He felt sorry for the young man. *Damn you, Dorfrichter,* he thought, *how many more lives are you going to wreck?* Lieutenant Vanini was no model officer, but Kunze never saw any special glory in being one. General Wencel was one, and Captain Moll and probably Landsberg-Lövy, who had to be especially correct because he was a Jew. What was there in the army that attracted them all, men like Gersten and Hedry and Hodossy and Dugonich and even Dorfrichter, drawing them like moths to a flickering light?

"You'll be drummed out of the army, Vanini," Kunze said when the lieutenant remained silent. "You'd better tell me all there is to tell, or by God, I'll have you put behind bars for the rest of your natural life. Answer me! Did you provide Lieutenant Peter Dorfrichter with the cyanide?"

"I did not!" The young officer seemed on the verge of tears.

"Look here, Vanini. Up to this point the whole thing has been between you and me. It may stay there, but only if you're willing to cooperate. A man was killed in a painful and cowardly way. We have a suspect. Your friend Dorfrichter. Many people would like him to get off the hook. A. Because he is an exceptionally talented man. B. Because his conviction would cast a black shadow over the army. Whether I personally agree with them or not is immaterial. I've been given the assignment of investigating this case, and I'm trying to do just that. The inquest has already involved several innocent people, some tragically. I don't see any purpose in dragging it out. Dorfrichter is either innocent and in that case must be set free or is guilty and should face the consequences. You won't save him by remaining silent, not anymore. Things have gone too far. But you can save your own reputation and career by speaking up."

Vanini fixed his dark Italian eyes on Kunze's face. There was no warmth in them. "I have nothing to say."

"I'm offering you a deal, Vanini. We all have to make deals in this life if we want to survive."

"I'm not sure I want to," Vanini said morosely. "Not on these terms."

Kunze gave him a long look, then decided to give an energetic turn to the thumbscrew.

"Don't pretend to be Sir Galahad, Vanini. You're a cheat and a fake. Living by your wits and hiding behind that uniform. Don't stretch your luck. Let's get down to business. Did you or didn't you supply Lieutenant Dorfrichter with potassium cyanide?"

Vanini's voice was barely audible. "I didn't! I mean, I didn't give it to him. *He took it.*"

For three months, Emil Kunze had been waiting for this moment. Longed for it and dreaded it. Without it, Dorfrichter's guilt was a mere hypothesis, a bold assumption based on unrelated bits of information, stationery available only in Linz, small cartons used for a sewing kit, the opinion of a handwriting expert, a mailbox on Mariahilferstrasse, a train that arrived at the Western Railroad Station in Vienna at six in the morning, a dog that refused to swallow worm powder without wafer capsules.

"What do you mean—he took it?"

"I was in trouble because of the promissory note," he whispered. "There was no way out—only five days till expiration. When Dorfrichter found out about it, he said he'd talk to Landsberg-Lövy."

So it was a promissory note. Worse than a debt of honor, especially if Vanini signed a fellow officer's name to it. An unpaid debt of honor made a man a social outcast, but forgery put him in prison!

"You forged Landsberg-Lövy's signature, didn't you?"

Vanini shrugged. "The lender wanted a guarantor of good credit. I was considered a bad risk."

"How could you do a fool thing like that?"

"I was counting on an inheritance from an aunt," Vanini explained. "She'd just passed away. Then it turned out she'd left her money to the church."

"So Dorfrichter volunteered to talk to Landsberg-Lövy about redeeming the note?"

"That's right. To my utter surprise he was successful, made Landsberg-Lövy fork over the two thousand kronen—"

"And in exchange Dorfrichter wanted the cyanide!"

"No! Not in exchange! He took it because—" Vanini pulled out his handkerchief and wiped his face. "He also took my service revolver, even the bottle of aspirin I had. I was in a rotten mood. I wasn't going to wait for his talk with Landsberg-Lövy. Why should a Jew want to save me? I thought. He never impressed me as a warmhearted man. I wondered what a rich Jew like him was doing in the army anyway. No, I didn't want Dorfrichter to talk to him. I was prepared to blow my brains out, but not to kiss asses—"

"You mean, Dorfrichter took the cyanide from you to prevent you from committing suicide?"

"Yes, sir."

"Did you tell him you would?"

"That I don't know, sir. I was drunk most of the time. Sarajevo wasn't my kind of place. It was filled with hatred: The Bosnians hated the Turks; the Turks hated the Austrians; the Austrians hated the Serbs; the Serbs hated everybody—and everybody hated the Sephardic Jews. The air felt heavy when you walked down Mutevelic Street. There was no social life, only cliques. The locals, whether Christian or Mohammedan, lived behind shuttered windows and locked doors. No women to talk to, except army wives and whores. Anyway, I never should have chosen the army, sir. Perhaps it'll be all for the best if I get kicked out."

Kunze felt the pity of an older and wiser brother for the lieutenant. He had seen many like Vanini, boys in uniforms tailored for men, trying to prove they would grow into them.

"I'll do my best to spare you, Vanini," the captain promised. "But you'll have to cooperate and answer my questions honestly."

Vanini nodded. "Yes, sir."

"Dorfrichter took the two sticks of cyanide from you. Did you ever ask him to return them?"

"Well, yes, I did."

"When was that?"

"Before my transfer to Nagykanizsa. I received my orders on the second of November. I was to report to my new regiment on the twelfth. I'd been friendly with a lady in Linz and wanted to take pictures of her for a souvenir. I borrowed a camera, and when Ritzberger refused to sell my orderly the cyanide, I asked

Dorfrichter if he still had the two sticks he got from me in Sarajevo."

"What did he say?"

"He said no—he'd thrown them away."

"Did you believe him?"

"Of course! What would he have needed two sticks of cyanide for?"

"When you read about the Charles Francis circulars and Dorfrichter's arrest, didn't it occur to you that there might be a connection?"

"Yes, sir, it did," he said reluctantly.

"Why didn't you come forward and report it?" Kunze asked it although he already knew the answer.

"Because it would have brought the business of the promissory note to light. I followed the case very carefully, sir. Read every newspaper item published about it. I knew the stumbling block in the investigation was the lack of proof that Dorfrichter possessed any cyanide. If I'd given you the information, he might've retaliated by telling about the Landsberg-Lövy affair. Besides— believe me, sir—I wanted to protect him. He'd been a good friend. I didn't want to be the one delivering him to the firing squad."

"The hangman!" Kunze corrected. "He'll be hanged."

"It's all my fault," Vanini admitted. "You'd never have found out about it if I hadn't sent my orderly to Ritzberger's. What did I want pictures of that woman for? She was a big fat cow, and I didn't even like her!"

XV

IT was one of those magic days when suddenly, from the blue distance of forests, spring wafted down the Ring in Vienna. The sky was still overcast with clouds threadbare like the sheets of the poor. A layer of honeyed air scented with the odor of last autumn's leaves spread through the city. There was the rich promise of flowers yet to bloom. It acted on the city like an intoxicating drug; more children were conceived and more suicides committed than at any other time during the year.

Kunze had arrived the night before with Vanini. Although the lieutenant was no longer under arrest, the captain had ordered him to remain in the court building overnight in one of the unused offices.

In the morning he had Vanini's testimony witnessed and recorded by Lieutenants Stoklaska and Heinrich. Both the promissory note and the forged Landsberg-Lövy signature were omitted from the deposition. Then Kunze sent for Peter Dofrichter. He hadn't seen him since their venomous confrontation on the day the lieutenant had been handed the newspaper report on his wife's Riviera escapade. The provost with the Kaiser Wilhelm mustache had been replaced by a tougher, older man, who was ordered to watch Dorfrichter and make out a daily report on his conduct. He had nothing much to report, however. The prisoner retained his habit of pacing the floor with the window open in his cell, of engaging in interminable monologues and doing push-ups at night. He kept himself clean and neat, displaying an attitude of placid indifference toward his guards.

When he was brought in, Stoklaska and Heinrich were at their customary places, Kunze was behind his desk, and Vanini was seated in a chair at the far end of the room. The triangle—provost beside prisoner, guard one step behind them—marched to the desk, snapped to attention, and executed its stiff salute, the provost reporting the delivery of the prisoner in a voice much too strident for indoor use. Kunze recognized the report, dismissed provost and guard, while the prisoner remained rigidly at attention, staring at the wall above the captain's head. He may have sensed the presence of a fourth person in the room, although his field of vision was narrowed by the blinders of military discipline.

"At ease," Kunze said.

There was a rustle as Stoklaska, Heinrich and Vanini resumed their seats.

"Sit down, Dorfrichter," the captain told the lieutenant.

As Dorfrichter turned to pull the chair placed for him in front of the desk, he caught sight of Xavier Vanini. His outstretched hand remained in the air as his glance met the Italian's.

"Well," he said, then: "Well" again. His eyes remained locked with Vanini's. A crooked smile turned up the left corner of his mouth. He threw him a greeting. "*Servus.*"

"*Servus,*" Vanini echoed, his voice trembling.

"Sit down, Dorfrichter!" Kunze repeated.

Picking up the page containing Vanini's deposition, Kunze began to read in the slightly nasal, Austrian upper-class tone that often made a death sentence sound intimate and inviting. When he finished, he looked at the man who faced him in rigid silence.

"Any comment, Dorfrichter?"

The prisoner shrugged. "Lieutenant Vanini seems blessed with a very vivid imagination."

"You mean he is not telling the truth?"

Dorfrichter laughed. "I don't recall having taken any cyanide from him!"

"You took it from him along with his revolver and a bottle of aspirin," Kunze snapped.

"I remember the revolver, and I may have borrowed some aspirin. His antics were disturbing enough to give anyone a headache. But that bit about the cyanide is pure invention!"

Kunze turned to Vanini.

"Come forward, Lieutenant, and face the suspect!"

Vanini rose slowly and shuffled toward Dorfrichter. His lips trembled, and he blinked nervously.

"Will you repeat to the suspect what you told us about the cyanide?"

Vanini's eyes on Dorfrichter's face held a mixture of desperation, apology and a plea for mercy.

"When you were looking for my revolver, Peter," he explained, "you pulled out the dresser drawers and in one there was the aspirin and the two sticks of cyanide in their original wrapping—I kept them in a glass jar—and you read the labels and said that you wanted to make sure I wouldn't do something stupid and took them—"

Calmly Dorfrichter shook his head. "I don't remember it."

"That was a day or two before your meeting with Landsberg-Lövy—"

"I don't remember the meeting either," Dorfrichter said. "You asked me never to— And I gave my word."

"Jesus Christ!" Vanini groaned. "Don't crucify me. Without you I wouldn't be alive today. I haven't forgotten that—I haven't—"

Kunze rose and crossed to him.

"Once again, Vanini, do you maintain that during the latter part of August, 1908, Lieutenant Dorfrichter took two sticks of potassium cyanide from you and never returned them?"

"I do, sir." Vanini groaned.

Kunze turned to Dorfrichter. "You heard the lieutenant. He's been testifying under oath. Do you still say that he is telling a lie?"

"I do!" Dorfrichter said firmly.

"What could be his purpose? He is your friend. Why would he lie?"

"Don't ask me. I didn't make a deal with him. You did!"

Vanini paled, his lips twitching as though he were about to burst into tears.

"The lieutenant had no choice but to tell the truth, Dorfrichter," Kunze pointed out. "He may be in trouble because of you. He should have reported your taking the cyanide from him three months ago and not have waited for us to track him down. It'll be up to the court-martial whether or not his silence has made him an accessory."

"I'm sorry, Peter," Vanini muttered. "Terribly, terribly sorry."

Dorfrichter's face showed no reaction as he stared at the neighborhood rooftops through the open window.

"I have a bit of advice for you," Kunze told Vanini after Dorfrichter and the two lieutenants had left the room. "Get out of the army before it's too late. Leave it with your good name intact. You're still young. It won't be difficult for you to find your place in the civilian world. You said you liked the sea. Join the merchant marine. This time you've escaped by the skin of your teeth and the charity of Captain Landsberg-Lövy. The next time you put a fellow officer's name on a note, the man won't be quite as charitable as the baron. I'll let you go now, but I'll be watching you. One more false step, and I'll see to it that you get kicked out of the army!"

XVI

ROSE wore a turquoise crepe de chine gown trimmed with black lace and in her hair ostrich feathers fastened with a diamond clip. She looked radiant. The corps commandant's ball was her first social appearance with Kunze since their engagement had become official. With her late husband, a cabinet minister, she had moved in the staid and rather dreary circles of higher government officials. The army was a new world for her, and she was both surprised and thrilled to discover how highly respected and well liked her fiancé was. Officers of all ranks, as well as illustrious names, sought them out, wishing them luck with a warmth that filled Rose's eyes with tears. Up to now she'd regarded the army as an organization controlled by cold, often inhuman rules, but on this February night she learned about the secret adhesive that held it together: the proud and affectionate solidarity of its men. These strangers in their gold-braided uniforms were Emil Kunze's brothers, who had shared the years of his lonely bachelorhood with him. Aware of their searching glances, she hoped they found her attractive and presentable, the stuff of which good army wives are made. What she experienced was more than happiness; it was an almost religious sense of fulfillment: she stood on the mountain of Nebo, ahead of her the Promised Land.

Kunze wished he could match her mood, but he was unable to rid himself of a numbing sensation of hopelessness. The view from his mountain of Nebo was a flat desert with no woods in which to hide or find shade. He was tired and under a strange pressure. Ever since Vanini's testimony, he found himself remembering the occupation campaign in Bosnia in 1908, when he had been a member of a court-martial which had condemned a young soldier to death. The picture of the boy—his body reacting to the impact of the bullets, then collapsing into a heap of pike-gray rags, spotted with what looked like slowly blossoming crimson flowers—now stubbornly superimposed itself on the spectacle of the ball. At times the young blindfolded face dissolved into that of Peter Dorfrichter.

At supper he and Rose found themselves seated at General Wencel's table. Lily appeared tired and unusually subdued. She wore a simple dress and practically no jewelry, as though Ash Wednesday were not five days off. The general looked resplendent in his full-dress uniform and wore the mien to go with it. Gallant and attentive to Rose, he emitted gay sparkles in all directions like an overcharged Roman candle. The talk at the table concerned war. One of the younger officers mentioned an article he had read in the Paris *Monde*. The Germans supposedly were abandoning the Schlieffen Plan, supplanting it with one that would call for an all-out attack along the Alsatian border. Everyone agreed that the *Monde* report was sheer fantasy. The French would prepare for an onslaught there as a matter of prestige. Someone speculated on the chances of Russia's entering the conflict, but General Wencel thought that she would need at least twenty years to recover from her defeat at the hands of Japan. It was of vital importance that Serbia be eliminated before the great powers could feel sufficiently prepared to start a war. Russia had a commitment to defend Serbia, so the campaign in the Balkans had to be quick and thorough, possibly without a formal declaration of war. Franz Josef would never agree to that, a major general retorted heatedly, and neither would Franz Ferdinand. Attack without a formal declaration of war would be dishonorable and foolhardy, too, and certainly likely to affect the morale of the entire Officers' Corps. War should start in the traditional way: ultimatum, declaration, attack. Throughout the heated discussion the orchestra played the "Merry Widow Waltz."

"Let's dance," Kunze suggested to Rose. "Since next week is Ash Wednesday, this may be our last ball for a long time."

Looking around the dance floor, he found that they were the oldest couple in the crowd. The faces that whirled past were fresh and glowing, the dresses white, pale blue or gentle pink, the uniforms bearing no more than one or two insignia on their choke collars. He wondered if any of the young men were really as anxious to attack Serbia, with or without a formal declaration of war, as their elders seemed to be. His vision of the barracks yard with the felled private gave way to another image: in a bleak country along the Bosnian-Serbian border, line after line of human figures, in closed formation, approaching a row of belching cannon. With each burst of fire a line went down, bodies falling neatly sideways like ripe wheat under a scythe.

"What are you thinking of?" Rose asked.

"Nothing much," he lied.

"But you look so grim."

He forced a smile. "I do not. I'm having a very good time."

"Congratulations, Captain. Everyone is enchanted with your fiancée," Dr. Goldschmiedt told him.

He had phoned for an appointment. First he had suggested lunch at the Sacher, but Kunze evaded the invitation with the excuse that he'd been booked for days, so they settled on a talk at Kunze's office.

"My wife hopes," Dr. Goldschmiedt went on, "that we'll have the pleasure of meeting Frau von Siebert soon."

"Thank you, Doctor. I'll tell Frau von Siebert. I'm sure she'll be flattered."

Kunze didn't want any social contact with the Goldschmiedts. He'd never liked him, but lately he resented him even more as though by cuckolding Dorfrichter, the attorney had affronted him personally.

Goldschmiedt had arrived on time, exuding charm and goodwill. His chatter, while amusing, was time-consuming. Quite evidently his visit had a purpose other than that of congratulating Kunze on the choice of his future wife, yet he was very slow in coming to the point. Finally losing his patience during a breathing spell between two amusing stories, Kunze quickly threw in a question: "What can I do for you, Doctor?"

The interruption produced a total solar eclipse on the attorney's face.

"I am here on behalf of Frau Dorfrichter. As you know, I represent her. Frau Dorfrichter intends to divorce her husband."

Shocked and also disturbed by an odd sense of guilt, Kunze asked, "What made her decide?"

"It's really a family decision," Dr. Goldschmiedt answered. Ill at ease, he evaded Kunze's eyes. "Frau Gruber is selling her store and wants to leave the country, taking her daughter and the child along. She has a married sister in Murnau, a small town not far from Munich, and that's where she wants to settle."

Kunze gazed at Goldschmiedt, the aging caricature of a dandy, his helpmate in breaking Lieutenant Peter Dorfrichter, and knew he should have been pleased with this development. Instead, he wished he could turn back the clock to the moment when the handwriting expert had first uttered Dorfrichter's name at the War College archives.

"I'm afraid we can't let Frau Dorfrichter leave the country. Not while the investigation is in progress. We might need her testimony."

"She won't be of much help to you. Not in her present condition," the attorney reported. When he saw the captain's raised eyebrows, he added: "She's suffered a breakdown and is in Dr. Breuer's sanatorium."

Kunze had known that much, but spending a few weeks in a fashionable sanatorium did not always mean that the patient was sick.

"Well, I'll have to tell Lieutenant Dorfrichter about his wife's wish. I imagine he'll consent to the divorce, so you won't have any problems. I'll let you know his reaction."

Immediately after Dr. Goldschmiedt's exit, Kunze went from the court to the prison section of the building. He hadn't been in Dorfrichter's cell since the night he had informed him of the birth of his son. Several times during the long walk across corridors and up and down stairs, he felt an urge to turn back and stage the encounter within the physical and emotional security of his office. It was hard to guess whether the intimacy of a cell would reduce or elevate him from judge to man. The guilt he'd felt before was still heavy on his mind. He should probably have sent Stoklaska to Dorfrichter with the message, arriving after the blow had been struck. That would have been the sensible thing to do. After all, he was still the judge and Dorfrichter the prisoner.

The two men on duty in the guardroom were playing twenty-one at a table in the corner, jumping up like flushed partridges when they sighted the captain. He had deliberately avoided calling the provost; that would have been the regular procedure. The men stood at stiff attention and stared at him stupidly. The room, overheated by an iron stove, was heavy with the smell of perspiring male bodies and cheap tobacco.

He asked for the key to Number 6 cell, indicating that the guards remain behind. They complied, and if they were astonished, it failed to show. The embezzler in the Number 1 cell had been convicted and moved to the Mollersdorf Military Prison; his place occupied by a young second lieutenant who had killed a comrade in a duel. Number 3's inmate was a young dragoon charged with conduct unbecoming an officer. In a state of drunkenness he had led his unit in a mounted attack against the police headquarters in Lemberg.

Peter Dorfrichter lay stretched out on the bed, his head resting on his crossed arms, his eyes focused on the ceiling. Evidently thinking it was the guard who entered, he turned only when he heard Kunze's voice. He blinked nervously as though trying to clear his vision.

"I have something to tell you, Dorfrichter."

The lieutenant sat up, swinging his legs over the side of the bed. "The last time you came here you told me I'd become a father. What is it this time? Something of equal importance?"

As usual his mocking tone made Kunze bristle.

"That's for you to decide. Your wife wants a divorce." Now it was out. It had not been difficult. The hostile grin on the face of the prisoner had helped.

"Does she now?" Dorfrichter frowned. "A divorce? I might not give it to her! Do I have to?"

"You may contest the suit or retort with a countercharge. I didn't ask her attorney how he intended to proceed, but at this point she'll probably sue on grounds of adultery."

At the words "her attorney" the lieutenant winced. "Is she still represented by that man?"

"At this moment, yes. I imagine when it comes to the suit, she'll have someone else." How grotesque it would be to have Dr. Goldschmiedt call Dorfrichter an adulterer, Kunze thought.

The captain stepped to one of the chairs and sat down. Dorfrichter was hunched on the side of the bed, his head propped up by his cupped hands. The fireworks Kunze had expected failed to materialize. The news had stunned the lieutenant but had not enraged him.

"Why?" He looked questioningly at Kunze, and for the first time, his eyes were free of animosity. "Why? What's happened to her? It's not like Marianne!"

Kunze felt oddly let down by Dorfrichter's lack of furor. "You know her. I don't."

With an abruptness that made Kunze start, Dorfrichter jumped off the bed. "I must speak to her," he said sounding determined. "I can't make a decision without that. I don't care if it is against regulations. I'm still her husband, and she is my wife. And this is something strictly between the two of us. It can't be settled by go-betweens or lawyers!"

"What if she doesn't want to see you?"

"Then I'll contest the divorce! I'll find means. In civil cases I'm entitled to be represented by a civilian attorney just like any other citizen." He crossed to Kunze and looked down at him. "You will arrange it, won't you? A meeting, I mean. You owe it to me."

The captain rose. They stood quite close, their bodies almost touching. He felt the lieutenant's dark, knowing eyes boring into his own. He was seized by an aching desire to throw his arms around the man and to acknowledge what he was, honestly, fearlessly. His arms moved, then slackened. Holding them back was not the knowledge that this one gesture could demolish his entire future, but the realization that the man facing him was expecting it, relishing in advance the taste of victory over him.

Kunze moved to the window, out of the magnetic sphere of the man.

"I'll see what I can do," he said when he felt sufficiently in control of his voice. "I can't promise you anything. All I can tell you is that I agree with you that the meeting should take place."

Without looking at Dorfrichter, he started for the door. The upheaval had not yet completely subsided in his body, but his

...

hands no longer trembled as he pressed the door handle down. "You'll hear from me," he said.

There was the sound of Dorfrichter's heels snapping together, and a murmured "Thank you, sir."

Kunze quickly slammed the door, twisting the key in the lock.

The meeting took place on a brisk, windy evening in early March. At first, Dr. Breuer was against it, but he changed his mind after a talk with Frau Gruber. He agreed with her that Marianne had no chance for a normal life unless she left Vienna, and the sooner the divorce was granted, the better.

There had been a decided improvement in Marianne's condition. She was still withdrawn, but in a more serene and at times even gay mood. Frau Gruber visited her regularly, occasionally taking the baby along. Marianne seemed glad to see the child but didn't ask for him when Frau Gruber left him home.

On the military side, the decision to let Dorfrichter meet his wife was made at the office of the commandant of the Vienna garrison, Baron Versbach von Hadauer, after a two-hour discussion attended by Captain Kunze, General Wencel and Councilor Stukart of the Security Bureau. Before the agreement was reached, the commandant consulted with Minister of War von Schönaich on the phone, obtaining his consent.

It was decided that the meeting between the Dorfrichters take place at a late-evening hour, mainly to evade the vigilance of the press. Since the Vanini testimony, Dorfrichter's guilt was no longer doubted by either the ministry or the corps command. Kunze was warmly complimented by both the commanding general and Councilor Stukart on his exemplary conduct of the inquiry.

Marianne Dorfrichter was accompanied by Dr. Johann Frazer, an attorney with Dr. Goldschmiedt's law firm, and a male nurse from the sanatorium. They arrived in a closed fiacre at the side entrance to the Military Lawcourt, where they were escorted upstairs by Lieutenant Stoklaska. The nurse remained in the anteroom while the young attorney and Marianne were ushered into Kunze's office.

At first sight, the captain could detect no sign of ill health in Marianne. She wore a dark-gray winter suit from her prepregnancy days, the skirt longer than the current fashion, a scarf and a muff of moleskin, and a red velvet hat. Her hair was neatly combed except for a few wind-loosened ringlets. She moved with a placid dignity, reminding Kunze of a swan gliding across a lake. When he had last seen her, she had been at the end of her pregnancy; now she seemed ethereal by comparison. The attorney, not realizing that she had met Kunze before, hastened to introduce them. Proffering her hand with a smile, she said that she was pleased to see him again. Then she took the chair offered to her and sat quietly listening to the strained small talk with which Dr. Frazer and the captain filled the minutes while waiting for the prisoner.

Kunze had given orders to the provost to escort Lieutenant Dorfrichter to the threshold of his office, then let him enter alone. As Dorfrichter stepped into the room, the light of the chandelier fell on the guard's fixed bayonet, transforming it into a sharp, glistening exclamation mark. As the door creaked, Marianne turned, but if she saw the bayonet, she gave no sign, recognizing her husband with a vague smile. Dorfrichter took a few steps forward, stiffened to attention, and saluted the captain. He appeared composed, although he bit into his lower lip to still the trembling. He acknowledged the attorney's greeting with a quick nod, not taking his eyes from his wife.

"Good evening, Marianne," he said gently.

She frowned, crossing her arms in front of her abdomen.

"Don't look at me!" she cried out. "I'm a sight. You promised not to look at me—not till I've had the baby. You promised!"

Dorfrichter seemed caught off guard. He opened his mouth to speak, his lips formed a word, but no sound escaped. He shook his head as though trying to clear his ears, and his eyes, startled and questioning, moved to Kunze's face. The captain answered with a nod, and Dr. Frazer broke the silence, his much too loud voice out of place in the small room.

"Lieutenant, I must warn you that your creating problems will merely lengthen the proceedings but certainly won't keep my client from obtaining her freedom," he rattled.

Dorfrichter stared. "Keep your mouth shut!" His tone caused the young man to swallow with indignation.

"My dear Lieutenant—" he began, the expression on Dorf-richter's face cutting him off.

Dorfrichter went up to Marianne and, reaching out for her hands, pulled her into a gentle, cautious embrace.

"You've had the baby, Marianne." He touched her chin, tilting it. "Don't you remember?" He stared at her searchingly as though trying to find the key that would unlock her mind.

She smiled at him, shaking her head.

"Do you know who I am, Marianne?"

"Of course, I know who you are," she said, laughing. Then pushed him away.

"Are you angry with me?" he asked.

"No." She shook her head. "No," she repeated, but this time with a question mark. Suddenly she seemed confused, burying her face in her hands. When she dropped them, there were tears in her eyes.

Nervously Dr. Frazer stepped closer. "You must understand, Lieutenant, that your wife has been a patient at Dr. Breuer's sanatorium."

"Leave us alone, will you? I do understand. Just leave us alone!" Addressing Kunze, Dorfrichter raised his voice. "Tell him, sir, to get the hell out of here!"

The young man sputtered, but Kunze cut him short. "You might as well wait outside, Dr. Frazer. I'll be staying, so you won't risk anything if you do as the lieutenant asks you."

"He didn't ask me—he ordered me!" The attorney hesitated for a moment, then made an abrupt about-face and strutted from the room.

"Marianne," Dorfrichter asked, "do you know where we are?"

She smiled through her tears and shrugged.

"Do you know the captain?"

"Of course, I know the captain." She sounded slightly irritated. "I've already said so, haven't I?"

"Do you know why we are here?"

She didn't seem to hear the question.

"I'm tired," she whispered. "Isn't Dr. Breuer coming tonight? He always comes around this time."

Dorfrichter led her to the sofa in the corner, and they sat down. "Listen to me, Marianne. Things have happened that are hard to explain, but you must remember one thing: I love you very much. I never wanted to hurt you. You are all I have in this world. Do you hear me, Marianne? Do you?"

She gazed at him with the expression of someone listening to the sound of faraway music. Lifting her hand, she touched his cheek.

"You need a haircut," she told him. Leaning closer, she spoke in a clear, lively voice. "The baby had black hair when he was born, but it all fell out, and his new hair is blond, almost white."

"You see—I told you that you had the baby." Dorfrichter's voice was heavy with pleading and hope, but like a shooting star, her lucidity had already flickered out.

Kunze had been sitting behind his desk with his back to them, wishing he could bring an end to their painful dialogue. He knew embarrassment and remorse and was—for the first time—filled with a deep and tender pity for the woman.

She was getting restless, asking again for Dr. Breuer. She reminded Kunze of a well-bred child who'd been taken to an adult party, behaved like an angel up to a point when, suddenly tired of the grown-up talk around her, refused to stay another minute. It was also obvious that Peter Dorfrichter realized he was talking to the empty shell of the woman who used to be his wife.

"I think, sir, she might as well be taken back to the sanatorium. This is wearing her out."

"I'll call Dr. Frazer," Kunze said, and left the room, allowing the lieutenant to say his farewells in private.

When he returned, he found them seated side by side on the sofa, Dorfrichter's arm around Marianne, her head on his shoulder. She appeared calm now, and there was an expression of peace and contentment on her face. In the past, she must have sat like this often, feeling the fabric of his tunic under her cheek and her nostrils inhaling the mixed odor of a clean male body, soap and tobacco, an odor particular to one man in the world, stirring up feelings in her that no pleading or persuasion could have awakened. She had not really recognized the man, Kunze mused, only the touch of his hand, the embrace of his arms and the feel of his body against hers—only the melody, surely not the words.

When the nurse came to take her, she was unwilling to

move. Finally, the warning that Dr. Breuer would be angry made
her obey, and she left the warm nest of the familiar arms.

Kunze had not invited the attorney back to his office, telling
him that he'd discuss the matter of divorce with Dorfrichter and
telephone him the decision. He saw Marianne to the anteroom,
although he was aware of the risk of leaving an unguarded prisoner in the office. It seemed an act of cruelty to Kunze not to
grant the lieutenant a few moments of solitude.

As Marianne Dorfrichter crossed the threshold of the corridor,
she turned back to the captain, a cold but lucid look in her eyes.
"I know who you are! Had I known you'd be here, I would
not have come!"

Kunze found Dorfrichter still seated on the sofa, elbows propped
on the table, chin cupped in hands. Engrossed in his thoughts,
he failed to hear the captain's return, jumping at the sound of
Kunze's pulling out his desk chair with a suddenness that sent
an ashtray flying to the floor. The captain picked it up.

Dorfrichter apologized when he saw that the ashtray—an ala-
baster souvenir from Venice—showed a crack. "I'm sorry, sir. It
doesn't look like government issue—it might have been a gift."

"No. I bought it the last time I was in Venice. But forget it!
I'll get another when I'm in Venice again. There is always a next
time."

It suddenly occurred to him that for the man he was talking to,
there'd be no next time in Venice or any other place.

"I told the attorney you'd consider the divorce and tell me your
decision. Take your time. Don't let them press you into anything."

"I've made up my mind," Dorfrichter said. "I won't contest
the divorce. She should have it. The sooner, the better." There
were deep shadows under his eyes, and for the first time his face
seemed devoid of the glow of youth that had made it so appealing. The process of age had molded a young man's features into
those of an old man during the past hour.

Kunze longed to tell him how sorry he was, for Marianne, for
him, also for himself, but knew it was the wrong moment.

"Do you want me to give your message to Dr. Frazer in the
morning, or shall I wait a few days?"

"Don't wait, sir. I won't change my mind."

"I've been told that Dr. Breuer is very optimistic. He thinks it's only a question of time and your wife will recover fully. It's not uncommon for young women to suffer breakdowns after childbirth. With your wife it was the added anxiety: your arrest and—"

"Nothing will change my mind, sir," Dorfrichter cut in, a hint of impatience in his voice. "Even if she recovers tomorrow, even if she tells me herself that she doesn't want a divorce, *I want her to get it!* Her mother is right. They should leave the country and settle where they're not known. Marianne is much too young to be buried under the ruins of what used to be our life together." After a pause, he added: "Anyway, thank you for your kind concern, sir."

This was new: the first "thank you" that sounded as though it were meant, possibly the first white flag of surrender. Anyone else in Kunze's place would have quickly summoned a witness and a recorder and begun firing questions at the prisoner. Kunze reached for the bell to summon the sergeant on duty, then let his hand drop. The man in front of him was a target he couldn't bring himself to take a shot at.

"I think I'll dismiss you now," he said, offering Dorfrichter a cigarette. "You need rest."

Later that night the captain was called on the phone by Dr. Klein, the physician on duty at the Military Prison, and informed that the prisoner had asked for a sleeping pill, the first such request during his imprisonment. Kunze gave his consent, wondering if it might not be a good idea to ask for a pill for himself.

XVII

KUNZE'S wedding day fell on a Tuesday. For a long time it had seemed that the fifth of March would never come. The date had hovered in the distance like Vesuvius over Naples, distinctly outlined against the sky, emitting little whiffs of smoke, but never presenting a live threat. Then suddenly, almost without warning, the mountain tumbled down on him. He put on his dress uniform and a pair of new white glacé gloves at eleven in the morning and climbed into a rented fiacre with Hans von Gersten, his best man. He had been to the magistrate's office with Rose the previous afternoon, so legally he was already her husband. Now he was headed for St. Michael's Church to make his marriage doubly valid.

"You're very quiet," Gersten remarked with a chuckle as the fiacre was turning onto the Ring. "Scared?"

"No. Just thinking."

He *was* thinking about marriage: what it would be, what it would give him, and what it would take away. He had slept with Rose before, so it wasn't sex keeping them together. What then? To belong, to be "we" instead of "I," a second face in the bathroom mirror in the morning, a hand to hold in the hour of death? To love and to cherish? Oh, but did he love Rose? Wasn't love the most brazenly exploited word in the dictionary? Probably not for the young. They had the capability of loving. On the threshold of middle age, he tried to conjure up his twenty-year-younger self. He had been able to love then, easily and uncritically: his mother, the eldest Hartmann boy, teachers, friends. What he had missed and sought he knew was being loved. With his precocious self-discipline he had managed to hide this longing even from himself, but it was there, gnawing at his insides like a bloodsucking parasite. It had seemed to him that only reciprocated love could make him really exist. Without it he would remain forever a ghost, a non-being, a nullity. Now, at thirty-eight, he no longer felt like a ghost. He was a person, even more than a person, a world in himself. He had found his place, learned to live alone and be complete, no longer craving the affection of others. The years had cleared away all malice, leaving in its stead tolerance lightly tinged with urbane cynicism. Goodwill, benevolence, charity he could dispense freely, but without any deep personal satisfaction, because he was unable to add the mysterious ingredient of love to them. Did he love Rose? he asked himself again. Did he feel a glow of tenderness when he looked at her; did he miss her when she was away? The answer was no. He tolerated her the way he tolerated the rest of humanity. Yet he *was* capable of tenderness. It welled up within him whenever his hand glided over Troll's bushy head, and he had felt it for Peter Dorfrichter as the younger man had sat hunched with grief on the hard government issue sofa in his office. At thirty-eight, in the midst of a billion creatures who inhabited the earth, Emil Kunze felt an emotion that could be termed love for only two: a murderer and a dog.

Was he being fair to himself and to Rose? The answer was simple. To Rose, yes; to himself, no. The fact that she was marrying a man who didn't love her was of no importance; she was marrying a man whom she loved blindly and unconditionally, and no woman could wish for more. The burden of the marriage was to be borne by him. He'd accepted her love, and since he couldn't repay it in kind, he would cancel the debt with tact, patience and solicitude. Out of weakness and emotional laziness he had allowed her love to grow until it threatened to devour him. A man of character would have killed it long ago. Peter Dorfrichter would never have married Rose von Siebert.

The candles in the church flickered palely as Rose walked up the aisle on the arm of her brother-in-law. She wore a beige spring suit and a matching wide-brimmed hat trimmed with black ribbons. The only thought that leaped to Kunze's mind at that solemn moment was that she would surely catch her death in the icy draft. Women were incredible; they would rather be fashionable than alive. To them the beginning of spring was not when the snow melted but when the couturiers showed their new lines.

Monsignor Olden, family friend and father confessor to the Sieberts, officiated. Rose, looking tired and nervous, approached the altar, staring straight ahead, with a fixed smile on her face. Kunze could never understand why women had to crowd their days with the most exhausting activities before their wedding. Of course, there had been the obligatory social calls on his comrades and superiors and Rose's staggeringly large circle of friends. Luckily, no call had to last longer than the conventional ten minutes; often leaving their card sufficed when the hosts were not at home. Nevertheless, the visits were wearisome and time-consuming. In addition, Rose insisted on buying a trousseau, from lingerie to bed linen, which Kunze found incomprehensible, since for the past two years they'd been comfortably sleeping together on old sheets. Wedged between social calls and fittings for her new wardrobe were the preparations for the wedding itself, conferences with the monsignor and the headwaiter at the Sacher Hotel, even with the formidable Frau Sacher. Kunze refused to take part in them, preferring a small, quiet wedding. They had compromised on an elegant *déjeuner* in one of the hotel's private dining rooms.

Throughout the ceremony, Kunze felt more like a bystander than a participant. Not a religious man, he nevertheless loved the rites of his church, their symbolism and Baroque splendor. This time, however, the monsignor's mellifluous delivery and trite phrases left him cold. He and Rose were not young innocents —they were two very mature adults—and they should have been spoken to—if at all—in a tone more befitting their intelligence. Throwing a glance at Rose, he was surprised to discover her listening spellbound and with tears in her eyes. *Oh, dear,* he thought, silently apologizing to the monsignor, who, evidently, was a better judge of the female psyche than he.

The *déjeuner* at the Sacher turned out to be a very satisfactory affair. From Kunze's world, the Wencels, Lieutenants Stoklaska and Heinrich, old General Hartmann and his wife, their daughter, Paula, and her husband and Hans von Gersten attended; the rest of the guests were from Rose's circle. Surprisingly, the two sets mixed well, the toasts were short and witty, and everyone, including the newlyweds, had a gay time. After a few glasses of champagne Rose relaxed, no longer the sentimental old maid she'd been at St. Michael's. The monsignor had stripped off his honeyed unctuousness along with his chasuble and was now telling risqué jokes to Lily Wencel. In Kunze's eyes this expiated his performance at the church.

Kunze had requested and been granted a week's leave, which he and Rose were to spend at the Bauer Grunwald Hotel in Venice. He would have preferred Venice later when the weather would be more predictable, but Rose had insisted on a honeymoon. She was getting married, and by God, she was going to do it the traditional way, blessed by Monsignor Olden, feted at the Sacher, and carnally possessed in a sleeping car on the way to the Adriatic Sea. It mattered not at all that she'd been through the entire ritual twenty years earlier.

From the Sacher, Kunze took his bride home to her apartment, then went on to Traungasse to collect his luggage. As he entered, he found Fräulein Baldauf waiting for him with a message.

"There was an urgent call from your office at the Military Court, Captain," she reported. "They tried to get you at the Sacher but were told that you'd left. They want you to call back."

The telephone was still a rather capricious means of communication, and it took Kunze a few minutes to reach the sergeant on duty.

"I know, it's your wedding day, sir," the man apologized, "but you told us to contact you any time if—"

Kunze cut in impatiently. "What's happened?"

"Lieutenant Dorfrichter wants to see you, sir. Staff Provost Koller says he's never seen the lieutenant in such a state. He's already had Dr. Klein look at him, but it didn't do much good—"

"All right, Sergeant, I'll be there in ten minutes."

It was four o'clock in the afternoon; their train for Venice was scheduled to leave at six. Kunze decided to go straight to the Military Prison, find out what the prisoner wanted, then decide about postponing or canceling his trip. No need to upset Rose unless absolutely necessary, he thought. He asked Fräulein Baldauf to send his suitcases over to Zaunergasse and scribbled a note telling Rose that he would be back in time to take her to the station.

The ride to Hernalser Gürtel seemed interminable. He'd found no fiacre at the stand, only an *Einspänner* with a drunken cabman and a horse afflicted with a bad case of the heaves. At last, at four thirty, they reached the prison, where he headed directly for Dorfrichter's cell. Both the staff provost and Dr. Klein were waiting for him in the guardroom. Kunze asked for the key to the cell.

"Don't you want us to go with you, sir?" the staff provost suggested. "The lieutenant seems to be in a rather bad frame of mind. The guards say he was up all night, pacing the floor like an animal in the zoo. He won't be the first man I've seen crack up. With your permission, sir, I wouldn't go into that cell alone."

Dr. Klein nodded agreement.

"I'll take the chance," Kunze said. The man's solicitude irritated him. "I'll ring the bell if I need you, Koller."

The staff provost went with him to unlock the cell door, then returned reluctantly to the guardroom.

Dorfrichter, standing at the window, didn't give the impression of a man about to go berserk, and although he looked pale and had deep rings under his eyes, he seemed composed, almost serene.

"So you have come, after all," he said. "At first, Koller refused to contact you. Tried all sorts of excuses. You weren't available, were out of town, on sick leave; then to top it all, you were getting married—"

Kunze nodded. "I was."

Dorfrichter gave him a quizzical look. "I'll be damned! But you've come anyway. I appreciate it. I had to get this thing over with. I couldn't have endured another day, another night—"

"What thing?" the captain asked.

Dorfrichter's expression indicated that he found the question absurd.

"My—well—I don't know what to call it. *My confession!* Yes, that about covers it." He was no longer calm. There was desperation written all over his face. He sat down on the cot and leaned against the wall. "I never thought I'd reach this point— Don't for a moment think, though, that you got me where I am! You haven't, despite your brilliant conduct of the investigation. It was a combination of things. The meeting with my wife—I couldn't get over it, not in this goddamn cell! No books, no reading matter, no pen, no paper, nobody to talk to, nothing to do all day, but look at the bloody ceiling or out the bloody window! Counting chimneys, cracks in the ceiling! The Spanish Inquisition was more humane. The thumbscrew or the rack. I would consider them a diversion. But the endless waits between interrogations! Why the hell was there so much to investigate? The very first day you had enough circumstantial evidence to get me convicted and sentenced to twenty years in prison. But no, you're a goddamn perfectionist. Nothing less than the firing squad will do for you!"

Kunze felt the sudden taste of bile in his mouth. "Don't count on the firing squad," he snapped. "The rope is more likely."

He swallowed hard, trying to suppress an attack of nausea, resentment at Dorfrichter's insolence as strong as ever. In a more tranquil tone he went on. "Let's get down to facts! Do you admit mailing ten circulars, each containing two cyanide capsules, to ten of your War College classmates on the fourteenth of November last year?"

Dorfrichter nodded. "I do."

Kunze knew he should have been elated, triumphant, gratified, but he wasn't. All he felt at this moment was leaden fatigue. He rang for the provost. Soon Koller entered.

"I want the lieutenant taken to my office," Kunze ordered. "I also want Lieutenants Stoklaska and Heinrich. They might not be home, so have them located. They're to report to the office no matter what condition they're in!"

He left the cell without looking at Dorfrichter and hurried to the Lawcourt Building. It was five o'clock. Nervously he cranked the phone and told the switchboard operator to connect him with Rose's number. The cook answered.

"Thank God, Captain," she wheezed into the transmitter, "we've been so worried. Where are you? Frau Kunze is afraid that you'll miss the train—"

"Let me talk to her!" Kunze said harshly. He was anxious to talk to Rose before the prisoner was brought in.

He heard Rose's alarmed voice from the other end. "What's wrong? Where are you?"

"Rose, this might upset you, but it can't be helped. We can't leave today."

"Why not?"

"I'm calling from the office. Something's come up. I must stay."

"Oh, Emil." He could tell she was crying. "I've been looking forward—so much—to this trip. Can't you do something? This isn't fair, Emil—"

He felt a flush of anger and raised his voice. "Listen here, Rose. You're no longer the widow Siebert. You are an army wife. And army wives know that the service comes before everything else. If they're not willing to accept this, they shouldn't be army wives! So stop crying and go over to the travel agency and have them cancel our reservations and refund the money."

"Does that mean we won't be going at all?" she whispered.

"We will—eventually. Right now, I don't know. We'll see—"

"But Emil, what shall I tell our friends? They all think we're on our way to Venice."

"Tell them we are *not* on our way to Venice. Anyway, it's none of their damn—their business." He took a deep breath. "Oh, Rose, can't you understand? I didn't plan it this way. It just happened."

"It's Dorfrichter, isn't it?"

"I'll tell you when I get home."

"Whatever's wrong, can't someone else substitute for you? I'm sure if you talked to General Wencel, he would assign another judge advocate. For instance, Lieutenant Stoklaska. He's been on the case from the very beginning!"

Kunze was losing his patience. "This is something I must handle myself! Because that's how I want it!"

"Oh" was all she uttered.

There was a knock on the door, and the sergeant on duty entered to report the prisoner's presence in the anteroom.

"I can't talk now, Rose," Kunze said into the phone. "Do as you're told!" Hanging up, he turned to the sergeant. "Have the prisoner brought in!"

Flanked by the provost and followed by the guard, Peter Dorfrichter entered and advanced three steps. At the distance prescribed by regulations, all three halted stiffly and stood at attention. Kunze wondered how many times the same pantomime had been performed in his office and what difference there was between the past and the present occasions. The guard was the same, probably not the man himself, but the cold, sharp edge of the bayonet, and the cold, sharp stare of the eyes. The staff provost? Now there was a difference. Old, chubby Tuttman had had asthma and a compassionate heart; Koller possessed neither. He was efficient, dependable and indifferent. As for the prisoner, the change was startling. There was a new man in the same body. The fight had left him. The defiance was gone.

Kunze dismissed both guard and provost and offered Dorfrichter a seat.

"We have to wait for Stoklaska and Heinrich," he told him. "Anything you say before they get here will remain between us."

"There's nothing I can't say in front of them. Perhaps just one thing—I am *not* sorry."

"Not sorry about what?"

"The circulars, the cyanide, even Mader. Yes, I would do it again; only I'd do it better." He spoke calmly but with a deep sadness. "For my wife's sake. I've destroyed her and that's terrible. I should never have been caught!"

Kunze stared with disbelief at the handsome face. "You're insane!"

"No. I am perfectly sane. You have the report of three psychiatrists in your files to corroborate it."

"Don't you feel any guilt?"

Dorfrichter shook his head. "None whatsoever."

Kunze was both amazed and envious. A man who didn't know the agony of guilt, Adam having eaten the forbidden fruit and enjoyed it to the last bite.

"You killed a man and tried to kill nine more. You can't justify that!"

"I certainly can. Perhaps not to you, because you've purposely shut your mind to my reasoning, but to myself. That's probably the reason why I don't feel guilty."

"I wish to God I could understand you. You must be mad."

"I'll try to explain my reasoning to you," Dorfrichter said patiently. Rising, he paced the floor.

"Let me go back to last November. The Advancement List was published in the *Gazette*. It didn't contain my name. I was to remain a field officer, in case of war commanding one company

—about two hundred men—while as a staff officer I could have controlled the fate of thousands. Take Mader, for instance. He was assigned to the Telegraph Office. The days of the commanding general observing the flow of battle through binoculars from a hilltop are over. He was to sit in his office far behind the front, keeping in touch with his men by telegraph and telephone. The fate of a whole army corps might depend on the competence of the staff officer in charge of communications. I happened to meet Mader by chance last year when I was in Vienna on leave. We both were mildly tight and got into an argument. A very amicable argument about army matters. Mader was bright and well trained, but his views were last century. Our Telegraph Office hasn't been substantially modernized since Königgrätz. Staffed with men like him, it wouldn't be reorganized until it was too late. What I'm driving at is this: The aim of any war is to kill the maximum number of the enemy while saving the maximum number of your own men. You put officers like Mader in charge of vital operations, and the result is that you lose more of your own men and less of the enemy."

"When I think of Mader, I see his hands," Kunze said, his voice low and dispassionate. "His nails torn from their beds, dripping blood. His views on warfare may not have been as visionary as yours, but he didn't deserve to die like he did because of that."

Dorfrichter gave him a sober look. "I thought you wanted to hear my motivation, not my defense. Because I won't defend myself. It would be useless. I'll be hanged or shot. No matter how deeply convinced I am that it would be in the country's interest to have me on the General Staff instead of any one of the nine promoted men, I'm no fool to offer that as a mitigating circumstance. No court would accept it, least of all a court-martial. What's the use? Let's talk about the weather." He slumped down on a chair. "Did you really get married today?"

The switch confused Kunze.

"Married? Yes, yes—I did."

"In that case, congratulations should be in order. Only I'm not exactly in favor of marriage right now. It could be a good man's undoing." Then with a bitter grin he added, "A bad man's, too. I'm afraid Frau Kunze won't feel too kindly toward me. I certainly chose the wrong day for monopolizing her husband's attention."

Kunze remained silent. For the past months he'd been looking forward to the day when the lieutenant would speak the magic words "I did it!" Now he had, but they solved nothing, except the case of the Charles Francis circulars, which suddenly seemed unimportant.

The two of them were alone, probably for the last time in their lives, and matters should have been settled between them because if they weren't now, Kunze knew they never would be. He felt a desperate urge to reach out to the man, but an invisible wall still separated them. With his confession Peter Dorfrichter had pronounced his own death sentence. He was already a dying man, while Kunze was destined to go on living.

"You goddamn fool!" Kunze flared. He wanted to hit the prisoner, pummel him with his fists, bloody his pale, unsullied face. "Didn't you know that you'd be caught? Are you so damn conceited that you thought you could outwit the whole bloody army? On the day I was handed the case, I knew it had to be you: a man passed over. All I had to do was dig out a few term papers at the War College archives and show them to a handwriting expert. And I'm no genius, just a very ordinary jurist. Genius—that's you! Oh, hell." He felt a sharp, dull numbing pain behind his left temple coupled with a wave of nausea, the onset of a migraine attack.

Dorfrichter stared at him baffled, but also oddly moved. "I am sorry," he said, then quickly corrected himself. "Not about the charge—I've told you, I'd do it again. Only to have made such a shambles of it all: Marianne, Vanini, Friedrich Gabriel, Anna, you—"

"Me?"

"I know you wish you'd never been assigned this case. It was no joyride for you. You're much too decent to deserve a lousy thing like this."

The pain inside Kunze's skull became sharp and piercing. "You're wrong," he said. "I wouldn't have missed it for anything. And not because I'm holding the winning hand. In spite of it! But goddamn you, why did you confess?" he exploded. "And if now—why not earlier?"

The lieutenant buried his face in his palms. "I confessed because I wanted to put an end to it. I botched the damned job, that's all." He looked up. "Sorry for having caused you nothing but aggravation." He smiled. "I even ruined your wedding day."

Stoklaska and Heinrich came bursting in, both glowing with postwedding euphoria. They were steady on their feet, though Heinrich's consonants sounded slightly slurred. After the breakup of the party, they'd continued celebrating at the Café Sacher, where one of the searching parties dispatched by Provost Koller had found them. They were tactful enough not to comment on the captain's presence behind his desk, instead of in a sleeping car headed for Venice.

When they had taken their places, Kunze began the systematic interrogation of the accused.

"When did the idea of the poisonings first occur to you?"

XVIII

IT had been one of those days when nothing happened right. The weather had turned nasty and a cold downpour
churned the mud left by previous rains. Lieutenant Peter Dorfrichter had to be at the casern at the ungodly hour of six to take
the company inspection. He usually left it to his adjutant, except
that the man was on leave, having a gay old time in Vienna. After
inspection the company marched to the drill grounds, and he
went to his office to handle administrative matters, dropping in
on his way at the garrison hospital to see a sergeant whose left
foot had been injured when the wheels of a soup kitchen cart had
rolled over it. Of all the regimental officers, Lieutenant Dorfrichter enjoyed the most satisfactory relationship with enlisted
personnel. His was a persistently model company with no cases
of insubordination, desertion or even absence without leave. He
felt close to his men, even to the raw recruits, peasants and mountain boys, clumsy, bewildered, smelling of sweat and manure.
Nothing pleased him more than to see men transformed into
neat, alert, intelligent soldiers, not just a horde of tamed cattle.
Troop duty was not exactly his dream, but whatever the assignment, his goal was to excel at it. He longed to be able to relax
and not drive himself, but no one who watched him perform with
such seeming ease could detect the effort behind the perfection.
What was it that caused his fellow officers to slow down, to come
to a standstill? Did they lack his ambition, his willpower, his
pride? Were they really as contemptible as he thought them to
be? Weak, dull-witted, lazy?

He remained a good ten minutes with the sergeant, then looked in on a private recovering from an appendectomy. The private was from Salzburg, his hometown, and Lieutenant Dorf-richter came right after the Father, the Son and the Holy Ghost in the private's world. The adoration in the young man's eyes amused and flattered him. Simplicity and innocence never failed to move him, and he knew that was why he was especially fond of animals. As a boy he had talked his mother into serving a veal roast instead of his pet pig for dinner and kept the pig for three years. It was ultimately run over by the first automobile ever to appear on a Salzburg street. People still talked about both in Salzburg, especially the pig. It had been the only housebroken pig in existence.

From the hospital he walked to the command post and collected his copy of the *Gazette* containing the November 1 Advancement List. He had deliberately postponed getting it, for he anticipated disappointment. In May he'd been transferred to Linz and given field duty. By then rumors were circulated that Conrad von Hötzendorf had decided to cut down on the number of War College graduates eligible for the General Staff. Up to 1909 the thirty highest ranking graduates of each class became assigned to the General Staff after four years in various garrisons. Since he was number eighteen, and until he heard the rumors regarding Conrad von Hötzendorf's decision he had had nothing to fear.

He found the bad news on the second page. The Advancement List named only fifteen graduates from the War College class of 1905 promoted to captains and permanently assigned to the General Staff Corps.

He read the names: 1. Ahrens. 2. Einthofen. 3. Schönhals. 4. Gersten. 5. Widder. 6. Hohenstein. 7. Dugonich. 8. Mader. 9. Landsberg-Lövy. 10. Hrasko. 11. Trautmannsdorf. 12. Moll. 13. Messemer. 14. Oblonsky. 15. Hodossy.

His first reaction was a numbing lassitude, followed by the reaction of a man who has succeeded in climbing a murderous mountain only to discover he has climbed the wrong one.

If he had been alone in the room, he would have relieved his anger by cursing, but he felt, or imagined, eyes focused on him. As always, there had been speculations about the November promotions. Others in the regiment, captains who hoped to be majors, majors who longed to be lieutenant colonels, were disappointed, too. Ever since General Conrad von Hötzendorf had become chief of staff, he was determined to raise the standards of the Officers' Corps, and many a career had fallen victim to his zeal for improvement.

He stuck the copy of the *Gazette* into his greatcoat pocket and started out for Römerstrasse. He knew he'd find his wife home, for she didn't go out much since her pregnancy had become noticeable. He was still two houses away from Number 77 when he heard Troll bark. The dog always recognized his steps, alerting Marianne. As he mounted the stairway to the apartment, she was already standing in the open doorway, Troll beside her.

She greeted him, breathless and relieved, as if she had feared that he would never return. She embraced him as no woman ever had, with the ardor of an Andromeda freshly freed from her chains. He often wondered about her power over him. It certainly wasn't her beauty; that was only part of her allure. What he could not resist was her absolute dependence on him. She was not a separate person, but a component part of him; torn from him, she would no doubt waste away like an amputated limb.

"I hope you like living in Linz," he said to her.

She gave him an astonished look. "I do."

"You'd better! Because we'll be here a long time!"

And he explained to her about his having been passed over.

"I know, you're terribly disappointed," she said, kissing him. "But I don't mind staying. I love this apartment. It's our first real home. And with the baby coming, it would've been difficult for you, too. You know how little help I am. It would have meant a lot of work for you."

He never minded work. When one didn't have money and still desired perfection, one had to be a jack-of-all-trades. Electrician, plumber, painter, upholsterer.

Since May he had been making repairs in the apartment, stopping finally to see whether he'd be transferred. Now he knew.

The mental numbness of the shock began slowly to give way to fury. There wasn't one among the lucky fifteen who possessed Peter Dorfrichter's qualifications. They may have been better athletes and horsemen, but if General Conrad wanted physical fitness in his staff officers, why put them through two years of a nerve-racking grind at the War College? He had excelled in most of the courses and, in addition, could speak, read and write six languages! Of course, he'd fallen off more horses than Prince Hohenstein and uhlan Oblonsky. But the next war wasn't going to be fought through cavalry attacks like the charge of the Light Brigade!

The turmoil in his mind grew unbearable. He thought work would help, but it did not. He decided to get out of the house, taking Troll for a walk. As he left, the landlord's wife, who lived on the ground floor, stopped him.

"Keep an eye on the dog," she warned. "Some scoundrel scattered poisoned meat around the neighborhood. I've heard that several animals have been killed."

"Has the man been caught?" Dorfrichter asked.

"Of course not. He never will be. No one has seen him do it, so how can they prove it's him?"

After the walk he returned home, his anger still mounting. He sent the maid for a carafe of wine and drank two glasses before dinner and the rest with the meal. Marianne was silent during the meal, realizing there were no words to comfort him.

After dinner he decided to work on shelves he was building. Needing more sandpaper, he reached into the cabinet for it, and his eyes fell on the jar containing the two cyanide sticks. It was by sheer oversight that he hadn't discarded them in Sarajevo. The orderly who packed for him had placed the jar in a crate. The unpacking in Linz was done by Marianne. She hadn't known what the jar contained and had placed it on a shelf in the larder, the door of which was always locked. It sat there among cans of paints, boxes of nails and pots of glue.

Mesmerized, he stared at the sticks, and his plan was conceived. It would grow, take shape, and be given birth. A hardy plan, which could bravely withstand fear, concern, hesitation and scruples of honor.

"Yes, sir," Dorfrichter said to Kunze, "that was the moment. From then on I had no doubt that I would carry it off!"

"You had the plan, and you had the poison. What made you decide on the circulars and capsules? Getting the cyanide to your intended victims through the mail?"

Dorfrichter shrugged. "That was the only way. With the least personal risk. I couldn't possibly ask them to dinner and feed it to them in chicken soup!"

Of course, the monster who had parceled out poisoned meat in the neighborhood had had it easy. He could rely on the hunger of hollow-flanked strays. But what would seem equally irresistible to well-fed, sated men? And how to get it to them? In a candy box? In some beverage? Too complicated and too dangerous. They might share it with others: women, children, friends.

The idea of the poison capsules had come to him one morning as he was reading the *Neue Freie Presse,* in which he discovered at least six or seven advertisements offering various kinds of patent medicine. Twelve thousand physicians recommended Sanatogen, a tonic supplying nutritive and invigorating substances most natural foods lacked. The people who produced Kola-Dultz claimed it to be a bracer stimulating the functions of the brain and the nervous system in general. Any reader sending in his name and address was promised a trial package of the fabulous Kola-Dultz. The same lucky reader was also entitled to a free sample of Bokalin, another great restorative.

As if destiny were showing him the way, a few days later he himself received a circular advertising a nerve elixir called Miracithin. According to the text, the small round pills—six were enclosed in a small paper bag—were guaranteed to alleviate the symptoms of sexual neurasthenia. As an experiment, he took them over a period of two days—one after each meal—as the text suggested, although God knows he didn't need them. After having gulped down the first, he was suddenly gripped with panic. What if some unknown enemy had stumbled on the same idea that was brewing in his brain? What if he had just swallowed his death? He felt dizzy. Was it the pill making his head swim, or was it fear? He started for the bathroom to make himself disgorge it, but regained his equilibrium by the time he reached the door. A feeling of shame swept over him; lack of self-control was a weakness he could never forgive himself.

The plan, still nebulous, had to be carried out without delay, however, before General Conrad once again changed the rules regulating promotional selection. One could never be sure of General Conrad.

Dorfrichter was as uninformed as most laymen about the effect of various poisons. Potassium of cyanide was no doubt one of the deadliest. Quick death. He couldn't risk buying medical textbooks or even borrowing them. The encyclopedia would have to do. The deadly dose was only one-tenth of a gram, and he had enough to wipe out the whole General Staff, including Conrad von Höt-zendorf.

Some months before he remembered having treated Troll with a worm powder administered in wafer capsules. A large supply of capsules was still in the medicine chest.

One evening when both Marianne and Aloisia, the maid, had gone to bed, he got the sticks from the larder and unwrapped one. To his surprise it crumbled under his touch, probably because of having been stored in a closed glass jar over a long period of time. Whatever the reason, handling the poison was less complicated than it might have been.

He studied the number of the expendables. At first, he thought of five men, but the number didn't promise to be effective. Not likely. How could he be sure that *three* men out of five would feel the need of a sexual stimulant. Some people were born pill takers; some were not. Three out of six? Seven? Eight? Nine? Ten?

"But why these ten?" Kunze wanted to know. "Why these men out of sixteen—rather eighteen, as you included Hedry. How did you make your choice?"

Dorfrichter gave the captain an arch look. "That's what has been puzzling you all along! My relationship to the men. Trying to find the clue to the whole case through my personal feelings for the men!"

"So you did leave the choice to chance?"

"Not really. I'm afraid you still don't realize that I am not a common murderer. An error was made, and I felt destined to rectify it. It may have been presumptuous of me, but I weighed the men and that's how I made my choice."

This wasn't true, at least not about every one of the "expendables." Lying awake at night, he'd go over the fifteen names in the Advancement List, repeating them soundlessly like the litany of all saints: Ahrens, Einthofen, Schönhals, Gersten, Widder,

Hohenstein, Dugonich, Mader, Landsberg-Lövy, Hrasko, Traut-mannsdorf, Moll, Messemer, Oblonsky, Hodossy. He conjured up every face, recalling the peculiarities of each man, weighing his qualifications. He would select the ones ripe for retirement. That the retirement in this case was synonymous with death was beside the point.

Ahrens? Number one. The son of an army tailor. A hard-working, talented, reliable officer. The General Staff needed men like him. And men like Einthofen and Schönhals. They had quali-ties that entitled them to assignments of heavy responsibility. Gersten? A good man, but a pacifist. During their second year at the college the class had once debated the importance of Italy as an ally. Ahrens and the "war party" decided that as an allied participant in a conflict, Italy would be more of a liability than an asset, a neutral bystander with knife poised against the mon-archy's back; the smart thing to do would be to stage a surprise attack and render her harmless. Gersten was outraged. He didn't believe in preventive aggression, especially not against an ally, calling the idea criminal and immoral. Thus Gersten became *ex-pendable!*

Widder was in the same category as Ahrens. Useful and am-bitious. Prince Hohenstein? Would he have rated number six if he hadn't been a prince? No doubt, he'd be a general before any-one else, command a division, although his disposition and in-terests ideally qualified him to a professorship at some provincial university. Having to put archdukes in commanding positions was a big enough risk; the army would have been better off without them and, no doubt, without the minor princes.

Prince Hohenstein was judged expendable. And so was Baron Landsberg-Lövy. The baron had brains and talent, but esthetes didn't belong in the General Staff. Neither did Francophiles. The ideal staff officer should be impervious to everything outside the sphere of his profession. Landsberg-Lövy would rather sacri-fice a regiment than fire a single shell at—for instance—the Ca-thedral of Rheims. Besides, he was a Jew. Even in an era of liberalism, some of the troops objected to Jewish commanders. *Expendable.*

Moll was the next. Although certainly no Francophile, he was Prussian and would have made an ideal field officer, meticulous,

correct, courageous, blindly obedient, a good staff officer in the
Kaiser's army, but not in that of Emperor Franz Josef. There was
an enormous difference between the two corps. The Austrians
had been taught to think, which the Germans were strictly forbidden, and Moll was a nonthinker. Also, a born hypochondriac,
addicted to headache pills, cough drops and prophylactics, he
was the one man who would try a free sample of a patent medicine. *Expendable!*

Oblonsky. A lanky Pole, a fine horseman. Like most uhlans,
he would have made a great circus performer and a gallant
eighteenth-century warrior, but his belief in the efficacy of cavalry
attacks made him *expendable!*

Hodossy. As typically Hungarian as Oblonsky was Polish. Another eighteenth-century man. The army could certainly function
without him or any Hungarians, for that matter. In 1848 they
rebelled against Franz Josef. Who could guarantee that they'd
be willing to fight for him in 1910 or later? Every Hungarian was
a troublemaker, even a good fellow like Hodossy, hence *expendable!*

He was still four men short. For safety's sake he would have
to add one whom he outranked to throw the inevitable investigators off the scent, forcing them to search among the graduates
from number twenty on up!

Lieutenant von Hedry had rated number nineteen. Another
Hungarian, but of different fiber from Hodossy's. Volatile, con-
tentious, a scourge of women and horses. A marauder in white
glacé gloves! The best swordsman in the class, one did not tangle
with him unless one wanted one's ear or nose nicked. A man
without fear, the kind of officer who'd always be the first to jump
from cover and lead his platoon into an enemy barrage to receive
posthumously the Gold Medal for Valor. If anyone, he was certainly *expendable.*

Dugonich! He could see his silhouette sharply outlined against
the inner darkness of his eyelids. Long, lean body, a hawk on
horseback. Jokes had circulated about his prowess in the bedroom. While everyone had been too goddamn overburdened with
cramming for examinations, riding drills, language lessons, Dugonich always managed to find time to play. He had it easy, that

rich Serbian son of a bitch, raised in the saddle, his way to success paved with his father's gold. *Expendable!*

Would eight circulars do, he had wondered? Eight, including Hedry, whose extinction was merely of tactical value. It occurred to Dorfrichter that when going over the names he had repeatedly skipped Messemer. The reason must have been that he had trouble remembering the fellow. A man with an impressive personality should not fade so completely from one's memory in four short years, so it wouldn't hurt the army if it had to get along without Messemer!

Completing the count, he had to admit to himself that from the very beginning he'd considered Richard Mader as one of the expendables. Mader, lifesaver and witness to the most humiliating moment of his life. For months after the incident on the Castelnuovo beach he'd been harassed by a recurrent dream: He was drowning and Mader, convulsed with laughter, stood on the seashore, feet apart, rocking back and forth on his heels, not moving an inch. The louder he, Dorfrichter, screamed for help, the louder Mader laughed, until the two sounds melded into an earpiercing shrillness which woke him up. After graduation they had served tours in different garrisons, meeting a few times by chance. On each occasion he had tried to avoid Mader, feeling trapped and ill at ease when he couldn't. The other three men at the picnic had been Landsberg-Lövy, Hoffer and Gabriel. Hoffer had obligingly killed himself, and Gabriel had resigned from the army. As for Landsberg-Lövy, while he never gave any indication during their meetings in Sarajevo that he'd been aware of the incident, still his name was among the expendables.

"Wasn't selecting Mader—who'd saved your life—going a bit too far?" Kunze flared.

"I've confessed having sent him the poison. Isn't that enough?"

"I'm not ashamed to admit that you're an enigma to me. You want me to believe that you plotted your murders with an almost scientific detachment. This I can't accept. What about your antagonism to the cavalry? Doesn't the fact that most of the men on your list were cavalry officers have anything to do with your personal aversion to them?"

Dorfrichter leaned back in the chair, closing his eyes. Cavalry!

He saw himself marching at the head of his men on the road leading from Linz to Sommerau. The sun was mercilessly hot. He was perspiring, and his feet felt like freshly amputated stumps, chafed and bleeding in the coarse infantry boots. And then a small yellow cloud formed where the horizon met the sky, and as it grew larger, its kernel turned out to be a squadron of hussars stationed in Enns. Galloping past his platoon, their horses' hooves stirred up geysers of dust. He felt the dirt settle on his face and mix with his sweat, while his men shouted obscenities at the hussars.

"There isn't much love lost between infantry and cavalry," he admitted. "But that didn't influence my selection."

"Now about Hodossy? Wasn't the Brassay affair a factor in your choosing him?"

"I don't think so. I chose him because of political considerations. I've told you before I distrusted Hungarians in the army."

"And Lansberg-Lövy? It was Vanini's cyanide you used, and Landsberg knew about your connection with Vanini."

"Next you'll ask why I didn't send Vanini a circular?"

"Why didn't you?"

"Because I never expected him to betray me. He was my friend, and I trusted him. Caesar and Brutus."

He hadn't seen much of Vanini in Linz. A General Staff hopeful had to be careful of his associations. In Sarajevo, Vanini's commanding officers were willing to attribute the boy's performance to the wretchedness of the garrison; in Linz they could find no such excuse for him, and he was written off as a man without a future.

"Before leaving Linz, Vanini asked you about the cyanide and you told him you no longer had it. Did you think he believed you?" Kunze asked.

"I'd never before given him reason to doubt my words!"

"What was the secret of your hold on Vanini?" The captain continued his probing.

"I had no hold on him. We were friends."

"All right, Dorfrichter. What kind of contrivance did you use for copying the circulars?"

"On November eighth, I was on night duty at the casern," the lieutenant answered. "I happened to remember a small secretarial office equipped with a hectograph, unused since the summer maneuvers. The key to it hung in the ordinance sergeant's room. While I kept the sergeant busy checking stores, I took the key, went over to the office and made the ten hectographed copies."

"With nobody the wiser?"

"That's right, sir," Dorfrichter said.

When asking for a leave of absence, he had mentioned Salzburg as his destination, although he knew he would be going to Vienna. With a little luck he could make the trip without being seen on the Vienna train. In that case the regimental records would place him at a distance of 313 kilometers from the capital during the crucial hour when the circulars were mailed.

But things didn't work out quite that way. A major in his regiment had taken the same train to Vienna on the night of November 13. They had saluted each other, leaving no doubt in his mind that the major would remember their meeting. Also, he had Troll with him, and the dog was known to the entire garrison. Taking the dog had been a spur-of-the-moment decision. As he was leaving the house, it had occurred to him that Troll wouldn't be safe in Linz alone with Aloisia, who hated the animal, resenting its shedding and wiping its mouth on the sitting-room rug.

The train had arrived in Vienna on time, at six thirty. He had thought first of mailing the circulars from the station, then decided against it. A bakery was open across the street, and he ordered Troll to sit in front of its entrance and wait for him there. It would have been risky to be seen at the mailbox with such a large, shaggy dog.

He dropped the letters into the Mariahilferstrasse mailbox, just as the investigation had assumed. Then after collecting Troll, he took a streetcar to the Ninth District, where his mother-in-law lived.

"Your wife told me you spent the rest of the morning playing with her sister's children," Kunze interrupted.

"That's correct, sir."

"How could you!"

"How could I what?"

"Goddamn it, Dorfrichter, you'd just condemned ten men to

death! Didn't you feel, at least, uncomfortable face-to-face with
those children who probably loved and trusted you?"

Dorfrichter answered with a dry laughter. "Uncomfortable?
Don't you for a moment think, sir, they wouldn't have approved
of what I'd done? There's no animal more cruel than a small
child!"

"One more question," Kunze said, and, turning to Heinrich,
asked him not to record the answer. "Haven't you ever felt any
regrets? You once told me you hadn't, but I can't quite believe
it. You're no savage—you're a civilized man, a Christian. You had
tender feelings for your wife, for friends, your dog. How could
you so completely render yourself insensible to pity?"

Dorfrichter rubbed his forehead pensively. His eyes were fixed
on Kunze's face as though he were appraising the depth of his
perception before giving him the answer.

"I am a professional soldier," he said at last. "Trained to kill.
From the very beginning of my schooling I majored in murder!
Despite all the noble trappings of my profession, the truth is that
I am a mercenary. Rather, a gladiator. When the emperor gives
me the thumbs-down signal, I kill my own brother."

"But there was no signal from the emperor."

"No. But had he given it, I'd have obeyed. And my fellow officers would have, too! For instance, when the shadow of suspicion
first fell on me—just the shadow, mind you—one of my best comrades at Linz left his service revolver in an open drawer for me to
shoot myself. The same friendly gesture was extended to me by
General Wencel. And to others before me. To men who couldn't
settle a debt of honor, who with some thoughtless act had disgraced themselves or the army. Then there were the duels. A man
gets drunk, drops a careless remark, and two days later either he
or the insulted party is killed in the presence of four placidly ap-
proving seconds. From the day a man puts on an officer's uniform
he's destined to be a killer and be killed. If war breaks out tomorrow five of my ten intended 'victims' would be dead within a
year! I was merely going to shorten their waiting period in death's
anteroom." He shrugged. "Now I've shortened my own!"

Kunze shook his head. "You're mad!"

"You're repeating yourself, sir. Anyway, how could you understand me? You've never been one of the gladiators."

Pulling out his watch, Kunze glanced at it. "Ten past ten."
They had been in the office more than five hours. Both his aides,
especially Heinrich, the recorder, seemed exhausted. There were
still a few details left to be cleared up. Ringing for the sergeant
on duty, he asked him to send out for food and a few bottles of
beer.

During the past months, Kunze—although not a daydreamer—
had often wondered in what mood and under what circumstances
Peter Dorfrichter would finally make his confession. He'd visualized a drama, tears, stormy emotions, anything but this relaxed
late-night snack in his office, accompanied by the odor of hot
frankfurter and beer and freshly grated horseradish. They all
were hungry; Dorfrichter hadn't eaten since his midday meal and
the others since the wedding lunch. The four men, Kunze mused,
looked very much like cardplayers resting between rubbers of
bridge or tarots. Of the four, Peter Dorfrichter looked like the
one ahead in the game, and Kunze appeared to be the heavy
loser, for he knew there were deep rings under his eyes and very
little color in his face.

It was past midnight when the final wording of the confession
was recorded and Dorfrichter could sign it.

"How strange," the prisoner said, examining the pen, "the same
type pen point I sent a boxful of to Lieutenant Dielmann." He
grinned at Kunze. "One of my errors."

"You didn't make many."

"A few—but big ones! I should have sent a circular to myself,
too, not only to Hedry. I almost did, but then I thought: Why
draw attention to my own person? It's safer to remain incon-
spicuous. Also, I shouldn't have written the addresses in longhand. I thought I'd be safe if I used cartographic script. I was
mistaken. Above all, I miscalculated the reaction of the army. I
expected the inquest to be halted the minute suspicion fell on an
officer."

"You damn near guessed right," Kunze murmured.

"I still think it was a mistake to track me down. The army won't
gain anything by my conviction. On the contrary. It'll hurt the
untainted image of the entire Officers' Corps. And in times, too,
when prestige of the corps is of national importance."

The scene was beginning to take on an unreal quality, Kunze

thought. The criminal discussing his crime with the judges in the lighthearted chatty vein of a Schnitzler comedy. In no other country or city could such a conversation have taken place, among no other type of men, save those officers of Franz Josef's army. A band of gypsies playing beneath the window was the sole missing touch.

On his wedding night, Captain Kunze slept in the rented flat on Traungasse. He left the Military Lawcourt a few minutes after one, knowing Rose would be waiting for him, but the day had been too long, and too much had been crowded into it. Always a solitary man, he needed especially on this night to be left alone with his thoughts. The church with its flickering candles seemed a thousand miles and a century away, while closer to him in time and space was the man who had just signed his own death sentence.

He called Rose the next morning, informing her that their trip had to be postponed indefinitely. Her reaction was a low moan, but no comment, and her husband decided she was an army wife now.

General Wencel received the report on Dorfrichter's confession with mixed feelings. He congratulated Kunze warmly, patting him on the back, but the captain knew him too well not to notice the uneasiness lurking beneath the approval. He commiserated with Kunze for having to break up his honeymoon, but the captain knew that wasn't what disturbed the general. "I'd better give the news to Archduke Franz Ferdinand in person," he said as he saw Kunze to the door. "His Highness has always shown great interest in the case, and I'm sure he'll want to give us his recommendations."

"We have a set course of procedures to follow. I don't see what recommendations he could make."

"He may have ideas," the general replied lamely. "He always has. He's at Konopischt and is not expected back to Vienna before the end of the month, so let's find out about the train connection. We'll get off at Beneschau and take a carriage from there. We should get to the Konopischt Castle either shortly before noon or after four in the afternoon. The archduke is in the habit of taking a nap after lunch."

Kunze frowned. "Did you say *we*, General?"

"Certainly. I want you to come along. After all, you've been in charge of the case and can give a more detailed account than I. When we know the time of our arrival, I'll wire Colonel Bardolff, His Highness' aide, for confirmation."

Kunze had never met the archduke before and never wanted to. He did not believe in advancing his career by worming himself into the good graces of the heir to the throne, partly because he knew that the amity of august personages was a rather perishable commodity and partly because Franz Ferdinand was known to be the most capricious of the lot. People attributed his whims to sheer frustration. Heir apparent, restricted to meaningless representative duties, he'd been impatiently champing at the bit for twenty years while the octogenarian remained seated on the throne, immovable and unmalleable—as though he were his own monument carved out of solid rock.

Despite the army's decision to keep Peter Dorfrichter's confession a secret, it was somehow disclosed to a reporter on the Socialist *Arbeiterzeitung*. About the time the first screaming newsboys began hawking the extra edition all over town, General Wencel received Colonel Bardolff's answer to his inquiry. The archduke would see them in two days, at noon sharp.

"We'd better take the train tomorrow afternoon," Wencel told Kunze, "and sleep in Beneschau. I've been informed that the countryside is badly flooded around Konopischt, and we might have to make a detour to reach the castle."

Wencel, annoyed because the city was astir with excitement over Dorfrichter's confession, blamed Kunze for the leak. Certain of the archduke's pique, he dreaded their encounter. Franz Ferdinand was not the kind to forgive news having reached the public before it reached him.

Having weathered Wencel's displeasure, Kunze now had to clear things with Rose. That night, for the first time since the wedding, he slept in the Zaunergasse apartment. He also had the first real fight of his married life. Rose wanted him to share the wide connubial bed in her room, while he insisted on occupying the small suite where he had lived as her boarder. In tears she showered him with recriminations, and he—as no doubt other husbands before him—learned much too late that compliant and undemanding mistresses did not necessarily make compliant and undemanding wives. Nevertheless, he spent the night in his familiar single bed with Troll stretched out on the silk comforter at his feet.

In the morning, as Kunze entered the anteroom to his office, a man rose from the bench along the wall. The face was familiar, yet he could not remember the name that went with it. For an inexplicable reason, his dark mood turned a shade darker at the sight of the man.

The caller approached him. "May I have a word with you, sir?"

"Friedrich Gabriel!" Kunze exclaimed, wondering why he hadn't recognized him immediately.

"Yes, sir," Gabriel said, bowing slightly and clicking his heels.

"What can I do for you?" he asked more gruffly than he intended.

"May I have five minutes alone with you, Captain?"

The man was neatly dressed, his somewhat shiny black suit freshly pressed, his white shirt immaculate, his shoes polished. Neither anger nor ill will showed in his face. Although he had aged somewhat since they'd last met, his bearing—despite the mufti—was, as always, unmistakably military.

"Of course. Come in, Gabriel," Kunze said, opening the door to his office. They jostled lightly on the threshold, each wanting the other to precede. Inside, Kunze offered his visitor a seat and a cigarette.

"How have you been, Gabriel?" he asked.

"Very well, thank you, sir," Gabriel answered stiffly.

No complaints. The man's reserve managed to disturb Kunze.

"I heard you'd left the post office. Assume you found a more suitable position." *It seems I am a glutton for punishment,* he scolded himself silently.

"In a way, yes, sir. I've been employed on a large dairy farm in Hadersdorf. That's about a half hour from here. Bookkeeper, overseer, factotum. Not a bad position. Have my freedom, decent lodgings, friendly people. Nevertheless—" He stopped, seemingly searching for words. "To come to the point, sir, I wanted to see you because I need your assistance. I'd like to rejoin the army, sir."

Transfixed, Kunze stared at him. "You do?" He wanted to add: "After what it has done to you?"

"Last night I read in the papers that Lieutenant Dorfrichter had confessed. That clears me from all involvement in the case. I resigned from the army with an unblemished record and have preserved my good reputation as a civilian. I want to ask for your support, Captain, when I hand in my application to reenter active service."

"You have my unqualified support," Kunze told him. "Anything I can do. Don't answer if you feel I'm intruding, but what made you decide?"

"On the contrary, Captain. I'm grateful for your interest. I want to return to the army because that's where I belong. I've been a civilian for four years, and that was like living in exile. From my tenth year to my twenty-sixth I wore a uniform among men in uniform, spoke their language, obeyed their rules, conformed to their standards."

"But how can you approve of those standards—after what they've done to you?" Despite Kunze's resolution not to touch the past, the protest slipped out.

"I wasn't brought up to approve, but to accept. That's probably why I'm unfit for civilian life. There you're constantly faced with the problems of right or wrong. You must pass judgment, and if you avoid it, you're a shirker. Call me a coward, Captain, but I'm tired of being a responsible adult. It's much simpler if I revert to boyhood and have no obligation to think, judge or correct. All that is done for me! Do I make myself clear?"

"Yes and no," Kunze said.

Later that day, sharing a reserved compartment with General Wencel on the Prague train, Kunze brought up Gabriel's case. Wencel raised his eyebrows.

"The fellow is out of his mind!" he exploded. "His kind doesn't belong in the army!"

"What do you mean by 'his kind,' sir?" Kunze asked, irritated.

"He was involved in a scandal!"

"What scandal, sir? He was unjustly accused, put under arrest, his wife driven to suicide!"

The general pulled himself erect in the seat, finding the captain's voice much too shrill, but deciding to ignore the lack of respect.

"His wife—she slept around, didn't she? Let's suppose Gabriel's wearing the uniform again and bumps into Moll or Hohenstein or Gersten? Men who cuckolded him. Can he pretend to ignore it when the whole world knows? As an officer he's obliged to challenge them. If he doesn't, he is a coward. Both ways it reflects badly on the army."

With great self-control Kunze suppressed a quip about cuckolded husbands. The general changed the subject, and Gabriel's name was not mentioned again.

They arrived in Beneschau late at night and stopped at the Hotel zum Löwen, an establishment certainly not in the Ritz class. Wencel had sent his orderly ahead to see to it that the rooms reserved for the two officers were thoroughly cleaned, beds sprinkled with insect powder and gasoline-filled saucers placed under the furniture legs to discourage surviving nightly invaders. A fiacre was ordered for the following morning to take the gentlemen to Konopischt Castle.

Kunze's information proved correct. The country around the archducal residence was indeed flooded. A sudden thaw in the mountains had turned a small stream flowing through the valley into a wild river. The castle, built on an elevation, had been spared, but large sections of the park still lay underwater. The entire personnel of the country's military posts had been put to work, repairing roads and bridges and also collecting the fish that floated to the surrounding farms from a small artificial lake in the castle park. Finding fat pikes and carps thrashing in the mud of their ruined fields seemed like meager compensation to the flood victims. They had hardly carried the fish home, however, and lighted stove fires, when the soldiers pounced on them, demanding the fish be returned by orders of the archduke. Cartload after cartload of dead fish, taken to the castle's compost heap and dumped there to rot under layers of straw, was to be used later as fertilizer in the rose garden. As Kunze learned from the waiter who served his breakfast, the action didn't exactly enhance the archduke's already slender popularity among his good Czechs.

The ride to Konopischt in a brisk March wind took several hours over muddy roads and around collapsed bridges.

General Wencel had been to the castle before and, as they entered the grounds, pointed out the sights of interest to his companion.

"His Highness' private museum," he said, indicating the square, two-story building protected from the flood by a high barricade of sandbags.

"I didn't know he was an art lover."

"He isn't, not really. He only collects statues and paintings of St. George, the dragon killer. They say he identifies himself with the saint."

"That's right, I remember now," Kunze remarked. "A few years ago there was an uproar in art circles when he bought a St. George done by an old master and had some dilettant repaint the saint's face to resemble him."

Stiffening, General Wencel threw a reprimanding glance at Captain Kunze. "I don't seem to recall that," he snapped.

They arrived half an hour early at the castle and waited in Colonel Bardolff's office until noon. This suited them, for they needed that long a time in which to thaw out.

At noon sharp they were led into the archduke's study, a long, narrow room, where it was necessary to walk its full length before reaching the man seated behind the desk. They halted and snapped stiffly to attention. Franz Ferdinand rose halfway from his seat, to extend his hand first to General Wencel, then to Captain Kunze.

"Thank you for coming, gentlemen," he told them in a bored monotone. "Please be seated." He turned to the colonel. "You, too, Bardolff!"

No one spoke during the next minute or two, while the archduke stared at the ceiling, dreamily examining the intricate design of the cornice. He was a tall, corpulent man with carelessly unmilitary posture that made his shoulders appear rounded and his embonpoint obvious. His face with its double chin, thick brushlike mustache, and cold eyes was without distinction. There was nothing imperial about that face, and no bejeweled crown could ever make it seem so. To Kunze it seemed the cap of a chef or hotel concierge would have better fitted that head.

"I've read about Lieutenant Dorfrichter's confession," Franz Ferdinand said finally. "A most unfortunate affair!" He addressed neither man but spoke instead to the cornice. "Too bad one must learn about such developments from the newspapers!" At last, his gaze shifted from the ceiling to General Wencel. "I wish you had notified me before you gave the news out to those scribblers."

"Unfortunately, sir, there was a leak. We couldn't help it," Wencel explained. "It's simply impossible to keep anything from the press nowadays."

The archduke rose. The three officers jumped at once to their feet. After crossing to the huge porcelain stove, he placed his hand on its side.

"The press!" he said. "Rotten, liberal and Jewish! Its sole aim: to undermine the monarchy. It must be stopped before it's too late and muzzled! Unfortunately, one has to wait for that. Yet one can't just sit idly and watch everything going to damnation." He turned and faced his visitors. "That confession must be retracted!"

General Wencel blinked nervously, then looked at Kunze, as though asking if he, too, had heard the edict. The captain's eyes, quizzical and slightly amused, remained on the archduke.

When it became evident that General Wencel chose to remain silent, Kunze said, "With Your Highness' permission, I don't know how this could be done."

"Very simply, Captain," Franz Ferdinand said, his skin turning pink. "He confessed under duress. In a state of mental derangement. Under hypnosis! He simply regains his senses and retracts his confession!"

"But, sir, he did not confess either under pressure or hypnosis. He was in full possession of his faculties," Kunze pointed out.

"I know, I know—" the archduke answered nervously. "That's beside the point!"

"His Highness means," Colonel Bardolff attempted to explain, "that you may use any of his suggestions when you give out the news of the retraction to the press."

Kunze pretended to be dim-witted.

"What retraction, Colonel? What if Lieutenant Dorfrichter isn't willing to retract anything?"

"You make him!" the archduke snapped.

"How, sir?"

"You know how! You made him confess, didn't you?"

"I did not, sir. It was the evidence brought to light against him. The last and most important bit—his having obtained the cyanide from a fellow officer—made Dorfrichter realize that any further denial was hopeless. Besides, the investigation had worn him out. He knew that even without a confession he'd be found guilty—"

"And what if he's found not guilty?"

"But he *is* guilty, Your Highness! There is not the slightest doubt about that."

The archduke crossed to Kunze, stepping so close that their bodies almost touched.

"I insist that the man retract his confession! I won't allow this stigma on my Officers' Corps! I simply won't!"

Kunze looked straight into the large pale-blue eyes of the archduke. He was somewhat shorter than Franz Ferdinand, but the man's hunched posture canceled the difference. *It's not your Officers' Corps,* he thought. *Not yet.*

"With Your Highness' permission," he said, "the stigma is there. Has been since the day of Captain Richard Mader's death. Nothing will remove it."

The archduke moved away, turning to General Wencel.

"The captain doesn't seem to understand my point. Do you?"

Wencel snapped to attention. "Yes, Your Highness!"

Franz Ferdinand shrugged. "Well, then, there's no reason to discuss it any further. How was your journey?"

"Very pleasant, sir," Wencel replied eagerly.

"Are the roads to Beneschau still flooded?"

"Some. Our coachman had to take a few detours." Then quickly, to assure the imperial host that the invitation had been appreciated: "Beautiful country! Gorgeous! And the air! Exhilarating. Literally reinvigorates one."

Especially if one doesn't freeze to death first, Kunze thought acidly.

Despite the archduke's initial displeasure with the captain's uncooperative attitude, the two men were asked to stay for lunch. The meal was served in the family dining room. The Duchess of Hohenberg, née Countess Chotek, the archduke's morganatic wife, presided at the table.

She was a handsome woman with a well-proportioned and well-rounded body and the cool, resentful dignity of a dethroned queen. Her attitude toward her guests—and probably all humanity—was one of tense watchfulness; ever since her marriage ten

years before, she had lived among people who either wished for
or expected her downfall. She couldn't look at a new face—royalty
or commoner—without suspecting an enemy behind the mask of
deference. At one time she'd been a sunny, radiant girl; now, at
forty-two, having married the prize catch of the monarchy, she
was a bitter exile, marooned in the no-man's-land between her
own world, which she'd left forever, and her husband's, which
she had lost hope of ever entering. Konopischt was the only place
where she felt at home. There she was the mother of three children and the wife of the man she adored. The minute she set
foot outside her retreat, she was faced with the cruel and humiliating decrees of Spanish etiquette, which seemed to have been
created to constantly remind her of her own inferiority.

They were nine at the table, the archduke, the duchess, Colonel Bardolff, the castle chaplain, a lady companion to the duchess, an aide-de-camp to the archduke, General Wencel, Captain
Kunze and one other guest, Mr. Linton, an English botanist.

The chaplain said grace, not the customary brief prayer, but a
rather elaborate sermon. The archduke and the duchess sat motionless, eyes closed as though in a trance, an expression of rapt
exaltation on their faces. *Good heavens*, Kunze thought, *they are
communing with God right here at the lunchtable, while the nice
hot soup gets cold in the plates.* At last the prayer ended, everyone crossed himself except the Englishman, whom Kunze decided
was evidently a Protestant, and host and hostess returned to the
material world.

For Mr. Linton's benefit, the conversation was conducted in
English, which the archduke spoke badly and the duchess quite
well. The botanist had been invited to Konopischt to help Franz
Ferdinand achieve one of his life ambitions: the growing of a
black rose.

"Last summer I thought we almost had it," the duchess informed them. "We crossed a *Rosa rugosa* with a *Rosa canina*,
and one bush had buds that looked pitch black. Unfortunately,
when they opened, the inside petals turned a dark reddish
purple."

"Beautiful," the archduke added, "but still not black!"

The lady companion, an elderly Czech countess, broke in. "Isn't
there a superstition about a black rose?"

The archduke frowned, and the duchess lifted a finger to her lips, signaling silence. But the countess evidently failed to notice because she continued blithely.

"Oh, I remember now!" she chirped. "Doesn't one know that a murder and a war are to follow when the black rose blooms?"

"That's the most idiotic nonsense I've ever heard," Franz Ferdinand barked at her in German. "In the future, kindly refrain from repeating such trash, Countess!"

Obviously the archduke's mood was spoiled for the rest of the meal, and he now focused his resentment on Kunze.

"Isn't it true, Captain, that when Lieutenant Dorfrichter was first interrogated, you handed him a revolver with the suggestion that he pass judgment on himself?"

The question left Kunze speechless for a moment.

"I'm afraid, Your Imperial Highness, I can't recall any such incident," he said finally.

The archduke ignored his denial.

"If he'd shot himself, he would have died without being administered extreme unction. I'm amazed you were willing to bear the responsibility for condemning a Christian soul to eternal death!"

"Your Imperial Highness, I did not hand Lieutenant Dorfrichter a gun or suggest that he shoot himself!"

"But you considered him guilty before anyone else did?"

"Based on the report of the handwriting expert, yes, Your Highness."

"You staked your career on his guilt, didn't you?"

"Certainly not, Your Highness. No judge advocate of this army would want to further his career at the cost of an innocent man's death!"

"He was a valuable officer, wasn't he?"

"That he was, sir. Very talented. He would have made an excellent staff officer. It's the army's loss that he wasn't chosen for the General Staff Corps."

"In case of war, would he be an asset to the army?"

"He certainly would, sir."

The meat course was served, and for a while Franz Ferdinand focused his attention on the food. Suddenly, he turned to the botanist.

"In your country, Mr. Linton, what is the general opinion regarding the war?"

The man seemed perplexed. "What war, sir?" he asked.

"A future war. Let's say, between England and Germany."

"I don't think there is a chance of that, sir. I mean the people don't think so. Why would they want to fight Germany?"

"And what if there were a war between Germany and France?"

"It wouldn't concern us, would it, sir?"

"Hardly." Franz Ferdinand agreed.

Mr. Linton took a deep breath. "May I be so bold as to ask a question, sir?"

"Go ahead."

"Does Your Highness expect a war between the major powers to break out in the near future?"

The archduke reflected for a moment.

"I do," he said. "It's inevitable. What's more, a necessity. Europe's like a man with a bad boil. A boil called liberalism. Better said, a lot of little but nasty boils. They have to be cut open, or the bacteria will invade the bloodstream, causing the body to rot alive!"

"But doesn't one need a cause for a war, sir?"

"Oh, there is always an incident or conflict, in itself insignificant, that can be blown up and exploited by the party determined to start a war, provided the timing and circumstances appear propitious."

Mr. Linton had no more questions, staring instead at his plate in quiet bewilderment. During the rest of the meal, topics closer to a botanist's understanding, such as the various methods of growing wormless apples and healthy house plants, were discussed.

Wencel and Kunze departed shortly after lunch.

"How will you go about making Dorfrichter retract his confession?" the general asked the captain as the carriage left the castle grounds.

"I won't, sir."

Wencel raised his voice. "You won't what?"

"Won't make him retract his confession. That would be a mockery of justice, General."

It took Wencel some time to digest Kunze's answer.

"You heard the archduke, damn it! His wish is that we let the man go!"

"I know."

"You can't simply ignore his wish. He may be emperor tomorrow."

"That's right, sir. Tomorrow. But today he is not."

XIX

CAPTAIN Kunze set the alarm clock for six in the Zaunergasse apartment but was awake long before it rang. He got up, opened the window, and inhaled a few deep breaths. The early-morning breeze felt like the caress of a rough hand on his cheeks. The promise of a premature summer wafted in from the vineyard-covered hills of Grinzing. Soon green wreaths would appear above the entrance doors of the hunchbacked little houses indicating that the owners were ready to sell their new wine. There would be tables and benches set up in shady backyards and —especially on Sundays—thousands of city people swarming all over the crooked Grinzing streets like ants over a piece of pastry dropped from a platter. The people would arrive sober, leave drunk, and the city-bound trams would be noisy with harmonica music and the air heavy with alcohol-laden vapors.

He brought in the morning paper from the letter box in the entrance hall. Edward VI was to be buried on the following day, and the preparations for his state funeral were the dominant news, luckily overshadowing the Dorfrichter court-martial. Franz Ferdinand had left days earlier for London to represent the emperor. Nine crowned heads, among them the Kaiser, a galaxy of princes, and a former President, Theodore Roosevelt, of the United States, were to follow the casket on horseback or in carriages. As Kunze read the anecdotes, gossip and quoted remarks that inevitably spice such occasions, he had the feeling that the most alive member of the entire gathering was the man they were to bury. Personally, he felt grateful to the jolly, fat king. His death had called the archduke away from Vienna at a time when his presence would have seriously complicated matters.

He wondered how Peter Dorfrichter was feeling on this balmy May morning. Since his trip to Konopischt he'd talked to the lieutenant twice. Once when Dorfrichter signed documents in connection with the divorce suit and, again, when he handed the prisoner the list of officers selected to serve on the court-martial. He went to see Dorfrichter in his cell still undecided whether or not to suggest that he retract his confession. The temptation was almost irresistible. The image of the young soldier executed in Sarajevo kept haunting Kunze with alarming obstinacy. And then, in another vision, he could imagine the lieutenant walking down the Ring, his shako jauntily askew, his spurs jingling, a free man, exuberantly grateful to be alive. One well-chosen word could change a bleeding corpse into a gay man about town. It would be the simplest thing to accomplish. Wasn't he, Kunze, under orders to bring about such a transformation? Nevertheless, by the time he entered the cell, he knew he would not carry out the archduke's command.

He found Dorfrichter engrossed in *The Truth About Port Arthur* by E. K. Nojine, a recently published essay. Since the confession, the lieutenant was given books to read, allowed to write to and receive visits from members of his immediate family —father, mother, sister and brother-in-law. Marianne Dorfrichter had been discharged from the sanatorium and was staying at her mother's apartment but had made no attempt to see her husband.

Dorfrichter appeared calm, relaxed and friendly. The acerbity was gone; even his looks had changed, no doubt because he had abandoned his physical fitness program. Instead, he read voraciously and worked on a treatise which dealt with the influence of the new century's discoveries in metallurgy, chemistry and biology on modern warfare. Work, while buoying up his spirits, had left deep rings under his eyes. He had lost weight, and his pallor, in Kunze's opinion, caused him to resemble a nineteenth-century poet, elegant, romantic and moribund.

On his last visit, Kunze had stayed more than an hour. He could have left in ten minutes, for Dorfrichter had shown no curiosity about the men who were to be his judges. Kunze had stayed simply because he couldn't tear himself away. He loved this man. He loved the way his eyes lit up when he became interested in a subject, the gestures of his long-fingered, narrow hands, the way he crossed his legs. And he had reached the point where he was no longer ashamed of his feelings. Surely there could be no sin in an affection almost completely devoid of carnal desire, an affection that filled one with a throbbing awareness of being alive and at the same time with a sense of deep sorrow.

They talked primarily about subjects relating to the lieutenant's work. After four months of complete isolation, reading to Dorfrichter was like water to a man dying of thirst in the desert. He had always been alert, but now he sparkled. He hoped to have time to complete, besides his present work, a dissertation on the defensive use of the projectile—bullet and shell—combined with field entrenchment. The necessity for such measures might arise whenever an offensive was brought to a halt by insurmountable enemy resistance. This could most easily happen on the Russian front. He felt that the greatest danger of a war against Russia would be a victorious opening campaign, with the Austro-Hungarian forces sucked into her soft, spongelike vastness and trapped there by a pitiless winter. The only solution had to be penetration in easy stages building up a defense system simultaneously with the attack.

Kunze, not really interested in military tactics, listened not to the substance of the talk, but to the music of the voice. It lulled him into a state of euphoria, short-lived and never to be recaptured. This voice would soon be silenced and the slim body buried, and he would have to go on living in the knowledge that a word from him could have saved the prisoner.

When the provost entered to ask if the lieutenant was ready for his dinner, Kunze felt it was time to leave. Seeing him to the door, Dorfrichter placed a hand on his shoulder for a brief moment. Years later, whenever Kunze recalled that hour, he could still feel the sensation of the soft, weightless touch.

Now it was the nineteenth of May. At six thirty, in full-dress uniform with waist belt and shako, Kunze was on his way to the Military Lawcourt. The streets were surprisingly alive despite the early hour. The sudden mildness in the air had lured people from their stuffy apartments, and they sat on the park benches, turning their faces to the sun, like the faithful waiting to be blessed by the Pope at St. Peter's.

A small courtroom on the second floor had been chosen for the trial. All unauthorized persons were barred from it and from the corridor between the courtroom and the heavy iron door leading to the prison wing as well. Scores of newsmen gathered in front of the entrance to the building and a fairly large crowd thronged on the viaduct over Hernalser Gürtel, one of the spots where there was a direct view into the courtroom. The only other point where one could view the courtroom was a balcony on the Ottakring side of the house across the street. People packed like sardines there made the captain wonder whether the railing was strong enough to hold them all.

At eight o'clock sharp, two buglers posted at the courtroom door blew the signal, and the members of the tribunal, delegated by Baron von Hadauer, commander of the Vienna garrison, filed in, led by the General Staff colonel who was to preside. Following them were Kunze, two captains, two first and two second lieutenants, all wearing full-dress uniforms and shakos. They proceeded to a long table surrounded by eight chairs, one with a somewhat higher back, placed on a dais at the end of the room. The colonel took the chair with the high back, with Kunze on his left, the captains flanking them, the first lieutenants next to the captains, and the second lieutenants in the end seats. All this was executed in a solemn pantomime to the accompaniment of jingling spurs and chair legs scraping the floor. The rows of benches below gaped empty, for the public was not admitted to the trial.

A second bugle call signaled to Staff Provost Koller to escort the defendant in. The trio—prisoner, provost and guard—marched to the courtroom and halted. The guard remained posted outside the door as the provost turned about and walked away. Peter Dorfrichter alone stepped inside.

He wore his regimental uniform and cap and was minus a sword. He seemed composed, yet his cheeks were flushed as though he were running a fever. After moving through the small gate that closed off the section with the empty rows of benches, he stopped to face the colonel, snapped to attention and saluted. The members of the court-martial rose, acknowledging his salute with curt nods. They resumed their seats as the colonel threw a mumbled "At ease!" at Dorfrichter.

"First Lieutenant Peter Dorfrichter," the colonel addressed him. "Have you been notified regarding the composition of this tribunal? Names and regimental affiliations of its members?"

"I have been notified, sir, regarding the composition of the tribunal," the accused answered in clipped tones.

"Have you any objection to a member or members of this tribunal?"

Dorfrichter's eyes combed the eight faces staring woodenly at him from behind the long table. On meeting Kunze's gaze, they lingered for a moment. The hint of a smile lightened the grim hardness of his expression, an oddly mocking smile, it seemed to Kunze. It brought to mind Max and Moritz, the bad boys of the German humorist Wilhelm Busch.

"I most respectfully report, sir, that I have no objection to any member of this tribunal." Dorfrichter rattled off the answer in a proper military staccato.

The colonel heaved a little sigh. So far so good. He motioned to the officers, and all rose. Lieutenant Heinrich, who had been designated as recorder, stepped forward to administer the oath to the court-martial.

The officers resumed their seats. Captain Kunze, who had picked the top folder off the stack of documents neatly arranged on the table in front of him, remained standing. He began reading the indictment. After the description of the offense, he presented the evidence and quoted the defendant's confession.

Dorfrichter had been listening with the polite impatience of a man who is being told a funny story which he knows he can top with a much better one. Halfway through, the colonel instructed Kunze to sit down so the defendant could also be seated. Dorfrichter thanked him for the consideration, but asked permission to remain standing, which was granted, though not without a puzzled frown.

"Do you, First Lieutenant Dorfrichter, confirm your confession as made to Judge Advocate Captain Kunze on the fifth of March, 1910?" the colonel asked.

Dorfrichter said slowly, emphasizing every syllable, "With the colonel's permission, I hereby refuse to confirm my statements made to Judge Advocate Captain Kunze on the fifth of March, 1910."

Kunze was the first to comprehend fully the meaning of the words.

The colonel blinked repeatedly, letting the monocle drop from his left eye. The six officers in their resplendent gala uniforms remained motionless, like figures in a wax museum.

The colonel erupted. "What the hell, Lieutenant! You mean you want to change your plea?"

"With your permission, sir, I wish to plead *not* guilty," Dorfrichter announced in a clear, loud voice.

"You retract your confession? Why?"

Dorfrichter looked the colonel straight in the eye. "I retract my confession because I made it under duress and in a state of mental derangement!" he announced.

Kunze threw back his head and closed his eyes. The wording was familiar. However, something was missing. Concentrating for a moment, he found the omitted phrase. The lieutenant had left out "under hypnosis."

The colonel lifted the monocle back to his eye and squeezed it into place. "Well, is there any additional statement you wish to make at this point?"

"With your permission, sir, I wish to state that I am innocent of the charges preferred against me. I did not send ten letters, each containing a circular and two cyanide pills, to ten of my comrades and had no knowledge of the crime prior to the day I first read about it in the newspapers and no connection whatsoever with its perpetrator or perpetrators!"

"Good God, man, you *did* confess. Of your own accord!"

Slowly Dorfrichter shook his head, his eyes fixed on the president's face.

"I wish to repeat that my confession was made under duress and in a state of complete mental and emotional collapse."

The colonel turned questioningly to Captain Kunze, who responded with a gesture indicating ironical bewilderment.

As established under Maria Theresa, the military criminal procedure called now for the signing of the trial record by the defendant, after which he was led from the courtroom, to be returned at the end of the trial for sentencing. All eight members of the court-martial were fully aware of the absurdity of the law but were powerless to change it or even to protest against it. The same law that placed defense and prosecution in the hands of one man, the judge advocate, decreed that the accused be absent while the question of his guilt or innocence was presented to the seven officers who—with the judge advocate now functioning as a member of the tribunal—were to decide about his fate.

The record of the morning's proceedings was completed in dead silence. Rising, Lieutenant Heinrich took it over to Captain Kunze, who stepped to the accused. "Lieutenant Dorfrichter, would you kindly read this document?"

"As you wish, sir," Dorfrichter said stiffly.

He reached for the paper, avoiding Kunze's eyes. He glanced over the pages quickly, then handed them back to the captain.

"Have you found the record true to facts?" Kunze asked him.

"I found it true to facts, sir."

"Will you then sign it?"

They stepped to the clerks' desk, where Kunze picked up a pen, dipped it in ink, and handed it to the accused. Their hands touched as the pen passed from one to the other; Kunze was aware that the lieutenant's palm was cold and damp.

"Thank you, sir," Dorfrichter muttered, quickly scribbling his signature. As he straightened, their eyes met at last, their glances locked together like harpoon and fish. Then the captain mercifully turned away.

The colonel dismissed the defendant. As though by magic, the provost materialized, and the guard with fixed bayonet moved forward from his post at the open door. Leaving the door to the empty corridor ajar was a symbolic arrangement conforming to the statute which decreed that the trial be held in public.

Dorfrichter saluted smartly, made a swift about-face, and joined the escort waiting for him. In complete silence the tribunal listened to their steps receding in the distance.

Captain Kunze then asked the president to grant a recess and a re-convening again at three in the afternoon, explaining that the defendant's unexpected plea of not guilty made it necessary for him to revise his trial strategy. The colonel agreed to the suggestion, after which Kunze went to his office on the third floor and immediately settled down to work. He cursed aloud as he recalled how smug and safe he'd felt when he'd learned about Franz Ferdinand's absence from Vienna. It had never occurred to him that the archduke's fine hand might have shuffled the deck long before his departure. Now in four short hours, Kunze realized as he attacked the transcripts in feverish, defiant haste, he had to amend the toil of two months. If Stoklaska hadn't ordered two frankfurters and a glass of wine for him from a nearby café, he would have gone all day without eating.

"I've found the key to the puzzle!" Stoklaska reported as Kunze ate hurriedly. "Remember about two weeks ago when General Wencel went to see Dorfrichter in his cell? Wencel wasn't alone. He had Colonel Bardolff with him."

The fork dropped from the captain's grip, landing on the plate.

"How do you know it was Colonel Bardolff?"

"One of the guards had served in his regiment. The Fifteenth Dragoons. He recognized him."

"I'll be damned!" Kunze invoked a hearty curse against General Wencel. Relieved, he picked up his fork again. "I thought something like that must have happened. God help the country once the archduke becomes emperor! He has the obstinacy of a mule. And the brains, too!"

During the afternoon and the rest of the week, and again from Monday until Wednesday, Kunze sat facing the tribunal, reading aloud the results of the six-month-long investigation. His voice droned on, buzzing into the ears of the seven men, lulling them to a numbing drowsiness. He tried to speak animatedly, determined to keep them awake, and they were equally determined to stay awake, but despite their best combined efforts, at times chins dropped on gold-braided chests and snorelike snorts escaped from drooping mouths. Unless the 1768 law determining military criminal procedure were changed, there was no way of changing the trial methods. Reading page after page, Kunze wondered whether participants in the mid-eighteenth-century court-martials had been blessed with more endurance and vitality than their 1910 counterparts.

Sunday was a welcome rest for both the tribunal and Captain Kunze. By Saturday evening he had lost his voice completely and was able to read only in a hoarse whisper. To the disappointment of both Rose and Troll he stayed in his study and worked throughout the day. In the late afternoon, a placative little walk reestablished him in Troll's good graces, though not in his wife's. She went along but never stopped grumbling.

When her lamentation—like a dentist's drill—finally touched a live nerve, he exploded, "For Christ's sake, Rose, you were no wide-eyed virgin when you married me! You'd lived with me for two years, ample time to find out what I was like. If I was a cold, heartless son of a bitch, that's what you took, for better or worse. So don't try to tell me you've been cheated."

"You never have time for me. You don't even talk to me anymore," she said, her eyes growing moist.

"How can I when all you want to talk about is how disappointed you are?"

"That's not true," she said. "I've asked you many times how things were at court! Like the trial right now. You never tell me anything. Do you think I'm not interested in your work?"

"What do you want to know?"

"For instance, what Peter Dorfrichter is like? People keep asking me and I can't tell them a thing."

"Why would they ask *you*?"

"They know you're assigned to the case. There's so little in the papers about him, and people are curious."

"Perhaps that's why I don't tell you anything. So you can't pass it on to the curious people."

"I won't if you don't want me to!"

For a while they walked in silence. The lilacs were in full bloom, and tiny wild marguerites dotted the grass. Troll, disobeying "Keep off the grass!" signs, was chasing pigeons.

"What is he like?" Rose asked again.

"What is who like?"

"Peter Dorfrichter!"

Kunze stopped, half-turning to look at her face.

"He is a man with talent, courage, imagination, obstinacy and a minimum of conscience. A man who'd fight his way through a phalanx of Roman legionaries to take Christ off the cross, so he could nail him back more securely. So he'd never be resurrected! In Dorfrichter's opinion the only good pacifist is a dead pacifist and the utterance of the words 'Peace on earth' should be punishable by death."

Rose's reaction was a troubled frown.
"I wish you wouldn't talk blasphemy. It disturbs me."

The trial continued on Monday morning at eight, Kunze reading
the rest of the transcripts. During the early hours on Tuesday
the tribunal was briefed on the paragraphs of the military criminal
code concerning the crime and the standardized punishment for
similar offenses. Finally, the captain could push aside the legal
papers piled on the table and embark on a discourse which
summed up the evidence and his own views of its value. He spoke
freely and at times extemporaneously, without glancing at his
notes. After four days of utter tedium, his eloquence and lucidity
dispelled the court's lethargy, and the seven men listened to him
with interest and concentration.

He described the defendant's character, his background, boyhood, education, the quality of his work at the Military Academy
and his performance in the service. He depicted Dorfrichter as
exceptionally gifted and deserving of a brilliant career in his
chosen field. It was the army's loss that a man of his mental powers and devotion to duty had been passed over when appointees
to the General Staff were selected. The fault, he suggested, lay in
a system which rated physical fitness above intellectual excellence,
a perception left over from past centuries when battles were decided in face-to-face combat. Modern warfare called for officers like
Dorfrichter, not fighters, but scientists, diplomats, visionaries,
men able to keep in step with the great discoveries of the new
century.

After the portrait of the man painted in scintillating colors,
Kunze discussed Dorfrichter's motives and mental processes
which led him to the commission of the crime. Despite the plea of
innocence, Kunze repeatedly stressed the defendant's guilt. His
confession was the truth, retraction the lie! Even without the
confession, he argued, the circumstantial evidence was strong
enough to convict him. He was an egomaniac and a zealot, whose
great talents were coupled with Napoleonic ambition and a belief
that the norms set for ordinary people failed to apply to him.
However, the fact that he was incapable of recognizing that his
act was wrong did not exonerate him from guilt.

On Wednesday morning, having discussed all the mitigating

circumstances, such as the frustration and injustice suffered by Dorfrichter, and the horribly painful death he had condemned ten of his comrades to, among them a man who had once saved his life, Kunze made his recommendation for punishment. The lack of any direct evidence and the defendant's plea of innocence (his confession had become null and void when he retracted it) ruled out, by force of Paragraph 212 of the Military Criminal Code, the death penalty and a life sentence as well. In view of the strong circumstantial evidence, Captain Kunze asked the tribunal for a verdict of guilty and a twenty-year imprisonment with special restrictions in a military penal institution. Resuming his seat, Kunze had never felt so empty or deathly tired.

Twenty years in any of the dungeonlike military prisons of the monarchy, Kunze knew, was a death or near-death sentence. Even the most robust prisoner was known to contract a fatal disease or suffer a nervous breakdown. A few years were enough to turn a strong young man into a human wreck. If pardoned, he usually never recovered fully; anyway pardons were not granted easily, and most inmates served their full terms or left their cells wrapped in a shroud, in a wooden box. Kunze tried to visualize what Dorfrichter would be like after twenty years: Palsied? Prematurely old? Tubercular? Hardly alive? He hovered between wishing the court would override his recommendation, granting acquittal, and conviction. The private in Sarajevo had, in a fit of anger, raised his hand against his commanding officer, and for that he had been placed before a firing squad. His execution and those of all the others who had been made an example in the name of the emperor-king—and for the good of the fatherland and the army—would be common murders if Peter Dorfrichter were to go free. Kunze had no doubt that some members of the tribunal had been made to understand that an acquittal would please Franz Ferdinand, and he wondered about the outcome of a conflict between subservience and moral rectitude.

The colonel asked the members of the court whether they fully understood the case or needed any additional information or amplification, at which point the lower-ranking second lieutenant requested that Captain Kunze reread Private Boka's testimony concerning the incident on the Castelnuovo beach and also the defendant's statements in reference to the scene between him and Captain Mader. After Kunze had complied, the colonel asked for clarification on one point: the circumstances of Dorfrichter's taking the cyanide sticks from Lieutenant Vanini. Kunze read the relevant section of the transcript.

After that the colonel declared the formal examination of the matter in issue to be ended, thanking Captain Kunze for his exemplary performance in the conduct of the trial and proclaiming the tribunal ready for the careful weighing of all arguments and pronouncement of the verdict.

In accordance with the dictates of the Military Criminal Code, each one of the seven judges was locked alone in a room where he could reflect in complete solitude, listening to no voice other than that of his own conscience, and reach a decision free from outside influence. When a judge reached his decision, he knocked on the door and told this to the guard posted in front of it. He had to remain locked up, however, until every other member of the tribunal had done the same.

At five after eleven the seven men, led by the colonel, filed back into the courtroom. Captain Kunze, who had been waiting for them for more than an hour, scanned their faces wearily. Their decision was to affect not only Dorfrichter's fate, but his, too. While they'd been grappling with a verdict, he had had time to ponder his own problems. He knew he had to find a way out of the maze of his own uncertainties, but, first of all, out of Rose's soft bed, which smelled of lilacs and sour milk. He had to come to terms with himself and arrive at a point where he could say, "I am what I am"—and know relief.

The seven men took their seats awaiting his instructions. He explained the procedure to them. Each member of the court, himself included, had one vote; the president alone had two votes. The lowest-ranking officer would be the first to speak, free to pronounce a verdict either harsher or milder than that proposed by the judge advocate, without having to explain or justify his decision. The voting then continued according to rank, with the president and, after him, the judge advocate voting last. If the votes differed, they were then grouped, beginning with the mildest and ending with the harshest, the fifth in succession determining the final verdict. The members of the court-martial under oath vowed never to reveal their decisions or the proportion of the votes.

The colonel gave the signal, and the younger second lieutenant rose, his "Not guilty!" ringing forth. Dropping back into his seat, he stared challengingly at the empty rows of benches as though expecting a protest from them. The vote for acquittal brought with it a dead silence. Finally, Judge Advocate Kunze nodded to the colonel, who in turn motioned to the ranking second lieutenant. The officer rose, calling out a verdict of guilty and a sentence of twenty years in prison. Both first lieutenants agreed with him as far as guilt was concerned, but considered ten years' imprisonment an appropriate punishment. The younger captain acquitted Dorfrichter. The rest of the tribunal accepted Kunze's recommendation.

Since there were two acquittals followed by two votes proposing ten years' imprisonment and six votes opting for twenty years, the final verdict was twenty years in a military penal institution.

Kunze's immediate feeling was that the trial had lasted not six days but six years, and he should have been satisfied at the outcome. It was not only a personal victory but the victory of justice over the forces of Machiavellianism. The horrible death of Captain Richard Mader had been—if not fully—at least to some degree revenged. The archduke had failed to influence the court-martial just as he had failed to pressure Kunze into exonerating Dorfrichter. The not guilty votes, however, may well have been the result of archducal interference. But it was meaningless to ruminate on them, Kunze thought, now that virtue had triumphed so gloriously. Triumphed for the time being, that is, because he knew the incident would not be forgotten. He could already see himself after the enthronement of the new emperor being banished to some godforsaken garrison along the Russian or Serbian border.

Before sentencing of the accused, the verdict, signed and sealed, had to be submitted for approval to General Versbach von Hadauer of the Second Army Corps. It was his prerogative as commander of the Vienna garrison either to affirm the sentence, commute it or pardon the defendant. The ranking captain and a subaltern delivered the dossier to the corps command post, fighting their way through the swarm of reporters and the curious who congregated in front of the Military Lawcourt Building. The fact that two members of the tribunal were leaving the court indicated to them that judgment had been passed, and the first rumors of a death sentence spread rapidly. The two officers were still on their way to the post when an extra edition of a boulevard paper proclaimed in bold headlines DORFRICHTER MUST DIE! Then shortly thereafter, the "well-informed" word went around in the clubs and cafés of Vienna that Peter Dorfrichter would be pardoned by General Versbach von Hadauer. Even the baron's exact words supposedly justifying the pardon were quoted. During all this unsuspecting Versbach von Hadauer was having a leisurely lunch of young goose, fresh peas and cucumber salad at the Sacher. His adjutant interrupted on the direct line connecting the command post with the hotel, to report the arrival of the Dorfrichter verdict. The general breezed through the rest of his lunch and returned to his office.

The verdict bearing his note, "Approved, sentence to be pronounced and made public," arrived at the Military Lawcourt shortly before three o'clock in the afternoon.

Kunze had not gone out to lunch but had sent a man for a portion of goulash, which he ate at his desk. Then he went down to the courtroom. To divert his thoughts, he took along Freud's *Three Essays on the Theory of Sexuality* but was unable to concentrate on it. Both as layman and jurist, he was a great admirer of Dr. Freud and usually found his theories both helpful and enlightening, but this time Dr. Freud's sharp thoughts became lost in the fog of his perturbed mind.

The return of the verdict was reported to the colonel president, who had also been waiting in the building. The command "Sentence to be made public" was observed symbolically by opening both the courtroom windows and the door to the corridor. The two buglers blew the signal to announce the approach of the accused and his escort, repeating it three times when, as before, Dorfrichter entered alone. Still wearing his first lieutenant's uniform and cap, he proceeded with measured, steady steps to a spot about six feet away from the tribunal, where he halted, facing the president. He held himself erect with head thrown back, eyes staring straight ahead, past the colonel's graying shock of hair, even past the emperor's framed photograph. He seemed in control of his nerves, his sickly pallor alone betraying the anguish he felt.

With one quick gesture, he lifted his cap, tucked it under his left arm, and snapped to attention, greeting the tribunal with a mechanical nod.

There was a moment's silence; then the colonel pushed back his chair and rose and the seven men at the table followed suit. The president reached for the sealed dossier which contained the verdict and handed it to Captain Kunze. The colonel drew his sword; this was the signal to the buglers for the call. The lugubriously solemn sound reverberated three times through courtroom and corridor, escaping via the open windows to be swallowed up outside by the rumble of street noises. The people on the balcony across the street could hear it, though faintly, but it failed to reach the crowd on the viaduct.

The bugle call was followed by the tattoo of the drummers. During it all Peter Dorfrichter remained at attention. Kunze opened the dossier, took out the loosely attached pages, and read their contents in a voice deliberately kept even and emotionless.

"The court-martial found the accused guilty and sentenced him to be confined to a military penal institution for twenty years."

During the reading, Dorfrichter's eyes were focused on Kunze. There was a slight flutter of his eyelids, an almost imperceptible twitching of facial muscles during pronouncement; otherwise he displayed no reaction. When a bugle signaled the end of the ceremony, he saluted stiffly, executed an exemplary about-face, and strode from the courtroom. The thumping of three pairs of feet on the stone floor of the corridor receded rapidly. There was the familiar clank of the heavy iron door as it fell shut behind prisoner and escort.

The trial was over.

The Advancement List published in the June 1 edition of the *Gazette* announced that in acknowledgment of his distinguished services the highest authority had ordered Captain Emil Kunze's out-of-turn promotion to major. In addition, he was awarded the silver medal bestowed on the military for outstanding achievements in peacetime. This honor made it necessary that he express his gratitude to the emperor in a private audience, this time not at an early hour at Schönbrunn, but amid the solemn ceremonies of a reception at the Hofburg.

All this was a great step forward, and Major Kunze was now considered by all to be the man of the future at the Military Law-court. Most impressed with the honor bestowed on him was his wife, Rose, and least impressed was Kunze himself.

To be the wife of a highly respected judge advocate, member of an elite army clique, invited to every important social engage-ment, compensated Rose for the frustrations of her marriage. For the Kunzes had reached a *détente*. Like all married couples, they had their heights and their abysses. However, the heights were never really high and the abysses not too deep.

The days after the Dorfrichter court-martial became especially difficult for Kunze, who suddenly felt himself cut adrift. For six months, Peter Dorfrichter had been the center of his life, and Kunze was aware that nothing could fill the void he left behind.

After sentencing, he saw the ex-lieutenant only once, on the day in June when the prisoner was transferred to Mollersdorf.

Dorfrichter was brought to his office at the Military Court. He wore mufti for the trip, an ill-fitting gray suit, a raincoat and a green hat with a chamois brush. His family were expected to come to say good-bye, and Kunze had to be officially present at the meeting. Either the family was late or Dorfrichter had been es-corted up too early, but the two men spent half an hour alone. It was a strained half hour, with the prisoner acknowledging Kunze's small talk in cool monosyllables, then unexpectedly launching a bitter attack against him.

"Major Kunze sounds a lot better than Captain Kunze, doesn't it? Is that why you manipulated my conviction?"

For a brief moment Kunze was at a loss for an answer. "What do you mean—manipulated? You were guilty as hell!"

"That's beside the point! I would have been acquitted without you, *Major* Kunze!"

"Come now, Dorfrichter, we both know you were guilty. True, you did retract your confession, but I have a damn clear idea what made you do it. I also know that just because I didn't comply with the wishes of a certain high place, this promotion might be the last one I'll ever have in this army! So don't delude yourself. You aren't the victim of my ambitions. I am not you, Peter Dorfrichter —ambition wouldn't make me kill a cat, much less a man!"

"You would have put me to death if I hadn't retracted the confession!"

"I suppose so—"

"Did you want me killed because I couldn't be had any other way?"

Kunze almost asked: What other way?

"The nature of my relationship to you was that of judge to accused. Nothing else. It determined what I could or couldn't do for you!"

"You're so goddamn righteous it makes me vomit!" Dorfrichter shouted. "I am a bastard, all right, but what are you? A Iago wouldn't have stooped to the tricks you used in trapping me!"

"That does it, Dorfrichter," Kunze snapped, a feeling of defeat blunting the sharpness of his indignation. "No matter what you think of me, I'm very sorry for you, and I wish you all the luck you can have under the circumstances—"

"Your wish might come true sooner than you think. I won't spend twenty years in Mollersdorf, that is certain. I'll be free the day war breaks out!"

So those were the terms of the deal! Not very generous terms. The archducal offer for the changed plea had been in character; it was niggardly and shrewd.

"In that case I won't wish you luck," Kunze told him. "As you know, I am a confirmed pacifist."

His sentence decreed that Dorfrichter spend the first year of his imprisonment in solitary confinement, deprived of all privileges. His cell was on the second floor, but with its moldy walls and narrow casement windows, it might as well have been in the cellar. On the day of his sentencing, he'd been cashiered without any military ceremony, simply exchanging his officer's tunic for a plain blouse. Three times a week he was taken to the prison yard for a short walk, alone and under the watchful eyes of armed guards, once a week put on rations of bread and water, which was almost better than the regular prison fare. He was not allowed to write, read or engage in any activity which might relieve the monotony of his days.

During the weeks following his transfer to Mollersdorf, Major Kunze repeatedly telephoned the prison commandant to inquire after the ex-lieutenant. If this unusual interest in a convict shocked the commandant, he didn't care. On the whole, he stopped caring about many things, among them the deterioration of his marriage. He made a habit of coming home shortly before dinner and—if they ate alone or weren't going out—retiring to his study after the meal, reappearing the following morning. During the few occasions Rose and he communicated, the subject was their estrangement. Divorce, because of her devout Catholicism, was never considered. Even separation was unacceptable to her, but he hoped she would ultimately relent and set him free.

The bomb was dropped on a balmy end-of-June day. She usually slept late and missed breakfast with him, but on this morning he found her, dressed in her most flattering negligee, her face discreetly powdered and rouged, pouring his coffee and buttering his pastry.

"I have something to tell you," she began, sounding solemn, almost tragic. He held his breath. There was no doubt in his mind that she was about to utter the magic word that would release him. Instead, she told him that she was expecting their child.

For an interminable moment, he stared at her, speechless. The possibility that they should have a child had never entered his mind. She was in her thirty-eighth year, he in his thirty-ninth. As far as he knew, she'd never been pregnant, not even during her first marriage. Moreover, she had once or twice dropped hints about some female disorder which would prevent her from conceiving.

"Good God, how on earth did you do that?" he spoke thoroughly flustered at last.

"I didn't. You did," she answered indignantly.

He had to laugh, realizing the absurdity of the dialogue, even though she didn't, and guessing that the child had been conceived after the Vienna garrison commander's Easter party. The Kunzes had stayed till two in the morning, and when they reached home, Rose had remembered the bottle of champagne that had been cooling in the icebox since their wedding. They both were in an unusually lighthearted mood, the party had been more fun than the customary army affairs, and the wine had buoyed up their already-high spirits. They had made love right there in the salon, Kunze recalled, on the uncomfortably narrow and hard Biedermeier sofa.

"You want to have a child at your age?" Kunze asked, still slightly dazed by the revelation.

Immediately, Rose was in tears. "What do you mean—my age? I'm not seventy, even though you don't seem to be aware of that!"

"But Rose, be sensible. By the time the child is twenty you'll be fifty-nine."

"You sound as though you wanted me to get rid of it," she said in a low voice. "Murder it! Is that what you want?"

He lost his composure. "Hell—Rose, don't always be so goddamn melodramatic! You can't blame me for being surprised. How long have you known?"

"About six weeks, but I wanted to be sure before telling you—"

"You must see a doctor!"

"I did—yesterday."

"What did he say?"

"That I'm more than two months pregnant."

Finally, the brutal fact of the disclosure penetrated his consciousness. They were going to have a child. Not Rose alone, for it would be his, too. The mere thought of it was staggering.

Their marital relationship failed to change much during her pregnancy. There was one improvement, however, for she stopped resenting being left alone quite as much as before, as though she found the child inside her sufficient company. Also, her condition offered a fair excuse to him for staying away from her bed. Additional weight seemed to give her a bovine serenity, for she moved like a cow and, Kunze admitted ruefully, was beginning to look like one, too, a cow with warm, soulful eyes and a voracious appetite. Her happiness seemed so complete that at times she even confessed it to Kunze, which, in turn, freed him from the guilt of being a poor husband.

Rudolf Kunze—named for General Hartmann's eldest son—was born on November 11, 1911. The major had just arrived home from the lawcourt when the cook greeted him breathlessly with the news that Rose was in labor. The midwife had been called earlier, and the obstetrician was on his way. In the cook's opinion, having a doctor present was a superfluous precaution when no complications were expected, but Kunze had insisted, mainly because of Rose's age. He was not happy about the blessed event but would never have forgiven himself if something had gone wrong.

Nothing went wrong. His son weighed more than four kilos, and mother and child survived the ordeal in perfect condition.

Kunze spent the waiting hours in his study with Troll. Later he tried to remember how he had occupied himself. He had a faint suspicion that he had fallen asleep to be awakened by the cook's triumphant cry: "It's a boy! It's a boy!"

He was shown the reddish brown lump of flesh that was supposed to be his son and looked at it with the interest of a zoo visitor watching a rare, exotic reptile. He tried to analyze the reasons for his complete lack of involvement, deciding guiltily that he was not and would never be a father. He remembered his own fatherless childhood and felt sorry for a little boy for being condemned to the same fate. He vowed, of course, to respond conscientiously to the obligations that went with fatherhood and to hide as well as he could, both before the child and, for his own sake, before the world, his indifference.

The change in his plans occurred suddenly and unexpectedly when Rudolf was about eight months old. Adhering to the routine forced on himself, Kunze went each evening into the nursery to have a look at its inmate. The boy, in shirt and diapers, lay in his crib occupied with what appeared to be an inventory of his toes. He was a strong, large baby, active and alert for his age. When he heard his father's footsteps, he let go of his foot, turning to see who had entered. Kunze, stopping beside the crib, became aware suddenly of two small arms reaching out for him.

Cautiously he picked up the child, as though he were as fragile as a flower and was surprised to find the little body firm and muscular. Rudolf placed his arms around his father's neck, played with the buttons of his uniform and the star on his choke collar, and talked to him in a garbled language. When Rose came to give him his bath, she had trouble peeling him off the paternal chest, and Rudolf reacted to the forcible separation with an ear-splitting yell and remained inconsolable. His tear-filled eyes followed Kunze longingly wherever he moved in the room.

"He loves you," Rose announced.

"Don't be ridiculous! How could he? He hardly knows me," Kunze mumbled. He'd be damned, he thought, if he let Rose notice his state of confusion.

"He knows you're his father," Rose insisted.

"He does not! It's the uniform. The buttons and the braid. All children are fascinated with shiny things."

Friends were coming for dinner that evening. Among them was Lieutenant Stoklaska, and when the young officer arrived, the major took him straight into the nursery. "I want you to see my son."

The lieutenant, surprised, detected a note of urgency in his tone.

Rudolf was in his crib again, changed and bathed and powdered, whiling away the wait for his dinner with a monologue to his teddy bear.

"Go to his crib and say something." Kunze's order sounded oddly muffled.

Stoklaska gave him a puzzled look, then obeyed. The boy stopped his gurgling and looked up expectantly.

Stoklaska leaned over the crib. "Hey, fellow, how are you today?"

The child stared at him wide-eyed and remained silent.

"Pick him up!" Kunze ordered from the doorway.

Stoklaska gave him an astonished look.

The lieutenant reached down for the little boy. "Hope I don't drop him. I'm not what you'd call a trained babies' nurse!" Rudolf pulled away from the groping arms, emitting a frightened cry. Stoklaska turned to Kunze. "He doesn't seem to like being picked up!"

"Then don't!" Kunze said nervously. Crossing to the crib, he bent over it. In later years, whenever he remembered that moment, he thought of it as the turning point in his life, a miracle which, for him, equaled the budding of Aaron's rod and the raising of Jairus' daughter. Little Rudolf's sobs stopped abruptly; the drooping corners of his lips curved up into a grin; he sat up, then, grabbing the side of his crib, pulled himself almost to a standing position, chirping an excited greeting.

"I'll be damned!" Kunze said, sounding awed as he gathered the boy in his arms. "He knows me!"

Stoklaska chuckled. "Why shouldn't he? You're his father."

"I suppose so, but I wasn't sure he knew," Kunze said sheepishly.

XX

IT had been a beautiful summer. The major and his family had rented a villa on a hillside overlooking the water in Strobl on the Wolfgangsee. Rose, their son, the cook and the maid left for Salzkammergut early in June, and Kunze would join them in August to spend his leave in Strobl.

He minded not at all being alone in the apartment. Troll was his companion, a Troll graying around the muzzle and behaving with quiet dignity. Lately, Kunze had fallen into the habit of taking him to the office, where no one objected to his shedding, although Rose had at last become reconciled to the idea that if she wanted to keep the man, she had to accept the dog.

That June Emil Kunze once again lived the life of a bachelor. He ate most of his meals at a small restaurant in Weihburggasse and on balmy evenings took the streetcar to a suburb, usually Grinzing. He read a great deal, Strindberg, Galsworthy, Thomas Mann, Werfel, D'Annunzio, and discovered Proust. Years later, whenever he recalled this memorable month—memorable because it was the last safe and sane June in his or his generation's life— he pictured himself seated in a shady backyard with a mug of cool wine before him, Troll at his feet and the pages of his open book turned by a jasmine-scented breeze from Kahlenberg. A few late chickens scraped in the grass around him, daylight dimmed, the moon came up, and his host brought a flickering kerosene lamp from the house. Somewhere someone strummed a song by Leo Fall on a zither, in a neighboring yard a *Schrammel* band struck up the "Blue Danube Waltz," and from down the street came an Offenbach tune played on a harmonica. The incongruous melodies fused into one happy sound with the rustling of the linden trees and the clatter of fiacre horses on the cobblestones before the house.

One evening a family at the next table—father, mother and three young sons—unpacked a picnic basket. Out came thick slices of home-cured ham, sausage, headcheese, butter, almond cake and wonderfully crisp four-cornered Kaiser rolls. The family watched Kunze, the quiet major sitting with a book and no food before him. Finally, the wife mustered courage, asking if the major would find it presumptuous if she offered him a taste of her ham. Delighted, the major joined them, and the evening symbolized for Kunze everything that had been good and precious and happy in Austria. Soon the music was gone, and so were the rich picnic baskets, the mutual respect across class barriers, the fathers and the sons. The women alone were left behind, women with empty beds and no picnic baskets.

It was in the same backyard that the news of the assassination reached the major. He had gone there from the office, Gersten and Prince Hohenstein were to join him later, and they planned to drive in the prince's car to Kahlenberg and have dinner on the Schlosshotel terrace overlooking the city. The rendezvous was set for seven. At eight, a distraught Gersten dashed in with the news which, like a poison gas, had already spread through the nooks and corners of Vienna: Franz Ferdinand and his duchess had been shot to death in Sarajevo!

Kunze's first reaction was to consider bringing his family home. "War?" he asked.

Gersten shook his head.

"I don't think so. Who in this monarchy would be willing to fight and die to revenge Franz Ferdinand? *De mortuis nil nisi bonum,* but let's face it, everyone loathed the poor bastard."

The lunch at Konopischt flashed through Kunze's mind. He recalled the English botanist's question about the mechanics of starting a war and the archduke's bluntly cynical answer. "There is always an incident, or conflict in itself insignificant, that can be blown up and exploited by the party determined to start a war . . . !" Now, in retrospect, the words sounded frighteningly prophetic.

"He that killeth with the sword must be killed with the sword," Gersten muttered. "Did you know that Franz Ferdinand had a double-barreled Mannlicher constructed specially for him, because an ordinary rifle couldn't satisfy his mania for carnage? Those photographs showing him beside mountains of bagged prey always turned my stomach." Rather sharp words, Kunze thought, coming from the winner of an Olympic silver medal for trapshooting.

"I only hope certain people won't make a martyr out of him now," Kunze said wistfully. "I wouldn't be surprised if they did. Anything to serve their purposes."

The panic caused by the assassination, however, subsided within a few days, and Rose and Rudolf remained in Strobl. Her letters were happy, though lightly peppered with complaints about the weather (it rained too much), the servants (they took the word "vacation" literally), and the local merchants (overcharging summer guests). Then, suddenly, Serbia was handed an ultimatum, and mobilization was ordered. Kunze requested a day's leave and boarded the train for Salzkammergut to bring the family back to Vienna.

Although he hadn't wired Rose, he found her packed and ready to leave. Feminine intuition—as it had many times before—filled him with surprise and awe. The same Rose who grew hysterical over a fallen soufflé was calm and collected in the face of the most serious crisis of their lives.

Their world was fast being ripped apart at its seams. All army and navy leaves were canceled, all reservists called up, as well as many of the home reserves. The country resembled an ant hill scooped open with a spade: everyone on the move, lines formed at railroad stations, banks, post offices, police headquarters, recruiting depots, bakeries, butcher shops, and grocery stores. Queuing up, the order of the day, never again went completely out of fashion.

While Kunze tried to find a cab to take his family to Ischl, where they could make a direct train connection to Vienna, the monarchy declared war on Serbia. He passed the Strobl general store, probably the only shop in town that had a telephone, just as the storekeeper stepped out onto the landing, raised his arms and shrieked: "War! War!"

Kunze could never forget him, this little man in shirtsleeves, leather pants and fancy green suspenders, standing in the brilliant July sunshine in front of a window displaying swimsuits, fishing rods, candy, postcards, flyswatters and toys, amid the accouterments of summer happiness, standing there, his mouth open, screaming the fatal words.

No taxi, not even a farm cart, could be had for love or money, so they left their luggage at the villa in care of the landlady and took the train that commuted between St. Gilgen and Ischl.

"Will you be ordered to the front?" Rose asked.

"I don't know," Kunze told her. "I hope not."

He wouldn't have minded fighting, was even willing to go when others went, but the functions of a judge advocate in wartime, the thought of having to attend court-martial after court-martial, meting out wholesale death to deserters, spies and partisans, made him shudder. The laws and moral principles binding in peace, he knew, would no longer prevail. No military animal, he dreaded the day when his verdicts would have to be coordinated with the new legality.

The train to Ischl resembled six large sardine cans hooked onto an asthmatic toy locomotive.

"I can't breathe, Papa," Rudolf complained, as the five of them —father, mother, child, cook and maid—squeezed into a carriage. "Let's go back to Strobl!"

The boy, three and a half years old, was able to put anything he wished to communicate to his elders into precise and clearly pronounced words. He was not a handsome child—his forehead was too high and his mouth too wide—but he was smart and had personality and—what startled his father most—a sense of humor. This was the trait that had swept away the last thin vestiges of Major Kunze's resistance to conventional fatherhood.

The journey from Strobl to Ischl was a nightmare and from Ischl to Vienna even worse. The coaches were packed. A ride that normally would have taken six hours lasted ten because of stops at every station so the rails would be left free for troop transports. Scenes that were to become sickeningly familiar during the ensuing years were played out on platform after platform: women, old and young, dissolved in tears, seeing their men, some already in uniform, off to war. The contrast between their Hecuban grief and the young soldiers' noisy hilarity added a touch of the macabre to the picture. Patriotic exuberance grew more manifest the nearer they got to Vienna. Whether a regiment of Bosnians, still in their red fezzes, or Hungarian hussars, already in pike-gray, or a battalion of Deutschmeisters, the elite of the Austrian infantry, boarded the freight cars with the specification "6 horses, 40 men," the mood was the same. Men turned into boys were setting out on a glorious vacation, a wondrous outing to some place where the cumbersome responsibilities of adulthood were unknown.

There was no water or food on the train, and the toilets couldn't be reached through the ever-thickening mass of travelers in the corridors. Vendors at the stations had long before sold out their provisions. Little Rudolf behaved with remarkable composure, remaining curled up in his father's lap. The cook, who had two sons of military age, sobbed throughout the journey.

They reached Vienna late at night, but no one seemed to have gone to bed. On the ring, people spread from sidewalks to roadbed, shouting, singing, waving flags bearing crude likenesses of Emperor Franz Josef, the Kaiser and Victor Emmanuel of Italy. The crowd behaved as though the monarchy were already at war with Russia. Threats against the enemy mingled with cheers for the old emperor, who had suddenly become a paragon of wisdom and goodness. The word "war" had produced the intoxicating effect of hashish on the crowd, Kunze thought as he scanned the sea of radiant, shining, jubilant faces that seemed to be celebrating not the outbreak of war, but its final victory.

Whenever Kunze recalled the days following his return from Strobl, the image was of himself as a sane man locked into a lunatic asylum filled with raving maniacs. The image he knew to be somewhat exaggerated, for he wasn't the only one whose discontent had turned to resentment. Long before the outbreak of war, his position had allowed him an insight into certain intrigues, behind the scenes dealings—never reported by the press—that both disquieted and enraged him. The version of Serbia's part in the assassination—as presented to the public—was mostly fiction. Rumors of Russia's complicity were never satisfactorily confirmed. Many leading politicians of the Central Powers opposed drastic action against Serbia and later agreed to an ultimatum only as a compromise measure. The war lovers, led by Conrad von Hötzendorf, drafted an ultimatum that was both an insult and provocation to a self-respecting nation. To the dire disappointment of the Hötzendorf clique, Serbia agreed—though with some reservations—to nine of the ten demands.

At this point, there was a moment of general calm. It seemed as though cooler heads might win their way. Governments—even the Kaiser's—vacillated between appeasement and belligerence. Unfortunately, the peace advocates weren't aggressive enough to counteract Austria's single-minded determination to eliminate the "South Slav menace" once and for all. Austria mobilized, and suddenly wary armies were massed along the borders of Europe, ready to strike in order to keep the enemy from striking first. When eighty-four-year-old Franz Josef was tricked into signing the declaration of war, the last chance for peace was lost.

In the offices of the General Staff hierarchy there was a mood of triumph and elation. The excitement in the streets subsided, then flared up again on August 6, the day of the Russian declaration of war. By then France, Belgium and England, too, were up in arms against the Central Powers. Becoming an island in a sea of hostility suddenly had a sobering effect on the high commands of the monarchy and Germany. The louder the happy clamor grew in the streets, the more rapidly the exhilaration diminished in the war ministries. The gallant charge, the great, glorious adventure were beginning to bog down, despite the carefully worked-out plans; the deployment of an army of millions could not be achieved as smoothly as had been expected. Wheels creaked; screws came loose; at times the whole machinery threatened to grind to a halt. It was a new kind of warfare, especially to Austria, the kind she had never before waged: complex, brutal, illogical and intolerant of a centuries-old system of muddling through.

The worst surprise, both in the East and West, was the enemy's stubborn resistance: He shot back with remarkable accuracy.

The month of August was a time of farewells for Kunze. He remained at the Military Lawcourt, but almost all of the Vienna garrison and most of his friends were ordered to the various fronts.

One morning toward the end of August he had a visitor. In the field uniform of a home reservist private, on his way to the Russian front, Friedrich Gabriel called on him, admittedly to say good-bye, but in reality—as Kunze suspected—to add a bitter note to the defeat the major had suffered back in 1910, when he had tried to champion Gabriel's rehabilitation.

They'd last met in June of that year, when Gabriel's petition to rejoin the Officers' Corps had been finally rejected. Although it had not been within his authority, Kunze took it on himself to personally convey the bad news to Gabriel, thus somewhat alleviating the stupid harshness of the decision. Gabriel had accepted it calmly, even philosophically, saying that it might have been all for the best. Now he stood facing Kunze, in his government issue, ill-fitting uniform, with a mocking grin on his lips.

"When they called me up, I warned them that I'd be a disgrace to the army." He chuckled. "They said I'd do for cannon fodder."

Kunze was outraged.

"This is the goddamnedest thing ever," he muttered angrily, stepping to the telephone to call Captain Stolz, one of the adjutants to the minister of war.

Half an hour later he was facing the captain in his office, the resplendent room where one hundred and fifty years earlier Maria Theresa had presided over her war council.

"You're desperately short of qualified men," he pointed out to Captain Stolz, "entrusting whole companies to green boys hardly out of officers' training course. Then you commit the idiocy of degrading a first-rate man to private, instead of putting him where he could do you the most good!"

Captain Stolz, unused to such direct rebukes, rose stiffly and ordered a clerk to dig up all documents pertinent to the Gabriel case.

Kunze interrupted. "That won't be necessary. I can give you the whole goddamn story in synopsis."

"I remember it correctly," Stolz said. "The man was involved in some scandal."

"He was involved in no scandal!" Kunze flared, then gave the captain a summary of the facts. When he left an hour later, Friedrich Gabriel had been restored to the rank of first lieutenant, moved from the unit bound for the front and given orders to report for duty to his old regiment, the Deutschmeisters.

He was waiting in Kunze's office for the major's return.

"I have good news for you," Kunze told him as he handed Gabriel his orders. "There'll be First Lieutenant Fritz Gabriel carved on your tombstone. Perhaps even Captain Gabriel, if you last that long and aren't buried in an unmarked grave."

Gabriel grinned. "It seems you don't like the war."

"Do you?"

"No! I like the army and hate the war. I must be a freak."

"In that case I'm a freak, too."

"I don't think so, Major. I don't think you ever liked the army. And what always puzzled me was why you joined it."

Kunze sighed. "That question has always puzzled me, too, Lieutenant."

Peter Dorfrichter's petition for a pardon which, if granted, would allow him to rejoin the armed forces of the monarchy to "fight for his emperor, his country and a better future for his son" reached Major Kunze's desk on a day in mid October. The petition had been addressed to the Crown, but Baron Bolfras, head of the emperor's Military Chancery, had forwarded it to the major, leaving the decision to him.

He hadn't seen Dorfrichter for more than four years. Not that he hadn't wanted to. He had gone through periods of mental torment when the idea of freeing the man, finding a legal angle that would make an appeal possible, haunted him. Somehow his sanity—he called it cowardice—managed to curb such impulses before he could take decisive steps. Slowly, as the years passed, the daydream had faded into a dull ache lodged in the depths of his consciousness.

Now the Dorfrichter petition, written in the prisoner's beautiful calligraphic hand—the same precise and military hand that had betrayed him—lay on his desk. Kunze had agonized over it for days, unable to reach a decision.

Since the outbreak of the war, many officers and enlisted men serving time in military prisons had been pardoned on condition they volunteer to fight at the front. An archducal gesture four years earlier was routine procedure now. Nevertheless, the major wasn't ready to settle the Dorfrichter problem with a simple yes or no. He came to the conclusion that he must speak to the man first to find out if he deserved to be released. Since his crammed schedule allowed him no time for a trip to Mollersdorf, he ordered the prisoner brought to his office at the Military Lawcourt.

The four years had left their mark on Dorfrichter. His hair now a drab gray-brown, his cheeks hollow and ivory-colored, he looked like a bad passport photo of his former self. His eyes seemed to have sunk deep into the cavity of their sockets, fine lines criss-crossing the skin around them. He wore a rather tight-fitting civilian suit, the same one in which he'd left Vienna, and he had put on weight.

When they were alone, major and prisoner, Dorfrichter spoke. "How very kind of you, sir, to let me come. Even the short ride from the station was like a dream."

Remembering their last encounter, Kunze was prepared for arrogance and insults. The meekness of the man's tone took him by surprise. Had prison changed him, he wondered, or was this an act? The old Dorfrichter had never resorted to subservience; he had been brash, infuriating, egotistical, but never cunning. Had Mollersdorf broken his spirit?

He offered a chair and a cigarette to the prisoner, who took the seat, refusing the cigarette. He had given up smoking during his year of solitary confinement, he explained.

"I couldn't let a whole year pass without some achievement," he added, and there was a faint reflection of the old personality in his smile.

Kunze watched him closely, at the same time watching himself. It was as though he'd split in two—one of him was seated opposite the visitor, the other withdrawn to a dark corner, eavesdropping. He had looked forward to the encounter with a feeling of excitement, mixed with trepidation, and was now baffled to find himself emotionally numb.

"If they'd only let me read during the first year—at least newspapers! It was frustrating not to know what was happening in the world." Dorfrichter's voice held a plaintive tone. "And no letters, no visitors. Incidentally, my parents never came to Mollersdorf.

My brother-in-law told me—he paid me a brief visit in 1912—that Father couldn't forgive my having disgraced them and that Mother felt it would be too much of a strain for her to see me in that—that environment. The same went for my sister. You'll be surprised to hear who looked me up once when she was in Austria! Frau Gruber, my ex-mother-in-law. They live in Bavaria now—she, Marianne and the child. I'm sure you heard about the divorce. It was granted shortly after my court-martial. Frau Gruber told me that Marianne was improving. Slowly, but improving. She never visited me—her doctor wouldn't let her. He feared it would cause a relapse. I should never've been angry at Marianne—I should've known she was sick when she went away with that son of a bitch! Frau Gruber told me they hadn't seen him since Marianne's breakdown. The divorce was handled by that fellow who brought her to your office. What was his name?"

"Dr. Frazer."

"Yes, Frazer." There was a slight pause. "Frau Gruber offered to bring the little boy, but I didn't want her to. Not at that time. I felt it was better not to see him. I didn't even want to see pictures of him. I wanted him to remain unreal—fictitious. One can't get emotional about someone who doesn't exist. Of course, now all that has changed."

"In what way?"

Dorfrichter gave him a perplexed look. "Before the war I had to be as nonexistent for him as he was for me. There is no glory in being a convict's son. But now it'll be different. The day will come when I can say to him, 'I am your father,' and he won't have to be ashamed of me."

Kunze moved his eyes from the man's face to the petition still on his desk. *The fool takes it for granted he'll be pardoned,* he thought and felt his backbone stiffen.

"During that first year," Dorfrichter went on, "it was hard to preserve my sanity. There could've been a war on, and I wouldn't have known it. There was a guard—a real bastard—who used to taunt me. He said war had broken out, but I was not supposed to be told—because they wanted to keep me locked up. Like a damn idiot, I once mentioned the archduke's promise to him, and from then on he never stopped baiting me."

"Now you have *your* war!" Kunze snapped.

Dorfrichter, preoccupied, failed to detect the bitterness in the major's tone.

"Last week I finished a treatise on how the Central Powers should fight this war. What they've done wrong up to now; they waited too long. It's October. In no time, the roads will be impassable. By the way, have you ever heard of Colonel Burstyn?"

"I don't think so," Kunze answered, somewhat baffled.

"I was afraid of that. I've been looking for his name in the papers, but never found any mention of him, either. Five years ago, when I last saw him, he told me about an invention he had. A great invention! An armored machine-gun carrier that moved on caterpillar treads. You see, the trouble with any vehicle driven by an internal-combustion engine is that it can advance only on hard-surface terrain. Caterpillar treads would be the answer to that. But Burstyn said no one at our Ministry of War could see his point and he was going to offer it to the Germans. If he did, he didn't have much luck with them either, or we would've heard about it. Why is it that our people always prepare for the *last* war?"

"So does the other side." Kunze shrugged. Dorfrichter's zeal both amazed and antagonized him.

"We've certainly missed our chance for a quick victory," Dorfrichter pointed out. "What we should do now is consolidate and hold our positions and prepare for the spring. On the first spring day, launch a formidable attack! Not only against the front lines of the enemy, but simultaneously against the hinterlands, too. The Central Powers, surrounded on all sides, are doomed if they use nineteenth-century methods. They must strike swiftly and with all their might. Wipe out enemy capitals by aerial bombardment—with planes and Zeppelins—demolish factories, railroad stations, hospitals, churches! No enemy soldier will go on fighting if he hears that his wife and children have been killed in their beds! One fast blow, and the war will be over in a week!"

He spoke in a hoarse, excited whisper. Kunze wondered if the man were running a fever. Or had he indeed lost his sanity in the musty Mollersdorf cell? But if *he* were insane, others could be as well: Schlieffen, Joffre, Conrad von Hötzendorf or the Kaiser. Or was it merely that whenever he touched the subject of war, it turned him into a demon of destruction?

As far as Kunze was concerned, Dorfrichter had chosen a bad day to glorify the war. During the past six weeks the death toll among his friends and acquaintances had been staggering. Not only he, but millions had begun to realize that the world would never be the same again. He dreaded looking at the casualty reports. No single day passed without his finding a familiar name among them. He had also become aware of the helplessness and fear that pervaded military offices which only two short months earlier had reverberated with jubilation.

Old people, Kunze recalled, always opened their newspaper to the obituary page to see who of their contemporaries had died the previous day. The news of some acquaintance's passing did not necessarily always fill them with sadness, on the contrary, with a strange mixture of satisfaction and triumph. They had lost a friend, but also outlived him, which gave them a sense of achievement. However, when one was forty-three, the death of comrades in their prime had the same effect as watching lush green country turn to desert, trees dry to skeletons, lizards scurry where pheasants used to nest.

Titus Dugonich had fallen in Galicia in one of the last great cavalry attacks of the war; Prince Rudolf Hohenstein lay buried in an unmarked grave somewhere on the outskirts of Przemysl; and Baron Landsberg-Lövy, who had been assigned as liaison to the German Fifth Army, in the Ardennes, in the French soil he had so dearly loved.

On the morning of the Dorfrichter interview, Kunze had received two bruising blows. Captain von Gersten had been killed on the Bosnian-Serbian border, and Major Hartmann, General Hartmann's younger son, on the Russian front, in a battle south of the Vistula River. To lose two boyhood companions was like having part of one's own self buried along with them. Belatedly he realized how important they had always been to him, taking the place of kinsmen he had never had.

"I'm afraid, your theories are a bit self-deluding, Dorfrichter," the major told the ex-lieutenant. "The enemy might retaliate in kind and drop bombs on *our* children, you know."

Dorfrichter shrugged. "You can't win without taking chances."

Kunze was beginning to feel perspiration under his restricting choke collar.

"Captain von Gersten was killed on the Serbian front last week," he blurted out. It was a *non sequitur*, but he couldn't restrain himself from saying it.

Dorfrichter gave him a surprised look. "I beg your pardon, sir?"

"I received the news this morning that Captain von Gersten was killed on the Serbian-Bosnian border," he repeated. "He was with the Second army—in charge of a detail laying telephone lines around Valjevo. He advanced with his technicians into enemy territory—which he didn't have to do, because he could just as well have stayed behind. They were ambushed, and he was found dead by the vanguard of the regiment when it reached the spot."

There was the glimmer of a smug smile on Dorfrichter's face. "Service above and beyond the call of duty! So typical of Gersten. If I remember well, you and I discussed this—this heroism complex. You asked me why I chose the ten and not Ahrens or Einthofen. I'm sure Ahrens will never get himself killed unnecessarily." He paused for breath. "I'll give you ten to one, sir, that Gersten won't be the only one killed of my ten."

Kunze nodded. "You've won." A minute earlier he had felt warm; now he shivered. "Prince Hohenstein and Landsberg-Lövy are dead, too. I must say," he added in a flat voice, "that war outdid you. You got only one out of ten, and the war has already taken three. You are number fourteen now, Dorfrichter. If you weren't a murderer, you'd be eligible for assignment to the General Staff!"

Dorfrichter was about to reply, then perceived intuitively that he was treading on dangerous ground and quickly changed the subject.

"I do hope, sir, you will grant my most humble request to go to the front. I don't have to convince you that I'll discharge my duties to the best of my ability. I, as you know—"

The major was still not ready to discuss the pardon. Cutting Dorfrichter short, he said, "Have you ever felt any remorse?"

"Remorse?" Dorfrichter asked in a high-pitched voice. "You mean, sir, about the circulars?"

"What else?"

"Of course, sir," he spoke swiftly, almost eagerly. "A great deal of remorse. I wouldn't do it again, if that's what you want to know. It was a moment of madness—I should've really pleaded not guilty by reason of insanity. Of course, one always looks for mitigating circumstances about one's own deeds—I've found a few. Even though I admit that I did cause Richard Mader's death—"

"Why shouldn't you admit it? You're safe. You can't be tried twice for the same crime!"

"He died on November seventeenth, 1909. If he hadn't died then, he would probably be dead by now. Killed in action—just like Gersten and the prince. So actually what did I deprive him of?"

"Five years! Summers and winters, five springs—and five autumns! The fall, too, can be good, especially here in Austria." He rose. "All right, Dorfrichter. That sums it up. I wish I could say it was good seeing you again, but under the circumstances that wouldn't be true."

Dorfrichter rose, too, for the first time looking worried. "You mean I won't be pardoned, sir?"

"I didn't say that—I'll have to think about it."

"What is there to think, sir?" Dorfrichter asked bluntly. "The archduke made a deal with me. I had his promise. Without it, you couldn't have subjected me to four years in prison. Without his promise, I would have chosen the rope."

"The archduke is dead," Kunze said.

"Colonel Bardolff is still alive! He knows! Ask him!"

"I don't have to. I knew about the deal before it was offered to you."

"Well, then, there is no problem."

"That's right, Dorfrichter. There's no problem."

"So what's the decision?"

Kunze gave him a long, taunting look.

"You should know better than to ask, Dorfrichter. This is the army, remember? Your petition will be given due consideration, and you'll be notified of the decision by His Majesty's Military Chancery. I'm afraid that's all I can tell you now."

He rang for the provost. Dorfrichter stood with hunched shoulders, his face sickly pale. His eyes followed the major across the room as though he were contemplating a dash for the door or an attack at Kunze. At the entrance of the provost the tension in the room dissolved into a cold, undramatic leave-taking.

Kunze watched the exit of prisoner and escort, dull-eyed, realizing only now how exhausted he was. He felt a trifle faint, and his shirt under his tunic was damp and clammy with perspiration. He decided to go home, take a hot bath, and forget about Peter Dorfrichter until the following morning.

As he passed the desk on his way out, something caused him to halt. He couldn't tell what it was, the wailing call of a bugle from the prison yard or a ray of the setting sun, much too bright and gay for October, which fell on Dorfrichter's petition. Hastily, he picked up the pen, dipped it into the dark-blue depths of the inkwell, and scribbled three crisp words beneath the bottom line of the petition:

"Rejected. Major Kunze."